Praise for *Dying for Revenge*

"Barbara Golder joins the ranks of Chesterton's bloodthirsty heirs as she spins a tale that will delight mystery fans. With *Dying for Revenge* in hand, your beach experience is now complete!"
Mark P. Shea
Author of *Mercy Works*

"*Dying for Revenge* dives into the deeply personal place in so many hearts with "justifiable" reasons for revenge... but the face of mercy is entwined in the unexpected turn of events. You'll be captivated..."
Patricia M. Chivers
ABLAZE Radio WNRE-LP 98.1 FM
Catholic Church of Saint Monica

"*Dying For Revenge* is a darn good medical thriller — a page-turning plot and vivid characters — with a stop-you-in your tracks twist: the costs of revenge. It's a gripping story — I defy anyone to put it down."
Deacon Dennis Dorner
Chancellor, Archdiocese of Atlanta

"When medical brilliance and a riveting plot collide, you get *Dying For Revenge* — a story of intrigue, murder, and faith that will leave everyone suspect but only one guilty..."
Rev. David Carter, JCL
Rector, Basilica of Sts. Peter and Paul, Chattanooga TN

"I know it sounds cliché, but I honestly couldn't put this down. It isn't just who-dun-it, but it's the story of the power of understanding in a world that's afraid of self-knowledge."
Joan Watson
Director of Adult Formation, Diocese of Nashville

"Richly-woven characters whose depth exceeds one mere mystery. A savory trail of facts and supposition will keep you guessing until the final pages."
Carolyn Astfalk
Author of *Stay With Me*

DYING FOR REVENGE

Book #1

The Lady Doc Murders

by

Dr. Barbara Golder

FQ Publishing

Pakenham, Ontario

Dying for Revenge (The Lady Doc Murders #1)

copyright 2016 Dr. Barbara Harty Golder

Published by Full Quiver Publishing

PO Box 244

Pakenham, Ontario K0A 2X0

www.fullquiverpublishing.com

ISBN Number: 978-1-987970-00-5

Printed and bound in the USA
Cover design: Doreen Thistle
Front cover photograph: James & Ellen Hrkach
Back cover photograph: Stephen Golder
Author photograph: Stephen Golder

NATIONAL LIBRARY OF CANADA

CATALOGUING IN PUBLICATION

Published by FQ Publishing

A Division of Innate Productions

To my midwife for helping me birth Jane and company
and to my husband. You are NOT Dead John.

PROLOGUE

JUNE 5, MID-AFTERNOON

"Is Mitch there?" A pause, then another question, "Are you Marla? Marla Kincaid?"

A female voice, with a smokes-and-whiskey quality that made Marla feel superior. Mitch couldn't possibly have anything to do with someone this low-class. Without thinking, taken off guard, she answered yes and her world had exploded.

"It's Liz. Liz Norton, from the *Hollywood Inquisitor*. Mitch's ex-wife just tested positive for AIDS. It's our front-page lead tomorrow. Did you know? Has he been tested? Did he tell you before he screwed you the first time? How about the baby?" The questions came out in a rush, a miserable torrent of words that made Marla feel dirty just listening to them. The voice was matter of fact, no warning, no cushioning to let her take it in little by little. Marla's stomach knotted, and she felt her heart racing even as she was powerless to reply.

And then the woman made it worse. "She's in detox, heroin and crack. Says they shot up together all the time. Never mind the sex, he'd have it from the needles. He's got it for sure." There was a curious delight in that awful voice. A sort of pleasure in the sorry details she just kept piling on. Marla closed her eyes tight, as if shutting out the light of day would shut out what she was hearing. For sure. Nobody smart got infected anymore. That was for losers, for derelicts, not for superstars like Mitch Houston. For a long moment, Marla stared at the phone in her hand, then dropped it as though it burned her. She could still hear muffled sounds: a rough, wicked cackle and then her name repeated again and again: "Marla? Are you there?" After what seemed an eternity, blessed silence.

It had all been so perfect. How had it gone so horribly wrong? Marla Kincaid screamed at last, once, a scream that vanished into a whimper. Then she sat on the floor of the marble shower that she had retreated to after that call, trying to wash off the filth of that awful call, hugging her knees to her chest and sobbing as the water spilled over her and ran down the drain. There she stayed until the hot water turned warm, then cold, a long time because it was a high-end shower, made for indulgent people, and she was indulging herself and her anger. At last she stood up, knees wobbly, skin turning to gooseflesh. She turned the shower off and stepped onto the sea-green rug, wrapping herself in a towel, warm from the rack, and shaking her short, blond curls. She regarded her image in the foggy mirror. Her hand dropped to her belly, small and round and firm. It had been so perfect, just like she planned. What was going to happen to her now?

She dried off quickly and dropped the towel to the floor. She pulled out her daddy's old red flannel shirt from the back of her closet. It was so big it fell to her knees, and the sleeves were so long they hid her hands. She clenched the soft fabric in her fists and then hugged herself, pressing her head to her chest and imagining her daddy's arms around her. Then she sighed, looked around at the mess in the bedroom, and opened the big French doors. She stepped out onto the expansive porch, a hint of breeze ruffling the shirt and making her hug herself again, this time for warmth, if not for control.

The sun was just beginning to lower in the afternoon sky. She heard a rustle and watched a deer meander from the far edge of the woods, coming almost up to the house. She was surprised to see him out so early, but the deer near Mountain Village were accustomed to people, almost tame. He nuzzled and then nibbled the tender tops of the newly planted bushes. She shifted position, making only the faintest of noises, but it was enough to startle him, and he looked up directly at her. His antlers were just visible against the pale lawn now behind him. She counted the points, six to a side, a trophy buck. She gave a wry smile. Trophy buck. Just like Mitch. A trophy every woman in the country was after, a trophy she had managed to snag with determination and guile and feigned innocence that even Mitch had taken for the genuine article.

He'd found her on the set of his last movie, in a role supporting the famous actress he'd been dating and grown tired of. A year later, here she was, living the life she'd dreamed about, schemed and clawed for, since leaving Little Rock at eighteen to become an actress. There had been so many terrible jobs, so many terrible people who had taken advantage of her, but she was good, and she was determined, and she'd finally gotten herself noticed and cast into a real movie, not some grade-

B disaster flick that went straight to DVD. The last year had been better than she could have imagined. All those years of living in roach-infested flats and eating peanut butter and working three jobs while juggling auditions were worth it. All those lecherous agents and casting directors and money-men she had flattered for an opportunity and then endured on her way up faded into the background when she stepped out on the red carpet with Mitch Houston, wearing custom gowns and covered in jewels lent to her just because she was who she was. Because she was with Mitch. She'd been on the cover of *People* and the subject of too many gossip columns to count. She was important and she was pregnant. Mitch was over the moon about the baby, and she'd never have to worry about anything again. He would never leave the mother of his son. Children maybe? Heir and a spare, like Diana, like Kate? No, one was enough. He was hers forever.

Or so she had thought until his cell phone rang. That call. The one she answered because he was gone, buying some wine. Mitch had people to do everything imaginable for him, everything normal people took for granted. But here in Colorado, taking a break in this little mountain town, he liked to pretend he lived just like everyone else. He had a maid to do the cleaning, and of course he kept his personal trainer. But everything else, he did. Just another role, just another pretense in his life. He was out pretending to be an ordinary guy while she was left behind, pretending not to care that he'd been gone for hours while she was bored to tears. And he wouldn't even let her drink the wine, on account of the baby.

He'd lied to her. He didn't use drugs; he said so. Then she remembered those times he disappeared for hours at a time and then came home too tired to do anything but sleep with no word of explanation. Unable to think, she needed to do something to get rid of the fear and pain and anger that consumed her, anger at Mitch for his betrayal, at herself for being so stupid to trust him, angry that she was pregnant and he was going to die from AIDS and so was she and maybe even the baby would too. Or maybe just the baby. She saw the phone on the edge of the gray rug and kicked it across the room. She heard it hit one of the legs of the bed and ricochet into the wall behind.

She screamed again at the top of her lungs, and so long her throat hurt and she went dizzy from lack of breath. Then she cried, great, hot tears that soaked her sleeve when she wiped her eyes, tears that rose again as soon as her arm fell back to her side. Finally, she turned her frustration from herself to Mitch. She threw things, anything she could get her hands on. She picked up his Oscar, that precious statue, feeling its surprising heft in her hands and thinking that she was glad the little figure didn't have eyes and couldn't see what was happening to her. She heaved it at the big mirror on the wall above the dresser, damn the bad luck. What could be worse than what already was? It broke into a spider web of cracks. The jagged, shiny pieces fell to the floor in a glittering cascade. One long piece, curved like a scythe, stuck upright in the floor.

She yanked his clothes from the closet, tearing his silk shirts with her bare hands and ripping holes in his designer suits and linen slacks with the jagged piece of glass from the mirror. Still, she took care to sheath her hand in the towel to keep from spilling her own blood. What she couldn't tear or cut, she threw in the middle of the fireplace. She narrowed her eyes as she carefully pulled the clothes away from the gas jets at the base of the ceramic logs, then pushed the igniter button beside the mantle to start the blue flames. Gray, choking smoke spilled into the room for a moment or two before it began to course upward. The logs might be fake, but the gas jets and the chimney worked just fine.

At length, fury temporarily spent, she fell into the shower, hoping that she might be able to wash it all away. It hadn't worked and here she was, still waiting for him to return, knowing that he could never resist the opportunity to pose with fans, sign autographs, and schmooze because it was all that adulation that made his life worthwhile. His life hadn't changed at all, not even when he'd told her she was his special, only, once-in-a-lifetime love, and now her life was never going to be the same.

She watched the deer nibble a few more branches and then bound off again until he disappeared back into the woods. She shivered a bit and went back inside, too chilled to stay outside now that the sun was behind the gathering clouds of an afternoon rain, and the breeze was picking up. With a set of her jaw, she determined not to remain in the house any longer. She went to the dresser, stepping over the mess and started to pack her bags and leave. The little pearl-handled gun her father had sent with her — and taught her to shoot as well as he did — lay half-buried under designer camisoles and tees. She picked it up idly, thinking about the difference between the father who gave it to her, who wanted to protect her from everything, and the father of the child she was carrying, who protected her from nothing.

A sudden calm came over her as she felt the weight of the gun in her hand. It was almost as though she were back home, standing by her daddy as he taught her to shoot, first at big tubs of lard, then coffee cans, and finally rabbits and squirrels and doves and deer, squeezing off rounds two at a time just for insurance. "No use knowing how to shoot at cans, baby, unless you can shoot at something that matters when the time comes," he had told her. She had cried the first time she killed a squirrel, but after a bit, she learned to squelch the rising tears and shoot as well as any of her brothers. She wondered whether she still could.

A squirrel scampered across the edge of the porch toward the low-hanging branches of a fir at the edge of the woods, perhaps twenty yards away. Looking again at the pistol in her hand, Marla eased out onto the deck, tip-toed to the edge of the railing and waited, still and patient, for it to move on again from the limb. She knew from experience that if she waited long enough, it would tire of its post and move along, and it did. With practiced ease, she lifted the gun, tracked the animal, and fired. She knew she had missed as soon as she pulled the trigger. She had forgotten to take and hold that breath her daddy taught her to count time by, to account for the lead needed for a moving target, and she hadn't fired the two shots in succession he taught her to, just for insurance. But a falling twig told her she hadn't missed by much. Easy enough to correct and not an issue if the target was standing still. It would do, if it came to that. If it came to that...

Marla walked back to the dresser and tucked the gun back between her camisoles, pulled out a tee-shirt and jeans, and dressed. Perhaps a walk around town would clear her head. Besides, there was business to attend to. She just hoped the doctor's office in the Regent Building was still open and that she didn't run into Mitch along the way.

CHAPTER ONE

JUNE 6, EARLY MORNING

John had just touched my face in his familiar way when the phone startled me out of my sleep. It was one of those vivid dreams, the kind that it takes a minute or two to realize you've passed from it into wakefulness. I was especially unhappy, because since his death five years ago, the only way I ever saw my husband or felt his touch was in my restless slumber. The phone rang again, insisting that I answer. In my line of work, a call in the middle of the night is never happy news. It means that death has come calling, unexpected, or violent, or both. It's the time of night when teenagers run off the road, when drug deals go sour, when sick old men die, the man inside having given up the struggle to keep the man outside alive, when drunken spouses abuse each other to death. At the end of it all, somebody calls the medical examiner, and I am pulled out of my orderly world into someone else's dark night. I wondered idly what particular nightmare I was entering this time as I punched the keypad of my cell phone.

"Yeah?"

I am not particularly civil at three in the morning. Fortunately for me, the cops who are on duty at that hour — the ones most likely to call — aren't too sensitive. This time it was the sheriff of San Miguel County himself who answered. His voice called up his lanky frame, thinning red hair, pockmarked face and crooked nose.

"Aren't you just Dr. Mary Sunshine! Wake up, Jane Wallace, you've got a case." His gravelly chuckle broke up a bit. Call reception isn't always good in the mountains.

"Yeah, yeah, yeah." I rubbed my eyes and took another stab at civility. "What's up, Tom?"

I sat up, stretching my neck and trying to come to consciousness. Tom had used my first name, something he never did, preferring to alternate between Dr. Wallace when he was vexed with me, and Doc when he approved of the way I was executing the demands of my office as Chief Medical Examiner for the Western Slope of Colorado.

"Oh, big dealings right here in Mountain Village. We got ourselves a celebrity murder, we do."

The words were flippant and out of context with the somber nature of such early morning calls. There's a certain propensity toward inappropriate humor among those of us who work regularly among the dead and the degenerate. I wouldn't put it past any of my law enforcement brethren, least of all Patterson with his avuncular style, to string me along for the sake of a little joke to liven up an otherwise routine death. I could jest with the best of them.

"Just as long as it's not Mitch Houston, we'll be fine."

Houston, Hollywood's current favorite leading man and a very hot commodity, had moved to town several months before, buying both a trophy home in Mountain Village and a remote cabin on a thousand acres in one of the basins in the Wilson Peaks, in a display of conspicuous consumption excessive even for Telluride, Colorado, my adopted home on the western slope of the Rockies. The silence at the other end of the phone did not bode well for my career on the comedy circuit. I sat upright, awake, my mind suddenly clear and feeling dismayed.

"Are you kidding me?" I asked.

Any murder is a tragedy, but this one was going to be a pain in the ass to boot.

"Nope."

I heard him take a swig from his ever-present water bottle. I had been trying to train him not to take it into crime scenes and hoped he was calling from somewhere other than the immediate vicinity of the corpse.

"Damndest thing. A woman coming down on the last gondola saw Houston through the bedroom window."

I could believe that. It never made sense to me why someone would buy a multi-million dollar home that complete strangers had a bird's-eye view into, but they did.

"It took her a couple of hours of her boyfriend trying to convince her she was crazy for her to work up the courage to call but she did. Otherwise we probably wouldn't have found out until tomorrow, and Houston's cute little girlfriend would have been long gone. She plugged him right between the eyes," he added.

"Allegedly."

"Allegedly. However, when the deputy arrived, she discovered the alleged perp standing by the alleged but very dead victim, calm as can be. She was packing her bags. We found a literally, if alleged, smoking gun. Well, recently fired, anyway. It was in her underwear drawer. She's lawyering up and won't say anything, but it seems pretty clear what happened. Not much mystery to this murder, but we still need you up here." Tom paused for another swig of water. "I'll send someone around."

"Never mind. I'll drive myself."

Patterson gave me the address on Double Bogey Lane. I scribbled hurriedly on one of the pads I habitually keep scattered all over the house. I recognized this particular street as the main one in the priciest section in what amounted to a wildly pricey subdivision. The guy who laid out the place had a sense of humor, at least.

Half an hour later, I was standing in the over-lit bedroom of one of the most ostentatious log homes in Mountain Village, a place where overstated log and rock palaces grow like weeds in a garden. I was outfitted in the latest in crime scene investigator chic: blue booties, gloves, and jumpsuit. Tom Patterson — temporarily minus his water bottle — was there, along with short, blond, plump, and efficient Maggie Gleason, the deputy Tom had offered to dispatch to get me.

The master suite was bigger than my first two apartments combined, with an expanse of glass that looked out onto a porch and through an aspen grove that opened up on one side to reveal mountain peaks washed in moonlight. A corner door, ajar, led into a bathroom with pale green towels dropped carelessly onto a pink marble floor. A massive, open, stone fireplace complete with bearskin rug dominated one end of the room and an entertainment center, bar, and leather couch the other. The furniture was heavy log stuff, interior-decorator tasteless. The bed, unmade, was in the center of the room, to take best advantage of the view. An open, brown leather suitcase was half full of clothes. The gas fireplace was full of ashes, and the walls were scarred from the impact of a variety of nick-nacks that were lying around the room, including an Oscar surrounded by bits of broken mirror.

Across the undoubtedly expensive Navajo rug on the floor, Mitch Houston was sprawled, face up, feet nearest the doors that were open to the porch and what would be a dynamite view of the mountains. His vacant blue eyes were staring up at the hand-painted floral chandelier above him, the blood pooling beneath his head enough to ruin the rug's Two Gray Hills design. Sure enough, there was a neat little hole in his forehead. I knelt and bent over him to take a closer look.

"It's not a close shot, and it sure could be a .22. Is this girl good or unlucky?" The edges of the wound were clean and sharp, a dead-on hit with no powder marks. I felt the hand of the corpse. It was not as warm as it should have been, with stiffness starting in the joints. His face and hands were smooth and free of scratches. The room was a mess but, except for the hole in his head, Mitch Houston wasn't.

"Unlucky is my guess. When we got here, she was standing there, looking kind of dazed at the body. Like she couldn't believe she'd done it. We found the gun in the dresser. It's what my grandma would have called a lady's gun, small, even with a pearl handle, so help me God. Recently fired and a .22." Tom Patterson paused.

"Unlucky as hell," I agreed.

I've known .22 rounds to bounce off the front of the skull, where it's thick and when it's not a close shot, just tunneling under the skin and causing no serious damage. This one had gone straight through the front of Houston's skull just above the eyes. I lifted his head and felt, then looked, at the back of it. No exit wound, which was typical. The low velocity round had just enough energy to get inside the skull, then spent its time ricocheting around the brain case.

"Probably won't be much left of the bullet," I remarked, then stood up. "He's been dead a little while, Tom. Three, four, maybe five hours max, I would guess. It's not a recent kill."

I retrieved a thermometer, a scalpel and a syringe from my case and knelt beside the body. I pushed aside the Bluegrass Festival shirt, unzipped the worn jeans to expose his abdomen, and made a small incision in the skin, then the underlying liver. I tucked the probe of the thermometer inside, waited for it to come to temperature, and recorded it. Body temperature isn't much help in determining time of death, especially in this day and age of air conditioning, but a lot of lawyers still ask about it, so I do it just to shut them up when I am on the stand. Most of the time, when you get right down to it, the cops establish the time better than I ever could, by old-fashioned legwork and being downright nosy. Like this time. The last gondola ran at midnight, and it seems Houston was dead by then.

"Anybody hear the shot?"

"Not sure yet. Nobody called one in, anyway," Maggie offered. "It's not like I can interview the neighbors in the middle of the night. Give me a time of death, and we can ask some intelligent questions tomorrow."

Patterson glanced at his deputy, then squatted down on his heels by the body, the better to see what I was doing. I shrugged and got back to business. The real scientific data comes from testing the fluid in the eyeball. I wiped off the thermometer, laid it on the case, and uncapped the needle on the syringe. When I leaned forward to slide the needle into Houston's right eye, I noticed out of the corner of my own that Patterson cringed, turned his face away and quickly stood up again. It never ceases to amaze me what makes people squeamish.

I finished, satisfied with the sample I had been able to get, and stood, still looking down at America's heartthrob. He was handsome enough, but thinner than a man ought to be and shorter than he appeared on the big screen. His features were a little coarse-looking in death, and there were dark circles under his eyes.

"I'll have something for you later in the day." I swore under my breath as I realized the sharps container I needed was next to my forensic kit. I debated recapping the needle, then decided against it. Rules are rules. "Hand me that red box, will you, Tom?"

By that time Patterson had recovered. He handed the water bottle he had managed to grab when I wasn't looking to Maggie and retrieved the red plastic container we use to dispose of needles. He handled it gingerly and placed it carefully next to the body, as though it might bite him. Tom has an unhealthy respect for germs. I deposited the needle into it and disengaged the test tube with the sample from Houston's eye.

"Thanks. I'll give you a call as soon as I know something."

Patterson shrugged. "It is what it is. Not much doubt about this one." His homely face wrinkled in thought. "Damn shame, she seems like a nice kid," he added.

I refrained from comment. I've never had a lot of sympathy for murderers, and since my husband's death at the hands of a colleague, my supply had run out. Houston might have been a world-class jerk, but no one had the right to take his life. I just grunted and started processing the scene.

Ordinarily, one of my techs would have handled the grunt work and in record time, but I make it a point to handle call duties solo one week out of the month, just to keep in practice. It keeps me competent but not fast. Dawn was beginning to spill over the peaks when I finished, zipping Houston into a black body bag with the help of Patterson. I called down to the Western Slope Forensic Center to ask Jasper Quick, my right-hand man, to pick up the body.

There wasn't much reason to go back home to bed. "How long until the press gets wind of this?" I asked Patterson as we stepped out onto the front porch.

"Not long. Marla Kincaid — the girlfriend — told the maid to call her agent," Patterson said. Maggie, standing by his side with her customary patience, rolled her eyes, a smile playing around her lips but she said nothing. "These Hollywood types never cease to amaze me. I presume the agent will have the sense to call a lawyer but probably not before he calls the Associated Press."

"Great." I drew in a breath of mountain air, clean and fresh and smelling of pine and aspen in the June morning. "Guess I'd better get right at this, then. Life's going to get real complicated, real fast."

I glanced across the lawn, suddenly washed by the lights of an oncoming car. I recognized it as belonging to a reporter from one of Telluride's two competing papers. Watching the vintage Jeep pull up the long drive, I slapped the sheriff on the shoulder.

"Best of luck," I said as I pulled open the door of my green 4Runner.

As I pulled out of the drive, I heard Patterson's distinctive voice in reply.

"Sh...."

It didn't take me long to finish the autopsy on America's heart-throb. It was a single shot to the head, and as I suspected, it had rattled around inside Houston's head long enough to completely deform the bullet. I had dutifully retrieved and bagged it. It wasn't much more than a lump of lead, but it was bigger than I expected. It struck me as a little odd for a round out of the pistol Patterson had showed me.

More interesting than that were the enlarged lymph nodes and spleen, the raised bumps on the skin of his back and chest, and the white coating on Houston's tongue. Mitch Houston may have been America's leading man, and was, according to the papers, a health fanatic of major proportions, but it looked to me like he'd fallen prey to a major weakness of the flesh. I'd drawn a couple of extra tubes of blood to run a few confirmatory tests, but if my suspicions were correct, this autopsy was going to be a major tabloid bombshell.

I peeled the gloves off and dropped them in the waste. One stuck on the side of the bin, and I kicked the metal side—harder than I intended—to dislodge it. I washed off, up to the elbows, three full minutes, two separate lathers with antimicrobial soap, then dried my hands on one of the soft terry-cloth towels I kept by the sink. I tossed it in the laundry bin where it landed on the bloodstained gown I had worn. I kicked off my morgue clogs, pulled on my boots, and headed up the back stairs to my office. My steps reverberated as I took them two at a time, rolling down the sleeves of my shirt as I went.

When I reached the final landing I was out of breath. It's hard for me to admit that I'm getting older, facing my own mortality, but running upstairs tends to do it. I chastised myself for forgetting my phone again; my pounding heart reminded me that if I had my first, last and only heart attack in the stairwell one of these days, it might be weeks before anyone found me. Most of my staff was young, fit, entirely unaware of the ravages of time, and invariably took the elevator, leaving the stairs for me.

Once in my office breathing normally again, I flipped the switch on the coffee pot, booted up my computer, and started editing the autopsy report the dictating system had entered as I worked two floors below. The system is a good one, the best on the market, but it still occasionally garbles my words beyond recognition. I was scowling at the screen, coffee in hand, trying to decipher a particularly obtuse statement when Quick stuck his head in the door.

Jasper Quick is my diener, a fancy German word for morgue assistant. Jasper spent his first career as a medic in the Army, serving three tours in Vietnam and then anywhere else Uncle Sam decided to send him over the next thirty years. He's seen more blood and gore than I have and left undisturbed can finish a post-mortem in less than an hour, skin to skin. Quick had followed me to Telluride from Florida. He was there when I got the news about John, and his arms were the ones into which I collapsed in the middle of an autopsy. He held me, walked me to the Emergency Room, then finished the case for me. We never spoke of it again, but sometimes he reaches out just to pat my hand in the middle of a case, and then we move on. He kept me tethered to my calling when all I wanted to do was run. He still does.

"You got a visitor," he said.

He'd been frolicking with hair dye in the morgue sink again. The scattered silver hairs that had been there only yesterday were now shoe-polish black.

"Who is it—and what does he want?" I finally realized what I had meant to say, and I pecked at the keyboard, then looked up again.

"Says his name is Monaghan. Won't say what he wants, just says he needs to see you."

Quick ran a self-conscious hand over his tight, close-cropped curls. He's always a little embarrassed when he dyes his hair, but he's too vain to stop.

"Lawyer, cop or funeral director?" I asked.

We get few visitors of any other sort.

"Shoes are too good to be a cop and not shiny enough for a mortician." Quick grinned. "Got to be a suit. I expect it has something to do with that murder up in Mountain Village."

I looked at my watch. It was a little before noon, too fast, I thought for anyone to surface yet in the Houston case. We'd surely have peace and quiet for at least another few hours. It takes a little while to get to our little box canyon, even with a private jet. I was about to tell Quick to bring the fellow up when a tall, blond man elbowed his way into my office. Quick was right: his shoes, ostrich-leather cowboy boots, were far too fancy to be those of a cop, and no self-respecting funeral director would be caught dead in them. Or in the shiny black designer jeans he wore, either, for that matter. He adjusted the collar of his orange silk shirt, huffed his way to my desk and stood glaring at me. I tapped away at my keyboard in unconcerned silence. I've played enough lawyer games to know that the first one to speak loses ground. I had the advantage. This pushy mouthpiece wanted something from me. He cleared his throat. I struck a few more keys. Finally, he spoke up.

"Steven P. Monaghan. Monaghan and Cutler. L.A, New York, London. I'm here to see you about the Houston autopsy."

Either Kincaid's agent did a lot of calling or Monaghan had already been in Telluride. Probably the latter. I vaguely recalled an article in one of the local rags about Houston being deep in negotiations for a new movie, one to be filmed in the area. I looked at the computer screen, moused a correction, tapped the keyboard once more, and answered him without looking up.

"What about it?"

"You can't do it."

Now he had my interest, in spite of myself. Unless he'd figured out how to do a little time travel and stop me retroactively, this discussion was moot, but I thought I would play along.

"And why ever not?"

I glanced at him and smiled my most ingratiating Southern Belle smile. My Alabama-born momma would have been proud.

Monaghan shifted a bit and leaned in, taking body-language advantage of what he thought was a tip of the verbal scales in his favor. He shoved a neatly folded paper toward me.

"Because Judge Lotham says you can't. It's a violation of my client's religious rights."

He'd been a busy little lawyer this morning, and I was impressed in spite of myself that he'd managed to get in touch with a local magistrate in such short order.

"And what would those religious beliefs be?" I was curious, not concerned.

"My client believed that the human body is sacred. That on death, it should be returned unharmed to Mother Earth. Not abused and torn apart."

So Houston thought the human body sacred and not to be abused, I thought. Too bad he didn't show that respect to his body before it became a corpse. He might not see drugs and wanton sex as bodily harm, but I sure did. Still, I refrained from commenting on the absurdity of this preening little man's position.

My smile broadened a bit and lost its charm.

"Paul Lotham is a family court judge whose knowledge about the medical examiner office might—just might—fill a gnome's thimble. State law not only gives me the right to autopsy your client, it compels me to do so."

I stood up and leaned right toward him. I had an inch or two on him, even without my boot heels.

We stood there for an uneasy minute, like two cats staring each other down, until a commotion from the hallway diverted our attention to the door. A thin, scruffy man, who looked to be in his late twenties, with stringy blond hair and a mangy excuse for a beard burst into the room. He wore a roughly woven, gray tunic over a long, brown robe, and his bare feet were dirty, with overgrown nails and the little toe on the right foot missing. When you're a medical examiner, you tend to notice things like that.

He shook himself to collect his dignity and glanced in my direction before addressing the lawyer.

"Did you tell her? Did you stop it? You have to stop it!"

His voice was a surprise: a deep, rich bass, controlled in spite of his obvious anxiety. Although I'd seen this particular nomad wandering Telluride's streets, I'd never actually heard him talk. He had a reputation as an eccentric, even among the oddballs that made up Telluride's general population, and he spent a good deal of his time passing out flyers about his own version of pop-culture New Age religion on street corners and in Town Park. It had earned him the desultory nickname of Reverend Bedsheet. I usually gave him a wide berth.

I came out from behind the desk and interposed myself between them, another power play on my part.

"Sorry, can't be done," I told him. "I finished it about half an hour ago."

Bedsheet keened and covered his face. I was surprised at how anguished he sounded; this clearly wasn't a theoretical issue for him. I wondered offhand what Mitch Houston had meant to him. Putting one lawyer and one gentle eccentric together, I guessed that Houston — none too tightly wound himself — might have fallen for Bedsheet's religious philosophy which, as I recalled, was of the total passivist, let-nature-take-its-course variety. I wasn't too far out on a limb to suspect that Bedsheet and his followers looked at medicine in general and my brand in particular as some sort of cosmic insult to nature and humankind. It explained the lawyer's ridiculous position that doing my duty was somehow trampling on Houston's religious freedom.

The lawyer cleared his throat, and I turned my attention to him. His eyes glittered in predatory fashion, angry to have been bested.

"That's too bad. We'll just have to see you in court and teach you something about the First Amendment. Performing an autopsy on my client was against — clearly against — his deeply held religious beliefs." I wondered how deep these beliefs could be, given that Houston had only been in Telluride a few months and Bedsheet had little sway outside our own little box canyon, but no matter. This was a lawyer tussle, not reality.

Monaghan's eyes drifted over to the corner of my office and came to rest on the overstuffed chair there, prayer book open on the seat, crucifix on the wall beside it, and at present, a cobalt glass rosary threatening to slide off its open pages. I'd been interrupted the last time I used it, for I usually put it carefully away. I had carried it when John and I were married. Something blue.

I kept it close to me in the wake of my husband's death, but I wasn't sure why. From years of experience, I knew that people affected by violent death either turned to God or away from Him. My work had propelled me toward God years ago to make sense out of the victims and those who murder them. Now that John was dead and that violence was personal, not professional, I was as precarious as my cherished rosary, not turning away from God exactly, but not turning toward Him, either. I couldn't remain suspended forever, and lately I was threatening to slide off into who-knows-what kind of oblivion.

Monaghan looked back with renewed malice, and his words brought me back to the moment, back in balance — if still in darkness — for the time being.

"It looks like the only religion you are prepared to respect here is your own. I might just have to add on the fact that you are using government facilities to promote your own religious beliefs at the expense of others."

That's one of the things I hate, absolutely hate, about lawyers. Here this little Napoleon had come to try to keep me from doing my job by getting the county's stupidest judge to issue him an injunction that ultimately wasn't worth the paper it had been faxed on. You'd think that once he found out that he was too late to do what he came to do, the lawyer would have gracefully retreated. Instead, he decided to attack.

Bad decision. I'd had enough fun with him for one day, Bedsheet's sobbing was getting on my nerves, and I was willing to bet my coffee was cold. I went over to my file cabinet, leafed through a few folders, and pulled out a copy of a case. I handed it to the lawyer.

"Take a look at that, counselor. Chin-Ho v. Florida went all the way to the nine old men. Had to do with performing autopsies on young immigrant Asian men who died in their sleep. Their community sued the medical examiner—that would be me—for violation of the right to practice their religion, which forbade autopsies. The Supremes decided in my favor that the M.E. law trumps religious preference when there is a suspicion of foul play. Law of the land, counselor. All the land. Even here." I smiled again, baring my teeth. "Just for the record, I also argued the case." I nodded at the papers in his hand. "You can keep that. I have several copies."

I went back to my desk, sat down and took a swig of coffee. I was right, cold.

Bedsheet by now had sunk to the floor. His shoulders still heaved, but he was crying quietly. The lawyer grabbed a wad of tissues from the dispenser on the corner of my desk; it comes in handy in my business. He helped Bedsheet to his feet again and started for the door, his arm around the gray shoulders. At the threshold he looked back and spoke again. Poor guy, he didn't know when to quit.

"We'll see about that," he growled. "In any case, I am sure the ACLU will be happy to listen to me about that shrine over there."

He flung an angry hand toward the corner. He had exceeded my tolerance for fools.

"While you are at it, sue about those damn Buddhist prayer flags that are on the barn as you come into town," I snapped.

The presence of those tattered scraps of cloth irritated me every time I drove past them.

"And then take a look at the plaque on the door, counselor. This is my office, not the state's, not the county's and not the town's. I own the building, and I rent out the lower two floors—and only the lower two floors—for the M.E. facility. The rest is mine, private property. Which," I added, "I suggest you leave. And close the door behind you."

He did, with a bang. I swiveled in my chair to put my coffee cup into the microwave on the shelf behind me. The timer had no sooner rung than there was another knock on the door, and Quick stuck his head around the door again.

"Another lawyer, boss."

He winked, then pushed the door open for the visitor.

This time the offending professional was of the more low-rent variety and younger. Fresh out of law school, unless I missed my bet. Things were looking up; this one at least offered his hand and apologized for interrupting me.

"Eric Johanssen. I hate to bother you when you must be pretty busy with the Houston case."

Brown eyes looked out of a freckled face that had seen too much sun for its own good, and they neither wavered nor plotted.

"All part of the job." I shifted forward enough to shake his hand, then waved him toward one of the two chairs that faced my desk. "Have a seat."

"How did he know I'm a lawyer?" His forehead wrinkled in confusion. "I just told him my name."

The accent was local, and the name was familiar.

"Playing the odds," I said. "We've had a run on attorneys this morning. You're up early."

Johanssen nodded and pressed on. "That was Mitch Houston's lawyer I just passed, wasn't it?"

Local, but shrewd. "It was. But enough about him—what are you here for?"

I saw him recoil a bit. If this fellow was going to succeed in the fields of the law, he would have to get a thicker hide and a poker face. I softened my tone. "Sorry. He got under my skin. What can I do for you?"

"I represent Marla Kincaid."

He shifted in the chair but kept his eyes on mine. I let the silence grow as I waited for an answer to my question. Impatience got the better of me this time, and I sighed loudly.

"And....?" I added expectantly.

"She's been arrested for murdering Mitch Houston."

No surprise there, I thought. She was found standing over him with the gun hidden in her unmentionables.

"I need to know what you found out in the autopsy."

"Mr. Johanssen, the body's hardly cold and the report isn't even finished. When it is, I promise you a copy." I cocked my head a bit and looked at him again. "What's so urgent?"

He glanced down, then his eyes fixed me again. "Marla thinks people will believe she had a good reason to shoot him. She didn't. Shoot him, I mean. She may have had reason to, though."

"Needed killing, did he?" I asked. The lawyer's name finally rang a bell in the recesses of my mind. The youngest son of Montrose's most prominent and flamboyant attorney, he'd joined the family firm a few months ago. Marla would have needed someone fast, and Montrose was the closest place to get a decent lawyer who knew something about criminal law. Daddy must have been out of town; otherwise Eric would have been carrying his briefcase, and I would have had to deal with another blowhard. I thanked St. Swithen, my own personal patron and the saint of rainy days, for this particular bit of luck.

A small smile formed on Johanssen's lips. "Maybe not, but from what she tells me, I'll have my hands full if what she says is true. Then again, I might have a case for diminished capacity. If she were the killer, of course — and she isn't."

He paused.

"Marla is pregnant. I have reason to believe that Mitch put her and the baby at serious risk. She was distraught when she found out."

"Ah." Daddy Johanssen was going to be real proud of his boy. I thought back to the autopsy. Spun the right way, the fact that America's heartthrob had a very active HIV infection — and had very likely infected his lover and the mother of his child — might well get her off with not much more than a slap on the wrist. "That could be." I smiled back. "The report will be ready in a couple of days. Leave me your card, and I will see that you get a copy when I send the final report to the state's attorney."

Johanssen pushed his card across the desk. Tasteful black and white, no raised lettering.

"Thanks."

I called after him in spite of myself, the lawyer in me racing ahead to the fertile fields of litigation. "You thought about a suit against the estate? Might finance her defense." Marla Kincaid was a shack-up honey, not Houston's wife.

He turned back and grinned, hand on the doorsill. "Why Dr. Wallace, that would be premature. I'll wait for the report, but I think Telluride might be the perfect venue, don't you?"

God spare me from lawyers, I thought as I put my coffee back in the microwave yet again to warm — but he was right. I picked up the top folder on my desk and wondered what was coming next.

****

Isa heard him slam the door against the wall as he came in, drunk and loud as always. El Pelirojo, the only one of us, she thought, who could pass for American because of that red hair, even though he was as Latin as she was. As Latin and totally consumed with machismo, that arrogant, woman-defiling pride that plagued so many of her countrymen. That sense of worth and privilege so out of place in a man so poor and unskilled and incapable. And just plain ugly.

It came, she thought, from the fact that he had not had any real work to do, nor had his brothers or father or uncles. The women in his life coddled him. First his mother, who sacrificed everything to raise her worthless son, then a string of girlfriends and a wife back in Mexico. And soon he expected every woman to take care of him and swoon at his feet, enchanted by his sour, sweaty charm. Even now, here, when they all had jobs, he expected the women to take care of his every need, when the women worked two and three jobs themselves. And none of the other men would stand up to him — he was too mean, too powerful. He was the one who arranged the coyotes to bring family members across the border.

Cross him, and your money or your family — and likely both — would disappear.

She was not going to let her Pablo grow up that way. She would find a way to get out of this small house, stuffed to the rafters with people. She would not let him grow up thinking that El Pelirojo was the kind of man he should be. She folded a pair of jeans and smoothed them as she put them on the shelf that she shared with three other women, and listened as he crashed through the living room, swearing in Spanish. A chill ran up her back as she realized she was alone in the house with him. It was only a matter of time before he found her and took out his drunken rage on her because she was here, she was defenceless, and she was female.

She scooped Pablo up and put him, along with his blanket and toy cars, into the bathroom on the floor. Kissing him on his head, she admonished him to be quiet. She shut the door and turned back to the laundry on the bed, smoothing the front of her new, blue blouse. She would find a way out. Pelirojo crashed his fist against the wall outside her door, and she made the sign of the cross.

CHAPTER TWO

JUNE 6, EARLY AFTERNOON

I left my office only once that morning, just long enough to go up the street to my favorite breakfast joint for chorizo and eggs. I was back enjoying the relative quiet of my office by noon, away from the media circus that the Houston murder was cooking up in town, a veggie sandwich from the same shop a guarantee against my having to venture out again before heading up to the courthouse. Tom Patterson had called to tell me the first appearance for Marla Kincaid was scheduled for first thing in the morning. Don't let anyone tell you the rich don't get treated differently. Anyone else would have rotted in jail all weekend. The local judiciary was in overdrive, first Lotham and now whatever judge had fallen victim to the call schedule and was about to become the next in a long and undistinguished line of celebrity murder justices.

I opened a bottle of water, propped my feet up on my desk and started thumbing through the latest forensic journals, taking a few more minutes' respite before starting to go through the stack of reports on my desk. One in particular beckoned, a folder that Ben had left. "Urgent— Mom, take a look and call me right away" on a neon green sticky. I fingered it for a moment, then decided that nothing to do with the dead could be that urgent. In the words of Ben's generation, I needed some space.

I'd just finished an article on new methods of blood spatter analysis when the phone jolted me out of my thoughts. "Jane Wallace," I answered. I knew that Tina had already screened the call, and whoever it was had the right number.

"Dr. Wallace? This is Dr. Wallace, the medical examiner, right?"

I resisted the urge to tell the reedy female voice that Dr. Wallace was on vacation and replied, as kindly as I could, in the affirmative. God spare me from the ditzes of the world.

"This is Dakota, down at Regent Clinic. We have a patient in here who says she's been raped."

There was a pause and I thought I heard a catch in her voice.

"Dr. Brownmiller told me to call you."

Dakota was a relative newcomer to town, or she'd have known that Regent Clinic was up valley, not down.

Most people in Telluride use the local medical center, which has been here since time began, or at least since there were enough solvent people in town to allow a primary care physician to make a living. About a year ago, an entrepreneurial type who had just settled in the area decided it was time to establish a "world-class" medical facility. He headquartered it just past the cemetery on the outskirts of town on the tag end of land that once housed the outbuilding of a now-abandoned mine. A tag end of land that faced another development of high-end homes owned by wealthy clientele was sprouting.

The land was cheap, there was plenty of parking, and it was far enough out of the historic district that he could use his generic floor plan, though he had to pretty it up some to get it past all the necessary approvals. He sweetened the deal by adding some low-cost apartments with a floor of offices, home to a variety of local entrepreneurs, dirt lawyers and real estate agents, both temporary and more established. His plan was to siphon off the lucrative medical business from Mountain Village and the ski slopes as well as his immediate neighbors — wealthy visitors who, when feeling under the weather in town, would want to indulge their snobbishness as well as their illness, to get "boutique" care.

It was not well received. There was a pretty spirited fight when it came time to permit the place, and the doc-in-a-box had to compromise by offering regular emergency care to the community as well as its high-end services. Not too many in town had taken them up on it, making the expenditure for the brand-new, state-of-the-art emergency department almost pure loss for the company. Except for now. I wondered how a rape victim had ended up in the Regent Clinic.

Not for the first time did I also wonder how in the world I ended up getting called to do the rape exam myself. As always, the answer came back to Father Matthew Gregory. Matt Gregory is the newly installed, and nearly freshly minted, priest just a few years older than my oldest sons. He took over shepherding St. Pat's when the circuit got too busy for one priest to handle, and the deacon moved on to a mission parish in

Aspen. When funds — mine — suddenly became available to support a priest in this exorbitantly expensive town, Father Matt's relative youth was seen as an advantage in Telluride, and the bishop quietly overlooked the fact that he'd only been an assistant for a few years in sending him to the post.

He is one of the few people in the world who intimidates me just by his presence. At almost six-feet-even in my stocking feet, and with a pugilistic personality, it takes a lot to make me want to run for cover, but Father Matt can do it. He claims to be Irish and Italian, but I'm pretty sure a Russian peasant sneaked into the family tree somewhere. He's the very incarnation of Rasputin, six-and-a-half feet tall, with dark, curly hair, an uncontrollable beard, and a definite edge to his otherwise warm personality. We had a familiar, if sometimes uneasy, relationship. I find myself unable to decide whether he was genuine, rebellious, cynical or a showman -- or all four rolled into one.

He was in my office one afternoon when a letter from San Miguel Combined Services arrived asking me to take over processing the collection of physical evidence from rape and assault victims as part of the mission of the forensic center. As it turns out, Fr. Matt is as nosy as an old maid. He saw the letter and scanned it upside down, a skill much prized by those of us who like to get information on the sly and use it at the most inconvenient time. As we finished our discussion, he rose to leave, looming over me like a tower in a black cassock. He looked at me for a long minute before he spoke. There was a bit of cunning in his brown eyes.

"So are you going to do it?" he asked.

Given that we had been discussing nothing that even remotely involved my doing anything, I was perplexed.

"The forensic exams," he added.

I scowled. "No, I'm not. No way on God's green earth. That requires talking to people I do not know about things I do not wish to discuss, and I am no good at that even when there's not a crisis involved. Leave that to the trained professionals." I met his gaze directly and said again, "No. I am not. It's not something I am capable of. They need a clinician, not me."

One of the perks of my job is that few people want to tell me how to do it. Another is that I don't have to listen to my patients. And I certainly don't have to listen to a priest, or so I thought. A man who knows how to exploit silence as well as I do, he waited a few beats before he spoke again, and when he did, it was the cynic who spoke.

"A forensic exam is a forensic exam, whether the body is warm or cold. Don't lie to me, Jane, that it's beneath you. You can do this, you ought to do this and you know it. You know like few others what it means to be touched by violence like that. You've seen it all. You'll make sure everything is done right so there are no loopholes. You've survived the worst yourself. You should care about those who are in the middle of tragedy themselves."

His eyes never wavered but one eyebrow lifted. I squirmed a bit. Fr. Matt never raises John's murder with me, knowing how raw it still is, even after all this time. To play the empathy card meant he had some serious agenda, and it involved me. Still, I wasn't ready to give in.

"I don't think so, Father. I'm just not called to do that."

I played my trump card. Most folks with any sense at all will back off at that point, unwilling to trespass on such sensitive ground. Not Father Matt. He laughed, a short bark of a laugh that let me know he wasn't buying what I was trying to sell.

"Oh, please, spare me. You're called, all right—you just don't want to answer. Why not?" he asked, his tone brisk. "Not doing these exams is not going to bring John back, you know, and you don't have anything better to do. All you do is work—this is just a little more." His tone softened a bit, and he added, "Violence is increasing in the area, Jane, and it so often involves the migrants. They aren't wealthy or powerful or able to take care of themselves."

He paused, expectant. I thought of all the rich and famous and powerful who had slipped through the net of the law. Tommy Berton had tried that with John's murder, and I'd expended every last breath to see that he'd not succeeded. Perhaps I did know what Fr. Matt meant, more than I wanted to admit.

Fr. Matt took a long breath and continued, this time sounding very much the earnest and devoted — if presently conniving — young priest, appealing both to my mind and my heart.

"They're afraid to get help because they're afraid that it will mean being sent home. They need someone on their side who not only knows what to do so that legal justice is done, they need someone who's on their side and capable to see to it that social justice is too. That's you. Period."

I was tempted to argue back, tempted to explain that as far as I was concerned, sending illegals back was exactly what social and legal justice required, if only for all the others waiting in line, but something both angry and hopeful in his expression made me stop.

"Oh, all right," I snapped. I signed the agreement on the letter and thrust it at him. "Hand this to Tina on your way out, would you? Now get out of here before you make more trouble for me."

So here I was, a couple of weeks later, being called out on that moment of weakness. I got the necessary information from the jittery Dakota and trotted down to the morgue to collect my camera and evidence kit. I punched out on the assignment board, yelled to Quick where I was going, and headed off for the Regent Clinic at the far edge of town. I went out the back door and down the alley in hopes of avoiding the press. Because they were still taking the lay of the land and circling the courthouse in anticipation of Marla Kincaid's arrival, I succeeded. I cut through Town Park, walking cross-lots to come out on the road just across from the cemetery. From there it was a short walk to the Regent Building and the clinic.

A perky brunette in a set of pink scrubs embroidered with the name "Regent Medical Services" met me at the check-in desk and showed me down a hall with pale green walls hung with tranquil local scenes, to an oak door with a surprisingly ordinary-looking medical chart in the basket on its face. I took the manila folder, muttered my annoyance at Father Matt and his schemes and went inside. Sitting on the examination table was a petite, dark-haired woman, whose face and figure proclaimed her Latin ancestry. She was hugging her legs to her chest and rocking back and forth, chin on her knees, staring off into the distance. On the floor, a small boy, perhaps four years old, played quietly with a stuffed toy. A well-coiffed, bottle-blonde, botoxed woman of indeterminate age stood beside her, with her hand on the woman's shoulder. At least I now knew how she'd come to this clinic — the Mountain Village connection was alive and well. The hand was manicured, it sported a multi-carat diamond and there was a Tag-Heuer on the wrist.

I recognized the shirt the dark-haired woman wore as one I'd seen in the free box, a wall of shelves where locals leave their unwanted goods for the use of anyone who needs them. I had seen it a couple of days before when I dropped off some dishes and glasses. A group of Hispanic men had just pulled up with a pickup truck and were systematically examining the finds in the free box, sorting them into bags as they took what they needed. I remembered the bright blue top being tossed from one man to another, then stuffed in brown paper as they chatted in Spanish. Something about a new building project in Montrose.

I looked at the chart and spoke. "Isa Robles? I'm Dr. Wallace."

She raised her head and turned to look at me. The left sleeve and the bodice of the blue shirt were torn, and her right eye was swollen and bloodied. "Si." Her voice was soft, but steady, and she looked directly at me. Then she corrected herself. "Yes. I am Isa."

I was impressed. She looked frail, but there was some steel in that voice. I turned to her keeper. "And you are...?" I let the question trail off.

Steel in the blonde's voice too, but a different kind. "Isa works for me."

She pointedly ignored my question, probably unaccustomed to being questioned authoritatively by someone sporting worn jeans, muddy boots, a white oxford shirt, and unruly salt-and-pepper curls pulled back into a ponytail.

"Well, Mrs. Isaworksforme," I said. "I appreciate your help, but I'm here to talk to this young lady, and you're just going to be in the way. Perhaps you could take the boy out into the waiting room and watch him until we are done." I held the door open for her and flourished my hand, giving her the look my kids used to call 'Mom-means-business.' She hesitated, cast a disdainful look in my direction, and picked up the toddler. She left the room without a word to either of us.

I turned back to the woman on the table, who had now sat up straight and was looking at me with a curious expression. "Habla usted inglés?" I asked as I washed my hands in the sink by the exam table.

There was great dignity in her voice. "Yes. I speak English."

Relieved that my high-school Spanish wasn't going to get a workout, I pulled on some gloves and asked whether I could take a look at her face. She nodded, still wary. I took her chin gently in my hand and carefully felt the bruise around her eye. She winced but didn't complain. "Can you tell me what happened?"

A tear slid down the brown cheek, whether from my probing question or my probing fingers, I couldn't tell. She closed her eyes, then said simply, "I was raped."

I recognized the control in her voice, in her expression. It was costing her dearly to distance herself from what had happened to her, to try to make it be something that had happened to someone else, someone in a dream, if she were lucky. I also knew that she wasn't going to wake up from this nightmare any more than I had from mine. I explained as gently as I could that I needed to take some photographs and collect some samples from her for evidence in court. She pursed her lips and nodded her permission, and I set about the collection checklist I had brought along, making notes and getting information. I had just finished photographing the bruises to her face and arms and breast, just starting to purple, when the perky brunette came in with a pill and some water.

I turned to face her, angry at being interrupted. This was hard enough without an audience. "We aren't finished," I told her, stepping between her and Isa, who was clutching a sheet to her chest.

"Dr. Brownmiller wanted me to bring this on in and give it to her. There's no reason to wait. Here you go, hon." She extended the pill and cup. I noticed the nametag on her scrub top. *Sally, from Denver.*

Isa gathered the sheet in one hand and took the pill in the other, looking at it, small and white against her palm. "What is this?" she asked, voice suspicious and face a little fearful.

"It's your emergency contraception. It will keep you from getting pregnant. It will make sure that you don't have a baby from this."

We were both surprised, Sally and I, when Isa hurled the pill across the room with a resounding "No." Her eyes flashed with anger and indignation.

Sally beat a hasty retreat, leaving me in the awkward silence that followed. Not knowing what to say or do, I took the time-honored course of ignoring what had just happened. Isa's medical care was not my problem. Collecting evidence to nail her attacker was.

"Let's finish these photographs," I said, gently changing the subject and picking up the camera again. Isa relaxed a bit and dropped the sheet so I could finish what Sally had interrupted. One of the bruises on the upper part of her chest was beginning to show a peculiar, distinct form, a small horseshoe with sharp edges and tiny, dark points. "Does he wear a ring?" I asked. In another twenty-four hours, I suspected the bruise might well show the pattern of the design, one that might link the attacker very clearly to Isa, even if the DNA from under her nails and from the swabs didn't.

She nodded in reply to my question. "A big one, on his right hand. Gold."

I told her I'd have to see her again tomorrow to take some more pictures, and she agreed to come to the Center in the early afternoon. She paused uncertainly and went on.

"I cannot take her pill. It's wrong. I cannot."

This was not a discussion I wished to have, but Isa left me no choice. "It's your health," I told her as I helped her lay back on the table. "You get to decide. You don't have to take it." I was having trouble imagining why in her situation she wouldn't want to. Her decision astonished me. It made me think. It made me remember John. This woman faced the possibility of a baby from a man she must hate, the result of violence, not of love. Amazing.

As if reading my mind she said, "What is my shame compared to the life of my child? It will be my child, if God sends it."

Uncomfortable with the subject and anxious to move on, I did the rest of the exam, asking a few more questions as I collected the necessary samples. I was labeling the last of them when the door flew open again and a muscular woman, her brown hair cut short and gelled into spikes, burst into the room, a force of nature in a lab coat. A nametag identified her as Dr. Jennie Brownmiller, and she had rose tattoos on the forearms that stuck out of her rolled-up sleeves. Call me old-fashioned, but I find it hard to trust a woman physician with tattoos on her arms.

Brownmiller immediately set about confirming my prejudice. She had a big city bearing, tough and overwhelming. I found her a shock among the generally easy-going populace of Telluride. I suspected that was another reason the Regent Clinic wasn't doing very well.

"Sally tells me you don't want to take the morning after pill," she announced with no preface. "That's ridiculous. You can't run the risk of getting pregnant. You can't afford another kid. You can't afford the one you've got."

Again, that great dignity and resolve. "No. I do not want your pills. I cannot. It is wrong." Isa looked to me for support, but I kept silent for the time being. She was doing fine all by herself. "Wrong," she repeated.

Dr. Brownmiller snorted. "Oh, please. You'll feel differently when you're pregnant, and all you can think about is the rape. You'll beg me for an abortion, and believe me, sister, we aren't doing one for you unless that blond-headed bimbo of an employer pays for it. Now take this pill and let's be done with it." She shook the replacement in a medicine cup, ominously, under Isa's nose.

I cleared my throat, and Brownmiller shot an annoyed look in my direction. "It appears to me that Ms. Robles has declined your kind offer of care," I said in an even voice, but one underpinned with the slightest edge of a threat. "I think that if I were you, I'd document her informed refusal and leave it at that." I was getting tired of asserting myself to jackasses. Was there no end of them in this town today?

Brownmiller scowled at me but didn't back down. "In three months she'll be a psychotic mess. Believe me, she'll thank me when this is all over."

I laid the last labeled and bagged sample into my kit and clicked it shut, then turned to face Brownmiller. "I don't think so. And I think that if you don't leave her alone and respect her decision, I'll have your license on a silver platter." I paused. "I can do that, you know."

No need to leave any doubt about the matter, even if I was overstating the case just a bit. Well, quite a bit. Lawyers learn to use even empty threats effectively. Then I gave her a conciliatory look. "I'll be happy to help you draft the butt-protecting language you need to stay out of court if she does change her mind."

My tone warmed and Brownmiller caved. Feeling the serious need to find another line of work, I jotted a refusal of care on Isa's chart and sent Dr. Brownmiller on her indemnified, if confused and unhappy, way. I spied a female deputy from Montrose County languishing in the hall, and I motioned her in. Isa lived in a house on the outskirts of that town and the rape happened there; Tom Patterson would be spared this case.

"I've got everything I need," I said. "I'll send my report over as soon as it's typed up."

She gave me a tight half-smile and edged past me to introduce herself. Her voice was quiet and reassuring and I saw Isa relax a bit. I remembered what Father Matt had said about illegal immigrants not wanting to talk to the police. I eavesdropped for a moment and then I dialed Father Matt. If anyone was going to take care of a woman with this kind of starch in her drawers, it ought to be he. And for the first time in days, I smiled at the prospect of Father Matt's schemes rebounding on him as I closed the door of the examining room.

****

Tom Patterson slammed the phone down in irritation at Simon Clark, the state's attorney who had fielded the Houston case. Damn fool still wanted to charge Marla Kincaid the next morning. Patterson had brought her in on suspicion, hoping to jar loose something that would seal the case against her, but that hadn't happened.

She'd maintained a distant, frightened silence after calling her lawyer.

He picked up Maggie Gleason's report. The case had been called in by a voyeur.

Houston dead as the proverbial doornail on the bedroom floor. A .22 found in the dresser, one shot gone, recently fired. The maid said that she'd heard an argument between the Kincaid woman and Houston just before leaving the house after cleaning the kitchen, a detail that tended to damn the suspect in custody. He smiled as he read on and found Maggie was an equal-opportunity reporter of unflattering facts. It seems the maid complained that it took her until almost ten to clean up the kitchen because Houston was both a messy cook and an exacting employer.

That put Houston alive and in Kincaid's presence at ten, he thought. The peeping Tom—if that was a term he could apply to a woman— said she saw a body on the floor of the bedroom around midnight. We found Marla Kincaid standing over the body at about two in the morning. It was her gun, found it in her dresser. There was no one else in the house. It had to be her.

Still, he thought, Clark was rushing to judgment. Doc Wallace's report was still out, no ballistics, no fingerprints, nothing hard and fast to show a jury. Patterson had been a lawman long enough to know that no matter how tidy a case looked at first glance, there was always room for something to screw it up, especially when lawyers got involved, even the ones paid by the state. He disliked having the case out of his control before he had had a chance to finish it from his end. He tossed the papers back on his desk, rocked back in his chair, put his hands behind his head, and closed his eyes to think.

Any other perp and he'd be cheering Clark on. Hell, he'd have cheered him on when he first caught the case. What was it he'd said to Doc Wallace? Not much mystery to this murder. But that was before he'd arrested Marla Kincaid. Before he'd had a good long look into those storybook eyes.

He sat up abruptly, the legs of his chair rapping sharply against the floor. *You're getting old and soft, Patterson,* he scolded himself. *Good thing you don't have to show up in court tomorrow.*

CHAPTER THREE

JUNE 7

The San Miguel County courthouse is a picture-perfect building that dominates town, symmetrical, made of red brick with a tower, clock and silver roof so photogenic that I'd be willing to wager not a single tourist gets out of town without at least one image of it.

It meant dodging reporters and fighting my way past crowds, but I wasn't going to miss the bail hearing if I could help it. My curiosity was up; this case was on the fast track for sure, and I wondered why. I supposed there was no harm in an early charge, given that there really wasn't room for any honest doubt that she had shot him. The lawyer in me understood that there are all kinds of mitigating circumstances that make guilt less than guilt. Even the Catholic in me understood that — depended on it, no less. The widow in me had no time for such soft-hearted nonsense.

The crowd around the courthouse doors was ten-deep, assorted journalists and onlookers all hoping to catch a glimpse of Marla Kincaid. I pushed myself through the crowd, forestalling angry comments with my badge upheld. I'd always considered the practice of giving the medical examiner courtesy law-enforcement status more an ego pleaser for my male colleagues than a necessary adjunct, but I had to admit that it had its purposes. This was one of them.

Even with San Miguel County's finest on crowd control, the courtroom was standing room only. I slid past a familiar deputy who gave me a wry look, and took a place along the back wall of the courtroom. It was all wood, ornate balusters, and leather, not much changed from its glory days but for the microphones, modern paintings and 50-star flag. It also wasn't designed to accommodate an event of this notoriety.

Still, it wasn't the first celebrity trial in these four walls. There had been several high-profile cases in Telluride in the past, including the crash of helicopter carrying a load of glitterati, and the murder some years ago of a well-known designer. Telluride was used to publicity, good or bad. Even William Jennings Bryan had delivered his "cross of gold" potboiler to enthusiastic crowds in town, though he'd had the good sense to set up a stage in front of the local hotel. Still, the crowds that day weren't much less pressing than this one, if the old photos in the museum could be trusted.

The crowd was restive and the room hot and sticky. The noise level grew as time passed with no sign of the judge. Craning my neck, I caught a glimpse of Marla Kincaid at the defense table. She was wearing the clothes required of a female defendant: dark skirt and white blouse. I wondered if she owned them already or if her agent and stylist had sent them with the pricey lawyer at her side. Probably the latter. Telluride isn't exactly tailored skirt-and-blouse country.

I recognized Johanssen and his father, both in serviceable navy suits, both deferent to the shorter, balding man standing between them and Marla Kincaid. Like theirs, his suit was navy blue, but even regarding him from the back of the courtroom, I'd be willing to bet that you couldn't have bought his suit for the cost of everything — including rings and expensive watches — that Johanssen, father and son, were wearing.

Judge Carnegie finally entered from the side door, a sturdy, middle-aged woman I knew was no-nonsense, well-read and fair. I took inordinate pleasure in the fact that, unlike many of her female colleagues on the bench, she refrained from affecting a lace jabot at the neck of her robe to declare her sex. Her robe was unadorned black silk, and the edge of a garish plaid blouse peeked out from the velvet placket at the neckline. We all stood, and she gaveled the courtroom into silence and got on with business as though she were dealing with a routine DUI. She glanced at the bailiff as his signal to get her judicial show on the road.

"State vs. Marla Kincaid," said the bailiff in a flat, uninterested voice that betrayed his Midwestern origins. "Does defense waive reading?"

Daddy Johanssen answered for the team. "We do."

The Hollywood suit might be calling the shots, but odds were that he wasn't admitted to the Colorado bar. Marla Kincaid looked at neither of them, her eyes on the younger Eric.

Judge Carnegie flipped through the folder on her desk, looking out over the top of her glasses, those half-bifocals middle-aged women buy by the gross at the local discount house because they are so easy to lose. These were pink floral, a jarring contrast to the somber robe and glowering demeanor, but they confirmed the taste of the woman who'd picked out the plaid shirt.

"Charges?"

"Murder in the second degree."

The state's attorney was a tall, thin, older man with graying hair. I was surprised he'd let go the bargaining chip of murder one right out of the gate, but I approved. More often than not, high profile cases are lost because of grandstanding by the prosecutor and charging more than he can honestly hope to prove. The judge cocked an eyebrow, nodded, then went back to examining the documents in front of her. There was a long pause as she shuffled through them for no apparent reason other than to exercise her control over the proceedings. Every eye was on her, and the silence was palpable.

Another look from Judge Carnegie over her glasses. "Plea?"

This time it was Marla who spoke in a thin, unsteady voice. "Not guilty, Your Honor."

Right. I found myself unreasonably annoyed by the amount of time and effort it was going to take to sort out this simple, clear-cut matter of murder once the lawyers and the press got done with it.

"Bail?"

No one could accuse Judge Carnegie of grandstanding. She even made me look flamboyant by comparison. Her Scots ancestors would be proud of her parsimony with words.

"The State asks ten million, Your Honor."

"Outrageous. This young woman has never been accused of so much as speeding before today." Daddy Johanssen leapt into action, and the proceedings suddenly became interesting. A short exchange ensued, Johanssen and the State attorney returning volleys as crisply as a Chinese ping-pong team.

"The defendant has no ties to the community and is at risk for flight."

"Miss Kincaid lives here, in fact, owns two properties in the county jointly with the decedent and is prepared to proffer her passport against the risk of flight. She has no access to funds of her own, and all joint funds she held with Mitch Houston are frozen."

"A bit like the man who killed his father asking for mercy because he's an orphan. The defendant's actions are responsible for the freezing of those accounts."

"Miss Kincaid is at this point functionally indigent, Your Honor. Ten million is excessive, unconscionable."

I almost gasped at the temerity of the assertion. Lawyers are good at making words mean what they don't; it's our stock in trade, but this was remarkable. I reflected that some of the truly down-and-out I saw in Montrose and Grand Junction, when I sallied forth from the protection of Telluride's box canyon would be gratified to know that they at least were the real thing, not mendicant posers like Marla Kincaid. Judge Carnegie interrupted the discussion with her own wry comment.

"She is the most well-heeled indigent this court has seen for a long time. I am sure that she can leverage some assistance to cover bail, Counselor. Start with those two properties you were talking about. Bail is set at two million."

Daddy Johanssen is no fool. He knew when he'd overstepped and when to cut his losses and remained silent, quieting his California associate with a dark look and an off-putting hand. A few more tactical points, a discussion or two, and the guards led Marla Kincaid off again. The courtroom emptied quickly as soon as she was gone, confirming my impression that the turnout was roughly akin to slowing down to rubberneck at a car crash. As I slipped out the back door, I noticed that the Johanssens and their colleague were deep in conversation with one of Telluride's more prominent real estate agents, probably cooking up a way to pledge the properties for bail. Marla Kincaid would be on the streets and relaxing in her rural second home before sunset. I would release my hold on the crime scene when I got back to the office, but for now the Mountain Village property was off the table.

Father Matt came up the stairs as I was leaving.

"You missed it," I said. "All done in record time."

He paused midway up the steps. "What did she plead?"

"Not guilty." I saw the faintest shadow cross his features and wondered why it mattered to him. "There will be quite a trial. She'll either plead self-defense or diminished capacity. Lots of room for a sympathy verdict. A waste of time and energy, this trial. There's no room for argument about what happened." I knew I was treading on thin ice, legally and ethically, and hoped that there wasn't a journalist lurking nearby to report my comments. I cast a furtive glance around to be sure. The place had cleared out. Father Matt and I were alone, not another human being in sight or earshot.

"Jane, you know very well she has a right to put the state to the test. Maybe there are mitigating circumstances. Maybe," he paused for emphasis, "she's innocent." He leaned against the balustrade, arms extended on the rail, one of those people who takes rest whenever and wherever it comes.

I let go an unladylike snort. "I know the theory but even in law school, I never understood the need to pretend that facts as clear as the light of day needed proving. There just was no other explanation for Mitch Houston's death than the stark reality that Marla Kincaid shot him. Willfully. Intentionally. With malice aforethought, even if just for an instant." I glared at Father Matt. "Marla Kincaid could present her sob story in the sentencing phase just as well as she could to a fawning jury," I said. "The difference is that a clear-headed judge — not twelve unruly jurors — would hear it, and her odds of getting off easy wouldn't be so great."

"There's some truth to that," Father Matt agreed. "But is it such a terrible thing for her to look for a little mercy?"

I shrugged. "She didn't have much for Houston. The law is about justice. In the end, it's going to be the same: she'll be guilty in some form or another, but only after a huge amount of expense and a lot of weeping and wailing about how she's really the victim. Spare me."

That shadow crossed Father Matt's face again. "Not everyone is as strong as you," he finally said. "Some people need to work up to accepting the truth, even when it's clear to them. You'd do well not to judge her, Jane—I see the same need in you."

That stung, but I managed to swallow a retort and keep the conversation on an even keel. I changed the subject.

"Have you seen Isa Robles?"

"I have. The social worker is taking care of getting her some money and some clothes—she's not going back to that house—and a few toys for her boy. We'll figure out where to go next." He paused. "She said you stood up for her."

I shrugged again. "Part of my job. She'd already been abused once. No reason to let that nitwit doctor do it again." I thought back to the exchange. "Besides, she's perfectly capable of standing up for herself. Tough lady." I remembered the bruise, the mark of the ring. "Can you make sure she comes by the Center tomorrow? I need to photograph some of those bruises again. I'll get better images for court. "

Father Matt nodded. "I'll get her there. In the interests of justice." He looked directly at me for a long minute before he straightened up and allowed me to pass. He followed me down the steps out into the street, where our paths diverged once again. He headed up the street toward the church. I headed down to the precincts of the dead, wondering what new work waited there.

****

Marla Kincaid looked around the hotel room one more time and shook her head. It wasn't a dream, it wasn't a set, it was real. It wasn't as bad as she expected. The sheriff had closed down the house in Mountain Village as a crime scene, and after the appearance in court, she had to take lodgings in the big, luxury hotel in the middle of Mountain Village. It was festival season, and all of the good suites were taken. She had to settle for some second tier room. It was clean, but it was small, smaller than any of the guest rooms in her real house.

Was it still her house? It really belonged to Mitch. She wondered if she would be able to stay there after the sheriff released it. Mitch was supposed to have put it in both their names, but she wasn't sure that he ever did. Marla was suddenly seized with the fear that she was, after all this, homeless. Her eyes clouded with tears, and she collapsed on the bed with the bought-by-the-dozens bedspread and wept, pounding her fist into the mattress in fear with utter frustration. It would never have passed for a scene from a movie, but then this wasn't a movie. It was real, too real. She could tell by the knot of fear that filled her stomach and refused to go away.

The worst of it wasn't really the fear of what would happen to her. Her agent had gotten her a good lawyer in town. She was surprised when the good looking blond man showed up at the house to spirit her away from under that sheriff's nose once the bail arrangements had been made. It hadn't taken long. Marla knew the sheriff was sure she had killed Mitch, but he'd have to prove it, wouldn't he? And he wouldn't be able to do that.

The lawyer brought her here and paid for the room, told her to stay put in the hotel, eat room-service food, and stay out of sight until her other lawyer arrived and they had a chance to figure out what the sheriff knew and didn't know. Her own pricey attorney should be on his way before tomorrow. Until then, she was stuck in a 20-by-20 room with a window that looked out over a parking lot instead of the mountains.

She had been here only a few hours and already she was restless. It wasn't the room so much as the sheer boredom of being tucked in a place with nothing to do, nothing to look at except a TV, and nothing to read that was making her restless and afraid. It had been years since she was this alone with herself, if ever at all, and she was as much afraid of what she would find if she looked inward as she was of what her own, familiar lawyer would say when he finally arrived. At least with him, she had the chance of flirting, pouting, playing the overwhelmed little girl. She didn't have that luxury with herself.

She rolled over on the bed and wiped her eyes with the back of her hand. She lay staring at the ceiling for a long while. Outside her door in the corridor, she heard the clank of the maids' cart and their chatter in Spanish as they moved down the hall. She waited until she couldn't hear them anymore. Then she got up with a determined look, changed into a non-descript pair of jeans and a plain tee-shirt from the half-packed bag the lawyer had grabbed as they left the house, tied a scarf on her head to hide her trademark hair, donned a pair of oversized sunglasses, and headed out the door. She took the back stairs out of the hotel, winding through a corridor on the very bottom floor that led her to a service entrance by a smelly dumpster overfilled with trash and sadly in need of emptying. She squared her shoulders and walked confidently around to the front of the hotel, half-expecting to see a crowd of reporters but saw only summer tourists coming and going.

She fell in behind a mother and daughter, both tall and brunette, with carefully coiffed hair, acrylic nails, and rhinestone-studded tops. *Texans,* Marla thought with disgust. Tacky people. Still, they provided her a sense of cover as she strolled with controlled anxiety toward the lift station that would take her into town on one of the big, gray gondolas.

The line was not long, and she blended into the crowd of people, most of them in groups, without attracting attention. Marla sat in one of the cars with a family from Iowa who couldn't stop talking about the murder that had happened just the night before. She turned her head away before they could engage her in the conversation and watched the town of Telluride come closer and closer and didn't say a word.

Marla stood for a moment outside the lower station, unsure what she would do now that she was free of the hotel and walking the streets of town. She pulled out the few dollars she tucked into her pocket as she was leaving the hotel room: enough for a drink or a coffee at that little shop on the main street of town, but not much more. Her credit cards were back at the house; she had not had time to pack them, and they were probably cut off anyway. Now that she was here, she had no idea what she wanted to do. She thought it would feel good to be out of the hotel; instead, it felt disorienting.

Then she remembered the trail on the other side of town that led to a pretty little waterfall. It wasn't a long trail, and it wasn't a strenuous walk. The thought of standing behind the waterfall and watching it cascade in front of her had sudden appeal. There was a little grocery not far from the lift station. She could stop by there and get a bottle of water and an apple and take a hike. There was still plenty of light.

Marla started off down the street, careful not to catch anyone's eye and walked with purpose, like she knew what she was doing. She walked the short distance to Fir Street and turned north. She was almost at the corner of Pacific when she saw them: a crowd of reporters clustered around the yellow brick building on the corner and lounging on the sidewalk in front of the grocery store, two satellite trucks parked nearby. A chill ran up her back and she stopped, uncertain what to do.

It was her downfall. One of the crowd nearest her, a tubby, middle-aged man holding a camera with an enormous lens, spotted her. He looked at her for a moment, uncertain, cocking his head in thought as she stood frozen on the sidewalk. His face split into a leering grin as he recognized who she was, lifted the camera, and aimed it at her.

She took a deep breath and turned, starting back the way she had come, hoping no one else had seen, but it was too late. She heard the crowd coming after her, their shouted questions barely audible over the noise of their running. She broke into a sprint, dodging from one side of the road to the other, aware that now everyone on the street had stopped to stare in fascination at her and the pack of humanity pursuing her. In her confusion, she turned away from the gondola station, running headlong toward the town park, the pack of reporters closing with every step. She saw one of them — younger, fit, and athletic — break away and sprint ahead, jumping over a low picket fence and a toddler on a tricycle to get ahead of her, almost running into a green SUV that was coming down the street in her direction. He swore at the vehicle and shook his fist at the red-headed driver, then dodged around back and started toward her himself. The SUV surged forward and swerved to the middle of the road, cutting him off and eliciting another round of swearing. The SUV edged forward, closing the distance to Marla. She could see the driver motioning her inside. Grateful for any escape, she pulled open the door. The driver extended a hand to help her climb inside.

"Ben Wallace," he said with a friendly grin. "Get in! Let's get you out of here."

She pushed down the lock and crouched down so that she could neither see nor be seen. The SUV pulled slowly forward, the driver impervious to the shouts of the crowd and certain they would move out of his way, whistling along with Eric Clapton as he maneuvered his way out of town.

CHAPTER FOUR

JUNE 8, MORNING

Silly me. I thought that once the arraignment was over, things might die down in town. Unfortunately, it was a slow news week, and because of bail and an acute lack of funds precipitated by the fact that almost everything was in Houston's name, Marla Kincaid was stuck in Telluride. I was amazed at how quickly the news-hounds multiplied in the twenty-four hours following the bail hearing. Both towns, venerable old Telluride in the valley, and Mountain Village, created to service the ski industry on the mountain, were choked with news vans sporting satellite dishes and reporters shoving microphones in the faces of passersby and the festivities showed no sign of dying down. I preferred to hide out in my office, and did so happily, avoiding the reporters seeking to score an interview with the pathologist who had cut Mitch Houston open and laid all his secrets bare. Six or seven of them camped out on the doorstep of the Western Slope Forensic Center, known in these parts as simply The Center, badgering my staff for access to me.

The Center is housed in a renovated brick warehouse I resurrected as the home for my pet project when I retreated to Telluride after John's death. Between the grocery and the bakery that are just across the street, the area is pretty well-traveled. The crowd was making a bottleneck in our quiet little town, right in front of my office, and because of the proximity of food, the reporters had no particular reason to disperse. Finally, Tina, the receptionist, came to my office in disgust.

"Will you just please go talk to them so they will leave us alone? I can't even get across the street, and I want to go home. They keep pestering us, but it's you they really want."

I scowled at Tina, who was pushing her hair back from her forehead in frustration. I took a leaf from my old Granny's book of stock answers.

"Wantin' ain't gettin', Tina. I have absolutely no desire to talk to them."

I was surprised at her acidic response. "Well, neither do I. Nobody around here cares about what you want, Dr. Wallace. You get paid the big bucks, and we're getting the problems. Now you get down there and talk to them."

She stood, hands on hips, clearly not willing to move until I rescued her from the hordes milling about. She had a point. My hiding wasn't making the problem go away, and it was making life miserable for my staff. I stood up, dropping the file I had been working on — a printout of Houston's autopsy findings and the lab results that Norman had just brought that confirmed my suspicions — onto my cluttered desk.

"Come on," I said.

Tina stood fast.

"No way. You go clear the trail. I'll stay here, thanks."

She watched me with aggravated eyes as I passed her and stepped into the hallway. I heard her muttering under her breath as I passed.

She wasn't kidding. The lobby was empty because Tina had had the sense to lock the glass doors; I could see the keys dangling from the lock. Outside, I counted three cameramen, seven reporters, four women, three men, in various states of costume from suits to jeans, clutching notebooks or dangling foam-topped microphones, their rectangular station flags upside down in anticipation of being pressed into service. When they saw me through the glass, they snapped to like a well-drilled platoon, pens at the ready, and microphones at attention. I scowled, strode to the door, and turned the key. The unruly horde threatened to surge through the door as I swung it open. I was having none of that.

"Get back," I barked in my best courtroom voice. "If you want to talk to me, it's going to be outside, not in here." I planted myself in the center of the doorway and dared anyone to defy me. I haven't lost my touch. Either that, or they were so anxious for information that they were willing to curb their reportorial instincts for the greater journalistic good. I stepped out, let the door swing shut behind me, and backed up against it for good measure to keep them from sneaking by me and foraging in the office on their own. I pulled out my cell — in my pocket for once — and called my office. Tina answered. "Get down here and lock these doors behind me."

I heard a chuckle, and the line went dead. I stared down the reporters until I heard the lock click behind me. I turned to glimpse Tina giving me the thumbs-up and a cheeky grin.

Sensing that to be some sort of starting gun, the throng erupted into a barrage of questions. I caught the occasional word, but it was worse than being the token conservative on CNN, each one talking over the other and no chance for me to get a word in edgewise.

"Knock it off," I finally shouted, then remembered with annoyance that the cameras were running and the mikes recording, and that I would undoubtedly be on the evening news with that resoundingly inane remark. *Oh well, at least the soft, yellow, brick façade of the building would make a nice backdrop.* I took a deep breath and tried again.

"I am happy to answer your questions, " I said. "But one at a time and that's it. I am not here to be harassed and neither is my staff. Mind your manners —" I cringed again, that wouldn't play well either, " — and let's get on with it."

A bearded man in a green polo shirt with the logo of a Denver station spoke first.

"What did you find at Houston's autopsy?"

"He was shot."

"Anything else important?" He eyed me, fishing for information.

"Depends on what you mean by important. Nothing much more important than the bullet that kills a man, at least in my book." I hoped it was enough of a non-denial denial to throw him off track. It wasn't, but another of his colleagues picked up the scent.

"What about the rumor that Houston had AIDS?"

"I don't listen to rumors."

"Did you test for it?"

"We took the usual post-mortem tests for infectious diseases and toxicology."

"When do you expect the results?"

This from a petite blonde in the front row, probably the only person in Telluride history to walk the streets in broad daylight in an elegant, powder-blue St. John's suit and Manolo Blahniks. Probably from one of the cable entertainment networks. *They must pay well.*

"They won't be released until day after tomorrow."

"Why so long?"

This bunch was as bad as a pack of jackals. No wonder Tina lost patience. I tried the honey-not-vinegar approach.

"I know it seems like a long time, but really, that's pretty prompt. Big city offices would take a week or more." I smiled, only baring my teeth a little. "I'll issue a statement sometime that afternoon." The fact of the matter was that the autopsy was already complete; I was just waiting on ballistics to sign, seal and deliver it.

The guy in the jeans circled back.

"Were there any physical findings that led you to suspect AIDS?"

"You're going to have to wait for the press release for details. I don't discuss autopsy findings on sidewalks in the hearing of every Tom, Dick, and Harry in town. It's not respectful to the decedent, nor the family."

"So let us inside. That way you can keep the family's privacy."

The fellow was persistent, I had to give him that. I gave the appearance of consideration before answering, although it was the original no-brainer.

"No, I don't think so. My office has work to do and doesn't need you folks cluttering up the place. I'll release a statement in a day or two. Until then, I would request that you leave me and my staff alone." I smiled again, more teeth. "I do hope I won't have to call on Sheriff Patterson to maintain the operations of my office."

"Is that a threat?" This from an indignant, middle-aged woman wearing a long skirt, a sleeveless tee-shirt and no foundation garments. She was busily scribbling on a notepad, and her expression was thunderous.

"It is not. It's a request for you to conduct yourselves like professionals. And an assurance that, whether or not you do, I will." I held up a hand as the crowd started to murmur again. "That's it, gentlemen and ladies." I knew this would annoy the woman in the tee-shirt, and I watched with satisfaction as she bristled outwardly and scribbled again. I needed to make certain for whom she wrote; this would definitely be an article to add to my scrapbook of assorted hate-mail and other assorted defamatory clippings.

I hadn't noticed Tom Patterson coming up the walk. His voice boomed out over the backs of the reporters.

"Nobody gets the report until we do, and we don't have it yet. Break it up for today. My office will see you get any information as soon as we do. No need to bother Dr. Wallace. Besides, the more you push, the more she'll drag her feet. Keep this up, and we'll be lucky to get that report by next Christmas." His homely, good-natured face and honest smile defused the situation and prompted the reporters to disperse.

I did hear a variety of uncomplimentary references to me and my lineage as they moved on.

"You sure do have a knack for annoying people," Patterson said. "Didn't they teach you to make nice?"

Patterson is a good lawman, but he's also an elected official, mindful of the need to calm waters, soothe ruffled feathers, and appear to be everyone's friend. A few years ago, a celebrated Aspen politician declared to the owner of a vacation home in the area that he didn't have to listen to anyone who could not even vote for him in the local elections. Unfortunately, an ever-vigilant member of the fourth estate was nearby, and the remark made headlines. He discovered to his dismay that the remark did not sit well with the 47% of the local populace that actually lived there and didn't vote for him in the last election, and they — and a few assorted owners of those expensive vacation homes who were being ignored — were able to sway enough of his own constituents to make, as they say in the political trade "a difference." The fact that that particular politician was no longer a mover-and-shaker in Aspen politics was not lost on Tom Patterson.

"Where? In law school, where they teach verbal kung fu from day one? Or in pathology training, where I spend my day with dead folks? No, Tom, they didn't teach me to make nice." Well, not exactly. John tried, and could usually cajole me out of a contentious mood, but that time was long past.

"Figures," he replied. "Got a minute to talk?"

I motioned to Tina, who had by now reassumed her place at the desk. She opened the door for us.

"Thanks," she said. "It was getting kind of tough."

"Keep it locked," I instructed. "I don't trust that lot any farther than I can throw them."

Tom Patterson added, "If there's any trouble, call me. I know you've got the cell."

In point of fact, I was pretty sure Tina had the sheriff on speed dial. I suspected his arrival hadn't been entirely fortuitous. I knew I should thank Tina, but the phone interrupted me.

"It's been like that since we opened the doors. And it isn't even noon." Tina looked apologetic. And tired.

"Put them on forward," I said. "Send it through to my cell, and go home. It's going to be a long day."

I hoped that would suffice for gratitude. It seemed to. Tina sprinted to the desk, punched a few buttons, and the cell in my pocket began magically to jangle. Patterson grinned as I answered, listened to yet another reporter, and more or less politely told him to buzz off.

"It's not going to let up until you release that report," he said.

"No kidding. And then it will just be different questions. Want a cup of coffee?" I punched the elevator call button, deciding that I'd had enough exercise for now, and we rode up in silence and continued it for the few steps from the elevator to the kitchen that was down the hall from my office. I had long since drunk up my own personal pot of coffee, but knew that there was always some in the kitchen. Quick was addicted to the stuff and had a pot going day and night. Tom took his coffee black, which was a good thing, since I noticed the half-and-half carton in the trash by the fridge. The pot had been on since Quick came downstairs at six, so the coffee was thick and dark and more than a little bitter. Penitential coffee, John would have called it. Whenever he found such an overdone pot, he'd poured it out and made fresh. I just suffered through it.

Patterson shared my pedestrian tastes in caffeine and took a long draw on his cup as I was pouring my own. He leaned against the counter, crossing his legs at the ankles, the sole of one scuffed brown, metal-toed boot visible. A hole was developing in the middle of it. Tom would have to visit the town cobbler, a Guatemalan man who had set up a portable shop near the coffee trailer in a small park near the east edge of town. I sipped my own coffee. It was truly foul, worse than usual.

"What's up?" I asked.

Patterson put his cup on the counter beside him and folded his arms across his chest. In any other man, it would have been aggressive, or threatening. In Tom Patterson, it was just a way of being comfortable.

"I'm not the press. What do you have on Houston?"

"He had AIDS, complete with opportunistic infections. No drugs on board, but looks like he shot up. A little booze. Otherwise, pretty good shape. Thin, muscular. Liver, heart and lungs okay. Brain, not so much."

"Range on the shot?"

"More than a couple of feet. She could have been standing by that dresser, dropping him where he fell on the rug."

"That piddly little pepper-pot kill him?"

I could never tell whether Patterson's affinity for archaic firearms terms was an affectation or just part of his down-home folksy persona.

"Well, the slug was too deformed to match." I took another sip of coffee. "Is there really any doubt?" I suppressed my own concerns that the lump of metal from Houston's brain was too big to be from that .22.

My mind returned to that "just-a-bit-too-big" wad of lead. I suddenly found myself concerned that the state's attorney, well seasoned but with a bit of a reputation for grandstanding, had jumped the gun, charging Marla Kincaid right out of the box instead of waiting a bit for my report. I wondered why. Patterson drained the mug.

"Not in my mind, but she claims she didn't kill him. Says she fired the gun earlier in the day, shooting at a squirrel from her porch." Patterson frowned. "Just doesn't make sense to me. No reason for her to do that, and we'll never prove it one way or another. She says she just wanted to see if she could still shoot."

I had my doubts, too. A gunshot in Mountain Village would have resulted in a dozen 911 calls. Not only were the wealthy residents a little nervous about security, they also opposed guns in any form.

"What's her story?"

"Says she went into town to walk around, went to the library, did a little shopping. Problem is, she didn't buy anything. And people in this town are either so starstruck they'd claim they saw her even if she was in Timbuktu at the time—or so indifferent that they wouldn't notice her." He uncrossed his legs and straightened up. "I've got my guys poking around, but I sure could use a match on that bullet. To punctuate my report." That was Tom's version of attending to detail. "Johanssen is keeping her wrapped up pretty tight, but she posted bail within an hour of the hearing. I want to be on solid ground when the time comes. Wonder if she'll change her story and plead self-defense?"

I thought about the crime scene again. I had to admit that Patterson's story hung together well; it sure looked like Houston had been shot by an angry woman. He'd not been armed, and there were no scratches or defense wounds that would indicate a struggle. If I had been asked my opinion—and someday I would be—I'd say he'd been caught off guard.

"I can't see self-defense, Tom. Diminished capacity—who knows?"

Tommy Berton had tried that ploy, but the D.A. had been able to circumvent it, if only because I had bird-dogged him so long that he finally put together the whole story of Berton's meticulous, diabolical planning. I had no way of knowing whether Marla Kincaid had plotted. My heart wanted it to be so, but my mind's jury was not only out, it was hung. Such dichotomies of mind and spirit were becoming increasingly common. *Sign of a soft mind,* I thought. *Or a hard heart.* I shook off the thought and returned my attention to Patterson again.

"I agree, but what do I know? I'm just a dumb cop. Johanssen's been pretty civilized, but Houston's own lawyer has been driving me nuts—mostly trying to get me to file charges against you, I might add, for abuse of a corpse."

"Let me know how that works out. My job description is pretty much abuse of corpses. He's harmless, just pissed and full of himself."

"Yeah, I know. He'll get tired and go away as soon as Johanssen files suit against the estate. I gather he's just waiting for your report. Marla Kincaid's other Hollywood lawyer, the one who handles the entertainment stuff, is due in town tomorrow. That's when the fireworks will really start." Patterson contemplated his empty cup for a moment. "When do you think you'll have the autopsy report?"

"It's on my desk." I finished my own coffee and put my cup in the sink. "Come on, I'll get it for you."

Patterson set his cup next to mine and followed me to the office. I handed Tom the review I'd been reading when Tina called. His face brightened as he scanned it. "Looks pretty clear-cut to me."

"I'd like to take credit for it, Tom, but it's a pretty easy case. Shot and killed, dropped where he stood. The lawyers will argue about what went on in Marla Kincaid's head, not about what happened in that room."

"That's good. Nobody will be coming after my crew on the stand, then." Patterson snagged an empty folder from the corner of my desk and slipped the report into it. "That will be an interesting discussion," he said. "I have to tell you, if some randy bastard gave my baby girl HIV, I'd be inclined to shoot him myself."

I didn't like thinking of my own girls in that context, and raised a quiet prayer that they remembered the values they'd been taught as children now that they were out in the vicious world. Still, I remembered John, and the parking lot, and the fruits of revenge. I pushed Zoe and Beth out of my mind.

"Houston was someone's baby, too, Tom. She shot him in cold blood." I remembered myself and the defamation laws and amended, "Allegedly."

"Allegedly," Peterson agreed. "Johanssen will call it the heat of passion—you wait and see." He waved the folder at me. "Thanks, Doc. Keep me posted. I'm headed down to Town Park for Huck Finn Day. You coming?"

I shook my head. "No thanks, Tom. I've got work to do. I'll give you a call if I turn up anything else of interest."

I went back to the papers on my desk. There wouldn't be anything else. I already knew the whole story. *All of it, every last word and, God help me, every last feeling.*

****

Pete Wilson loved Huck Finn and Becky Thatcher Day, if he could be said to love anything at all. He was drawn to the fact that Telluride had the decency to kick off its summer festival season with a program just for kids...well, sort of. There were a couple of other events that came first in the schedule, and the town felt compelled to make it Huck and Becky instead of Huck and Tom. But there was a parade — there was always a parade — then costume day in Town Park with a fishing contest. It was fun to see the ones in torn pants and checkered shirts, barefoot, with painted-on freckles, plying the pond. Almost none of the girls wore old-fashioned dresses, and most of the kids confined their "costume" to a straw hat. Still, it was a day just for them and he liked it. Too much of the town was all about adults, even when people intoned with great solemnity that it was "for the children."

He cast a glance up at the sky, which was clouded over and starting to spit rain, as he walked down to the park. The parade was over, and the town was making its way toward the green-space. He passed a poster in a shop window advertising the event and wondered again why it was Huck Finn and not Tom Sawyer who got top billing. After all, Tom and Becky were the best of friends, and Huck Finn starred in a book that no one in Telluride would read out of political correctness.

He smiled to himself. Fitting in with the crowd, at least on the surface, was a small price to pay to escape Chicago and the crime beat. Nothing much ever happened here, Houston's murder being the exception that proved the rule. He would be glad when the horde of reporters that had invaded as soon as Houston was murdered finally left. They were thinning some already. They figured out that Marla Kincaid wasn't going to do anything spectacular as long as her lawyer had her under wraps, and the trial was a long time away. Even so, a few of them were still camped so determinedly around the hotel in Mountain Village that the poor girl was held a virtual captive, especially after that fiasco on the street yesterday when she tried to go out for a walk and was swarmed by the press.

Wilson shook his head, banishing his reflexive grin at the thought with a grimace. That was the difference between real reporters and these scriveners of fluff that covered the celebrity circuit. A real reporter would have known the best way to get a story on Marla was to leave her alone, lull her into a false sense of security. The way these idiots acted, she'd gone to ground like a frightened fox, and she could stay holed up there longer than they could mill around on the sidewalk, assuming she didn't get cabin fever again. And assuming that another one of those idiots didn't get himself arrested by posing as a maintenance man and crashing into Marla's room.

A green SUV with a red-headed driver crawled past him on the street, easing its way out of town. The last time Pete Wilson had seen that particular vehicle and that particular driver was during Marla Kincaid's ill-fated walkabout. The driver rescued her from the pack of reporters and whisked her off, presumably back to the safety of Mountain Village and, curious, he'd loitered around long enough to see the young man heading back to the hotel twice more that evening. Wilson put two and two together and wondered what the medical examiner would think if she knew that her son was cavorting with a sweet young thing who was charged with murder?

The town pond was already lined with kids trying their hand at fishing. Once in a while, one of them would shriek with delight and pull up one of the small fish that resided in the dark waters. The adults in charge would duly make a fuss, measure the catch, and gently return the traumatized fish to the pond to risk capture again. He stood for a while, watching, then took a few photos and interviewed a few of the participants for the next edition of the paper.

It was a good turnout, but the park was far from full and most of the people were concentrated by the pond and the refreshment concession run by the Elks. A couple played Frisbee in the field that would become an ice rink in the winter months, and three girls in matching pink tee-shirts raced their mountain bikes around them, deftly dodging both the people and the flying plastic disc with shrieks of delight. Wilson's eyes followed them a fraction of a second, thinking how the drizzle had dampened their thin tee-shirts to show just how well they were beginning to fill them out.

It was early in the season. A few weeks and no matter what was going on, Town Park would be packed and the campground full of vacationers and festival-goers, the backbone of Telluride's summer economy. Wilson found he was enjoying the last few days of relative calm before Telluride's summer-long storm of visitors. He turned his attention from the girls on the bikes as one of the Elks took a microphone.

"Time to line up for the costume contest!" he said in theatrical tones. He smiled and waved a hand to the double handful of children who had actually turned up in tattered pants or the other accoutrements of Mark Twain's long-ago Mississippi. A ragged line was beginning to shape itself when a sound, sharp and hard, rang out and reverberated in the tiny box canyon. People looked around in surprise. But Pete Wilson knew a gunshot when he heard it. And then he heard another.

A woman screamed. Wilson looked around to see the stocky brunette who had been playing Frisbee, frozen in place, shrieking and pointing. The man she had been playing Frisbee with lay crumpled about a hundred feet away, the Frisbee on the ground just ahead of him.

The crowd stood as frozen as the woman for a long moment, then exploded. Mothers swept up their children. The Elks herded those nearest into the warming hut and bathrooms. People ran in any direction, running into each other with shouts and deprecations, shoving each other aside and jostling the smallest children to the ground. One father huddled with his toddler, pressing the child against the stones of the barbecue pit and shielding him with his body as he looked desperately around at the crowd roaring past him. They ran in every direction except toward the man on the ground. The woman who had been with him — his wife, girlfriend, mate of the day? — still stood screaming, motionless as a statue.

Pete Wilson had the sense to shoulder his camera and fight the exodus to get the first photo of the young man lying dead on the ground before he pulled out his cell and called 911. Some habits never die.

CHAPTER FIVE

JUNE 8, AFTERNOON

The sirens — an unfamiliar sound in Telluride — made me look out my window. The street was uncharacteristically empty. I saw a knot of people huddled in the porch of the bakery across the way. They were cramped, close together, pushed within the confines of the doorway, almost as though they were trying to escape a cold winter wind. Then almost as though they had received some mysterious signal, they darted back inside.

When a tall, muscular, gray-haired man passed, walking casually with hands in pockets and head thrust back to the day, one of them darted out and called, motioning him in. I saw him stop, stiffen, look around hurriedly, and dash inside with the others. I let the shade drop back and turned back to my desk, a familiar sense of unease making me too restless to sit and accomplish anything. I paced the long rectangle of my office for ten minutes by the clock before the call came that explained it all. It was Tom Patterson.

"Need you down here in Town Park," he said without preamble. "There's been a shooting."

Technically, a shooting in Town Park would have been the marshall's problem but, by common arrangement, the Sheriff's Office handled all homicides in the county. It saved on resources. I continued to pace, thankful for the headset that Ben had insisted I have, if for no other reason than he was tired of explaining to others about his Luddite mother and her unreasonable distrust of technology.

"When?"

"Fifteen minutes — give or take — ago."

"Who did it?"

"Damn it, Doc, I don't know. I just have a dead body and a panic on my hands, and I need you down here to help me make sense out of it."

Tom's words were sharp. It was unlike him to lose his temper. I've always thought that that phrase about blood running cold was hyperbole, but I found out otherwise.

"Tom," I said cautiously, "is the scene secure?" Cop and Medical Examiner code for 'is it safe to come out'? Suddenly the empty streets made sense. A shooting in broad daylight in the middle of Town Park. I heard a sigh.

"Doc, I don't know," he repeated. "I think so. There were a couple of shots. A man was killed. All hell broke loose at the Huck Finn Day party. All I can say is that Pete Wilson has been here taking photographs and trying to interview the man's girlfriend, and nobody's shot him yet." There was a pause. "Though I might consider busting a cap on the son of a bitch myself." Another pause. "You know I wouldn't call you out if I didn't think it was safe. This looks like—feels like—a single, deliberate hit. Get down here. I need your help."

I paused in my course around the rug, closing my eyes against the rising fear, taking a long breath in and letting it out slowly before I replied.

"I'll be right down. But just me. I'm not sending any of my crew."

"Thanks, Doc."

The two words held a world of relief, and then the line went dead. I reconsidered my commitment to go alone, dialing Quick and grateful to hear his voice.

"Jaz here."

It was one of his two standard phone-answering phrases. The other was "Morgue," in appropriately melancholy, drawn out tones. I occasionally countered with my own "Ma's mule barn, Ma speaking," but this wasn't the time for levity.

"There's been a shooting in Town Park. Care to come along with me?"

Quick wasn't a forensic technologist, but his battlefield experience and common sense made him an invaluable colleague. I had a feeling Patterson might welcome him as well.

Quick let out a low curse, another of his trademarks.

"Where the hell they think this is? The Bronx?" I could hear him opening a cabinet. "I'll get the kit. You get that camera of yours. I'll be ready in five minutes."

I met Quick in the lobby of the center. By now, the word of the shooting had spread all over town, and my own staff had taken refuge in the interior of the building, away from the massive front windows. They were listening to the local radio station, which had interrupted its usual eclectic music format to provide running commentary on the shooting. The volunteer deejay alternated between reading a single statement from the town marshall — Patterson still had his hands full — and taking calls from people who had been at the park when the shooting happened. If you believed them, the shooter(s) was (were) a lone (pair of) tall (short) black (white)(Indian) men (women) who were by the stage (soccer field) (Bear Creek trail) and were last seen driving (running) away from the scene in the company of a brown (black) Lab (mutt).

So much for eyewitnesses. What their sight confused, their ears did not. Every caller I had heard as I pulled out my camera and tape recorder and checked batteries and memory cards was confident. There had been two shots in rapid succession. Not one. Two.

It took us only a minute or two to walk the few blocks to the edge of Town Park where a deputy ushered us to the scene. A nondescript man of middle age, expanding paunch, and thinning hair plugged with recent transplants, lay on his side. A bright yellow Frisbee was on the ground a few feet away.

"Fill me in," I said to Tom as I pulled on my gloves.

"He was tossing the disc with his girlfriend over there in the field. She overthrew and he went after it. She says she heard a sound and he just fell."

"One sound?" I asked, remembering the callers.

"So she says. Why?"

"Everyone who's calling in to the radio station says two."

"They're right." Pete Wilson had materialized at my elbow. Tom Patterson's face became a thundercloud. "There were two shots. Close together, but two."

I turned to face the reporter. "Did you see him fall?"

Pete Wilson shrugged, the noncommittal gesture without concern for the dead man. "No. I heard the shots, then heard the banshee screaming. He was already down. Hard to tell where they came from, even, everything echoes so bad."

I turned back to Patterson. "I need room to examine the body. Get him out of here." Wilson wasn't the only one who had a cold heart.

Patterson brightened considerably and took Wilson none too gently by the elbow.

Quick and I knelt by the body to take our first good look at the dead man. He had dropped where he stood, face down on the grass; there was only a pool of blood beneath him, no trail in the surrounding ground. That was unusual. Hollywood notwithstanding, most people move around a bit even with a fatal gunshot wound unless it's one to the head, like the one that killed Houston. Even with a shot to the heart, it takes a few seconds to lose enough blood to lose consciousness. Dropping someone in his tracks generally takes a combination of a good shot and a round with a lot of stopping power.

I was surprised when I finally flipped the man over, after photographing him from every possible angle, to find a pair of tiny holes in the front of his shirt. I scowled and pointed them out to Quick.

"What do you think of this?" I asked.

"Looks like a .22 to me," he said, running a brown, gloved finger around the edges of one of the holes in the blood-soaked shirt. "Don't make a lot of sense to me. Something that small don't usually kill a man right away."

I straightened up, standing with my feet on either side of the man's own feet and looked around. Fixing my sights on the Frisbee, I stood motionless for a minute, my hand drifting involuntarily to my chest, touching the same spot where the gunshot wounds were on the unfortunate corpse. I looked down at Quick, still kneeling at the man's side. "Can you stick a probe in that to get me an angle of the shot?" I asked.

"Sure thing."

It wouldn't be perfect, but of where the shooter — no doubt long gone by now — might have been. I watched as Quick slid two thin, steel rods into the holes left by the bullets. Tom Patterson had taken his place next to me by that time, and as soon as the probes settled, we both stood still and silent, imagining the trajectory and looking out at the park for a likely spot. He saw it before I did — the cluster of trees at the top of the sledding hill. Straight, uninterrupted line of sight, sufficient height to account for the downward drift the probes were indicating, and enough cover from any angle, even the hiking trail above that with the park being crowded, no one would have seen anything at all.

"Get up to the top of that hill and see what you can find," Patterson barked to one of the deputies. The man loped off, motioning to one of the others to come along.

Quick straightened and reflexively brushed his hands off on his jeans, leaving a small smear of blood. I frowned at him and he gave me an apologetic look.

"I'll change them as soon as I get back with the wagon and a body bag. And," he cast a look at the deputies who were just cresting the hill, "I'll bring a metal detector. I expect those boys can use it."

He was off before Patterson could thank him, and we both watched him for a moment before turning to look at the body at our feet again. Tom finally broke the silence.

"This is no damn good," he finally said. "No damn good at all."

I was inclined to agree.

****

Isa finished filling the yellow bucket with warm water and closed the tap. The smell of the cleaner reminded her of the tall pines that she could see through the windows. She wasn't supposed to use ordinary cleaner, only some expensive liquid the woman who lived here called green even though it had no color at all. It didn't work, either. Isa smiled and nodded whenever the woman fussed at her for using something different from the grocery store, then did as she pleased. Clean was better than not clean, so she was using the real cleaner, the brown, not green, kind. She liked the scent, it worked, and with the man dead and the woman arrested, there was no one to fuss at her today.

The woman always called her Eva, because she could never

remember Isa's name and out of spite, Isa never used hers, though she remembered it because it was so pretty. Marla. It was always Marla who fussed at her though she knew it was the man, Mitch, whose idea it always was to complain. He was a lot like Pelirojo, always using someone else to do the things he wanted done but did not want to take the blame for. Like fussing at Isa for the cleaner. And making her stay late that night to clean. At least she was not here when the murder happened. She hunched her shoulders, trying to shield herself from the effects of all that violence, but it didn't work. She shuddered in spite of herself and whispered a quick prayer to La Guadalupana.

She worked methodically through the empty house, ending in the big bedroom. It was filthy, with broken glass on the floor and walls marked by the things the woman had thrown around. It was all made worse by some sort of fine, black powder scattered over the surfaces of the furniture and the gold statue of the man with no face. It was as much a mess as the kitchen had been on the night the man was killed, the night it had taken her until ten just to finish cleaning. She had been almost to the house in Montrose when the tiny phone in her bag rang, and the police called her back.

The last time she had seen the room, the police were there, and the dead man, and his woman, who had thrust a paper at her and told her to call the number and tell the woman who answered she had been arrested. The woman policeman was angry and yelled at both of them and tore the paper out of Isa's hand, but not before she had memorized the number. Isa was good with numbers, and she was good at doing the little things that got her work and kept it for her. Like calling the number later that evening from one of the downstairs bathrooms, making sure her voice was soft enough not to be heard through the door by the woman policeman who went with her, and passing the message on.

Like cleaning the place up yet again from the excesses of these crazy Anglos. The woman's lawyer had told her to get the place ready to be shown, whatever that meant. She was glad to have the work because it was the last she would likely have from this house. And the blond woman who had taken her to the clinic the day before had fired her as soon as the doctor left, saying that she was afraid that having Isa around would put her family at risk if Pelirojo found out she had been the one to take her to the clinic. The priest had told her not to worry, that he would find her other work, but for now she was glad to still have this job.

She twisted the mop in the big roller and slapped it down on the wood floor. The big, gray rug was gone and she could see where it had lain. The red wood was darker where the sun had hit it.

Can wood get a suntan, she wondered, and giggled a bit at the thought.

Then she sobered again, remembering the sight of the man, so handsome and so dead, lying on the rug. She was glad no one expected her to clean the rug. There was so much blood. She sighed and swished the mop around in broad circles and tried not to think about anything more than the floor. By the time she got to the edges of the room, Isa's mind was settled, and she was humming one of those children's songs that Pablo was so fond of, this one about a bus with wheels that go round. She smiled to herself.

Of course they go around, she thought. *What else do wheels do?*

She broke into the words as she finished mopping the spot where the broken glass from the mirror had been. She noticed a glinting shard caught in the molding and bent to remove it. It was stuck fast. She was afraid she would cut herself if she pulled too hard, so she laid down the mop handle and went to find a washcloth so that she could remove it, conditioned by weeks of employment not to leave even the tiniest bit of dirt or disorder lest she risk a scolding if the lawyer was as temperamental as the man had been.

As she walked into the bathroom, she noticed a neat, round hole at the edge of the doorframe. It was almost obscured by the pattern of the earth-colored wallpaper.

She traced the edges of the hole with her finger and then shrugged. There was nothing she could do to fix that. She took a washcloth from the marble shelf by the shower and went back to extract the glass. It came free easily but left a tiny crevice in the polished wood.

Isa held the shard in the palm of her hand for a moment and regarded the baseboard and the scratches and tiny holes that the pieces of the broken mirror had left on this part of the shiny, beautiful floor. She tossed the piece of glass into the trash with the others, thought for a moment and then stood by the dresser, looking in the direction of the bathroom door. She tried to remember where the man's body had been in the middle of the pale spot. She paced a few steps back and forth until she was sure she had it right, raised her arm level with her eyes and cocked her head, squinting at the distant doorframe.

Dios mio, she thought and went back into the bathroom to look for a nail file.

This would be harder to remove than the piece of glass had been, and she didn't want to make the hole any worse. It took her a moment to pry the soft metal out of the wood of the door. It was wedged at an angle, held in place mostly by the soft plaster of the wall. She eased it out on the tip of the file, and it skittered down the wall when it worked free. She caught it with her free hand, rolled it over in her palm, and dropped it in her pocket. Then she smoothed the edges of the paper that had frayed as she worked it loose, pleased that the hole was no more noticeable than before.

She was back downstairs in the room off the kitchen emptying the last of the wash-water into the big metal sink when she heard a knock at the back door. It was the priest, come to take her back to the lady doctor for more photographs.

Isa smiled as she let him in, put the mop and bucket away, and ran water into the sink to wash away the last of the bubbles. The priest held the door for her, and together they walked around the side of the house to the long driveway in front where the priest's car waited. They had just rounded the big rock planter when Isa remembered the key in her pocket, the one the lawyer said to leave on the kitchen table. She hurried back, leaving the priest to wait.

When she returned, he was in the deep shade of the house, leaning up against the stone wall, one long leg crossed over the other and his arms folded. She could not make out his face in the shadows, and anyway, it could not have been this kind and gentle man. But seeing him brought back a sharp memory of another tall figure in the shadows of the house the night of the killing.

I must remember to tell the lady doctor, she thought as she fingered the bullet in her pocket.

CHAPTER SIX

JUNE 8, AFTERNOON

"Pull over, Quick! Let me out here."

The big morgue van was just nosing into the alley behind the Center when I saw Father Matt heading toward the big main doors, Isa Robles in tow. In the chaos of the afternoon, I had forgotten they were due to come by for me to take additional photographs of Isa's wounds. I didn't even wait for the van to come to a full stop before I jumped out of the passenger's side, thumping the rear fender with the flat of my hand as I jogged around the back calling Father Matt's name as I went.

He paused and waited for me to catch up. Isa scurried behind him as I approached. Standing next to him, half-hidden by him, she looked more like a child than a grown woman. Her medical record put her at twenty-six, but she could have passed for a teen with her diminutive frame and smooth skin, marred though it was by the bruises that had come to full flower. She had quite a shiner, and I had no doubt that the bruise I was interested in would show some interesting details. I made a point of speaking to her first. "Hello, Senorita Robles," I said, remembering my momma's admonition to always give people the most respect possible.

"Isa," she replied simply.

"Isa," I affirmed. "Con permiso."

I smiled and pushed the door open for her to enter, then followed behind leaving Father Matt to fend for himself. I nodded to Tina as we passed. She was back at her desk, still looking a little unnerved with the radio giving updates in the background. Father Matt listened intently.

"Another shooting, Jane?" he asked, disbelief obvious in his voice.

I shrugged. "Town Park. Broad daylight during the festival. You know as much as I do."

It was as clear a signal I could give that this was not a subject for discussion. Isa's eyes widened, but she said nothing. Wherever the two of them had been, it clearly wasn't within earshot of a radio, and it sure wasn't in town. Quick came in through the security door that separated the public areas from the morgue itself.

"Body's inside, boss. Want me to get it ready?"

I considered the time and the events of the day. Suddenly, I was tired, and all I wanted to do was go home. I expected he did too. I shook my head. "It can wait until morning. Bring me up the camera, then why don't you lock up and go home? All of you."

Home for Quick and the rest of my staff was one of several apartments on the fourth floor of the building, but at least it wasn't the morgue or the office.

"Sure thing."   He nodded to Father Matt and Isa.   "Miss. Reverend." Then to me, "Be right there."

I left Father Matt in the lobby listening to the radio and ushered Isa into my office. "Have a seat on the couch. Can I get you something to drink?"

She shook her head and we sat in awkward silence until Quick reappeared with the camera bag from the van. He handed it to me without a word and ghosted out of the room. I turned up the dimmer on the overhead lights. The architect who designed the space was a fanatic for light. Ordinarily, I hated the bright intensity of the overhead spotlights, but they would come in handy now. I put on my business face and stepped over to Isa.

"Let me take a look." I took her chin in my hand and tipped her face upward. She squinted at the light but did not protest. The bruises, only faintly red when I first saw her, had purpled and swollen, much more impressive than they had been when I first saw her, and much easier to see. She'd taken quite a beating in addition to the rape. I wondered whether the good Dr. Brownmiller had thought to get x-rays of her face; with this much bruising, she could easily have a broken cheekbone. I made a mental note to check the records to be sure, and I took un-Christian delight in the possibility of making the good doctor bring her back in for more studies if she had not.

Isa winced and wrinkled her nose when I touched her eye, but this time there were no tears in her big brown eyes. I straightened up and stepped back, recovering the detached attitude I needed when working with living, breathing people.

"Let's take a few shots of these bruises," I said. "Can you hold the scale for me?"

She nodded, and I retrieved a small ruler from the interstices of the bag and handed it to her. I kept up a meaningless chatter to fill the silence, hoping to keep Isa at ease and to distance the news of today's murder. It seemed to work. She even giggled when the edge of the plastic tickled her under her chin, then flushed with embarrassment. At length, I had documented all the visible bruises, and it was time to move on to the money shot, the one I hoped would pin the attack on the culprit. She unbuttoned her blouse and pulled it down to show the bruise on her chest, now a perfect representation of a horseshoe, complete with a few pinprick hemorrhages from the prongs.

"It is what his ring looks like," Isa said, looking down at the bruise, her chin nearly on her chest, her fingers pulling the skin tight so she could see it better. This time, I noticed that her eyes were glistening. Isa was brave, but this was a lot for her to handle. I knew from experience that revisiting the reality only made it worse, not better. I grabbed a tissue from my desk and handed it to her.

"Yes, it is," I said briskly, "and that's going to make it easier to convict him. Good thing, yes?" I handed her the ruler. "Can you hold this for me?"

Isa nodded. I positioned her hand and tilted her chin out of the way to eliminate the shadow across the bruise. Three quick snaps and I was finished.

"I'll get these off to the sheriff first thing in the morning." I had finished my initial report, but the events of the last few days had kept me from talking to anyone from the Montrose Sheriff's Office.

"Thank you." I was struck again by the great dignity in Isa's voice. "Will they put him back in jail?"

"Back in jail?"

"They took him away right after, but he is not in jail now. My friend told me so. She told me..." Isa hesitated, then continued with more resolve, "to be careful."

I wasn't surprised her assailant was back on the street; after all, Marla Kincaid was walking the streets, and she had killed a man. But how to explain the vagaries of American justice to this woman?   I sighed.

"I agree. It doesn't seem right. But maybe this will help convict him. Evidence like this, it's very powerful in court."

Her face brightened.   I congratulated myself on scoring an emotional victory.   She handed me the ruler and buttoned her blouse again. I was reviewing the images on the screen of the camera when she cleared her throat and extended her hand to me.

"I found this at the house I was cleaning. The one where that man, Houston, was killed."

She dropped something hard and heavy into my palm. I was stunned. It was a wad of lead about the same size, if tactile memory was any judge, as the slug I had removed from Mitch Houston. This one retained some of the general shape of a bullet, a discernable base and a flattened nose. It was definitely not a .22 round. I raised it in the light and twirled it between my two fingers as I tried to take in what I had just heard. Isa sensed my confusion.

"It was in the wall of the bedroom. I found it when I was cleaning. It is important, evidence, sí?"

Trying to remain calm, I asked her, "Where, exactly, did you find this? In what wall?"

"The one where the door to the bathroom is. It was in the wood."

"In the wood?" I still couldn't believe what I was hearing.

"In the wood. The edge of the door, the side. I had to pry it out."

"Pry it out?" I was beginning to sound like a parrot. I strode across the room to buy myself some time, mentally reviewing the scene and my processing of it. This was a mistake of major proportions on my part, and it changed everything about the case.

Everything. I dug on the desk for my report and muttered under my breath, "You've been watching too much CSI." I was surprised when Isa replied.

"What is that?"

I had not intended to be heard. I looked up from the report, which confirmed my recollection that Tom Patterson told me that there was only one shot from the gun in question, not that that mattered, given that this explained why the bullet I had recovered seemed the wrong size. It was still my job to comb that room, and I missed a bullet hole. Isa was glaring at me. She clearly didn't know what I was talking about, but she had caught the sarcasm in my voice. A bad habit of mine. I instantly regretted my indiscretion and my blame-the-bearer response. She had not meant to do any harm.

"It's a television show," I explained. "One about crime technology. About collecting evidence." *One that makes everyone in the world think he can do it,* I added silently to myself.

"So this is important? Yes? "

I took a deep breath and closed my eyes briefly. "It could be. But it won't..."

I paused, unwilling to explain that her removal of the slug dashed any hope of its ever being used in a trial, not to mention that prying it out eliminated the chances of being able to make a ballistics match, despite the fact that it was relatively intact.

Isa made the connection instantly.

"It won't be used? Porqué?" She immediately corrected herself. "Why not?"

I sighed again. "Because you found it and took it out. It means I can't match it to anything, and I can't prove where it came from."

"But I am telling you. And I was very careful. Even the paper on the wall is no worse than it was."

"I know. And I believe you. But there are rules we have to follow. Like when I came to see you at the clinic. I had to do that, not Dr. Brownmiller."

"Then why didn't you? You were there, I saw you. If it is your job, why didn't you do it?" A momentary pause, then a moment of doubt herself. "Did you miss something with me too?" She added, "Maybe you don't watch enough CSE."

I could hear panic edging in as she considered the possibility that her assailant might go free because of me and my incompetence. I winced. I deserved that. I had insulted her and let Tom Patterson down.

"CSI. And no, I don't. Maybe I should." In spite of my growing sense of dread, my reply sounded absent-minded, my mind racing with the full implications of that bit of lead. If it matched the other one, officially or not, odds were very, very good that Marla Kincaid was innocent. And there was that other two-shot murder, the one I had just come from, with nasty implications of its own.

****

Pete Wilson was passing by the White Deer as Ivanka Kovacs, the old woman who owned and ran it, was locking the door. It wasn't late for a summer evening, and Wilson was surprised the avaricious old bat would pass up the chance for an extra buck by closing so early, but he guessed that there hadn't been much business since the shooting. Most of the shops had closed their doors; only the restaurants and the bars — mostly the bars — were busy.

He'd done a profile on her when he first came to town, and she'd impressed him as being canny and sharp and as tight with a dime as the bark on a pine tree. Still, Wilson had to admire her. She worked every day in the shop or at the family ranch where they raised the sheep for the wool that went into the sweaters and scarves and shawls the little shop sold to anyone with enough money to afford three digits starting with five for a simple pullover. In the shop, she was known as a tyrant, not putting up with the lazy ethic of the town's work force, importing her own staff from God-knows-where in Eastern Europe, something Wilson heartily approved of. The girls who worked in the shop were sexy in an over-ripe, slightly tawdry way, mostly brunette-turned-blond and filling out the inventory in a most inviting fashion. And like their boss, they were never seen without their makeup: dark-lined eyes, lots of mascara, and bright red lips. On them it looked great; on her, sad and out of place. On the other hand, he gave her credit for trying to keep up appearances, at least. He liked the natural look well enough, but too many of the women in this town took it to extremes. A little paint now and then wasn't such a bad thing.

Most of the people he had interviewed this afternoon had been women, partly out of preference, but mostly because they were the ones most likely to have their cameras and phones out to record any happening that involved their precious offspring. He'd criss-crossed town, following one lead after another, knocking on doors, wheedling and cajoling until he amassed an electronic folder of videos and stills taken at the day's festivities. He'd even gotten releases for them, in case he wanted to use one or two to accompany the article he was already writing in his head.

He stopped by the market and picked up a frozen dinner on his way back to his little down-valley house. Like many who lived in the area, Wilson couldn't afford to live in town proper; instead he rented a 20-by-30 foot bungalow, not much more than a shack, really, that perched between the highway and the river just below the site of the old uranium mine. It wasn't much to look at, he reflected, as he unlocked the door, but it was cheap and Internet and cell phone access, the lifeblood of his occupation, were consistent at this particular spot. He dropped his backpack on the couch he'd salvaged from a remodel of one of the hotels in Mountain Village, stripped the wrappings from his frozen meal, punched time into the microwave, and fired up his computer.

His inbox was stuffed with mail, almost all of it with attached image files. He started sorting through them. Most of them were unimpressive, often grainy, usually taken at the most inopportune times, with the subject's eyes closed or mouth open, the sort of thing only a mother could treasure and only a mother could take. He scanned them with practiced ease, finding nothing of interest and nothing he could use on the front page of tomorrow's paper. He glanced at his watch. He was hard up on his deadline, and the story still needed to be put together, a first person report.

The microwave buzzed, and he retrieved the organic macaroni and cheese he'd bought, dousing it with Tabasco sauce, a habit learned from the men who worked in the slaughter pens in Chicago. He was on his second bite when the image loaded on the screen. It was so unexpected, he had to put the plate down and focus in on it to make sure he wasn't seeing things.

He wasn't. There, in profile in the background of a shot taken of a tow-headed child by her doting mother, was the sledding hill and the small grove of trees that had so interested the cops and the Medical Examiner. And right there in the middle of it, he could see a small flash of flame. Talk about a lucky shot. Right place, right time, right angle, and right in front of him.

Wilson sat back in his chair excited and satisfied. Persistence paid off. With a little cropping and enlargement, his front page, above-the-fold story would be accompanied by a picture that showed the very instant of the shooting. He wondered whether the AP would pick it up and smiled to himself as he took another bite of macaroni. He bet they would.

CHAPTER SEVEN

JUNE 9, MORNING

I slept in as long as I could, if you could call the fitful tossing and turning that passed for rest these days sleep. Even after my mind was fully awake and the sun was long up, I remained in bed, staring at the ceiling and trying to make sense out of the past two days. Two murders in three days in a town where no one ever intentionally killed anyone else. It was one of the reasons I chose to locate the Center in Telluride; that, plus the fact that I had wrested the house I lived in out of my former partners at ten cents on the dollar in settlement of my suit against them. I wanted to be in a place where murder was remote, and I was in control of how and when I entered into its domain.

Montrose or Grand Junction would have made more sense, especially since they both fell under the generous jurisdiction the state had given me. But I enjoyed the luxury of showing up, calm and collected an hour or two after the call, leaving the initial response to associates I had appointed in every town of any size on the Western slope. I had planned my life carefully so that I had to go calling on murder; it didn't come calling on me. I had encountered death on my own doorstep once before. I never wanted to again.

Man proposes, God disposes. Here I was on a bright June morning, with not one, but two deaths in rapid sequence, if not on my doorstep, at least in my front yard. I stretched, got up, and pulled on my clothes. Lucky for me Telluride was the kind of place I could go to Mass in jeans and boots, and Father Matt was the kind of priest for whom it would matter more that I was there than how I was dressed.

I encountered Ben in the front hall, tucking his shirt into his khaki pants. He was better dressed than usual for Sunday morning. A sophomore in college, Ben was deep in the throes of doubt, but he knew that as long as he lived under my roof and lived off my bank account, he had no choice in the matter of Sunday Mass.

"You look nice. Going somewhere?"

His neck colored, telegraphing that he was about to lie to me. "Mass with you."

Okay, not an outright lie, but the crimson just above his collar told me there was more to it than that. I considered pushing but decided not to, and he wasn't volunteering anything else. We walked the short distance to St. Patrick's Church in soft summer sunshine, the air clean and fresh.

The church was abuzz when we arrived, a larger crowd than usual, every pew on both sides filled, the chatter among the faithful filling the little building to the rafters.

"What gives?" Ben asked. "There's hardly ever this many people here."

Technically, Ben was right. It was literally SRO in the main part of the church, though our customary places in the loft, right in front of the statue of St. Anthony, were open. Summer often brought large turnouts, especially since both faithful and curiosity seekers were drawn by Father Matt's introduction of the Latin Mass, but nothing like this.

"Two murders, one in broad daylight. People are nervous. Nervous people go to church."

I knew from experience that killings close to home made people think about God. They either ran to Him or away, but they almost never ignored Him. Seems that the good people of Telluride, permanent or transient, had more faith than I gave them credit for. More than I had. They were here looking for solace.

I was here only out of duty, out of sheer, longheaded obedience. I was still mad at God for taking John from me, and I was in no mood to forgive the man who'd been the agent of my grief. Still, holding on to the barest remnants of our life together, I financed the parish generously in John's memory. I kept coming to church out of fidelity to his rock-solid faith, though my angry mind rarely gave me a moment's rest, and I never went up for communion.

That had been a source of confusion for Father Matt. He had a little trouble understanding why I would come week after week and infuse massive sums into parish activities when I might as well have been a board on the wall for all I participated. Ben thought me a hypocrite for attending church at all, but he was at that stage where I was damned if I did and damned if I didn't and, frankly, I didn't care what he thought. I was keeping him in church for John's sake, and that was all that mattered. And I was finding that, in the midst of the darkness that seemed to be my lot in life these past few years, I was drawn, compelled almost, to this little parish. I never missed Sunday, made most daily Masses, and even stopped in from time to time just to sit in the quiet of the balcony, looking down on the empty pews. I wasn't sure why, really. It just seemed the thing to do. Most of my life these days was on autopilot. This was no exception.

Father Matt kept it to under an hour and I was in the morgue, discharging my other Sunday duty by doing the post-mortem on the unlucky Frisbee player. Quick already had the body on the table when I arrived, a tray of instruments laid out, bottles labeled, and camera ready. We worked together in near-silence, so familiar with each other's ways that he anticipated my needs, and I stayed out of his way. It was like the macabre dance of two experienced partners who looked neither at their feet nor at each other, but spent the time lost in thoughts and worlds of their own making. I surfaced from mine long enough, once, to wonder what Quick was thinking; for myself, I was trying not to remember John and trying to squelch the rising knowledge that this was not going to be the last two-shot murder in my jurisdiction.

It was a straightforward autopsy, two shots to the chest, remarkably close together. I retrieved the bullets, one of which was just beneath the skin of the back, having traveled through the man's heart and between two ribs. It was enough to kill him, but what probably dropped him on the spot was the other bullet, the one that lodged in the innards of the pacemaker he had implanted. I'd have to do a little research, but I was pretty sure that the bullet caused either excruciating electroshock or a sudden disruption in heartbeat that prevented the man from moving. I was willing to bet the shot to the pacemaker came first, the shot to the heart second, though it hardly mattered. He was dead either way.

"I'll finish up, boss." Quick broke the silence as I dropped the last bit of tissue onto my stock jar and screwed the lid on tight.

I shook my head. "I'll help. Nothing better to do."

I returned Sig Monson's — that was the man's name, a well-heeled young man whose daddy had made a fortune in real estate — vital organs to his body and stitched up the y-shaped incision that had given me access to all his secrets, including his enlarged heart that had been pierced by a sniper's bullet. I put a stitch in the scalp to hold it in place where I had cut it to get at his unremarkable brain, then I took a cloth and washed the dried blood from his face and torso, hands and arms, feet and legs, finally holding him up off the table as Quick took the sprayer and hosed the table and the man's back clean.

It always cost me something to finish up a case this way. It was a dropping of those medical examiner defenses I had learned over the years to cultivate so well, and I always felt a fresh stab of pain, displaced grief for the victim and the family, unwelcome for the hurt but the only way I knew I was still among the living. It was my nod, perfunctory though it was, to the person who had been a person before he was a body in my morgue and, like going to church, it was something I simply had to do. It fed some deep and unspoken need, though I had no clear idea what.

At length, the body was tidy. Quick and I transferred him onto the gurney, a new body bag around him and a clean toe tag with all his information in place. Quick returned the gurney in the cooler to await its transport to the funeral home in Montrose. I thanked him, washed up, and headed back upstairs, carrying the pacemaker and the free bullet with me. The autopsy was finished, but just like in the Houston case, the trouble was only beginning, and I wanted a little time to get out in front of it, if only by a nose.

****

Hunter DiManio had run into Jim Webster on the sidewalk in front of the Steaming Bean. It was a beautiful, clear Sunday morning, the town just beginning to come alive with people crossing the street in easy conversation, careless of traffic, for it always stopped for them and there wasn't that much anyway. It was easy to tell the residents from the tourists from those who lived down valley, he thought. The residents dressed in one variation or another of faded shorts, well-worn tees and scruffy sandals, accented by a variety of tattoos, piercings and dreadlocks. The tourists were more self-conscious in matching, but oh-so-current, outfits crisp from a well-packed bag. The down valley folks were generally a bit older than the Telluride hoi-polloi, and ran more to jeans, boots and cotton shirts: ranchers, carpenters, plumbers, tradesmen.

He stepped aside as a short, white-haired woman, erect and intent on her destination, made her way down the street, eyes fastened on some distant goal, face set, mouth unsmiling. She wore rancher's denim, but clean and pressed and a straw hat, and she carried a black book with ribbons for markers in the crook of her arm. Her face was made up with dark-lined eyes and a too-red mouth, startling in contrast to her clothes and bearing.

Down valley, he thought, *and tough as nails.*

He watched her catch up with a tall man, slim-hipped and barrel-chested, as erect as she was. He slipped a protective arm around her as she slowed her steps, her goal obviously accomplished. They were just within earshot. He heard the man call her by name.

"Ivanka, my love!"

He smiled at that. It seemed off to hear something so extravagant from a man so very old.

Jim had come out of the Steaming Bean just then, coffee in hand, sandy hair still damp from his morning shower. He stood under the trademark oval sign and bent down to pat the head of a yellow hound someone had left outside.

"I'm heading up to the Ophir Wall to do a little easy climbing. Interested?"

He named a spot in a miniscule town, a face of rugged rock that had become a playground for local climbers. Sipping from the brown cup with the brown corrugated collar, he waited for an answer, stepping aside to let a middle-aged man pass by. Belatedly, Jim recognized the sheriff, who stopped at the side of a county SUV parked in the middle of the street opposite the Bean. He waved and the sheriff waved back, shouted a wish for good climbing and drove away. Jim turned his attention back to the man before him.

Hunter's eager face telegraphed his enthusiasm for the invitation. Interested? Interested in a little climb with a man who'd bagged all the fourteeners by the time he was himself fourteen, who'd summitted Everest and K2 twice each? Interested in a little climb with the best-known free-solo climber in the country — maybe the world — author of books and star of documentaries? Interested in climbing with a man who hadn't let the last name he shared with the Washington luminary who was his father keep him from his dreams of mountaineering?

"Hell yes, I'm interested!"

Jim patted him on the shoulder, smiling. "Good deal. Let's go."

They walked together down the street to the little half-Victorian Jim had bought by violating that first rule of trust funds: never touch capital. It had a neat little patch of lawn and a bed of columbines, just starting to come into bloom. It had been a late, cold spring, but the weather was warming now. Jim was throwing a cooler in the back of the Jeep when the old woman passed them, alone again.

Jim smiled and spoke, "Nice day."

The woman slowed her steps, paused, turned and smiled back. Her face was creased with wrinkles and browned by the sun.

She had an accent when she spoke. "Yes, it is." Then, "What is it you are doing? So much baggage!" Her "Y" sounded like a "Ch."

Jim laughed and tossed the gear bag and ropes onto the cooler in the back. "A nice day for a climb on the Ophir Wall."

The woman shook her head and continued up the street, muttering, "Foolishness. So dangerous."

They saw her climb into a dilapidated, faded red Toyota truck with the image of a deer in white on the side of the driver's door, faded and scratched by too much time in the sun and too many encounters with the landscape. They watched it head off down the street, sending up a cloud of dust and rattling as it went. Hunter wondered aloud whether he'd ever be that old and scared.

"Not if you keep climbing. We tend to check out early."

He climbed into the driver's seat and turned the key, and they were off. They passed the red truck on the way up to Ophir, careening into the oncoming lane on an almost-blind curve, testing their nerve and their luck as they passed the rattletrap with the ancient engine not making more than 35 miles an hour up the steep slope. Hunter saw the white head shake in disgust as they passed.

The rock was dry, and the sun hadn't topped the wall, an imposing face that stretched up to the morning sky, as close to vertical as God and climbing allowed. Only the reverberation of a contractor driving pilings down in the town marred the perfection of the morning; construction took no days off when the weather was good and there was money to be made. Ophir wasn't a hot bed of building, though it was picking up. Hunter surmised that the only day the pile driver would be free to do some work in this tiny town was on a Sunday when all the rich folks in Mountain Village or Aldasoro or wherever would want their peace and quiet.

The rhythmic slam-slam-slam of steel against steel echoed against the rock, leaving the silence in between strokes all the more potent, making the wide space at the foot of the wall, just off the road, seem unexpectedly part of civilization when it wasn't intended to be. Here was where the very edge of nature reared itself up: a huge face of rock, crabbed and streaked with planes and angles, crevices and overhangs, a rubble of stones, large and small, piled up at its feet. Talus, geologists called it, for ankle, the ankle of the rock as it rose from the earth. Talus, because if you tried to climb it, you hoped you'd be lucky enough that only your ankle would suffer misfortune.

Hunter pulled out the gear and laid it on the soft grass on the clearing at the bottom of the wall. It was unusual that they were the only ones there: no other climbers, no other hikers, not even the invariable passerby just checking out the real estate. He heard a couple of cars pass on the road, but no one pulled in.

Business in Ophir, he guessed, maybe part of the construction crew arriving late. The crunch of tires on gravel was the only sound apart from the rhythm of the pile driver.

Jim handed Hunter an energy bar and a bottle of water. The two men chatted, leaning against the Jeep in the warming sun, swapping climbing stories for half an hour before Jim decided he had enough adulation from this third-tier climber and stood up to prepare for his ascent. He peered up at the wall for a long minute while he stretched his hands, his shoulders, his legs, his core; Hunter could tell he was prepping the route in his mind. Hunter started to lay out the ropes, belay devices, the carabiners, the cams and hex-bolts, the harnesses and helmets as he watched. Jim's routine was impressive and methodical. By the time he was done, not even the small joints of his toes – life or death to a climber – were left untested, unattended. When he finished, Hunter tossed a spool of tape, and Jim began to wrap his hands as methodically as he had broken in his body.

"Toss me the chalk bag."

Hunter looked up again from his unpacking to see Jim pulling on his sticky shoes. He caught the bag with one hand and powdered his hands.

"I think I'll take a little warm-up climb."

Hunter watched him as he ascended the nearly-sheer face of the wall, eking out holds where none was visible. His ascent was smooth, brisk, and graceful. *Time* magazine had described him as a human Daddy Longlegs, powerful arms reaching to improbable lengths to find a grip and strong legs to propel himself upwards. There was no reason to be taking a warm-up, Hunter thought, other than to show off, but damn! The man was good.

It was almost like watching music, and Hunter wondered how long it took to develop that sense of internal coordination, so that as soon as he made one hold, he found another, three points on the rock at all times, ascending like he was a wave in the rock itself, pulsing upward. He was nearly a hundred feet up. Hunter glanced at his watch. There were people who couldn't walk down a street that fast.

****

In a grove of aspens, a figure aligned eye and scope, watching the man on the face of the rock, tracking his progress until it was easy to anticipate his moves. He had a pattern, a preference, so characteristic that it gave his climb an even, rocking quality as he arced from side to side in his climb. It would be enough to be close. The fall would kill him.

Still, the shooter was confident. Listening to the pile driver, counting in time, watching the climber. Patience. Patience. One more cycle, across, back. The finger that caressed the trigger was skillful, and it pulled twice. The cracks of the rifle were drowned by the sounds of construction.

****

Jim arced to the right almost to the overhang where he would have to power himself over. Surely he'd turn around there. Hunter watched intently, saw him reach for the ledge, then stiffen and jerk. Improbably, the long legs lost their footing, the hands let go. As the pile driver kept up its rhythm, James Madison Coolidge Webster IV fell, and Hunter Dimanio screamed like a little girl.

CHAPTER EIGHT

JUNE 9, AFTERNOON

Quick's call about the climbing accident and the intrepid reporter from the more reputable of the two local rags cornered me at the same time with news of Webster's death. I was mailing my weekly letter to Seth. I maintained the archaic habit of writing a real, handwritten letter to one of my absent offspring every Sunday after church, usually in the quiet of my office or, on days like this, in the shade of a tree in the quiet of Town Park. I figured that way my children might someday have a few scraps of correspondence to remember me by.

I had just stepped out of the sterile, new post office building when my cell rang. It was Quick letting me know to get my sorry bones down to the morgue to do the autopsy. Pete Wilson loped up as I finished. He wanted a scoop. I was seeing entirely too much of that man lately and I scowled as he approached.

Fortunately for me, Wilson is usually one of the more reasonable members of the fourth estate. A big-city reporter who got tired of the rat race and retired to Telluride, he's sensible and easygoing, even if his politics — like most of the denizens of this granola-laden part of the world — are almost far enough left to make him a card-carrying communist. That particularly annoys me, given that the Telluride economy, the engine that keeps him in business, is the complete and utter result of unbridled capitalism at its best and worst.

"So what do you think, Doc? The scanner said he fell free-soloing on Ophir Wall. What's that going to look like? Did he suffer much? Was it quick?"

Wilson kept pace with me as I hurried past the library. I could see the morgue hearse coming up on the broad double doors that marked the rear entrance. Quick was on the sidewalk shooing a gathering crowd away. The jungle telegraph works fast in Telluride, and this celebrity death hit home more than Houston's had. Webster wasn't exactly a local boy, being the scion of a Back-East political dynasty, but he was a local hero.

I thought of the little house along the main street I had seen Webster coming and going from. He seemed like a nice kid, polite, cheerful, and—except for his penchant for scaling high mountains and vertical surfaces without much assistance — reasonably level-headed. I remembered seeing his exotic, doe-eyed — and very pregnant — wife standing in the doorway waving him off. He was a fool, I thought, to be tempting fate by climbing mountains and rocks and whatever else he encountered when he had a wife and an almost-family. There were too many other things in the world that would conspire to snatch him away without his cooperating with them.

I turned reflexively away from the crowd gathering down the street, looking past Pete to the mountain that stands sentinel at the end of our box canyon and watching the course of Bridal Veil Falls for a moment before I answered. The thin cascade against the rock quieted my angry thoughts just enough for me to be civil.

I shook my head, in part to communicate with Wilson, in part to rid it of the images of Webster that were already forming in my mind. Hollywood would have you think that you can sustain a multi-story fall and still look human, the only evidence of death arms or legs akimbo and a trickle of blood from the mouth. The reality is a lot different. After about five stories — and Webster had fallen from a greater height than that — the body is pretty well distorted: bones broken, skull shattered, spine telescoped, skin torn either by the force of the fall or the ends of protruding bones.

And there is blood, lots of it, everywhere. It's not a pretty sight. The Jim Webster on my slab wouldn't look much like the handsome, charming guy who had been a regular in the Steaming Bean and Sofio's. According to the report, he'd fallen about a hundred feet and had landed in a pile of rocks at the base of the wall. I'd be surprised if I found anything intact.

"Let me do the case and I'll give you a call. Off the record—I think it's a pretty damn foolish hobby for anyone, but especially someone with a family." Sometimes my judgmental side comes out in spite of my best efforts. We'd reached the door to the Forensic Center. "Give me a couple of hours, Pete, and try to leave the family alone." I added the last as reparation for my earlier comment.

Quick had rolled the gurney into the autopsy suite, and I helped him move the zipped, black body bag onto the steel table. We wrestled the body out of the bag and onto the cold steel, a process made more difficult by the fact that, as I suspected, there was hardly an unbroken bone. Moving it onto the slab took both of us.

Once we had Webster on the table, I sent Quick for the camera and stood at the head of the table, trying to steel myself for the unpleasant job ahead of me. This job was getting harder and harder as I got older, harder still since I no longer had a husband to help me keep balance when I lost my distance as I had with this one. The body in front of me looked more like a broken, battered doll than a once-vibrant young man about the same age as my own sons. I closed my eyes to shut out the image for a moment and breathed a quick Hail Mary.

Quick was back by then with the camera, and I did my usual photographs before starting my examination of the body. I started by cutting off the bright red tee-shirt, stained with blood and dirt and torn, front and back. I laid it out on the spare table, smoothing it, looking at it more out of forensic habit than out of the expectation of really finding something. As I ran my hands across it, I noticed a neat, round hole over what would have been the mid-back. Once I noticed it, it stood out glaringly, a tidy defect in a shirt otherwise in tatters from rocks and the ends of bones. Puzzled, I returned to Webster's body, face up on the table, and had Quick help me roll it over again.

Like the initial move, it was hard, because there wasn't the usual resistance of an intact skeleton, something every M.E. learns to use like a set of tools to move a corpse around for examination. We managed with a minimum amount of swearing, and sure enough, I found it. It took me a while, because of the scrapes and tears that the fall had left. Patience is power, though, and by methodically covering every inch of the back, lens in hand, I found it amid the blood and the dirt: a corresponding hole, beveled edges and all, that told me this death wasn't an accident.

Quick saw it then, too, and whistled low as I ran my gloved finger reflexively over the edges of the wound.

"Damn," he said. "That ain't good."

"Nope." I straightened up. "Let's get some x-rays and see what we've got here."

I stepped back and watched him roll the gurney down the hall to the x-ray unit. Within an hour, I was looking at a full set of computerized x-rays on the mortal remains of Jim Webster: adventurer, husband and about-to-be father. Among the broken bones I expected, just under the skin just below what would have been the upward arc of the ribcage, there was a tiny, flattened shard of metal, the remains of a bullet. He must have had his body flat up against the rock when he was shot. I made a mental line between the hole in the lower back and the spot that more or less corresponded to the exit wound. The shot had come from below. No great surprise there.

Well below, the trajectory I envisioned was sharply upward. I'd soon be using my reconstruction software to get a better angle; then we could head back out to the wall and try to figure back from the height on the wall to where the shooter might have been. I wondered what the first responders had seen, heard, and written down in their report.

Not for the first time, I blessed my compulsive mentor who taught me to do everything according to the book, every time. This wasn't the first murder I had discovered simply because I never skipped a step. It probably wouldn't be the last, either. Jim Webster might have been a risk-taking daredevil, but someone had murdered him, counting on a through-and-through wound getting lost amid all the damage that a ten story fall would create.

I closed the computer file and pushed my chair back from the counter. "I've got to make a phone call," I said.

The sheriff was not going to be a happy man when I told him; best to get it over with. I climbed the stairs to my third floor office, my steps echoing in the narrow well.

"Tom? I need you to meet me out at Ophir Wall."

"I just got back from there. I was on the other end of town when that climber fell. I've got his buddy here giving me a statement."

"You might want to keep him, and bring him along. It wasn't an accident. Webster was shot."

I heard his trademark epithet again, just before the line went dead.

"Shit!"

When I came into my office, I found my son Ben putting a file on my desk.

"What are you doing here?" I asked.

His neck gave him away again, something that was getting to be too much a habit. My boy was getting ready to tell me another whopper just like the one on the way to church, but his face was an odd combination of excitement and concern.

"You gotta see this, Mom. I found something pretty interesting in the files."

I noted he neatly sidestepped my question. Although the Center had been open less than a year, we had a decade worth of records that my youngest, an IT major at Georgia Tech, was entering into the system by a variety of low-budget labor. He'd been analyzing the data over the last few weeks, and I had grown accustomed to hearing various exclamations coming from his cube in the lab on the first floor. I was even more accustomed to his eccentric work habits. Like most of his peers, his attitude toward work was 'give me the job and I'll get it done in my own way and on my own time.' I hoped he would learn to punch a time clock with some regularity one of these days, but it hadn't happened yet.

"Can it wait, babe? I just found out that accident is a murder."

"The trustafarian?"

I looked puzzled. I wasn't quite familiar with Telluride slang, despite living here. Ben had arrived only a few weeks ago — I suspected as part of a well-orchestrated plot on the part of my family to provide me company — and he already talked like a native.

"Somebody who lives on a trust fund, Mom, an old one. The last of the line gets money his great-great-granddad left lying around. Was your victim a trusty?"

A remainder-man. That was a term I knew—someone usually banished with that money by a wealthy family to live outside the family sphere so as to avoid embarrassment, though I wasn't sure that was what had brought Webster to Telluride.

When I first arrived, I had been surprised to see some of the scruffier residents of town motoring about in expensive, late model SUVs and regularly taking cash out of the local ATM. It was clear to me that in Telluride, what one saw was not necessarily what one got.

"Webster had a trust fund, but he was a legit kind of guy," I replied. "He had made a name for himself. He worked, at least once in a while. He'd accomplished a lot. Why?"

"'Cause every death we've had since spring has been a trusty. Every…one."

"Come again?"

Ben pointed at his spreadsheet. "Look here. There have been four deaths before this week, all in the last two months, way, way above the average for Telluride. The explosion up on Silver Pick. Three cars off the road with no explanation, one on the Jeep trail above town, two on 145 coming into town."

I looked skeptical. "Those were accidents. This is a murder."

Even as I said it, something nagged at the back of my brain. This one might have been mistaken for an accident, too. A less exacting medical examiner, one with less time on his hands, might have made this a "sign-out" case, one in which massive injuries were documented only by external exam. I knew I needed to take a second look at those cases. Unfortunately, I didn't say it to my son, and the light faded from his eyes.

Ben folded his chart and looked at me, his fair face flushed, eyes now distant and vacant — what I called his "going to Timbuktu" look. It meant he had taken a mental vacation from me because he was so upset he needed to be somewhere — anywhere — other than in my presence. Odd man out in the family with his red hair and pale skin, he sometimes felt he had to prove himself to us all, and especially to me, these days. It didn't help that, as the baby, he really was often ignored, even when he was right as he often pointed out.

"It's just like the fire, Mom. I'm right, and you're not going to listen."

Ben had been about five when we were visiting his grandparents and fire had broken out in the nearby woods. The adults were all in the living room when he had come running in, telling us that the fire was in the back yard. We patted him on the head and ignored him until we smelled the smoke and saw the flames creeping across the wooded lot. It had become his oft-employed standard for being right and misunderstood. He was flying it now, and unfortunately, the metaphorical breeze was stiff enough to make it crack in my mind. I backed off. The sheriff could wait.

"Show me what you got."

Ben opened the chart again and walked me through his data. When he was done, I dispatched him with instructions to retrieve the files and meet me at home with a six-pack and a pizza for dinner. We had a lot of work to do. He gave me a quick hug and left my office smiling.

It took me a few seconds to finally stop staring at the spreadsheet he left behind and to pick up the phone. I was lucky and caught the sheriff before he headed out again. When I heard Tom's familiar voice, I broke the bad news.

"Looks like we might have a serial killer here in Telluride — and Jim Webster's the latest victim."

I filled him in briefly, promising more when I'd had a chance to look at Ben's data and hoping aloud for some luck when we processed the area around the bottom of the Wall. The crime scene would have been hopelessly contaminated, but perhaps there was something we could learn.

Life is never easy. And this time, neither was death.

****

I beat the sheriff by ten minutes or so, even though I was driving our Center SUV. I went past Society Turn at the base of the mountain and up towards Mountain Village, pulling through the curves with more care than dispatch, unusual for me. I'd gotten several warnings and finally one ticket from an exasperated deputy for taking the last turn into town on a rolling stop from a somewhat advanced rate of speed. After all, there wasn't a body to recover and the scene was already disturbed. Because the state program that established me as the Chief Medical Examiner for the Western Slope and the Forensic Center as its base also made me the head man in charge of all crime scenes, I did not have to wait on Tom Patterson.

Nelson Gorman, the tech on call for the day, and I started shooing the spectators away from the wall as soon as we arrived. We first made them empty their pockets and backpacks. In twenty years of medical examiner work, I have discovered there is no end to the ghoulish tendencies of on-lookers, who have been known to carry away all manner of evidence as souvenirs. As it was, we commandeered a few blood-stained rocks, a tattered piece of cloth that looked like it might be from Webster's pants, a broken carabiner that clearly had not been used by the deceased, a mangled triangular piece of metal that looked like a decorative plate, still bright with tiny nail holes to show where it had once been attached to something proud, and several tufts of rope, of equally dubious provenance. Gorman silently logged them all, bagged them, and took the names and contact information from everyone who was still at the scene. None of them had been there when the accident actually happened.

We were stringing crime scene tape when Tom Patterson roared up in one of the San Miguel County Sheriff's Office SUVs, spewing gravel as he pulled up by the Ophir Wall Recreation sign. The vehicle was still rolling when he popped the door, and it rocked to a halt as he slammed it into park as he exited. His expression was dark and his creased brow had leveled out his brows, which, when his face was at rest or in good humor, tended downward at the corners in a perpetually dreary way. He tilted his cowboy hat back and grunted at Norman and me. The day had started to warm, and his dark green shirt was already sweat-stained across his mid-back.

A young man climbed out once the SUV was safely stopped, trotting obediently and deferentially behind, wearing the red embroidered tee-shirt of the Telluride EMS. He carried a silver clipboard. Patterson motioned for him to hurry up, to bring the papers forward. He did, then melted back into the background. I gathered that our sheriff wasn't in the best of moods.

Patterson took a cursory glance at the paperwork, then shoved it at me.

"You'll probably need this. What the hell is going on? "

"Nice to see you, too, Tom." I replied. "What's going on is that someone shot Jim Webster, causing him to fall — though it looks to me from the trajectory of the bullet, he wouldn't have had much chance even if the fall hadn't killed him." I took out a computer-generated sketch showing the upward angle of the bullet in a man crouched in what I hoped was an approximation of the position Webster had been in while ascending the wall. "Here's what we have so far. "

I had already explained the findings; now he had a chance to see exactly what I was talking about. The clouds in his face deepened as he considered the sketch, and he made no comment. The paramedic loitered back by the sign, quietly watching the interchange between the sheriff and me, looking for signs of trouble. His expression told me that so far, at least, he didn't see any as far as he was concerned. Across the way, Norman was tying off the last bit of tape and striding back in my direction.

Patterson had nothing to add, so I pressed on.

"I need to have some idea where he was on the wall. If we can establish that, we might have a prayer of figuring out where the shooter was. "

I looked around. The base of the wall was a large clearing, with a couple of exposed rocks, but not much in the way of cover, except for a couple of scattered stands of aspens. They'd fit the bill, but which one was the likely spot?

"The other climber didn't see anyone, or so he says. In my mind, that means he's the most likely suspect in the shooting." Patterson glanced around, too, and it was clear his assessment of the situation was much the same as mine.

"It's always hard to tell," I continued, "but if I were a betting woman, I'd put money on this being a .22 rifle. That means we're probably talking about something within 300 feet, give or take, of impact, even if our shooter is an expert — and my guess is that he is."

Three deaths in as many days from .22 bullets. So much for the folklore that a .22 wasn't lethal for anything bigger than a rabbit.

"Maybe a little more than that if he was good enough to account for drop — the shot had to be into the air. Dimanio — that's the other guy — says Webster was up nearly 100 feet. I've got him locked in the back. You can ask him where."

Patterson strode back to the SUV, unlocked the back, and hauled out an obviously shaken man. He stumbled to get his footing. When he looked up at me, his dishwater blond hair was disheveled and his blue eyes red and bloodshot. They were still bright with tears. He walked unsteadily alongside Patterson, who made a cursory introduction to Norman and me when he reached us. I shook his hand; the palm was sweaty. Norman nodded. I noted again his intrinsic dislike of shaking hands, something he told me was a result of his upbringing. One of these days I would have to ask him why.

"I'm sorry," I said. "This has to be rough for you." Without waiting for acknowledgement, and not wanting to establish anything other than a professional interest, I hurried on. "Can you point out where Mr. Webster was on the wall when he fell?"

Dimanio looked determinedly at the ground, shaking his head, his breathing ragged. He took a gulp of air, looked up and perused the wall. He didn't hide his feelings well; from the play of expressions on his face, he was reliving the moment in detail. It took a while, but he proved to be of sterner stuff than I thought when he stumbled out of the SUV. At length, tanned and unlined face set, biting his upper lip, he pointed upward to the left of a large cleft that soared upward from the base of the wall.

"There. Just under that little overhang."

Norman took his rangefinder out of his pocket and played it on the site Dimanio indicated. Then he walked over to the M.E. van, opened the back and fired up his laptop. A few minutes later, he emerged with another sketch and an estimated distance for the shooter. Sure enough, off to the left, at 280 feet, more or less, was a copse of aspen trees.

The Pythagorean theorem is a beautiful thing, I thought as I surveyed it. In the morning light, without reason to look, it would have easily obscured a murderer. We'd at least found the proper haystack — now to look for the needle.

Patterson and I paced off the distance in silence, Dimanio having been returned to the locked rear of the SUV for the time being and Norman busy in the back of the van preparing to work the scene. We stood by the trees looking up at the wall.

"Damn fine shot," Patterson said grudgingly. "He'd have been a moving target. It means the murderer was pretty confident."

"I guess. He was working without ropes — maybe the shooter was just trying to scare him and make him fall. I know it wouldn't take much to get me to let go up there."

Patterson turned with a grin, the first good humor I had seen from him.

"That's because you aren't one of these idiot climbers. These boys have no nerves. They start climbing and all they think about is that rock. Good thing if you want to live to make another climb."

Then, realizing he'd committed a Telluride faux pas in referring to the climbers in the masculine, added, "Women too."

"Did Dimanio hear a shot?" I asked. The corpse wasn't very far from the spot where he said he had been laying out gear.

"Says not." Patterson cocked his head toward town. "Says that there was some construction noise going on. I can vouch for that. They were already at it this morning when I got here to check out a burglary in town. Noisy. Would have covered anything else."

It struck me as odd that Tom had been out on a burglary, but maybe he was short-handed. Anyway, it was good luck for us, confirmation of one piece of the puzzle. He removed his hat, wiped his brow with his forearm and replaced it.

"Better be off. Let me know what you find."

He turned abruptly on his heel, passing Norman as he headed up laden with metal detector, bags, brushes and assorted other implements of scene processing.

Three hours later, as the fading light made it hard to see much of anything on the valley floor, we packed it in, shoving three dozen labeled evidence bags into the locker and tallying the scene photos at over a hundred. Most of them would be worthless. We hadn't found what we wanted. Either the shooter had policed the area well or we were just plain unlucky — no shell casings, and nothing particularly indicative of human occupation, recent or otherwise. Norman slammed the rear door closed, and we headed back to Telluride in the gathering twilight.

****

Ben Wallace stepped off the gondola station near the market, enjoying the bright sunlight and glad to see a crowd of people milling around. There had been a big turnout at Mass, but the town of Telluride seemed almost deserted. He was surprised at how fast so many people could disappear from sight; he guessed they all came up here.

The market was almost as crowded as the gondola station. As he threaded his way through the aisles in search of something for dinner, he caught snatches of conversation.

"Right in the heart. He was shot right in the heart."

"I heard his girlfriend felt the bullet come by."

"It's a vet, gotta be a war vet with PTSD. Damn military."

"They have a kid. A two-year-old. He was in the park, can you imagine?"

"They say Bedsheet saw him running away."

All of it was spoken in hushed, conspiratorial voices, but Ben recognized the fear in them. He thought about the girlfriend and remembered the day his mother had come into his room — he was packing for a weekend trip to Tech to try out the dorms when it happened — to tell him about his dad's death. Hard to believe it had been almost five years. It still hurt.

"There she is!"

Ben looked around in the general vicinity of the voice, then cast about for the "she" in question. It wasn't hard to pick her out: brown hair matted, twisted into a knot and clipped indifferently on the back of her head, brown eyes vacant and red-rimmed, no makeup, staring absently at the contents of a freezer as though she had forgotten why she was there in the first place. He saw people duck and shake their heads, drop their voices to a whisper and skirt around her, afraid to say anything. He remembered how that felt. Even his friends had disappeared. He'd asked them later why, and the response was the same voiceless answer, a shake of the head, a shrug of the shoulder.

She was standing in front of the pizzas. Ben walked up quietly and stood next to her, regarding the choices, waiting for her to glance over. Eventually she did, her sad eyes catching his for only an instant before she turned them back to the pizzas.

"Too many choices," Ben said. "Thin, thick, organic, full of chemicals, veggie, meat, white, red."

She glanced back and tried a smile.

Ben cocked his head. "It's hard to decide. It's really hard to decide when you feel so bad."

The brown eyes widened.

"My dad was murdered a few years ago. It was months before I could even pick out the clothes I wanted to wear. Pizza was way beyond me."

It was a shading of the truth. It was months before his mom could function. The kid left at home, he'd had no choice but to keep it together, for her and for his dad.

"Yeah." The voice was small and shaky. Ben put his arm around the girl, who stiffened for an instant, then turned toward him for an honest-to-God hug.

"I'm sorry," he said and then went quiet.

He held her quietly until he felt her pull away. His shirt was damp, but she almost had a smile on her face. She opened her mouth to say something and then shut it again. He remembered that, too, how words wouldn't come. He opened the freezer and took out a couple of pies, handing one to her.

"This is a good one for kids. Lots of goo. Lots of chemicals. Not very healthy. He'll like it, especially now."

"She."

So much for eavesdropping.

"She'll like it then. The box is pretty. Let's go. My treat."

The two of them headed for the exit, Ben grabbing a six-pack, a bottle of milk and a bag of cookies on the way, juggling them as he ran interference for the woman. He paid for the groceries, loaded them in two ecologically insensitive plastic bags, and held the door for the woman.

"Where to?"

She took in a big, shuddering breath and let it out in a deep sigh, blinking in the sunlight, then named a time-share in the center of Mountain Village. They got in line for the gondola, waiting in silence, Ben a protective presence that dispelled curious stares and thoughtless conversation. He didn't notice the couple in line a few people ahead of him until he saw them step into a gondola, waving the others away and taking the car for themselves in a serious breach of summer, long-line etiquette. The woman was small and blond, the man massive with a curly brown beard and dressed in unfamiliar jeans and a cambric shirt. Ben stared, unsettled, a sense of foreboding and confusion making him forget for a moment the woman he'd taken under his wing.

What on earth was Father Matt doing up here with Marla Kincaid?

CHAPTER NINE

JUNE 8, EVENING

When I opened the door of the house, the smell of sausage pizza greeted me. Ben hollered a greeting from the kitchen as Caleb, my grizzled, drooling bloodhound, loped into the hall to greet me, followed by Zeke, the poodle-mutt I inherited when my daughter went to college, dancing on his hind legs. My two cats slinked up the stairway to avoid the ruckus, pausing halfway up to look at me with disdain for my traitorous affection to the dogs.

Ben was cutting the pizza when I entered the kitchen, dropping my bag on the desk in the corner. I washed my hands at the sink, crossing the kitchen to drop the towel I used into a hamper in the laundry room before sitting down at the center island where Ben was just pouring my beer. I'd never been able to break myself of washing hands in the sink, but years as an M.E. had at least made me careful not to re-use a towel once I did.

"Sorry I'm late," I said.

When I had called ahead, Ben had been a little irritated, a combination, I thought, of his enthusiasm for his findings, and the fact that he, like his maternal grandmother, generally had his day planned down to the minute and disliked any disruption of his schedule.

"It took a long time to process the scene, and we didn't find much," I took a bite of pizza, pre-fab, bake it yourself take-out from the market in Mountain Village. It was perfect, crisp, savory and just cool enough not to sear the roof of my mouth.

"Ahem," Ben said, reminding me of my manners.

I put down the slice, we graced the dinner, and I listened as he explained what he had found.

"I went through all the files we have. I'm in the process of getting all the photos I can, never know what you'll find. Especially since there's this."

He shoved a five-by-seven glossy of a wrecked Hummer.

I'm not much of a car buff, and it looked like any of the other Hummers in the area, except that this one was an outrageous orange, and had landed in the San Miguel River after a seventy-foot fall. The front was mangled, the front seats shoved up and protruding from the open top. Ben pointed to a spot on the passenger seat in a blow-up of the first photo. I took off my glasses, habit of the presbyopic and nearsighted who want to see clearly, up close. There was a tiny dark mark, with a hint of white in its center. I looked up expectantly.

"I think it might be a bullet hole," he said.

I considered the photo again. Ben was reaching, but he might be right. I remembered the case; it had been only a couple of weeks ago. At sunset, for no apparent reason, a car had driven off the road and into the river, at one of the few points along the way where there is no guard rail to prevent it, right where three large boulders had crashed into the river, the so-called Three Kings, in a mudslide several years before. The weather was clear, the sun was behind the car, not in front; and the driver of the car behind had given a statement that there was no reason to think the victim of the crash — there had been only one occupant — had been drinking, inattentive or speeding. One minute he was fine, the next, driving off the road.

A bullet through the windshield might just cause the driver to instinctively jerk the wheel. There was certainly lots of accumulated evidence to indicate that sudden projectiles of any kind through a windshield had deleterious effects on drivers, even on the safest of roads. That part of the shelf road into Telluride, high above the river, was anything but that. I put the photo down.

"We need to check to see whether the car is still in impound." The idea made sense, but it wasn't certain. Patterson would need proof.

"Done. It's there. Lucy and I will go over to Montrose tomorrow. It's in the wrecker yard there."

I wasn't surprised he'd elected to ask Lucy Cho rather than Norman to accompany him to Montrose. Lucy was tiny, friendly and just Ben's type, though I personally thought that she was out of his league.

He'd always been one step ahead of me, something that had made raising Ben a bit of a trial. This time, however, it proved to my advantage. I took another bite of pizza, washed it down with beer. Simple pleasures after a tough day. I looked over at my rusty-haired son, glad that he was there with me, aching for a mother back East who wouldn't have that pleasure again. He was deep in pizza and looked at me quizzically. "What?"

"Nothing. What about the explosion?"

"Not much to tell. The report said that it was a gas leak, but that's not certain. I did some research online. You might be able to explode a propane tank by shooting it." He grinned. "There are some awesome videos on YouTube. Problem is that most of them show people heating up the tank first. I'm not sure if that's necessary. If it is, I guess it means that the shooting theory is out."

"Was the tank even accessible? Most people bury their tanks these days. And how the hell did he get propane up Gold King anyway?"

I was constantly amazed at how far out people were prepared to live around here, and in spite of that, how many comforts of home they had.

"Gotta check," Ben replied around a mouthful of pizza. "And if they can bring ranch trucks up Silver Pick, they can bring up a propane truck. I'm going to check out what the cabin looked like with the realtor that sold it. Didn't have time this afternoon."

I nodded, smiling, impressed with my son's natural investigational abilities. On reflection, I supposed that tracking down IT issues and tracking down forensic evidence might not be so different, after all. I reached for another slice of pizza, and we finished dinner in a companionable silence, shuffling papers back and forth, poking at lines of text or details of photos and newspaper articles. Caleb and Zeke sat alongside looking patiently and hopefully from one to the other for a handout of leftover crusts. Pizza bones, my oldest, Adam, had always called them. I was rewarding them with just such a handout when the doorbell rang.

"I'll get it," said Ben, bolting for the door. He went so fast, it made me wonder whether he had some clandestine appointment he didn't want me to know about.

Apparently not. He came back into the kitchen with a grin on his face.

"You've got company, Mom. A lot of it."

He stood aside to let me pass, then followed me into the spacious front hall in which waited Father Matt, accompanied by a confused looking Isa and her dark-haired boy, two other women behind her, with two other children in tow, and a man I'd never met before, tall, and in his early sixties, but as muscular and fit as a much younger man. He had a face that was appealing now, but would have been brash and unfinished in his youth, before time silvered his hair and softened his edges. I found myself staring at him in a way that my Southern mother would have reproved. I shook my head, then nodded to the ones I knew and welcomed them.

"Father Matt, Isa, Pablo."

I glanced at the others standing behind Isa. One was a woman about Isa's age, blond-haired and blue-eyed, with two children, a boy about three and a girl of perhaps five, both brown-haired with wide brown eyes. The other was a woman who looked to be about fifty, erect, matronly, with graying black hair pulled into a bun and an ample bosom. Father Matt sensed my confusion and filled me in.

"These are Isa's friends, Pilar," the gray-haired woman nodded slightly, "and Lupe, and her children, Ignacio and Mariela."

He started to say more, but I cut him off and turned to the stranger.

"I don't believe I know you?" I extended a hand, but the answer came from behind him, from Ben.

"Mom, where have you been? That's Eoin Connor. The writer."

I recognized the face now from a display in the bookstore in the middle of town. Eoin. I hadn't known how to say it, but Ben pronounced it Owen. *Another of Telluride's transient stars*, I thought, who'd probably last only as long as he got top billing in the window. I wondered if the spelling was his given name or a literary affectation. A firm hand took mine, but the face turned to Ben and he winked with a familiarity that told me this was not the first time my son had met this man.

"That's me. Eoin Connor. I was looking to find your mother in town, and the good Father there was kind enough to point me the way."

Awkward silence again. Now I at least knew all the folk in my foyer, but I had no idea what brought them around at nearly ten at night. There was nothing for it but to ask. I smiled at Connor, and excused myself to turn to face Father Matt. His face, at least as much as I could see behind his unruly beard, had a cat-and-canary quality to it.

"Well?" I asked. "To what do I owe the honor of this unexpected pastoral visit?"

Isa stepped back, shoving Pablo behind her, obviously uncomfortable. The other two paled a bit. Pablo, like any toddler, made a break for freedom as soon as his mother's hands tried to corral him. He plowed right into Ben's leg. The other two children, older, stayed close to the younger, fairer of the two women whose names I had already forgotten. Ben scooped him up.

"Hey, Buddy, not so fast. How about we go check out the kitchen? We have dogs, you like dogs?" He nodded at Isa. "Is it okay if I give him a cookie?"

He was already headed off in the direction of the kitchen, Pablo in tow, when Isa's yes reached him. As he went by, he passed me a guilty smile. I had been right. There was something clandestine going on, and it clearly involved Father Matt as well, who now nodded at Isa, shooing her off after Ben's retreating form.

"Father Matt..." I started, but he held up a quieting hand.

"Ben was good enough to talk with me this afternoon when I came looking for you. You'd already gone over to Ophir, about that murder."

He made an involuntary sign of the cross. Father Matt did that with great regularity, more than any priest—any Catholic—I had ever known. I asked him about it once, and he said it was to remind him who and whose he was, because his memory was so bad. That might be the purpose, I reflected just now, but the man had a mind like a steel trap and I was about to be caught in it; I could feel it. I could also feel Eoin Connor's curious eyes on the both of us. Father Matt plowed ahead.

"Now, William," he said, using the nickname he had given me early on for my short temper, no Jane Wallace, he'd said, definitely a William. It meant he knew he was on thin ice and it meant he was serious. I narrowed my eyes. *This could not be good.*

"Isa needs a place to live. I put her up in the Victorian Inn, but she needs a more permanent place. She can't go back to that house she was living in. She's lost her jobs. She needs help. And so do Pilar and Lupe. They live with her at the house in Montrose. They can't go back. It's too dangerous. This man Pelirojo, he's a thug. Dangerous," he repeated. "They are not safe, and they need a place to live."

My mind fast-forwarded to what he was almost certainly going to ask.

"Oh, no. Not here. No. I can't put them up here."

"Why not? This place has six bedrooms and maid's quarters. You have plenty of room. You need the company."

I saw Ben's fingerprints all over this.

"I'll rent an apartment in town."

"Ridiculous. Isa needs a safe place where she can recover, not some lonely efficiency surrounded by rowdies. She needs Lupe and Pilar for support. Besides, it's a poor use of your money when you have space here."

"I can afford it."

"What you can afford is to take them in."

"They're illegal."

I expected pleading from him but got a derisive laugh.

"Please. First of all, you don't know that. It's not like you to jump to conclusions without information, Jane Wallace. More importantly, they are people. Isa's a person. She's been raped. You helped her once. Help her again. It's no skin off your nose. God knows you have enough room and enough money. It would be good for you."

I was surprised at the edge in his voice. It was too much. I was tired of people, especially my children, treating me as though my widowhood were something to be remedied, something to be cured. They could fill up the house with guests, and John would still be dead. Blue paint and broadsword came out, and I earned my nickname.

"How dare you?" I snapped. "Good for me? How? Another six people underfoot? A bunch of illegal aliens living with me — just the sort of ammunition anyone who wants to come after my law license, or my medical one for that matter, would need. An officer of the court harboring illegals? I don't need you, or Ben either for that matter, figuring out ways to keep me occupied. I'm fine. I don't need company, and I don't need any more aggravation than I already have."

I hadn't noticed that Ben had slipped back into the hall, Pablo on his hip with Ben's favorite chocolate-peanut butter sandwich cookies in each hand. Isa was beside him, with the same "going to Timbuktu" look Ben had perfected set on her face. He touched my arm with his free hand and just said, "Mom?"

I looked from Ben to Pablo, to Isa and back to Father Matt and the other women. The face of the older one, Pilar, was set and hard, an expression earned, I suspected, from many years of suffering indignity. A tear slid down Lupe's cheek, and she hoisted her younger child onto her hip, holding his hand, drawing him near. I knew when I was defeated, and if the truth be known, I was mortified at my outburst. If nothing else, John would have expected better of me. Time to be a better steward of his memory. My resolve to keep them out of the house crumbled when I saw the obvious pain and disappointment in Isa's brown eyes.

"I can't believe this," I said, but I suspect my voice lacked the sharpness I tried to convey in an attempt to save at least a little face. I sighed. "Ben, show Isa and Pablo and the others upstairs. Let Isa and Pablo have the suite. Let Lupe," I looked questioningly in the direction of the woman holding the child, and she nodded slightly, "have the big room next to the suite. Put Pilar in the guest room at the end. Make sure there are plenty of towels and that the sheets are clean."

"Why wouldn't they be?" Ben said. " No one has stayed there since you moved in. The beds might have a layer of dust, but the sheets are clean. C'mon Buddy, let's go find your new room."

Ben grinned, tickled Pablo, and headed up the stairs, edging past Father Matt and then taking the steps two at a time, pausing just long enough to cast a too-long look at Father Matt. I suspected there was more to come, but I had no idea what. As Isa followed, I reached for her arm.

"I'm sorry. I'm sorry. You are welcome here. It's just been ...difficult."

She pulled away, then nodded, but her expression didn't change. She hurried up the stairs with the others close behind. Pilar paused at the landing to cast a curious look back at me and then hurried up the stairs and out of sight. I doubted any of them believed me, or felt comfortable, and who could blame them? Could I have been a greater ass? I'd violated the first rule of Southern hospitality. I'd made a visitor feel unwelcome.

Father Matt looked like he wanted to embrace me, but my glare made him take a step back instead.

"Thank you, Sweet William," he said, taking some of the sting out of the nickname in a tactic he'd never used before.

He was getting too good at finding ways around me, too good at getting under my skin. He glanced back at Ben and his face momentarily clouded. He cleared his throat and his expression at the same time.

"I'll be back in the morning to get Isa and Pablo. The liaison is going to meet with her to see what we can do about regularizing her status."

There were so many Hispanics in the Telluride area, St. Pat's had added first one, then two, liaisons for immigrant services. I know. I pay the bill.

"Do that," I said dryly. "I meant it about the trouble, Father Matt. Make it go away. I can't afford to risk my job with the state and the feds."

"Like they care."

Father Matt looked at me for a long moment as the Seth Thomas ticked the seconds away. This time the silence worked against me. I was unsettled by this turn of events. I wanted control back, and I wasn't going to get it from Father Matt or even from my son. So I turned to the only remaining possibility: Eoin Connor, who had watched the proceedings with a faint grin. I wondered if he'd use it for color in some future book of his. Ben seemed to know what he was doing in Telluride, or at least what he did elsewhere, but I hadn't a clue. I decided to ask. I folded my arms and regarded him askance.

"And what do *you* want from me?" I asked.

****

What *did* he want? What he wanted was to snatch those big, round, black, owlish glasses off her face and revel in it. She took him completely by surprise, she did. He was expecting some half-aged twit of a woman doctor, all modern and feminist with no use for half the population of the world. She stood there, arms crossed, challenging, of a comfortable age and a womanly shape, and an unsettling confidence, nothing like those walking wraiths that chattered and chased after him, attaching themselves to him as soon as they recognized his face from his latest bestseller nestled among the offerings in the bookseller's window. This was a woman who would remember the things he remembered, even if she had experienced them half a world away and a few years younger. He liked that thought.

She hadn't said another word, just stared at him, eye to eye, waiting for his response. He noted with relief that it was an illusion, their equality. If she didn't have the height of her shoes, he'd have her by an inch or two, and that gave him a curious reassurance.

She wasn't beautiful, not really even pretty in the conventional sense, but he found her arresting. She had a sunset face, one that would get more interesting with age, not just older, unusual, he thought, in anyone. It was just a bit off, out of the norm for well-off American women obsessed with youth. Her face too long, her forehead high, the nose a bit crooked, and the lines on her face had begun to settle in. He noted with satisfaction that they seemed to be the kind that came from joy, not sorrow. Her hair had once been black but now was shot thoroughly full of silver, much more salt than pepper. Her brows, though, hadn't yet changed, still dark and wild, and her face was bare of makeup. He noticed her lips were pursed and got on with it.

"You could offer me a wee drink."

The wild brows lifted on one side. "I could. I haven't."

She had a tongue as sharp as a cheese knife, of that he was certain; he'd heard the edge of it when she spoke to the priest and he heard it now. He tried again.

"Surely you've got a drink in the interests of hospitality. It wouldn't hurt you. I need a favor from you, and you're more likely to grant it if you've a bit on board."

He kept her gaze, but it was hard, distracted as he was by the glasses. He was hoping he'd take her off guard by his comment, and he did.

She didn't smile, though, just shook her head. "Very well, come in," and turned on that boot heel to lead him like a spaniel puppy into the parlor. Then, "Have a seat," as she vanished presumably in search of ice.

There was whiskey in a decanter on the sideboard. He recognized the pattern, *Clare*, good, expensive, Waterford crystal. It was Fiona's choice; she had insisted they buy some for the house even when he was too poor to keep the two of them in bed and board. She probably had rafts of it now. Sad that he ever knew it by name. Sadder still that he recognized it after so many years.

The room was surprisingly sterile, more like a hotel than a home, everything in place and matched, its design-book perfection marred only by a motley collection of books, in all shapes and sizes, stacked two deep on the shelves and spilling onto the floor in disordered piles; and by a scattering of photographs. Uncharacteristically, he looked at the photographs first.

He was holding one of the pictures when she returned with the glasses and ice. She was in it, younger, but not much, and sitting on a pier, long legs dangling over the water, surrounded by children, six of them, in various raucous poses. There was a younger version of the likely, red-headed lad who had opened the door, and five others, three boys, two girls, all with brown hair and laughing eyes. He wondered what the father looked like; he'd probably been the one to take the picture. He replaced it on the shelf and took the glass from her, holding it as she covered the ice with lovely, amber liquid, knowing enough not to dilute it no matter how good and clear the water was in these parts. Her left hand was bare, not even a tan line on her ring finger; he wondered why, and then wondered why he noticed.

"You've a fine looking family." It was a good start to conversation. Good for ten minutes of non-stop bragging from most women, and most of the ones he knew only had one or two cubs to talk about. She poured her own.

"I do," she said, as though it were a matter of simple fact, but he noticed the corners of her mouth turn upward. "I do," she repeated, satisfied, then turned to him, all business, and all expectant behind those glasses as she asked him again what he wanted.

CHAPTER TEN

JUNE 9, EVENING

I handed Eoin Connor a glass and waited. He sipped it appreciatively. I had never been much of a whiskey drinker until John introduced me to it. A bit of Jameson's before bed, while we reviewed the day and planned for the future, was our ritual. It seemed odd to have offered it to this interloper, but hospitality demanded, and he seemed to appreciate it. He savored the sip for a good while before swallowing, either because he liked it or because he was trying to buy time. He finally swallowed and spoke, keeping his eyes on mine.

"Can I not just sit down?"

This was shaping up to be a real chess game, and I had already demonstrated that my powers were behind a cloud. All I really wanted was to get this man out of my house and go to bed. I sighed. "Of course. Please." I moved a tapestry pillow and sat down in the green overstuffed chair. My foot hit the stack of books at the side as I crossed my legs, and the pile toppled.

This was my favorite reading chair; it should do for whatever inquisition was to follow.

Eoin Connor sat himself opposite me on the sofa, a big man, broad-shouldered and square-faced. His seated form still hinted of those strong muscles under the cotton shirt open at the collar. He settled himself among the pillows, not bothering to move them. An abundance of pillows had been Kiki Berton's decorating trademark, and she'd indulged it to the hilt when outfitting this place.

"Comfortable," he said with some surprise. "Your home is grand."

Courtesy dictated that I respond with thanks, and I did. I still didn't think of this as my home, just a place to live, one I had wrested from my former partners in the settlement following John's death. I valued it more for what it represented than what it was; it made no real difference to me how it was decorated. Had I an interest, I would have thrown out all the matched, nouveau log cabin furniture and furnished it with Victorian antiques.

"You didn't come to see me this evening to discuss my house," I added. "What can I do for you, Mr. Connor?"

Another sip from the glass, and I saw him regarding me over the rim. He was definitely buying time.

"Right, then. On with it." He shifted his weight, then shifted it back. I was used to making people uncomfortable, but this surprised me. "I need your help with my latest project. My book. The Putnam murder."

I was perplexed. "The Putnam murder?"

"I am surprised you don't know of it. It happened about two years ago. Saul Putnam, the designer, shot at point blank range by his lover. The fellow then holed himself up in Putnam's house, took some hostages, and held the police at bay for a good long while. The trial was right here in Telluride, a few months later. Quite a production, though there wasn't any doubt how Putnam was killed and who did it. The lover claimed he'd been driven to it by Putnam's abusive nature. It's quite a sordid tale, in the end."

"Lovely."

I will never understand how people make a living writing about real crime. For that matter, I will never understand how they make a living writing about fake crime, either. There's enough disaster in everyone's life without looking for other peoples' sorrow. Or maybe reading about someone else's grand tragedy made one's own seem insignificant. Who knew? My own tastes ran to histories and biographies, the odd mystery thrown in, if it were improbable enough that I didn't bother to spend all my time criticizing it for lack of verisimilitude. Lately, I had even lost the taste for them.

"I'm afraid I wasn't the M.E. at that time. There's nothing I can do to help you."

Though I had to admit, the thought of dealing with a murder that wasn't mine to solve had a certain appeal these days. Anything to get my mind off the string that was building up in Telluride, more to come if Ben was right.

"I realize that. I've already interviewed the fellow who was coroner here at the time. He told me that there's a significant file with a good deal of background information. It would be a great help to me if I could see it. I'm trying to get the context of the murder, the lives it came from."

I noticed that he'd slipped from his charming Irish talk back into ordinary American. I wondered whether he used his accent for effect. The man definitely had a public persona and a private one, of that I was sure.

He took another sip of whiskey, almost draining the glass. "This is a peculiar sort of place. Not really —"

He searched for the adjective, and I supplied it in my own mind before he found it himself. *Real.*

"When I put that together with Putnam and his lover, it makes for an interesting tale — or at least so my publisher thinks."

Not real. It was as direct a description of this place as I had ever heard.

"Telluride does seem to operate in a sort of permanent suspension of the rules that make other places tick," I said.

Connor finished his drink and set it down on the coffee table.

"It does," he confirmed. "Anywhere else, this sort of tawdry story wouldn't be worth a second look. Gay lover kills boyfriend. But here, it takes on a different sort of significance. Putnam was a successful businessman, but he started out as an outcast from his Boston Brahmin family, a remainder-man, living on the leftovers of a trust that he inherited from his great-grandpa. A classic remainder man."

I started. The second time in a day I had heard that term, not exactly common commerce in everyday conversation. I was intrigued. "Go on."

Connor picked up his glass again and tipped it invitingly in my direction. "Will you cover the ice for me?"

His voice dropped on the word ice, giving the invitation a lilt, the accent back to the fore. I retrieved the decanter and covered his ice. I left mine alone. He tipped his glass toward me again, thanked me, sipped and began again.

"Putnam was a fellow who didn't belong in this world, so he made his own. Biggest sportswear designer in anyone's recollection. Made his own rules. Bought the biggest and best of everything. Master of his own domain."

"Dime a dozen in Telluride," I commented.

How this particular box canyon had come to attract so many of the glitterati, I had no clue. All I knew is that, on any given day, in the right season, I might run into — literally — aging folkies, trendsetting models, film stars — like Houston — or producers, TV personas or news anchors, even the odd five star general or rear admiral, not to mention at least one Anglican prelate of international disrepute. Telluride had some appeal to the rich and powerful; it was nothing I understood, but it was real even if the atmosphere it engendered was anything but.

"True enough. What makes it interesting, at least to me, is that Putnam had a great company of demons driving him. He'd made his name, but he wanted to be accepted by the very people who'd sent him away — his family. He'd been working on a reconciliation — even to the point of moving his headquarters back to Massachusetts — when he was murdered."

"Prodigal son returns home?"

Connor took on a reflective look. "I'm still not sure. If so, it's probably less of a story. Regardless of what drove Putnam, what drove his lover was his hatred of Putnam's family."

"So why didn't he kill one of them instead of Putnam?"

Again the tip of the glass.

"That is the reason for the story. And the reason I'm here. I need to see your files to be sure of the answer to that question. There's a gold mine in most morgue files. Never known a coroner that wasn't obsessive about collecting details — articles, pictures, impressions. Can you help me?"

I took exception to his characterization of forensic pathologists as glorified voyeurs and pack rats, and had half a mind to give him a quick lecture on the differences between medical examiners and coroners. I resisted, knowing instinctively that this was his way of teasing me into cooperation by tripping that switch in my mind that needed to set the record straight. Instead, I mentally went over the relevant laws and regulations on turning over files.

"I gather the trial is over?"

"Over with a verdict as tight as an old maid's purse," he replied. "After a terrible long ordeal, Kip Grimes, Putnam's lover, broke down in open court and admitted he'd killed the man. I'm told his defense lawyer was livid; he was sure he could get the man off. He's serving his life sentence without parole. Colorado Correctional facility in Canyon City. I've an appointment to see him later in the month, but I want to be prepared."

"No appeal?"

"None needed and none possible. I'll show you the transcript; even the King's own counsel couldn't get around his admissions. The stuff of TV shows, which I'm hoping this will be when I'm done with it. A morality tale for our time."

Another glass drained, he put the glass down with a certain wistful finality. "Good whiskey."

"Thank you. My husband's favorite."

I half-expected a question from him about John, but none came. Instead he circled back to his request. He was persistent.

"So, will you show me the files, then?"

There was that lilt again, voice dropping on the last word. I drained my own glass, put it down alongside his to signal that the discussion was done for the night.

"Let me see what we have. Right now I can see no reason you can't have a look, but I'll need to do a little research in the morning. Come by my office tomorrow, late morning or afternoon, and I'll have something for you. One way or another. No promises."

"Right enough. None needed. I thank you for your time, and the drinks."

He stood and took his leave without offering his hand. Instead, he ducked his head, touching two fingers to it as he said his goodbyes, gave me half a smile, and was gone before I had time to get to my feet or show him to the door. Odd man, to show up here uninvited, cadge a drink and then move on without so much as a by-your-leave.

Caleb shuffled in from the kitchen, prodding my hand with his head, begging for a pat. I stroked his head absentmindedly as I watched Eoin Connor walk down the steps of the house and into the lamp-lit street, hands stuffed in his pockets and head back.

I couldn't see his face, but something about his carriage told me he was very well-satisfied with his visit.

Caleb scratched my leg and dropped to the floor, begging a belly rub.

"You too?" I asked. "Seems like every man I meet today wants something from me."

Caleb whined and I obliged. Just, I suspected, as I would oblige Eoin Connor in the morning when he came by to poke around in the sorry past of Saul Putnam and Kip Grimes.

****

Tom Patterson enjoyed his evening walk along Pacific. Off duty, in jeans and a tee-shirt, sneakers instead of his boots, he greeted friends and enjoyed the quiet calm of the evening. There wasn't as much activity on the streets as he expected, no particular surprise with a man gunned down in cold blood and broad daylight in Town Park. He stopped in his favorite pizza joint for a white pie and a cold beer. The bar was almost empty, so he took his favorite spot on the corner and settled onto the bar stool, motioning the waitress. Kate was an old friend. She mouthed "The usual?" and gave him a thumbs up when he nodded.

"Thanks, Kate," he said as she slid the draft in front of him.

She'd filled it generously, the head spilling over the top and leaving a little puddle of foam around the base. He wiped it up with a napkin and took a handful of popcorn from the bowl on the counter. He glanced at the blonde who approached the seat next to him and gave him a beguiling smile when he turned her way. She looked a lot like the Kincaid girl, blond and tiny, but harder somehow, and older. She was already three sheets to the wind. Her foot slipped on the base of the stool and she nearly toppled over. He caught her arm and helped her onto the seat, then turned his attention back to his glass and the television.

The television over the bar was tuned to a news channel, sound muted. He watched the pictures and the text crawl along the bottom with little interest. Baseball wasn't big here in Telluride and there wasn't a soccer game just now; otherwise the screen would have been tuned to sports, and he would have missed it. He'd just taken a swig of beer when a photograph appeared on screen, familiar ground, Town Park, the sledding hill, the trees they'd searched in vain for evidence of the shooter who had killed that Frisbee player.

"Kate!" He barked. "Turn it up!"

She wasn't fast enough. He missed the first part of the story, but it was enough.

"....killed in Town Park. This photo shows where the shooter hid. If you look closely," here the camera zoomed in, "you can see the shot being fired. Sources in Telluride tell us that the police have no suspects in this daring, daylight shooting and the townspeople are understandably on edge. This is the third death in a week in this exclusive community. Movie star Mitch Houston was shot and killed in his home earlier in the week with a gun of the same caliber. And in related news, world famous mountain climber Jim Webster fell to his death in the nearby town of Ophir. Death seems to be stalking Telluride. Stay tuned for more details...."

Just what he needed. He supposed it was a pipe dream to hope that this would stay under wraps for long, but he'd hoped for a day or two. National attention would mean even more panic in town. It was an even bet whether there would be a drop in tourism from fear or an increase because of curiosity and thrill seekers. He'd bet on the latter, as long as there were not more deaths. Kate returned with a fresh beer he hadn't ordered.

"On the house. You can use it."

He rolled his eyes, nodded, and lifted his current glass to her in response. He and Kate went way back, all the way to high school in the days when Telluride was just beginning to take off as a result of the ski area, and ranching was still a part of the local economy.

"That's for damn sure. Thanks."

Kate lifted the pizza pan and swept a damp rag over the counter as an excuse to stay and chat.

"Any idea who did it?"

Tom Patterson smiled. "Now Kate, you know I couldn't tell you if I did. But the plain fact of the matter is, I have not the first clue." He paused, then corrected himself. "Not true. Clues I got. Ideas, not so much."

"It's pretty tense, Tom. That's all anybody is talking about. Nothing like this has ever happened here. Remember the killings in Virginia a few years ago? I was visiting my brother about that time. It feels like that. People are scared."

He could understand that. Telluride was a particularly placid place, almost devoid of violent crime. Lots of drugs, some theft, DUI and the occasional crazy-disorderly, but nothing personal.

"Believe me, I know."

Kate pursed her lips, and two small furrows appeared between her eyebrows. She looked right into Tom Patterson's eyes, unblinking. "Not sure you do, Tom. People are really, really twitchy. I hear a lot from this side of the bar. And every story I hear is worse than the last and crazier."

Patterson sighed. He had no personal experience with a panic-struck populace in the middle of a crime wave, but he'd heard, he'd read. The Virginia case was well-known, discussed in law enforcement programs as a classic. Worried populace, vague clues at who was responsible and almost as many crimes against people—less significant, but more histrionic than the actual murders — from the nervous populace as there were shootings. He hoped it wouldn't happen here.

"Oh, I expect we've seen the last one," he said with a confidence he didn't feel. "Even Paradise has its problems now and again."

Kate relaxed her lips, and one brow drifted upwards. She tilted her head a bit as she answered. "Right," she finally said. She didn't believe it either.

On the way home, Tom Patterson passed the deliveryman putting out copies of the paper for the next day. He snagged a copy, curious to see what Pete Wilson had written about the shooting. He stopped underneath a streetlight to take a look. There, on the front page, was a half-page photo of the hill, a flash of flame emanating from the trees and a banner headline reminiscent of the old days: "*Cold Blood, Broad Daylight!*"

Count on Wilson to add fuel to the fire, Patterson thought. Scowling, he crumpled the paper and tossed it in the waste bin. Then, thinking better of it, and knowing he needed all the information he could get, he walked back to the rack and pulled out a second copy. *Forewarned, forearmed*, he thought to himself as he ran through the options for pulling the plug on Wilson. If this kept up, there would be a full-scale panic in town—and Wilson hadn't had time to exploit the Webster murder yet. First thing in the morning, he and Pete Wilson would have a little talk.

CHAPTER ELEVEN

JUNE 10

Not long after John and I were married, in an attempt to make sense out of the brutality that was my daily portion and share, I started going to daily Mass. Now that John was gone, I still went mostly out of habit, but these days out of respect for John, whose name was on a shiny little plaque in a far corner of the church, memorializing his life and my grief. This day, with the town in an uproar because of Pete Wilson's sensational story and because almost everyone knew at least one of the dead men, I went to Mass to escape and to try to find a little respite from the phone, the reporters, the cops, and my restless mind.

It didn't work. I slipped out the door as soon as Mass ended, in no mood to chat with Father Matt and about half afraid if I did, he'd have yet another self-improvement project for me. Isa, Pilar and Lupe had decided to tough it out at my place despite my inhospitable treatment of them when they arrived. I had apologized in the morning, and we had reached an uneasy peace, but I had no desire to hear Father Matt's take on the situation or to endure his admonitions. I was about halfway down the street when I heard a voice behind me: male, deep, and Irish.

"Jane Wallace. Wait, hold up! I was just on my way to see you."

I turned to greet Eoin Connor.

"What brings you to Mass on a Monday?"

From my perch in the balcony, I had seen him at the end of the back pew, nearest the confessional with the procession bells on the side. Somehow he hadn't impressed me as a pious man, with his easy charm and his manipulating manner, but he'd looked as natural as Father Matt, kneeling there in preparation for the Mass, at the same time eyeing his fellow Mass-goers. I suspected that writers and medical examiners shared that particular curse: always keeping an eye out, always making mental notes, always sorting and coming to decisions based on what we see. Thirty years into it, I rarely even noticed myself doing it anymore, it was so second nature.

He caught up with me, a bit out of breath from the effort.

"I could ask the same of you. Poor sinner like me needs all the grace I can get. Besides, I like hearing the Mass in the old words. Comforting. Don't get that much."

I heard him turn on his Irish accent for effect, and it annoyed me.

One of the things I loved about Father Matt was his insistence on celebrating the Latin Mass as often as he could. The bishop had been leery of his plans, but had given him his head, and it had turned out to be a resounding success, turning the Hispanic and the Anglo communities from two into one, no small accomplishment even here in politically correct, inclusive Telluride. I loved the beauty of the words, the fact that I could get lost in sounds and feelings and for a blessed hour, could cease to think. When English words hit my ear, they triggered a cascade of thoughts, a verbal chain reaction that I could never control. The Latin soothed me into thoughtful quiet. That was hard to come by in my world, especially these days.

"I agree," I said. "One of my husband's colleagues — he was Swiss — would have agreed with you, too. I remember him telling me once that one conducted business in English, spoke German to animals, made love in French, but talked to God in Latin."

Connor laughed. "We've got a similar saying. 'Labhair Gaeilge le do leannán, Bearla lena madraí agus Laidin le Dia.'"

It was Irish, it had to be, melodic, complicated, with back-of-the throat sounds I'd never heard in the course of mastering bits and pieces of Yiddish, Spanish, French, German and Italian. It was lovely and enchanting, and I had no idea what it meant.

"Which is...?" I prompted.

"Speak Irish to your lover, English to the dogs, and Latin to God. You see, we Irish don't have a hand in business."

I wrinkled my nose. "It seems you think very little of English," I said. I expected him to demure, but he didn't.

Instead the green eyes crinkled. "Indeed, and with good reason," challenging me to rise to the defense of my mother tongue.

I walked on in silence, hoping he would lose interest and drop away. He didn't. He moved the conversation into a different court.

"Odd to see a coroner in church," he said. "Runs counter to my wide and varied experience with your fellows."

I was intrigued in spite of myself. "Oh? Are we all heathens in your experience?" I had to admit privately that we were in mine.

He settled into a comfortable stride alongside me, hands in his pockets. "Not really heathens, but dealing with the underside of humanity brings out the person you really are. Cops, they're all religious, even if they don't go to church, at least they are until and unless they go bad. They all believe in truth and justice, you see, and when they can't find it in their jobs, they look for it in the next world. Every mother's son of them believes in God and looks for His wrath and for Him to balance the scales."

I thought about the police I had worked with. He had a point. I shrugged assent, and he went on.

"Coroners like you — they're scientists. They believe in truth, all right, but they filter it through their own minds as the court of last resort. They can't believe what they can't understand and don't realize they have it backwards. Agnostics, most of them, either that or they take whatever bits and pieces they think fit and cobble together some sort of theology of the day that answers whatever problem they're facing at the time. Unusual to find one in a place that claims to be the one true church with the fullness of truth and a healthy dose of mystery in the bargain. Scientists are always looking for what doesn't fit. They're not ones to submit to someone else's authority, and they're not ones to live with uncertainty."

I was surprised at his insight. He was dead on.

"True enough as a rule, but not for me," I said.

"Clearly not."

He looked at me curiously. Had I really shivered when I recalled again why I started going to daily Mass? I thought it was in my mind. I shrugged, as much to cover the emotions I had stirred up as to dismiss his overture. He paused, and I glanced at him long enough to see his eyes were twinkling. He was enjoying this.

"Seems you avoided the trap of your other profession as well."

I might as well bite.

"Which is?"

"Lawyers. Hard shell atheists, all of them. Live in the world of reasonable rather than right, and in their world, reasonable is whatever you can convince a judge, or twelve men chosen for the fact that they have no opinions, hear no news and form no judgments can be convinced to say it is. Lawyers don't believe in truth, so they don't seek it out."

I stopped and turned to face him, annoyed at his familiarity as much as his accuracy.

"Do you suppose you could find something to discuss other than my two obviously inferior professions?"

We stood beside a lilac hedge, and the scent of the lavender and pink flowers was intoxicating. He looked genuinely chagrined. Either that, or he realized that his ill-mannered joke might cost him access to the information he needed for his book. He looked away, twisted off a spray of flowers, smelled them absently, and then twirled them in his fingers for a moment, collecting his thoughts. I hoped he'd just lapse into permanent silence and go his own way.

I never got to find out. I heard a loud crack from behind us, and then a second in the general direction of St. Pat's, then heard screams from up ahead. Before I could connect the sounds, Connor pushed me to the ground and elbowed me roughly into place beneath the heavy and overhanging branches. There were no more of the sharp sounds, but the screaming continued amid a rush of other noise: slamming doors, gunning engines, bikes clattering to the ground, and running feet. I counted the pounding beat of my heart and took deep breaths to quiet it. Hard to do, pinned as I was by the bulk of the man beside me.

One minute, perhaps, then two, three. The close quarters became even tighter, and I felt panic rising, my heartbeat escalating in spite of my mental admonitions to relax and the deep breaths I took. I squirmed, a rock prodding me squarely in the breast-bone, grass and a bit of dirt in my mouth and a dangling twig tickling the back of my neck. I mentally counted seconds, trying to judge the time.

"Stay put, you damned fool," Connor hissed. "Do you not know the sound of gunfire when you hear it?"

I felt him adjust his position and began to sort the sounds out. There were no more of the ordinary sounds of the street which had otherwise gone quickly and ominously quiet; even the screaming had stopped. There were no more footsteps, no crunch of bike tires on gravel, no idle chatter. Then from the distance, a bullhorn telling people to evacuate the area, and more distant, a siren.

"Coals to Newcastle," I heard Connor grumble. "Not a soul outside except for you and me."

Just then, my cell phone vibrated on my hip. Connor's bulk had me neatly pinned against the trunk of the biggest lilac tree, and I had to maneuver to retrieve it. My hand brushed against his shirt. With no small amount of pleasure, I elbowed him in the ribs for space. He grunted and shifted, but kept himself between me and the street. I rolled onto my side and lifted my head just enough to extract myself from the bush and to bring the phone to my ear. I already knew who was calling and what it was about. I just didn't know who was dead yet.

****

Half an hour later, Eoin Connor and I were sitting in the marshall's office waiting to make statements. The unfortunate victim had not even made it to Telluride Medical Center. Cosette Anira — a stunning brunette heiress and fixture on the glossy pages of the local lifestyle magazines as both model and accomplished local real estate agent—had bled out in the street just as the ambulance arrived. I'd made a cursory examination of the body at the scene, Eoin Connor standing far enough away to be discreet, close enough to know what I was doing. I sent him two steps backward with a sharp word, and a deputy closed ranks to keep him at bay. I despise voyeurs at a scene. The dead should at least have the dignity of eyes turned away.

The woman had died of one dead-on shot in the middle of the chest, another grazing her neck, ripping a hole in the blood vessels that pumped blood out at an alarming rate and sucked air in fast enough to stop her where she stood. I'd find a hole in the heart, a pericardium full of blood and a froth of air that stopped her heart cold in a matter of a few beats when I autopsied her later that afternoon. I hoped I'd also find an intact bullet. I was laying mental odds that it was a .22. From what the deputies were able to tell me, she had been walking up the street when she was hit. I had been right about the general origin of the shot.

Connor walked with me to the marshall's office after he apologized, both for his teasing and for his insensitivity. I should have thanked him for his instinctive protection, but I did not. Instead, I wondered why he responded so viscerally to the sound of the shots before there was time to think. It bespoke an unsettling familiarity with gunfire. There were layers to this man, it seemed, and not all of them good.

Now we sat side by side in uncomfortable chairs, in silence, waiting to be called. At length, Connor cleared his throat and tried again at ordinary conversation.

"A friend of your husband, you said back there. Your husband's favorite whiskey, you said last night. And a family. You're married, then?"

I was surprised at the details he remembered. Making mental inventory was a habit of mine, one I often regretted, but not one I saw in most other people, who were generally so wrapped up in themselves that information about someone else went totally unremarked.

"Widowed."

He looked sideways at me, and I saw his expression from the corner of my eye. It was kind.

"I'm sorry."

"So am I." My voice was sharp and hard. I wanted to make it abundantly clear that this was a closed subject, a boundary he would not be permitted to pass.

Connor was persistent but not stupid. He dropped the subject and moved on.

"I was hoping to get a look at that file this afternoon. Have you had the chance to look at it?"

I nodded. "Ben brought it up this morning. It's on my desk. Not much there, really, despite what your source told you. But you're welcome to it. You can stop by when you're done here."

"Would you have time to take a look at it with me?"

"I told you it isn't one of my cases. I won't be any help."

The last thing I wanted was to spend the afternoon with this man, with his uncomfortable insights and all-too-charming tongue. I knew I needed to keep him at arm's length, or even further, and something told me that might be difficult.

"Consider it an act of Christian charity."

I looked askance at him.

"I've never gone through one of these files but that there was something to throw me off. I'd consider it a kindness if you'd spare the time to answer my questions." He paused. "I'll be happy to pay you, since it isn't your case. Consider it a consulting job."

My sideways glance told me the good humor had vanished from his face. It was set and hard; he was clearly annoyed, almost as though I had delivered a personal rebuff.

I hastened to make amends, which is how I ended up with Eoin Connor in my office for the rest of the afternoon. Worst of all, I was trapped in the office with him. The marshall had difficulty finding the victim's next of kin. One of my personal rules is not to put knife to body until the nearest and dearest have been notified. I'd violated that rule in the Houston case, and it had bought me lawyer trouble. I wasn't going to violate it again.

Connor was a model visitor for the most part, asking occasional questions but otherwise so quiet that, had I not stolen the occasional look from my own work, I would not have known he was there. I had just made one such glance when he looked up himself and caught my eye. He grinned as if to say "Caught you!" then stood and stretched, the file in an untidy heap on the coffee table.

"You're right about the case," he admitted. "The facts seemed pretty simple to me on first glance, and there's nothing in this file that changes my mind. In a way, it's too bad for me. Better reading when there's something wrong in the investigation, but this looks pretty simple."

His comment irritated me, even though I hadn't had anything to do with this case and had no particular dog in this fight. Most of us in the business of investigating crime are committed and capable. I take exception to people who view us as either dupes or goobers.

"I'm glad it meets with your standards," I said dryly. "Though I am sorry that the meticulous nature of my predecessor means that you've wasted your time on this book."

"I didn't say that," Connor countered, face still pleasant. "I just said it makes better reading and an easier sell if there's a controversy about the evidence. Ever since the O.J. trial and all those true crime shows, the average man fancies himself a forensic expert. And it's just human nature to want to catch the expert in an error. Do that and you're guaranteed a bestseller. Turn it back around and prove that justice was served anyway, and you've got a movie or a mini-series. People still like to see right win out, vast amount of noisy sentiment to the contrary."

"You couldn't prove it by me," I said, then changed tacks, because I didn't like the route my train of thought was taking. "So what do you do now?" I was curious in spite of myself.

Connor bent to reassemble the file, tapping the papers back into neat order and handing it to me before answering. "Sure, a mistake makes better reading and an easier book. But the real story is never the science; it's the psychology. People read about murders for two reasons. Either they are simply nosy and the story is nothing more than written gossip, or they want to reassure themselves that that sort of thing could never happen to them. They want to know that there's something really abnormal about murderers, that they're safe in their homes and in their friendship. Which, around here, these days, doesn't seem to be the case."

A quiver went up my spine, and a knot formed in my stomach. I wondered when he was going to broach the subject of the series of killings stacking up in town. I had moved to Telluride to be safe, and it seemed murder was following me far too closely. I narrowed my eyes in aggravation. This man had a knack for treading on forbidden ground and doing so in a way that I found exceptionally irritating. My hospitality was at an end, and I wanted him out of my office.

"Murders happen every day. Ordinary people, ordinary means." I was stretching and I knew it.

"People ordinarily get gunned down in broad daylight in Telluride? News to me!" Connor had cocked an eyebrow and his look was a challenge. He had caught me out and he knew it. I shot him a hard look but didn't answer. He backtracked with a faint grin on his face, as though he knew full well what he was doing, and he was enjoying sparring with me. Putting together three shooting deaths with the information Ben had given me, not only did we have a serial killer, we had one who was rapidly decompensating. The killings were alarming, more frequent, and chancy.

"No, I suppose they don't," I said cautiously, but with enough ice in my voice that I hoped he would take the hint and drop the subject. I had not sorted out this series in my own mind yet, and it worried me. I knew from experience there would be more killings, and there was nothing I could do to prevent them. I had no thread that tied the bodies together, other than a crack shot with a .22 and an animus towards the rich and famous. Mostly, it seemed, the rich. Although these folks had some notoriety, it was mostly local and secondhand, family fame, not personal.

"You're right, of course," he admitted. "Most of them are. Ordinary, I mean. That's why I don't write about most murders. I choose my cases very carefully, either for the victim, the killer, or sometimes the survivor. Something readers will either identify with or recoil from, sometimes both."

I took the folder from his hands. "Well, good luck."

"Thanks. Can I get a copy of the file to take back? It makes fact-checking easier."

I nodded and picked up the phone. "Ben? Can you come make a copy of this file for Mr. Connor?"

Ordinarily, I would have asked Tina, but she had taken the afternoon off for a doctor's appointment. And besides, I knew that Ben would relish the chance to have a few minutes with Eoin Connor. He'd bent my ear at great length about the man at breakfast the morning after Connor — and Isa and the rest — had appeared on my doorstep, obviously the result of Ben's plotting to slide Connor in with the women.

I had barely replaced the phone when Ben appeared at my door, striding into the room with vigor, a half-eaten sandwich in his left hand. He extended his other hand to Eoin Connor, big grin on his face. I watched as I always watched my children — waiting to see how this man treated my son.

Connor extended his hand in return, as though my Ben were an old and respected associate.

"Good to see you again," he said.

Ben glowed, hesitated a minute, then turned to me to take the file.

"I'll just be a minute," he said more to Connor than to me, and backed out the door, taking another bite of sandwich as he went, his attention never leaving the writer.

Connor turned to me once Ben was out of the room.

"Learning the family business, is he?" he asked.

I shook my head. "Not really. Ben's a college student, studying computers, information technology. He's helping set up a new archive system for the center. He'll be back at Tech in the fall."

"That's the calling of the day, isn't it? Did none of your children follow you into medicine?"

I remembered that he'd seen a photo of us all when he'd come by a few nights earlier. His innocent, conversational question felt intrusive, but I answered anyway.

"Only Beth. One older than Ben."

"The rest?"

"Two in seminary. One housewife. One carpenter. One in med school. And Ben."

It was the minimum civility required, and I would say no more. I was spared the need when the power in the building went out, leaving the office in shadow, the only light filtering in from the long, rectangular windows in one wall.

"Well, now," Connor started, but I interrupted him, irritated about the inconvenience, but happy for an excuse to eject Connor from my office.

"This happens now and again. It'll be a while before it comes back on."

The powers that be had approved a generator for the building after repeated negotiations and once we pointed out the problems of losing our cooler, but our compelling argument only went so far. The generator, whose whine I could hear over the incessant beeping of my UPS, back-up computer power supply, powered only the morgue proper. I saved the work on my computer and powered it down, switching off the UPS to silence the irritating beep. Ben materialized at the door just as I looked up.

"I didn't get it done," he said with some chagrin, then, hopefully, "Maybe I can bring it to your place later on tonight?"

He was looking at Eoin Connor who regarded him like an indulgent uncle. I hurried to forestall that possibility. Somehow I didn't want my son striking up a friendship with this man; it disturbed me on too many levels. Not the least was my innate horror at Ben's finding friendship with a man other than his dad.

"I'm sure Mr. Connor will come back later to pick it up. Give me your number, and I'll have Tina call you when it's ready."

Connor fished in his pocket and produced a card with a cell number with an unfamiliar area code but a local address, one in Mountain Village.

"I'm renting a place at Sunrise," he said, naming one of the newer condo developments that overlooked the slopes. "Nice little place, not but a few steps from the local bar."

I scowled a bit to put him off as I put the card under a weight on my desk, then shooed Ben and Eoin Connor out of my office.

We emerged from the dim interior of the building into a brilliant summer afternoon. The streets ordinarily would have been full of the denizens of Telluride, gathering in groups on corners and around, chatting casually with each other, the power outage having provided a universal and welcome town coffee-break, but today they stood huddled together in doorways and in the shadows of overhangs, clearly needing to be outside, but wary of becoming a shooter's target. I saw one brave soul cross the street heading toward the bakery. His walk was hurried, and he soon broke into a trot, taking the steps to the cockeyed screen door in a graceful leap.

I turned to ask Ben a question only to find that he and Connor, deep in conversation, were already half a block down the street, headed in the direction of Town Park, Connor tamping tobacco into a pipe as he walked. They were the very image of unconcerned Telluride, from the days before the killings that now seemed to be our daily portion.

Funny how easily the routine fades away in the face of fear, I thought as I steeled my nerves at the sight of them walking in the open. There's already been one killing today. There won't be another. *Please God, not another.*

I saw Ben's hands gesturing animatedly as he talked, a trait he inherited from me. Connor's head was cocked in his direction, and he matched Ben stride for stride. I turned back and headed in the opposite direction, forcing myself to walk in the open to prove to myself that they were safe, cold in spite of the warmth of the pleasant afternoon.

****

Pete Wilson loitered in the shade of the grocery across the street from the Center, leaning casually against the wall as he watched Jane Wallace emerge in the company of her son and Eoin Connor. She didn't look happy. Then again, she never looked particularly happy in Wilson's experience, and another murder was not going to improve anyone's mood. He was surprised to see her turn away from the men and walk west, right in the middle of the street. Not that there was too much traffic to worry about. He watched her until she turned right and disappeared around the corner.

Dragon Lady's gone, he thought to himself. Might be a good time to poke around.

He sauntered across the street and pushed open the big glass doors, framing up what he planned to say to sweet-talk the receptionist. As it turns out, there was no need. The desk was vacant, no sign of her frizzy little head.

Probably gone to the bathroom, he thought.

He strode to the double doors with the red sign that said "Authorized Personnel Only." Hoping that the power failure meant that the electronic locks were disabled, he pushed tentatively against them. They gave and he slid through, hoping that the staff, like everyone else in Telluride, was taking advantage of the situation and enjoying a little break. Outside. He paused, listening for sounds of occupancy. Nothing.

The morgue was at the end of the main hall, steel doors still lit by the lights in the ceiling. He could hear the generator behind the doors and wondered for a moment why it didn't power the circuit for the doors. His good luck, he decided. He debated getting an image of this latest victim in the morgue, but only for a moment. No sense courting jail. He already had a shot of the victim from the street, taken as the EMTs loaded the body into the ambulance. Better to exploit this unexpected access in more subtle ways.

He tiptoed down the side hall, pushing in doors to look inside. Laboratory spaces of various kinds, all pristine and clean. Nothing too promising until the last door on the right. A common office with five desks, four of them neat, one cluttered. It looked a lot like the newspaper office. He wished he could find the idiot architect who decided that common areas like this fostered communication and… what was it? Community. Fostered community. What it fostered was time-wasting and a way for his colleagues to borrow his snacks and his ideas.

Thank God for messy desks, he decided. The four that were clean were also locked, the odd one a goldmine of papers and a clutter of empty drink cans and food wrappers with a half-eaten sandwich lying precariously on a pile of folders. He moved the sandwich and picked up the top folder, a thick one, labeled Putnam. It was an old case; he remembered the murder. Sensational enough, but only because of the people involved. Nothing like these last few days. He laid it carefully aside and picked up the next.

Toxicology on Mitch Houston. A blood alcohol in excess of the legal limit. No surprise there. The man drank like a fish. He made a mental note of the actual number though. It might come in handy.

Two more folders with names he didn't recognize. Finally at the bottom, he found something interesting. An unlabeled brown folder with a spreadsheet in it and a sticky note written in an irregular hand, a smear of chocolate in the corner. The spreadsheet contained information on four recent Telluride deaths, one a bizarre accident involving an explosion up Silver Pick Road. The note made him read the contents carefully, aloud but in a hushed voice, into the recorder on his phone.

He finished quickly, restacked the folders in their proper order, hurried out of the office and out the back door into the alley. The door closed behind him just as he heard footsteps in the main hall and a man's voice calling, "Who's there?" He thanked whatever journalistic gods had his back and forced himself to walk casually down the alleyway. He was already thinking about the headline he could fashion from the four words on the sticky note: All trusties? Serial Killer?

CHAPTER TWELVE

JUNE 11, MORNING

The autopsy on Cosette Anira was as routine as a homicide postmortem could be. She was a beautiful, dead girl with a hole in her chest and her neck, and I found exactly what I had predicted the day before. I wondered again who could possibly have pulled off such a shot, on Anira, on Monson, on Webster. A slug from a .22 long rifle — that's what I pulled out of Cosette Anira — was accurate up to about a hundred yards and dangerous enough, but usually because of the damage it created by ricocheting around the body. These folks had been shot with uncanny skill. I just couldn't reconcile the choice of weapon with the notion of a serial killer. Mass murderer, really. In either case, shooters tended to use high-powered, high efficiency guns. Not a small gauge rifle, no matter how accurate it could be. It was just odd, damned odd, as my grandfather would have said.

And she was a trust fund baby. Ben's little discovery was having very ominous overtones. Seven dead and counting. It didn't take a rocket scientist to figure out we had a serial killer on our hands, odd or not. I wondered how long it would take for Pete Wilson to stir the pot.

I took a break from fretting to sort through the morning's mail and reports. It was Tina's daily task to stop by the post office on her way into work and bring the day's missives to the office, sort and deliver them. There was usually a substantial pile, so much that Tina used one of the big city-style rolling carts to bring back the daily haul.

Not only did we get regular paperwork from all our outlying pathologists, there was a steady stream of inquiries from lawyers needing forensic assistance with various lawsuits. I liked the variety that being a consultant for hire provided, because it meant I got to use more of my medical brain and more of my legal one. The sad reality of life is that there's not a whole lot of novelty in medical examiner work. Murder is murder, and accidents are accidents. There's a fair variation in style, but nothing like the kind of variety that the rest of medicine provides. I read the mail with more interest for some than others until a voice interrupted me.

"Can I talk to you?"

I was startled out of my deep thought and put the letter down. No one ever enters my office unannounced; Tina is too good a guardian of the gates. I glared up at the intruder.

It was Marla Kincaid, dressed in white jeans and a simple, roomy tee shirt. She stepped into my office without waiting for my answer, but paused just inside the threshold, looking expectant and a little afraid.

I stood up, pushing the papers I had been reading away with my left hand. "No. No, you can't. I can't talk to you. That's why you have a lawyer. You have to leave."

I felt an unwarranted panic rising in my chest. She could not be here, not in my office. It was just wrong. I wanted to escape and it was my office. She had to leave. I straightened my spine, loomed as large as I could, and put on my most threatening face.

Her green eyes widened, but she stood her ground. "I just want to ask you about Mitch."

Her voice quavered a bit, but she had the look of a woman used to getting her way when she made a request.

"I need to know if it hurt. Did he feel anything? I need to know, it's important. Please tell me, did he suffer?"

Her voice rose with each subsequent question until, at the end, it was a fragile, tentative, little girl voice, and it threatened to break.

I shook my head, adamant, even with the panic still there. "Miss Kincaid, you have to understand. I will be a witness for the State in your trial. I simply cannot talk to you without your lawyer present. Not about this and not about anything. You have to leave."

I pushed out of my mind the report I had just read, the ballistics report on the bullet Isa Robles had pulled from the wall. It was bigger than the ones from the gun found in the possession of Marla Kincaid, a nine millimeter, not a .22. And explanation for my niggling concern about the weight of the lead I recovered from Houston. The gun in

Marla Kincaid's underwear drawer had not killed Mitch Houston.

It put a definite wrench in the works. In my mind, Marla was pretty much in the clear, but it wasn't my mind that counted. I wanted to stay above the fray that was about to ensue when the sheriff and the lawyer got the report. I reached for the phone to call Tina and looked down to dial. I'd find out how this woman got past her later, but I suspected I knew. Tina, bless her heart, was starstruck.

I was three digits into the extension when the sounds of retching interrupted me. Marla Kincaid was an unpleasant shade of green, and she was in the process of depositing her breakfast on my office floor. I dropped the handset and hurried to her side, snatching the wastebasket from the side of my desk as I ran. I managed to have it in place before the last bout, holding it in front of her and supporting her thin shoulders with my arm. *Great, just what I needed.* At least the mess had missed my Oriental rug, difficult to clean and one of the few things I had taken from my old home. From my bedroom.

After a few deep breaths, she straightened up, threatening to drag the back of her hand across her face. I held up a hand.

"Just wait. Go sit on the couch. I'll be right back."

I shoved her in the direction of the couch, none too gently, and fled the room at last.

Sudden nausea is not a phenomenon unknown in a medical examiner's office, and we're well-prepared to deal with it. I dampened two washrags with cool water and picked up a clean towel, then snagged a can of ginger ale and a plastic cup from the shelf above the sink. By the time I got back, Marla Kincaid was lying on the couch, her head propped on the heavily padded arm, eyes closed, forehead damp. She was even paler than I remembered from the hearing. I snapped the top of the ginger ale and poured some in the cup, then offered it to her.

"Here, sip this. Sips, not big gulps."

I waited as she drank tentatively. When she had put the glass on the side table, she wiped her face with one of the wet cloths, then I offered her the towel. Some motherly habits die hard. I squared my shoulders and suppressed my tendency to sympathize.

"Feel better?"

She nodded, face in the soft confines of the small towel. Her "a little," was muffled by the cloth. She looked up, eyes still watery, caught a whiff of the mess on the floor, and retched again. Fortunately, I had the wastebasket handy. I laid my hand on her back; she was so thin, I could feel every vertebra. When she came back up for air, I handed her the second cloth after she wiped her face again.

"Lie down, put this on your forehead. You'll feel better."

I crossed the room, called Quick, and asked him to rustle up the spills kit and clean my floor.

"I don't know what's wrong," Marla said.

Her voice was tentative; I recognized the reason. In the midst of serious morning sickness, even opening your mouth to talk gets to be scary.

"Sure you do," I said, reaching automatically and indifferently for her wrist. Her skin was warm and dry and didn't show any signs of dehydration. I felt absently for a pulse as I continued, "The first three months are the worst. After that it gets better."

"I'm just so tired all the time. And nothing tastes good. And lately, it seems I can't keep anything down."

I smiled, not really meaning it. Her pulse was rapid, much too fast for a young woman her age, and the vomiting hadn't been enough to elevate it. My mind raced though possibilities even as I continued the conversation in a light and pleasant vein.

"Been there, done that. When I was pregnant for the first time, it seemed like all I ate for three months was crackers and milk. And with Zoe, I was so tired that I took one of those long lawn chairs into my office so that when I wasn't actually working, I could sleep."

"Really?"

Marla struggled to sit up on one elbow and took a few more sips of ginger ale. I saw Quick, his bucket, mop and deodorizer out of the corner of my eye. I waved acknowledgement, and he smiled and went to work. He was done before Marla Kincaid put the glass down again. She gave a ladylike burp and sat up the rest of the way.

"I really am sorry. I didn't mean to throw up on your floor. It's so embarrassing."

Civility compelled me to reply, memory made it easier.

"Don't worry, you have many worse moments in store. Just wait until you are in the middle of a department store and your water breaks."

Not only in a department store, in the most expensive store in town, trying to find a suitable dress for a wedding a week away, thinking that you have six weeks to go. I remembered the chagrin, then the fear because the baby was far too early. Luke had arrived ten hours later, four tiny pounds, but he'd done all right, and the store eventually let me back in. Best of all, I was spared having to buy a new dress for the wedding.

I shook my head to clear the memory and continued.

"Kids have a way of embarrassing the pants off you even before they're born. Of course, when they are teenagers, you get revenge—it's your turn to embarrass them."

"How many do you have? Kids, I mean?"

"Six. Four boys and two girls."

Those round eyes got big again. "That's a lot!"

"These days," I agreed.

There should have been more, but I'd lost a baby early on and a complication with Ben meant an end to my childbearing days. I remembered how I had cried when I woke up from the emergency surgery to find they had had to take my womb as well as deliver my baby. John rocked me in his arms and stroked my hair as I wept for hours, days, weeks, nearly a year.

"Was it hard? Raising kids?"

She never seemed to get a thought out on the first try, always needed a second shot to make herself clear.

I shrugged. "Sometimes. They can drive you crazy, but it's worth it. You'll do fine."

What a platitude. She'd do fine if she wasn't in prison for murder. Which, I reminded myself, she probably wouldn't be. I was irritated at my ineptitude. There is a reason I deal with dead people.

"I sure hope so." She gave a small smile. "Maybe I better start reading up."

"Maybe so."

Marla Kincaid got to her feet, a bit wobbly. I put a hand under her elbow.

"Are you sure you're all right?" That pulse nagged at me.

"Yes. Thanks. I guess I had better go. I really am sorry about your floor." She started away, then turned to face me again. "You're sure you can't talk to me?"

I shook my head firmly. "No. Absolutely not. Have your lawyer explain. He'll understand."

"Okay. Well…thanks. That ginger ale really helped."

"Usually does. Keep some on hand. And soda crackers."

I bent over to retrieve the face towel, and turned to go back to my desk when I caught one last glimpse of Marla Kincaid as she exited my office through the glass of my door. On the back of her crisp white jeans was a spreading red stain. My heart sank, and I felt bile rising in my own throat. I dropped the linens and hurried to the door.

"Marla!" I shouted. "Come back in. Please."

She was startled, but I'd used my lawyerly voice, and she returned obediently. "What is it?"

I sent a silent complaint heavenward. I had no business taking care of this situation but, under the circumstances, I had no choice.

"Maybe we better have the docs at the clinic take a look at you," I said as evenly as I could. "Just to be sure. Come on in, lie down on the couch. I'll give them a call."

I was never any good at pouring oil on troubled waters. On my best day, I'm not a reassuring person; the kids always went to their dad for that. And this was far from my best day.

"What's wrong? What's wrong? " Marla's hand went instinctively to her belly. "The baby! Is the baby all right?" Tears were already spilling down her cheeks. She looked desperately to me for an answer.

I've never been good at lies, either. I put an arm around her as I guided her to the couch again, arranged her on her side and propped one of the back pillows under her feet.

"I don't know. You're bleeding. We need to get the doctor to see you, but for now just lie here and let me call."

She reached out a hand to grab my pants leg as I started away.

"Please, no. Don't leave. I'm scared." The tears were out in a flood, and she was already wracked with sobs.

I suppressed the urge to run. I am even less adept at dealing with hysteria than I am with impending miscarriage. Like it or not, Marla Kincaid was temporarily my patient. I sat on the edge of the couch and she grasped my hand tightly, still weeping. I knew too well the cold fear that gripped her, and I knew that there was nothing I could do to make it better. Still, I reached a tentative hand out and stroked her hair. Soft curls, like my own brood, but short and stylish, a cut they used to call gamine-like.

"Marla," I kept my voice soft and steady, hoping no measure of the fear I felt for her made its way in. "Let go of my hand. I'm going to call Tina and she'll call the clinic, and I'll be back just as soon as I do."

She kept muttering to herself, "What's happening to me? What's happening to me?"

Her words echoed in the recesses of my own mind. I wondered for an instant about a woman who worried about herself and not her child. My words had been of fault, not self-concern, when I was in the same situation. I'd said them to John when we'd lost our baby, convinced that I had done something to deserve such a terrible fate. Something unforgivable. In his no nonsense way, he'd shaken his head and held my hand.

"Jane," he told me. "Things just happen. It's our job to get through them. It's not your fault."

And he'd kissed me.

Remembering, and feeling John nearer than he had been for months, I stroked the curls again and again. Finally, she let go of my hand, her sobs beginning to subside. As soon as I called down to the front desk to tell Tina the situation, I was back on the couch. Marla lifted her head to make room for me on one end, then laid her head in my lap, quiet now but still crying, staring vacantly ahead, calm and afraid. I stretched my arm across her form, hugging her as tightly as I could from the awkward position of having the head of a weeping murder suspect in my lap, and feeling sharply, completely sorrowful for her pain. I remembered John holding me when we lost little Emma, and I closed my arm a little more tightly and smoothed her hair again. I was still stroking those blond curls when the paramedics arrived from the Center, and there was a patch of dampness on my lap from her tears.

****

It took almost two hours for Ben to find the salvage yard. Because Lucy wasn't there to give him directions, he got lost on the far side of Montrose, amongst interrupted streets that didn't end up going where they should have gone. It was almost noon when he finally pulled through the chain link gate into the gravel yard. A mixed breed dog loped up, tail wagging, tongue lolling, the very antithesis, Ben thought, of the junkyard dog of legend. He stepped out of his Jeep and scratched the dog's head. The owner, old and wiry, his face tanned by too many hours in the sun, his beard gray and his thinning hair pulled back into an improbable pony tail, held out a leathery hand.

"You must be the young fella from the coroner's office. Tom Patterson said you'd be by this morning."

The man spit a stream of tobacco juice into the weeds and wiped spittle from his mouth. Ben was glad they'd already shaken hands.

"I'm Ben Wallace. Thanks for letting me take a look at that car."

"No problem, son. It's right over here."

The man threaded a path through the various wrecked cars, brown dog trotting behind him as though it anticipated a treat.

"Hang on," Ben called after the disappearing form.

He retrieved a small plastic case from the back of his car and trotted, like the dog, after the disappearing form of the man, his boots crunching the gravel in double time. They stopped in front of a bright orange Hummer, much the worse for wear for having rolled over on its top and come to rest on its nose in the San Miguel River. The windshield was broken out. Even had the shards still been there, there would have been no way to tell whether it was gone from the impact of the car as it rolled down the embankment or had been broken out by gunfire first.

"It took a pretty good beating," the old man observed, spitting again. "Not much left. Good thing Patterson called. I was getting ready to crush it up and send it off. Not worth much except as scrap metal."

Ben peered through the hole that had been the windshield to look at the seats. From what he could see, they were in much better shape than the rest of the car, the leather intact, except for being bent out of shape, bloodstained and flooded by muddy river water, cramped by the intrusion of the front end into the passenger compartment. He craned his neck to see the spot that had caught his interest in the photograph. It was shaded and hard to see, so he retrieved a flashlight.

"Whatcha looking for?" the man asked, his curiosity aroused.

Ben played the beam of light on the brown leather. "A hole. I thought I saw a hole in the photograph from the day of the crash."

"You don't say!" The man was clearly intrigued and leaned forward over Ben's shoulder to look where the light was focused. "Musta been some kind of picture to see something like that."

Ben refrained from explaining that the photo was pretty ordinary, but his photo-enhancing software was first rate. He kept sweeping across the seat until suddenly he saw it. Right in the seam, a neat little round hole. He hadn't been imagining things.

"Bingo!" he exclaimed.

"I'll be damned," echoed the man.

The dog looked disappointed when Ben emerged from the hulk empty handed, but wagged his tail nonetheless and gave Ben's pant leg a sniff for good measure. Ben grabbed the camera and dove back through the window to photograph the seat. The dog cocked his head and sat down again to wait.

Pulling himself back out, taking care not to knock the camera, Ben made sure that the digital images showed the hole in all its forensic glory. Satisfied, he recapped the lens and knelt once again to retrieve a plastic bag and a pair of forceps, then paused to contemplate how best to reach the hole across the expanse of sharp crumpled metal that was once the hood of the Hummer. The old man, caught up in the enthusiasm of the chase for evidence, retrieved a couple of old padded movers' blankets and laid them across the hood. Ben climbed gingerly on top and leaned in, probing the hole.

"Yahoo!" Ben's exclamation was muffled, but enthusiastic. He sat up too quickly, hitting his head on the windshield frame, and very nearly losing the cylindrical piece of metal he held in the tongs of the forceps. It was from a .22 long rifle, unless he missed his guess, almost perfectly preserved by the padding of the seat into which it had been shot.

"Well, I'll be damned," the old man said again. "Ain't that something!"

With a self-satisfied grin to his crime-scene partner, Ben dropped the slug into a plastic bag and labeled it, then stood back in order to take more photographs of the car itself. Finally, something concrete to show his mother. Real evidence. Someone was killing trustafarians for months, and Ben Wallace was the one to figure it all out. "Hot damn!"

CHAPTER THIRTEEN

JUNE 11, AFTERNOON

Ben had spent the last half hour, between bites of sandwich and gulps of milk, explaining to me what he'd found at the salvage yard. He summed it all up by producing the bullet he'd recovered from the seat with a flourish.

"That takes care of one car accident," I admitted, "But not all of them. They were in different places, and we don't have photos or data or anything else to confirm that there was a shooting."

The fact that we had a string of serial murders in Telluride was now crystal clear; the length of the string was the only thing in doubt.

My last-born screwed up his face in concentration, reluctant, I thought, to admit to a gaping hole in his theory. Instead, he surprised me by presenting another one.

"There's a problem with the gas explosion, too," he said. "I stopped by the propane company on my way back. No way that a .22 could have penetrated one of their tanks. They said that the explosions I saw on YouTube were really pressure explosions—heating the gas caused such extreme pressure that the impact of the bullet causes the explosion. Nothing like that here."

I sighed. His theory was so attractive, so tidy, that I really wanted it to be right. I really didn't want to think that we had unrelated killings, and I was too skeptical to believe that purely accidental deaths occurred on such a regular basis.

"Get me the file. Let's take a look at it."

The propane tank explosion had occurred on a rare weekend when I was out of town, taking care of the business interests that sometimes threatened to overwhelm me. I'd left the Center in the care of a colleague; he'd done the case.

Ben scurried down to his office and returned with a manila folder.

Somewhere, I was sure, all this evidence was enshrined online, but I am an old-fashioned girl at heart. I think better when I can scatter papers around in front of me. My staff humors me with a hard copy of everything.

I started with the newspaper reports from the day after. The explosion had occurred just before dawn. A neighbor — a rare commodity on Silver Pick, where the houses were few, far between and, mostly, very expensive — had heard the blast as he was pulling out of his drive, saw the plume of fire and called the local volunteers. The house, a single bedroom cabin with a few outbuildings, remnant of an old ranch, was completely destroyed. The remains — it wasn't accurate to call it a body exactly — of the man who owned the house were found ten yards away, propelled away by the blast.

I studied the sketch of the scene my compulsive tech had included and pointed it out to Ben. "See this? If Norman was right, it made sense that Cooper was on the porch when the blast occurred."

I paused. That struck me as odd.

"Why would he be on the porch at sunup? It would be shaded, there's no view. Why?"

Ben took the sketch and pondered it, shaking his head. "Coming into town?"

"The car was off the back porch. Why wouldn't he leave from there?"

The cabin's small back porch opened onto a pasture, another remnant of the ranch. The utilitarian front porch was only steps from a stream house and stand of aspen, a tribute to the desire for convenience of the original builders. Water at the front door, by the kitchen and hearth; work out back. I was willing to bet good money that Cooper had used the back entrance almost exclusively.

I pulled out another clipping from the file, a newspaper article from the week prior to the accident. It was a profile of Cooper, one of the better-known eccentrics in Telluride's pantheon. Son of a former TV Western star who made millions by being at the front of the designer vegetable and organic meat wave, he'd convinced his father to let him try his hand at real ranching. Why he'd chosen this forbidding patch of land on the Western Slope was anybody's guess, but he was earnest in his attempts to tidy up the land and to start "running a few head," as he put it in the interview. I handed the article to Ben.

"It wasn't out of character for him to be up early," I said. "Looks like he was a real back-to-the-land type."

I pointed at the photo which showed Cooper in the light of a kerosene lamp. The cabin had propane for heat and cooking, but apparently he eschewed electricity. Perhaps chopping wood was too energetic and cold baths too off-putting. Cooper looked like a gentle soul, but he was effete. Plenty of the ranchers I knew were short of stature and light of weight, but they had a wiry heft and durability to them that Cooper lacked.

"Maybe he knew the tank was going to explode."

"So why not head for the car, get away as fast as possible? The tank was midway along the side of the house, according to Norman, no easier to go out the front than the back."

"Maybe something was in the way."

"Like?"

Ben's brow furrowed again. Much more and I'd have to send him for Botox. I could tell he was trying to fit all the pieces into his theory, while accounting for the facts. Good for him. At length, he pulled out a photo of the cabin the realtor had provided and spoke, his voice and expression cautious.

"The cabin had big windows on all the walls. The one that looked over the propane tank was in what would have been the kitchen. Suppose he was at the table reading, and someone shot in the window?"

Ben was determined to work in a gunshot; but then, so was I.

"Maybe he'd run out to get away from the shooter. In that case, he'd run for cover — the woods, not the car."

"Explosion?" I prompted. "And even if you're right, how will we prove it?"

Exasperated, Ben lost his temper. "I don't know, Mom. You're the M.E. You figure it out. I just know that it has to be connected."

I pulled out the autopsy report. The remains had been mutilated in the blast and charred by the fire. I skimmed through with growing horror. My substitute had just signed out the case, going on the basis of the external exam rather than doing an autopsy. I felt my heartbeat quicken and a pull in my gut, early warning system for my anger. I reached for the phone, punching in Quick's extension so hard my fingers hurt.

"Quick, I'm looking at that explosion case from Silver Pick earlier this month," I said as calmly as I could. "Can you explain why there wasn't a post?"

His hesitation told me he knew he was caught in a problem. I waited to see what he would do and, as I expected, he took the fall.

"I told the doc he needed to do one," he said. "But it was his last day, and he wanted to get out of here early. He laughed at me, said it was a waste of time. If he hadn't left so fast, I'd have done it myself, but without him here, I didn't think I should."

Another pause.

"I'm sorry, boss."

Still another silence, then he redeemed himself.

"I did x-ray everything, just in case."

I struggled with rising emotion. I had policies and procedures, and I expected them to be followed, and this was why.

"There's no excuse, Quick. Why didn't you call me?"

I struggled to keep my anger in check. I hate to be wrong, even by proxy.

No silence this time. "Didn't want to, boss. You needed to be away from here. I wasn't going to bother you with something that looked pretty simple at the time. You needed a break." He paused. "I'm sorry, boss. It's my fault."

Yes, it was, I thought. *And dammit, you know better than to let things slide. We never let things slide. When we let things slide, life comes apart. You should know better.* Instead I answered in as neutral a voice as I could muster. "We'll talk later."

I turned back to Ben.

"Pull up the x-rays on this," I said.

At least I could take a look at them while I mentally framed the request for exhumation I was destined to submit. One way or another, I needed to know what really had happened to Kyle Cooper. Ben hurried to pull up the films on the giant screen perched amid the bookshelves. This was going to take more detail than my desktop monitor would provide.

Quick had made a complete series of films, so that no part of Cooper's remains went unexamined, and from several perspectives at that. I scanned them briefly, confirming that the remains were, in fact, that of a man, of about the right age. Then I started mowing the lawn, taking my gaze from one side to the other in sequential rows, looking carefully at each portion of each film. I was not sure what I was looking for until I found it on the third film and confirmed it on two others. Deformed and almost lost amid bits of bone and shrapnel, but there it was, a lump of metal that could be nothing other than a bullet, lodged next to one of the upper thoracic vertebrae. Whatever else had happened, Cooper had been shot. I'd never be able to match that bullet to any gun, it was too deformed. But I'd stake my life, and I was staking my profession, on it being a .22.

I pointed it out to Ben. "Bingo."

His face lit up. God help us all, forensic experts, even temporary ones, get excited by the most terrible things.

"So they *are* connected. I knew it." His voice was triumphant.

I agreed, if reluctantly.

"I still want to know why the explosion," I said, irritated that that particular piece didn't fit. Propane tanks didn't just explode, and the convenience of this particular explosion was eerie. It had very nearly obscured a murder. Much like the climber's fall.

Ben started gathering the papers back into the folder. I put out a restraining hand.

"Leave it. I need to take a closer look at all this. Now scoot—I know you have work to do."

I'd put off the call to Tom Patterson until I had a convincing argument for his calling the parents to tell them their son had been murdered. Come hell or high water, there was no way I was making that call.

****

Lucy Cho was working late, finishing up the ballistics study Dr. Wallace requested on the bullet Ben had retrieved from the wrecked Hummer. She knew as well as anyone that the murders of the last few days were all related. She was surprised when Dr. Wallace had come in with something else to match, something from a case they'd all thought was just a terrible automobile accident.

"See whether this matches the one from Cosette Anira," she had asked Lucy.

Unlike most medical examiners she knew, Dr. Wallace always used both names when referring to a corpse under her care, though she was likely to refer to a living, breathing person just by a surname. Quick, Patterson, Wilson, almost everyone except her son and her techs, who, Lucy suspected, she viewed as simply other children.

She hummed as she seated the two intact bullets in the comparison microscope and adjusted the lenses to her own, nearly perfect eyes. From the tweaking it took, she suspected that Dr. Wallace had been in here playing with it.

The bullets, same general size, shape and weight, the same sort of ammunition, came into clear focus and Lucy looked from one side to the other, hoping to match the grooves in the base left by their transit down the barrel of the gun. The marks were clear and easy to see; both bullets were in good shape unlike the wad of lead—same weight—that had been recovered from Jim Webster. She peered down the tubes, frowned and sat up straight, not liking what she saw.

She took a deep breath and looked again. The images hadn't changed. The marks were there, some similar, most different. The bullets were not from the same gun. Dr. Wallace wasn't going to like that at all. Lucy sighed, took the photos and uploaded them to the main office drive, then sent an email to Dr. Wallace. This was news she'd rather not deliver in person. She wasn't sure she liked it herself.

CHAPTER FOURTEEN

JUNE 12

"Dammit, Doc! Don't you know better than this?"

Tom Patterson was standing, arms folded across his chest, blocking the way to my desk, his face flushed and the muscles in his jaw working. Tina had warned me he was waiting in my office, but I hadn't expected this. I suppressed the urge to respond in kind to his provocation. I have learned by bitter and repeated experience that taking up the verbal cudgel too soon has a way of backfiring.

"This?" I repeated in as calm a voice as I could muster. "Better than what, Tom?"

I skirted around the far side of the desk and took up my customary seat. Because I did it of my own volition, the fact that Tom loomed over me served not to intimidate me, but to tip the battle-scales in my favor. Calm in the face of a storm is surprisingly powerful.

Not, however, powerful enough to keep him from throwing well-thumbed copies of the morning's papers on my desk. The headlines were in larger-than-usual type, all caps, and surprisingly similar: SERIAL KILLER STALKS TELLURIDE from one, MURDER STALKS THE WEALTHY from the other. I reflected for the umpteenth time that I'd never seen a headline in which murderers and death did not stalk. Even in this instance death—and the murderer—seemed more to erupt than to stalk, but who was I to quibble?

The mental detour gave me sufficient time to scan the first couple of paragraphs. It wouldn't take a rocket scientist to string together the murders, so I wasn't surprised that the paper had figured out that a dedicated killer was on the loose. What surprised me were the particulars. In case I missed them, Tom's forefinger punched at the newsprint.

"Every damn detail. The jeep accidents, the propane tank, all there. What the hell were you thinking, telling him all that? You didn't bother to share that with me, did you?"

I cut him off. "Not me, Tom. You know I never talk to that pack of weasels unless I have to. I have no idea where he got this. What makes you think it's from my shop?"

"Because the damn thing says so!"

He stabbed his finger at the paper again. There it was, four paragraphs into the story: *A highly placed source in the Forensic Center....*

I felt my heart rate climb and my skin go cold. As long as I have been in the adversarial business of forensic medicine, I have never gotten over the stomach-dropping fear of being wrong in public. Doing something I ought not. Screwing up. It's one of the reasons for the redundancy in my policies and in my work. *I do not screw up*, I reminded myself, even as I remembered that missed bullet hole in the wall of Houston's bedroom, then added for Patterson to hear, "I do not talk to the press, Tom, and neither does anyone else in this office."

My staff knew talking to the fourth estate about anything that had to do, even remotely, with the office was a firing offense with no second chances.

"Then where did this come from?"

Give the sheriff credit for persistence; he was not going to be put off.

"I'll ask."

I tugged the papers out from underneath Patterson's hand and quickly scanned the rest of the articles. What facts were there were more or less accurate, but it was the tone of the article that made my face flush and my temper rise. Wilson had outdone himself in an attempt to paint both the San Juan County Sheriff's Office and the Forensic Center as incompetent, corrupt, indifferent or a combination of all three. On the other hand, they missed one important tidbit, one I hadn't had time to share with Patterson.

No time like the present.

"Tom, there's more than this. Lucy did the ballistics on the bullet from the Hummer yesterday. Same kind as the one from Cosette Anira, but different markings. A different gun."

Two shooters, I thought. A tag team, the worst kind because it meant there would be a lot of conflicting evidence before we sorted out enough to get an idea of who we were looking for.

Tom's face brightened immediately.

"Not from the same gun? Good. Lots of .22 rifles around here, people use them to shoot varmints. Without a match, those accidents are just accidents."

I could tell he was relishing the idea of pulling the rug out from under Wilson.

"There's that bullet in the x-ray of Kip Cooper," I reminded him.

"You think it's a bullet. Until we get it in hand, you can't be sure. Could be debris from the explosion. I'm not asking for an exhumation on that basis. Not without more."

"You know I can't get more without the exhumation, Tom, and I'd stake my life on that being a bullet."

"Go ahead. As far as I am concerned, we have only three deaths — not that that is a big improvement. Cooper, the car wrecks, all accidents. Come to think of it, Webster might be too."

"With a shot to the back?" I was open-mouthed at the thought.

"Lots of varmints in Ophir. Might have been an accident there, too. I can't believe someone would actually be able to pull that shot off."

He was warming to his topic, I could tell.

"Accident. That just leaves me with two, both in town. Nicer pattern, makes more sense. Just two. One shooter, one gun, two deaths. Bad enough, but it's not a long string of murders that I — that you," he added with a glare for emphasis, "missed."

"Interesting appraisal," I finally said. "Best take a tack and stick to it, Tom. Have fun."

I was furious; I held my voice calm and hoped he heard the underlying and unspoken threat. I would not be threatened, and I would not be maligned. And I know how to get my own recompense, if need be.

"Damn right, I'll have fun. I'll have fun telling Wilson how hard it is to run a decent investigation when the M.E. in charge can't keep her mouth shut!"

I counted to ten in Greek to control the urge to shout at him, my composure making a rapid retreat. I counted quickly, because Tom had grabbed the newspapers up and was stomping toward the door.

"Tom, it really doesn't matter where they got the information."

The tone of my voice, not quite what I wanted but not far off the mark, made him slow his step and then turn back to me when he got to the door. His big frame filled the space, he still glowered, and the muscles in his jaw still worked for a long moment. I waited and counted again, my version of patience and the only one that works for me. In Russian, Italian, French, and Spanish. I was up to six in Hebrew when he finally spoke.

"You're right. Dammit, you're right."

He wadded the paper up and thrust it toward the wastebasket by my desk. It rattled the rim but dropped neatly in. He walked back into my office and plopped down on the sofa with a sigh and ran his hand through his hair. "This town is so damn twitchy, I'm afraid it will explode. These people are losing their minds. They already see a murderer behind every bush, what's this going to do? I got nothing. Nothing," he sighed.

I got up from my desk and took the easy chair opposite him. We both put our boots on the scarred coffee table, then stared at each other for a few minutes. Tom spoke first.

"Did you know that I've had more than a dozen applications for concealed carry permits in the two days since the shooting in Town Park and that damn news story on TV? And that the local dealers have had a run on handgun purchases — all from Telluride?"

I furrowed my brow. "From this town?" I was incredulous. "Telluride is as anti-firearm as any community I've ever seen. They are actually buying guns?"

Tom nodded. "Lots of them. If this were anywhere else I'd take that as a good sign. Crime tends to go down when the local populace is well-armed—ask the Swiss. The thought of being blown away has a chilling effect on criminals. Problem is, most of these people haven't got the first clue about handling guns, and they're nervous as cats. Forty-eight hours and we've already had one surly German shepherd, one innocent potted plant and two front doors shot. Only a matter of time before some nitwit shoots his best friend or, worse yet, one of my boys."

I tried to suppress a laugh at the image of one of Telluride's citizens plugging a front-hall ficus. Sometimes, in my line of work, things are so bleak the only possible reaction is to laugh. I rubbed my brow, pinched my nose and snorted in sequence and increasing intensity. It didn't work. I started to giggle in spite of myself. I managed to choke out, "Has the state's attorney decided whether to charge plantslaughter?" before I dissolved in outright laughter. But it was the laughter of frustration and fear, not good humor, and Tom Patterson knew that. Still, the edges of his mouth curled up for an instant as I composed myself. It was a Herculean effort.

"Sorry, Tom," I said as I wiped a tear from the corner of my eye. "Nothing funny about it."

"Nope," he drawled. "But it's ironic as hell, that's for sure. And dangerous. And that article doesn't help at all."

I cleared my throat, the last vestige of a laugh banished, the cold fear remaining. I'd had a sobering thought in the middle of my breakdown. There was one plausible explanation for the leak, and I dreaded pursuing it. Ben was the one who had put all that together, and I had often seen him with Pete Wilson. For reasons I could not explain, my son liked Wilson and enjoyed his stories of the crime beat in Chicago.

I changed the subject. "It could be worse. Wilson obviously doesn't know about the ballistics on the slug from the wall at Mitch Houston's. Puts Marla Kincaid in the clear, I think, but leaves us with another unsolved murder."

"Does, doesn't it? I spent the first part of the morning arguing with the state's attorney about that one, too. If it's not Marla Kincaid, who is it? Nobody else there."

I thought for a moment, something rattling about the edges of my brain, something Isa had told me when I was making photographs of her bruises. I went still for a moment, eyes closed, in hopes the thought would settle where I could find it. It did.

"You better talk to Isa Robles again," I told Tom. "She was there that night, and she says she saw a tall man standing in the shadows by the back door as she left. Big guy, too, according to her."

I expected swearing, but all I got in reply was a tired sigh.

"Great. Another bushy-haired stranger," he said, harkening back to the staple of murder mysteries and defense lawyers. "Still, it makes as much sense as anything."

He stood up to leave, in a better mood than he'd come in, but still frustrated by an abundance of crime and a dearth of explanation. If Pete Wilson were smart, he'd avoid the good sheriff for a day or two.

I spent the rest of the morning trying to run Ben to ground. I knew his trip to Montrose to get the oil changed and the tires replaced on the 4Runner put him in questionable cell range, but it didn't matter. I wanted to talk to him, and I wanted to talk to him now. I used up all my available languages counting to ten between calls. In the end, I had to wait patiently until he returned to the office, whistling a now-familiar tune with increasing skill as he dropped the keys on my desk.

"All done, Mom. Good as new. And I ran it through the car wash and filled it up on the way into town."

I picked up the keys and pocketed them. "Thanks, Ben. "

"Sure thing." He smiled, picked up a cookie I had left from lunch, and started out the door. I hesitated, wondering how to approach the subject at hand. The schoolmarm in the back of my head reminded me he was my employee within these four walls, not my son.

"Ben. Wait a minute. There's something we need to talk about."

My offspring have enough experience to read my tones, and this one said I meant business. Ben turned around with a wary look on his face and cocked his head. He stayed in the doorway but answered me in a cautious voice.

"Sure. What's up?"

Another hesitation. Should I try diplomacy or cut to the chase? I cut.

"Have you been talking to the press about the murders?"

His face went pale, then bright red. "No, Mom! I haven't! I know better than that! All I ever heard was how sneaky reporters are and how hard they make your job. No, I haven't been talking to them."

A lifetime of maternal experience was not enough to divine whether this particular child was telling the truth. It isn't that Ben is a habitual liar or even a very good one; it's just that he doesn't have any reliable tells. His face could just as easily have been a result of his anger at my question as the run up to prevarication.

"I know you like to chat with Pete Wilson." I made it as neutral a statement of fact as I could, and forced my tone to follow.

That red face again, this time definitely anger.

"So I like talking to him. He has interesting stories. I like that. I like hearing about all the stuff he's done. It's really interesting. Kind of like what you do but without the science. He puts it together with words."

I nodded my head, considering. "Fair enough. What do you talk about besides his stories?"

"Nothing much. The food at Baked. Bluegrass, jazz. Movies. How I like town."

"Nothing else?"

"Nothing else. I swear I didn't tell him. Swear it!"

His words were forceful, and he punctuated them with a punch to the door frame. "I'm not the only one who knows about the wrecks and the explosion."

"I didn't tell you what I was worried about."

"Mom, do you think I am a complete idiot? I read the paper before I left for Montrose. I..." Ben hesitated and then said no more, his lips in a determined line and the muscles in his jaw working like Tom Patterson's had for a moment before he regained control of his temper and went on.

"I know better than that, Mom. I'm not a baby. And I'm not stupid."

I folded my hands and rested my chin against them, thinking for a moment. "Ben, there aren't too many of us who know about all this, and it says it is a source from our office. If it wasn't you — and I believe you," I hurried to add, seeing the temper flash in his eyes, "then who? How? Did you talk about it with anybody?"

"Just you and Lucy, because she was running all the tests, and Norman, and maybe Eoin." Flush again, this time guilty realization of his mistake.

"Eoin?"

I wasn't sure what irritated me more, the fact that my son had, in fact, carried tales out of school or the fact that he'd carried them to Eoin Connor, who apparently had become his buddy. Ben was right about one thing; he didn't talk freely with people he didn't like. He was like me in that, at least.

"Yeah. Remember, yesterday I couldn't make copies of the file for him, and I had to take it by his place later? Right where that girl was shot? Anyway, we just got talking and I may have...um...mentioned that I had found some interesting new information." Ben's voice trailed off; he knows that when in a hole the first rule is to put down the shovel.

Eoin Connor, who made a living writing salacious true crime books, who was a much better storyteller than Pete Wilson and no doubt a much more skillful interviewer. It wasn't a stretch for me to imagine him trading information with Pete Wilson over a couple of beers, nor was it hard to hear his glib tongue proffering Ben as the source. Ben may be naive, but as he says, he's not stupid. He connected the dots almost as fast as I did.

"Mom, Eoin would never do that either. He doesn't like Wilson any better than you do, he said so. There has to be another explanation."

I pinched the bridge of my nose for the second time that day, this time out of fatigue touched by despair. The situation in Telluride was getting out of hand, neither Tom nor I had any idea who the killer was, and there was no end in sight to the corpses that were piling up in my morgue. I wanted to cry. Or run away. Or both. When the feeling had passed, I looked up at Ben with weary eyes.

"Ben, just don't talk about anything from work with anyone outside this office. Ever. By all that's right and holy, I ought to fire you. But technically, Eoin Connor isn't the press, so you're off the hook. Just keep your mouth shut, okay? Not a word to anyone. Not Eoin Connor, not Pete Wilson, not anyone."

I turned back to the work on my desk with a dismissive air. Ben didn't bother to respond, but the flush was back on his face, and I was pretty sure I knew why. What I didn't know was who was killing people in my little town and why and who would be next. I fussed with the papers on my desk, but my mind kept going back to the headline. Who was killing the rich young people of Telluride? For that matter, who had killed Mitch Houston? Too many bodies, too few answers.

****

Isa Robles took a deep breath and pushed open the door to the church. They had told her that the priest was in the church when she dropped her son in the daycare. Pablo was so happy in the daycare center. It was safe, the people were nice, and he had children to play with while she went to work.

She was glad not to be working for the blond woman in Mountain Village anymore. She had fired Isa after the...after Pelirojo. Isa still could not will herself to acknowledge what had happened to her; she simply passed over it and went on with her life. But the woman had been concerned that Pelirojo might come to her house, looking for Isa, and she was afraid.

No matter. The priest knew several other women in the town, and she went with him when he asked them if they didn't need help keeping their houses. He was smart, that one, and charming. Isa could tell that the women weren't particularly interested in hiring any more help, but after a few minutes discussion with the priest, a story or two, smiles and even some laughter, she had five jobs, one for every day, and she cleaned for the priest, too. The families were nice. Two older couples, two younger ones, and a single woman whose huge house was filled with art, newspapers, and cats.

It was clear that this gentle Father was able to get almost anything he wanted. Hadn't he gotten Isa and Lupe and Pilar a place to stay with the lady doctor? At the beginning, it seemed like a bad idea, going from the house where they were in danger to live with this angry, bitter woman. She had told the priest so when he suggested it.

"She does not like me, Padre," she had said. "I am just a job to her, part of her work. Why would she want to take me into her house? Why would I want to go?"

The priest had smiled and taken her hand. This one, he touched people a lot, always offering a hand.

"I know Dr. Wallace seems unfriendly," he said, "But she has a good heart. And she needs you as much as you need her. You can't go back to stay at the house, it isn't safe. You have jobs now here in town. It makes sense for you to live here, where you can be near Pablo. Please, Isa, trust me. Give her a chance."

And so she had. That first night had been terrible. "Illegal!" the doctor had called her, as though she were somehow less than a person because of it. She had stayed the night only because the boy was so kind and because there was no other place to go. The next morning, however, the doctor had showed up at the breakfast table quiet and repentant. She had apologized, in strong words, without explanation. Isa found that odd. People usually made excuses. This peculiar woman did not, offering only her words and asking Isa to stay, please, and to influence Lupe and Pilar to stay, too.

Isa had done so, and in the days following had come to like the strange woman. Señora Doctora liked Pablo and when he crawled into her lap for a hug or a story, Isa could see her face light up, if only for a moment. Isa had the run of the house; the doctor had replaced everything that Isa and the others had left behind without question or comment and with, it seemed to Isa, even a bit of pleasure. It was clear that she was lonely, even with her son living with her. The women and the children, the children especially, filled up the house.

She caught sight of the priest, sitting in a pew. The church was an old-fashioned one like the parish church was back home, pews arranged on either side of the altar rather than front to back. The priest was there, bent over, listening to someone sitting by his side. When he leaned back, Isa recognized her, the woman Marla. What was she doing here? She had heard snatches of the doctor's conversation; she had been in the hospital yesterday because of fear of losing the baby. Perhaps she had; Isa concluded. Perhaps she was here because she had lost her child and was sad.

The priest said a few more words, made a motion with his hands. It looked like he was pleading from the way he reached forward, hands palms up, cupped and waiting. The woman's face was hard, anything but sad, no tears and no sadness, just hard like stone, like a statue, only not as pretty. Isa had the sense she was intruding on something she should not. She started to back out and bumped into the votive rack. It swayed and threatened to fall. She reached to steady it but it hit the wall with a great clang. By the time she turned in embarrassment, Father Matt was standing to welcome her, and the woman was gone. Isa heard a door close in the distance.

"Isa. Buenos días."

"Good morning, Father."

Isa never spoke back in Spanish to Anglos, and not even to her friends if she could help it. English was the language of opportunity. She wanted practice. She wanted Pablo to speak it well.

"What can I do for you?"

He was putting a rosary into his pocket, slipping his hand through the slit in the side of the cassock to do so. Then he sat again, patting the pew beside him in invitation.

Isa stood where she was, uncertain for a moment, thrown off by what she had seen. She remembered the tall man in the shadows of the big house the night of the murder. Frowning for a moment, she shook her head. *This priest is a good man,* she thought quickly, then just as quickly, *it is the good men that are so easily deceived.* Pelirojo, no one takes advantage of him. But men like this?

She shook her head again. No sense thinking about problems she could not solve. She hurried to the pew, speaking as she went.

"I need the key to the house. It is my day to clean. You forgot to leave it open for me."

"So I did."

He dug in his pocket and brought out a fat ring of keys.

"Just leave it on the table and leave the door unlocked if I am not back before you leave. I usually don't lock it myself."

Isa shook her head. "I will bring it right back. It is not safe to leave a house unlocked."

A thief believes everyone steals, wasn't that the saying? Isa wasn't a thief, but too many in this town were. And most of them had good houses and plenty of money, and the people they robbed blamed it all on others, usually the maids or the workers, never their friends.

"You are too trusting, Father."

Father Matt regarded Isa with respect. "I think you are right, Isa. I probably am. But it's my job to trust, verdad?"

Isa hesitated. She had no business advising a priest, that she knew, but something about the meeting she had interrupted troubled her.

"That woman, Father. The one who was here, Marla, she is not a good woman. Cuidado, Padre, cuidado."

It was a measure of her distress that she broke two of her own rules. She spoke in Spanish, and she used the woman's name. She made a quick sign of the cross as she remembered her grandmother's admonition to her: *don't speak the name of the devil unless you are ready to do battle with him.*

CHAPTER FIFTEEN

JUNE 13, MORNING

I wondered what I had done to deserve the fact that Pete Wilson was sitting in my office. Weakness under pressure, I suspected. After all, what I needed to do was tell Tina to send him packing when she called announcing his presence in the building. Instead, I had granted him an audience, partly out of the hope of figuring out where he was getting his all-too-abundant information. Bad choice.

It's never a good idea to try to outfox a weasel, especially if you're becoming something of a chicken. This string of murders had worn me down. That, added to the fact that there was a better-than-even chance that the leak really did come from my office, had put me uncharacteristically on the defensive. And Wilson was enough of a journalist that my usual trick of keeping quiet wouldn't work. He made a living getting people to talk about things they didn't want to talk about, and he was good at it. He surprised me, though, with his first question, which wasn't about the murders at all.

"So, did Marla Kincaid lose her baby?"

I answered promptly and with an unusually clear conscience. "I don't know. I haven't heard from her."

"She's out of the hospital. I saw her late yesterday afternoon, walking around."

I considered for a moment. First trimester bleeding is common, and about half the time, it signals a miscarriage. Marla Kincaid was showing some signs of stress when I saw her. I remembered her increased pulse rate. I knew from experience that chances of a miscarriage were pretty high, but it wasn't experience I was willing to share with Wilson.

"You got me," I said as non-committally as I could, beating back the thought that, if she had miscarried, she belonged in bed to recover, and if she hadn't, she belonged in bed to try to save the baby.

Then again, Marla Kincaid didn't strike me as too concerned with anything beyond her immediate desires, fame and attention being prime among them.

"I suggest you ask her."

"AIDS can cause miscarriage, can't it?"

I could see myself being cited as a source in a largely fabricated article about Marla Kincaid. I punted, crossing my fingers so my outright lie didn't count, given that I wasn't going to confession these days.

"I can't really remember, Pete. You'll just have to look it up."

In fact, AIDS would make no difference to the pregnancy, unless Marla Kincaid decided to abort her baby because of it.

Wilson looked skeptical. One disadvantage of being—and being known as—good at my job is that it seriously limits plausible deniability in situations like this. Wilson knew I was skirting the truth, but it seemed that Marla Kincaid wasn't the real reason for his visit.

"Any progress in figuring out the murders? Links between the seven victims, other than being rich?"

"Who told you there are seven victims? Tom Patterson says only two. And it's his job to figure out connections, not mine."

I was hoping he'd take the bait and go pester the sheriff. I also knew that the sheriff probably wasn't talking to him, which was the reason for his visit to me.

No such luck.

"Two murders with three gunshot deaths in town in the last week, not counting Mitch Houston. The sheriff is either dreaming or incompetent."

Now Wilson was baiting me.

I shrugged. "Take it up with Tom yourself. Not my problem. I just do the autopsies."

"How often do you see sniper murders with a .22?"

"Doesn't matter. We have them now."

"Any idea who would have enough skill to pull off shots like that?

Any ideas why there's not a single good description of a suspect?"

"No. And no."

"I hear there are at least two guns involved. If you count Houston, three."

Now I was annoyed. The ballistics report wasn't public knowledge, and I was sure Tom Patterson hadn't said anything. It was beginning to look like the leak really was in my shop. Either that or Wilson was bluffing.

"Where do you hear that?"

Wilson smiled. "Gotta protect my sources, Doc, you know that."

"Protect them all you want, but if I were you I would make sure they are reliable."

"Are you telling me there's only one gun?" Wilson leaned forward.

"I am not telling you anything."

"Then you aren't denying it, either."

I could already visualize that article in tomorrow's paper ...a highly placed source at the Western Slope Forensic Center did not deny there are at least two guns involved...this was a no-win situation. I changed the subject.

"Ask me something I can talk about, Pete, or quit wasting my time."

Pete Wilson grinned, clearly enjoying himself.

"Okay. Any idea why Marla Kincaid went to see that priest friend of yours yesterday?"

My surprise must have shown on my face, because he moved in for the kill.

"Third time this week according to my sources. He's even been riding the gondola with her. Not exactly keeping a low profile. And he was dressed in civvies. Quite a change for the man who walks around town in a dress most of the time."

Father Matt was not likely to escape local attention under ordinary circumstances. Aside from his imposing appearance, he insisted in wearing full clerical garb all the time, even gadding about town in a cassock in the heat of the summer. Fr. Matt told the reporter that it was just the way he dressed, but confided to me over coffee once that he was taking a leaf from the saints. Dressing like Bing Crosby in *Going My Way* made it impossible for the locals to avoid recognizing that there was at least one committed Catholic in their midst. Like St. Francis, he called it "preaching without words," and it was. Stares and comments followed him, at least among the visitors, and he was the subject of myriad, if brief, conversations. As he would say, it was a start. If he left it off, it was intentional. Under the circumstances, that worried me. This morning, Isa had looked up from her breakfast and told me in a quiet voice that she had seen a big man standing by the house the night of the Houston murder. Father Matt was a big, big man. I did not like the turn the conversation was taking.

"None. Take it up with Father Matt. But I'd remind you there are all kinds of reasons, chief among them the fact that her boyfriend was just murdered."

"Nobody's seen much evidence of grief."

I opened my mouth to tell him that grief takes many forms, then stopped myself. "Whatever," I said, channeling Ben.

He must have read my mind about Ben.

"She's hanging out with your son, too. He's up there every day, even brought her flowers."

It stopped me cold; in my business not much does. The room was filled with the silence I wanted, but it was working to Wilson's advantage, not mine. He let it grow for a long minute, smiled his predator's smile, stood and left. He had what he'd come for.

****

Lucy Cho opened the specimen cooler in the lab and took the vials from amid the ice packs in the Styrofoam box. It was a set of specimens from one of the pathologists in the northern part of the state, needing extended drug screening toxicology that wasn't available in his own area lab. It seemed a waste of time to fire up the analyzer for a few specimens, and even putting everything together, there just wasn't that much that needed to be done. Most of it was blood alcohol testing that arrived regularly from the various law enforcement agencies; Dr. Wallace had somehow finagled the state into using the Center as the reference forensic laboratory for the western half of the state. Every once in a while, something more interesting, more exotic, but not today. Still, Dr. Wallace insisted that things be turned around promptly.

"People don't like to wait for the answers," she told her when Lucy had pointed out the expense, the wasted reagents. "And they ought not have to. Justice delayed is justice denied. It's a cliché, but it's true. Just do it."

Lucy brushed her black hair over her shoulder and consulted the clipboard to make certain what she had to do. Check and double check was the rule of the lab. It was in every place she'd worked, but Dr. Wallace took it to extremes. There wasn't room for mistakes in her shop, even human ones, insignificant ones. Lucy remembered the time, when she had just arrived, that she had mixed up two blood typing reports, putting them in the wrong folder. Dr. Wallace had been at her desk before the end of the day,

"Lucy, you messed these reports up. Look."

Dr. Wallace had laid the two folders out in front of her, open to the serology tab.

Lucy had immediately seen the error and swapped the offending papers from one folder to another. Dr. Wallace wasn't satisfied.

"Do them again. These have to be right."

Lucy had been indignant. "I know the results are fine," she had protested. "I just put them in the wrong folder. No big deal."

Dr. Wallace had been patient, but firm. "Maybe so. Do them again, anyway."

She had stood by Lucy's side while she re-ran the results, quiet, unobtrusive, but making Lucy nervous all the same. She had been relieved when the results panned out the same as they had before.

"See. I told you."

Lucy had been annoyed at the waste of her time. If Dr. Wallace didn't have confidence in her work, she might as well look for another job. It would be hard to find one that paid as well, she reflected, or was in as nice a place, or came with its own apartment, even if it was on the premises of the center.

Lucy's annoyance had rolled off Dr. Wallace. She had taken the new reports and re-read the file with satisfaction. Lucy fidgeted in anticipation. She had never worked for anyone as distant and complicated as this woman. Finally, Dr. Wallace looked up from the folders and smiled, a rare occurrence.

"Good job, and thanks. I know it seems silly to you, and I know you think I'm way too compulsive, but I have my reasons. There isn't room for error in anything we do, Lucy. Lives depend on it, even though pretty much everyone we do work on is dead. Dead doesn't mean unimportant. I mean to see that we take every opportunity to make things right before they go out of the lab. You did a good job. Please humor me."

Dr. Wallace had flipped the folders closed and left Lucy to her work.

Lucy never mixed reports again. She checked and double-checked her work, and when she found an error, which wasn't often, she checked them again. Dr. Wallace never came into the lab to complain again, and they even sometimes had the odd technical conversation about this test or that or another. Lucy was surprised that a pathologist knew so much about the daily workings of a forensic lab. Most of them left that to the hired help, able to interpret the results well enough, but a disaster if they ever had to actually run a test.

Lucy knew Dr. Wallace could step in at the bench any time she needed to, and it impressed her. Her boss worked hard and long. She was here before Lucy came down in the morning, and there until well after she left, usually bent over her desk and piles of papers. She was fair to her staff, but she expected them to cover their shifts, even keeping the office open on Saturdays, and she expected hard work.

She had worked for other pathologists like that, always busy, always puttering about in their offices. One of the professors she had worked with in training had an office cluttered with stacks of papers and books and specimen jars, with an old-fashioned barber chair covered in thinning red velvet in the middle of the room. The professor had liked to sit in it and review reports; he had called it his thinking chair. Those guys — they were mostly guys — were nutty and didn't have much of a life, having run off their wives and divorced or never actually married in the first place. Forensic pathologists were an odd breed, she reflected, except for Dr. Wallace. She seemed sad but otherwise pretty normal.

Today's load was a total of ten specimens. Not much, but not bad, either. The analyzer beeped, signaling it was ready. Lucy pipetted the samples, loaded the tray, and was just about to seat it when the lab door opened. It was Dr. Wallace. Lucy experienced a momentary frisson of anxiety. Had something gotten past her in error?

"Looks like a light day."

Lucy relaxed a bit. This was a social visit.

"Very. Ten samples, that's all. And I have a little paperwork to catch up on."

"Finish those up and take the rest of the day off. It's beautiful outside, and we need a break. I'm heading up to the house, myself. I need to get out of here for a while, and you probably do too. Let's take advantage of a lull. Just keep your cell on in case something comes up."

Dr. Wallace waved a hand, closed the door, and was gone.

Lucy shook her head. Just when she thought she understood her rigorous, taciturn boss, Dr. Wallace started showing enough signs of life just to be confusing. Ah well, a free afternoon — no sense arguing. She seated the tray and punched the start button.

CHAPTER SIXTEEN

JUNE 13, AFTERNOON

I had left the Center in sheer desperation. I had gone over and over the data Ben had pulled out, and I had to agree. There was a serial killer at work. For my nickel, that series included those accidents, but I couldn't find a connection that pulled it all together other than being an heir to vast sums of money, and I had no idea where to start looking. A killer loose in town, one so clever as to avoid being seen in the middle of a crowd and such a good shot he could drop a man on the spot even with a varmint gun. All in all, a lousy day. Staying inside the Center ruminating on it made it just that much worse.

After Wilson's visit, I finally looked out my window at the clear blue sky and decided to call it quits. I walked home, opened the door, and went directly to the kitchen. I scrounged in the fridge for the makings of a sandwich — a late lunch — poured myself a glass of wine and went out onto the back deck. Isa and all the others so newly arrived were gone for the day, out on a picnic with one of the Hispanic liaisons from St. Pat's. They'd taken a trip to Owl Creek Reservoir, and I didn't expect them until after dark. It was one of those golden summer afternoons when the sunlight would last well into the evening.

Three kids in residence overnight had turned the clock back to a time when my life was filled with noise and vitality. As much as I loved it, I was unused to the energy that children demand. I had to admit that a few moments of solitude watching the sun dapple the trees as I sat and simply did nothing had appeal, especially since I knew the whole tribe would be back again this evening, noisy as ever. What had I been thinking when I offered them a place to live?

I needed to keep my mind away from the conundrum at the office that was driving me crazy. So I picked up the paperback I had been trying to finish for months, an entertaining bit of mind-candy involving murder on a culinary cruise and punctuated with recipes. I jokingly called this sort of escapism "reading professional journals," but it was a nice change to see a murder committed, wrapped in mystery, cleanly solved and the bad guy punished within a few hundred pages.

My life's work didn't usually turn out that way. Most of the time, the deaths I investigated were tragically ordinary, with no challenge to solve them, rather like the Houston case. Or, like the Houston case looked like at first. Now it was firmly wedged in the column of cases-I-can't-solve, and it was making my head hurt.

Aside from the headlines about a serial killer and the attacks on Tom's office and mine, the morning paper had a short article and a half-page photograph of Marla Kincaid two pages in. She was supposedly still confined to bed, but now at her luxurious home under the virtual care of an international expert on high-risk pregnancy. She looked wan and pale, propped up in bed and surrounded by pillows. I wondered whether the picture had been taken before or after she visited Father Matt.

The photo caught my eye because she kept surfacing at the edges of my world, reminding me of Houston's death and John's and the fact that all I ever did was pick up the pieces of murder. She had surprised me with her visit to my office. There was real pain in her voice when she asked about Houston, but something about it didn't fit. I frowned at the recollection.

This series of trustafarian deaths had me flummoxed, and there wasn't anything useful I had been able to uncover to help out my law enforcement brethren. Waiting for the next shoe to drop was what drove me to improbable novels and the fruit of the vine on a workday afternoon, when, if my interior barometer were correct, the next shoe was indeed due to drop.

I had just drained the last of my wine and put my grandmother's paper-thin Czechoslovakian wine glass on the table by my chair when the cell phone rang.

"Hi Mom, it's me, Adam."

My first-born had been starting his long distance communications — whether phone or letter — with the same words as long as any of us could remember. As if I could mistake that voice, or his trademark, illegible scrawl. I smiled to myself, but wasn't able to get my answer out before he pressed on. Also typical of my number-one son.

"We're all fine. I wanted to tell you because you're going to see it all on TV, and it really isn't as bad as all that. If I hadn't had the bishop with me, no one would have even noticed."

He had my heart in his hands. Adam has always been the daredevil of the family, though apparently possessing a guardian angel who himself is on steroids. At the age of not-quite-two, he pulled a child's rocker over to the dresser in his room, piled on a stool, and then some books on it to give it the necessary height, and clambered up on the teetering edifice to retrieve a toy I had taken from him and placed out of reach. I had walked in to see him balance precariously, snatch the toy from the dresser, and scuttle back off, oblivious to his peril. His judgment had not gotten appreciably better, and I held my breath, waiting for the rest.

"Actually, it was cool, awesome. It was amazing. I was taking the bishop over to Kotzebue in the float plane..."

This seminarian son had taken a summer position on the staff of the most recent "Flying Bishop" of Alaska, which entailed making jaunts all over remote Alaskan territory in various incarnations of small aircraft. He and the bishop were cut from the same bolt of cloth, both having gotten pilot's licenses while in college, both over the strenuous objections of their powerless mothers.

"...And we lost an engine just as we were coming in to land. I kind of missed the dock area, had to be towed in by motorboat, but we landed just fine, no worries. Problem was, it looked a little rough coming in, I did a...well, I stalled out a little...anyway, it looked worse than it was and somebody videoed it. It's going to be all over the news tonight, and I didn't want you to worry."

Mom rule number one is to never let them see you sweat, even when they are not babies any longer. I put a great deal more control into my voice than I felt. "But you're okay? And the plane will be fixed — what happened?"

In a voice of supreme confidence and indifference, he answered. "Not really sure, Mom. They'll have to take it pretty much apart. I guess we'll be here a little longer than we planned, but that's really awesome. We just missed the solstice, but it's light nearly all day. The sun never sets. It's really an amazing place, Mom, you'd love it."

"I expect so. Why were you flying the plane?"

"Bishop Leland had some kind of stomach flu — tossed his cookies as we landed. He figured I could handle it, so he turned it over to me.

It all happened so fast, he didn't have time to take over again."

It does happen fast, a life-changing event like that. One minute, you're flying along in smooth air, and the next minute you lose an engine and you're headed straight for a crash. One minute, you're a happily married woman and the next, some vengeful bastard mows your husband down in a parking lot, and you don't even get to say goodbye. Tears welled up in my eyes, and all the pain in my soul took residence in my constricted throat. I pinched the bridge of my nose so hard that it hurt, emptied my mind, and managed a reply that sounded almost normal. "Well, thank God." *And your guardian angel and your patron namesake Augustine, and whoever taught you to fly so well.* "Thanks for calling me, babe — I think I'll go find the story on the news. I want to see your aerobatics."

"Record it for me, Mom, will ya? They're going to interview me, and the bishop said I'm a real ace, that he couldn't have done it better."

Though he was well into his studies for the priesthood, my son sounded like he did when he won his first space derby with his own innovative — if eccentric and moth-eaten — fenestrated rocket.

"Sure, son, everyone should be able to review his near death experiences in HDTV." I paused. "Love you. Be safe. Don't crash. Say a rosary."

I stopped, hoping my silence wasn't too abrupt. I couldn't risk saying anything more. It wasn't. Adam charged ahead, still cruising on the adrenal dump that his unexpected landing and his new notoriety had produced.

"Don't plan to auger in, Mom, and the bishop says we'll all say the rosary together in the church after Vespers. Love you too. Bye, talk to you later."

I heard someone calling in the background, and he was off before I could warn him that nobody plans to crash.

I was in the kitchen, wine glass in hand, before it hit me. Adam, my first-born. The carbon copy of his father, with the same big, wide eyes, dimpled cheeks and wicked sense of humor, Adam had almost died. I stifled a sob, and made to put the glass in the sink. I missed, hitting the sharp ledge so that the stem broke with a crack, and, by reflex, my hand closed on the delicate bowl, shattering it in my grip. When I opened it to drop the shards, my hand was already red with blood, several deep cuts across the palm, one of which sprayed blood in the rhythmic pattern that told me I'd cut a small artery.

Curiously, I didn't feel pain in my hand, just deep in my heart. I grabbed a floral patterned towel from the counter, where Isa had left it neatly folded, wrapped it tightly around my hand and sank to the floor, finally giving way to tears, heaving great and inconsolable sobs, unable even to catch my breath. I heard the kitchen door swing open and then someone running towards me, long strides, heavy steps. Strong arms wrapped around me, pulling me up and holding me close to a plaid shirt that smelled of peppermint and pipe tobacco. Eoin Connor didn't say a word, but cradled me as I spent my fear and anguish in gulping sobs until I was exhausted and still. I hated that he had seen me cry. I hated that I cried so much these days.

Only then did he ask, "And what have you done now? Let me see."

The big hands that unwound the towel and coaxed open my bloody hand were rough and calloused, the hands of a laborer, not a writer, but they were gentle and competent. Had Ben told me that Connor kept a farm both in the states and in Ireland, to stay in touch with what he called his peasant roots? I couldn't remember.

He kept up a narrative as he examined my palm, spurting again now that the pressure was released, and then quickly wrapped the towel back around it.

"They told me you'd gone for the day. I was coming to see if you might want to join me for a bit of grub tonight, when I heard a noise and looked through the window. I saw you fall."

He finished the wrap with a decisive tug and tucked the end in on itself.

I still hadn't looked up at him, ashamed that he had been privy to my pain and oddly aware how I must look, with swollen eyes and a stuffy nose. Connor still held my injured hand in one of his, the other on the sleeve, now blood soaked, that ended at my wrist. I ran the other one across my face to soak up some of the moisture before I answered his unspoken question.

"I hit a glass on the counter. The glass broke in my hand. Idiot." I looked up with what I hoped was a smile. Connor's look told me he expected more explanation. I collected myself and shifted away from his surprisingly comfortable bulk, disconcerted and decidedly not comfortable. And suddenly in physical pain and weak at the knees. I staggered, and Connor caught me by the elbow to steady me.

"You're a bit green around the gills," he said. "Where are your keys? I'll drive you to the Medical Center."

I was in no position to argue, unable to steer and too shaky to walk. I gestured toward the back door with my bloody towel. "On the rack. The 4Runner."

Connor retrieved the keys, bundled me into the passenger seat, and refused to leave my side until I was tucked into an exam room waiting for the doctor and a surgical tray to arrive. I heard him exchange a few words with the nurse as he left, and he lingered at the door until she returned and slipped a paper in his hand, giving me a sideways glance and him a smile. The exchange had the aura of conspiracy about it.

I'd not met the fresh-faced young doctor that came in to stitch me up, but he was chatty and efficient. He injected my hand, which by now had begun to hurt like hell. I watched in detached fascination as he irrigated out the wound, expelling a few remaining shards and pulling another out with a pair of forceps. Courage failed when he began to stitch, however, and I turned away, counting the stitches by the pressure on my palm. Twenty-two. This fellow could be a seamstress in an atelier; the cuts just weren't that big.

By the time he finished, the light through the treatment room window was beginning to soften. As the doctor stripped off his gloves, Eoin knocked on the door and came in, bearing a bag from the pharmacy. He opened it and took out two brown pill bottles and handed one of each of the pills inside to me, one white, one a blue capsule.

"You're now masquerading as a nurse?" I asked.

The doctor, with the same conspiratorial look his nurse had shown, looked up at me from jotting in the chart.

"Painkillers and antibiotics. No need to wait, so I sent them on with Mr. Connor there to get them filled."

The metal cover of the chart made a sharp clang as he flipped it closed, one-handed with practiced ease, and looked at me again.

"Keep it dry. Take your antibiotics. And for God's sake, don't get near any autopsies. I'll see you in ten days to take out the stitches. Call or come back if it swells or you get a fever. You know the drill."

He extended a hand to Connor. "Nice to meet you, Mr. Connor. I enjoy your books."

And with that, he was off, leaving me alone in the exam room with Eoin Connor.

Connor dug around in the pharmacy bag and handed me a pink, long-sleeved tee-shirt proclaiming "Telluride" in teal letters and rampant with garish wildflowers.

"I thought you might want to change out of that bloody shirt before we go to dinner," he said, wagging the shirt at me.

I took it in my good hand and regarded it skeptically. "I'm not all that fond of pink..." I started to say.

"I figured as much," Connor interrupted, green eyes smiling. "It's why I bought it. Now be a good girl and change; the only blood anyone wants to see at the Chop House is on the plate with a steak."

He slipped out of the room and closed the door behind before I could ask him what in the world made him think I wanted to go to dinner with him, now or ever.

Breakfast, however, had been a long time ago, I hadn't eaten my sandwich, I couldn't drive with my bandaged hand, and the buzz the painkiller was going to give me made food a necessity. Dinner, even with a charming, if irritating, Irishman had a certain practical appeal. I pulled the top on. It was a bit snug. I wondered whether that was intentional, too. I hopped off the exam room table, still a little unsteady, and met Connor in the hallway. A few minutes to reckon the bill and stuff my bloody cotton shirt into the bag, and we were on our way, driving up Pacific Street towards the New Sheridan Hotel.

The maitre d' showed us to a corner table, lit the candle, pulled out my chair, flourished my napkin and shook hands with Connor as though he were an old family friend. I was suddenly aware of the awkwardness of the situation. I had rarely eaten out since John's death, and never with a man, alone. In fact, the last time I'd had dinner alone with a man other than my husband had been long before we were married, some thirty years ago. I gulped and buried my face in the menu, wishing as I so often did that my husband were back with me, and feeling more than a little guilty at the fact that I was finding even a little pleasure in other company. And more than a little surprise in the bargain. Without looking up from his own menu, Connor must have read my mind. Either that or my gulp was audible.

"It's just dinner, not adultery. I recommend the veal, unless you have some moral scruples against it."

In the recesses of my mind I heard John echoing his words. *"Dear Jane. It's dinner, and you need friends. Just enjoy it. It's fine, Mrs. Doe."*

I felt myself relax and looked up at my companion. I'd never really studied Eoin Connor's face before, considering him a grievous thorn in my professional side to be dealt with efficiently and dispassionately. He was now sitting directly across from me, and I could only study the menu, the flowers, and the art on the wall so long.

His green eyes returned my glance, not in an unkindly way, but full of curiosity. Below his still thick, wiry, silver hair and those tilted, unruly black brows, they had a perpetually quizzical look to them, as though everything he encountered were new, surprising, and delightful. His broad face was ruddy, lined and worn, with a scar across his left cheek I'd never paid attention to, but it was a comfortable, open, welcoming face. I was struck that this man was entirely at ease with who he was no matter where he was, and that there wasn't much of anything that could change that.

I closed my menu, dropped my eyes, and gathered my courage. Looking up again, I smiled. "I think I'll have the trout. And the macaroni. Comfort food."

I sighed, plunged in again. "Thank you for dinner. I don't know that I would want to be by myself just now."

"So I gathered," he replied, closing his own menu and motioning the waiter over. "Will you have some wine?"

The doctor in me screamed no, but the injured woman part managed to shove her into a metaphorical sound-proofed closet in the back of my mind and ignore her. *Who cared whether I got a little wasted tonight? I deserved it. I needed it. I probably shouldn't do it.*

"Sure, just a bit. Sauvignon blanc, if that suits."

Connor pointed out a selection from the wine list to the waiter and resumed. "It wasn't just the glass this afternoon. What happened?" His eyes fell on me again and the brows furrowed.

I took a drink from my water glass to buy some time. My hand throbbed. *None of your business,* I thought, *none of your damn business,* as tears welled up again. One splashed on the tablecloth as I fought to regain control. This tearfulness really had to stop.

"Sorry," he said gruffly and passed me a handkerchief.

How few men carry them these days, I thought, as I wiped my eyes. Like his shirt, it smelled of peppermint, probably from a stash in his pocket. He must keep his tobacco somewhere else.

I shook my head. "No, I'm sorry, really. It's all right. It really is." I quickly recounted what had happened with Adam. "I just couldn't bear the thought of losing him," I finished up, mopping up the rest of the tears that followed, finally handing the sodden cloth back across the table.

Connor looked at it ruefully, folded it, and tucked it into his right pants pocket, leaning back from the table as the waiter poured the wine. He took up his glass and extended it. "May the face of good news and the back of bad news always be towards us."

I clinked my glass to his.

"Forgive me for not knowing more about you. Ben says I am hopelessly out of it all. How did an Irish farm boy get to be the most celebrated crime writer in the world?"

A question right out of what one of my more gracious friends called Southern Belle 101. It ought to keep him going for a while.

I was surprised to see his face grow thoughtful. Surely he'd been asked the question a thousand times in his career, surely it was an answer that would roll off his tongue like legendary Irish blarney. He answered after a long sip from the glass, and it wasn't the glib response I expected.

"It started out as revenge. I started writing during the troubles, after the August riots, after I saw a boy killed when the RUC fired into his flat. He was just a lad, twelve years old. I wanted to make the whole world see what England had been doing to us. I discovered I had a flair for blood and gore, and that the rest of the world had an appetite for it."

Another sip of wine and he set the glass down deliberately, and turned his eyes on me again. "After a while, it got to be a job, one I was good at, no more, no less. It's served me well. My Da would be proud, after all those stories he told me as a cub, working side by side on the farm to make the time go easier."

"Not fond of the English, then?" I winced inwardly. Either the pills or the wine were making me mean. I'd better mind my tongue. I could see John frowning at me in my mind's eye. This was no way to return hospitality.

A faint grin crossed Connor's face as though he were remembering things long past, and pleasant.

"You could say that. You have to understand, in Northern Ireland, we had to fight to keep anything that was our own: our land, our language, our church, even our bloody dignity. It makes for a certain disaffection for those who are trying to take it away."

At this, he filled my glass.

"But if you don't break under the strain, it makes for a grand life. I decided early on that I wasn't going to let the English bastards take any of it from me. I bought back the old man's farm after he lost it to debt with my first book advance, and Mick, Joe, Terence, Molly and I work it to this day. I kept on speaking Irish. I kept the faith in the Church even when she kicked me in the teeth. I know who I am despite those soldiers that bullied me and mine. In the long run, it's served me well. I've made a comfortable life. And the reality is, I don't give a damn about the bloody English now, one way or the other." He paused. "I found out that revenge makes for great copy, not a good life."

I wondered what it would be like, to get to that point, where I didn't care one way or another about Tom Berton. I decided it wasn't possible, and said so. "I don't think I'll ever get past my husband's murder."

I was surprised that my voice didn't falter and my tears didn't start up again. It was almost as though I were talking about one of my cases, not myself. "I won a huge judgment against several national lab companies for insurance fraud. Huge. 75 million free and clear in my pocket alone."

I paused, took a breath and went on. "The day after the trial ended, one of my ex-partners, who was on the board of one of those companies, ran my husband over in the parking lot of the hospital. I'll always give a damn about what happens to him, as long as he's alive and John isn't."

I was aware how hard and set my face was, but there it was.

Connor regarded me with a curious combination of dawning recognition and amusement on his face.

"And then you testified in the partner's murder trial and then you sued the rest of them out of existence in record time," he said quietly. "You're *that* Jane Wallace. All the news reports called you Dr. Simpson. I never made the connection."

"*That* Jane Wallace?"

For a while I had been accustomed to people recognizing me, but only in my former hometown, one reason I had left. About half the town wanted to console me, the other half to lynch me. I wanted neither, and so I had escaped to Telluride, and I had traded in my professional name for John's.

"My next book. You're my next book. I've quite a raft of research on your case in my study, just waiting for me to take after it. You're quite a story." Connor suddenly looked uncomfortable and leaned back in his chair, bracing for the outburst he expected. Maximizing the distance between us, he made a quick look toward the door.

It took a few seconds for the import of this to sink in. Eoin Connor wanted to write a book about my husband's murder — one of his gritty, true-crime morality tales that invariably made the bestseller list, and from there to a made-for-TV movie or, sometimes, a Hollywood blockbuster. I'd fought so hard to maintain my privacy, to seal off that part of my life. And here I was, for the first time in years, having dinner with a moderately attractive man, who had, for whatever reason, asked me out. And whose next goal in life would turn my life even more upside down than it already was.

Oh, hell, who cared anymore? How much more uprooted could I possibly be? The irony of the situation struck me, and in spite of myself, I started to laugh. Slowly, at first, then uncontrollably, finally in tears again as I gasped for breath and tried to control myself. People were beginning to stare, not the least of whom was Eoin Connor. Eventually, my laughter was spent, except for a few momentary giggles, and I wiped my eyes for the last time.

"I'm glad you find the thought of my next book so amusing," he said, dignity obviously affronted, face thunderous.

"I'm sorry," I said, wiping my eyes with my napkin and suppressing a final chuckle. "It's just...funny. After everything that's happened lately, it's just too much. And, by the way," I settled the napkin back in my lap and took a sip of wine. "When hell freezes over and you present me with a pair of ice skates engraved with Satan's first name, we'll discuss your interviewing me for your book. Cheers."

I lifted the glass and cocked my head, a challenge on my face.

So did he, and we spent the rest of the dinner in comfortable conversation about travels, books, favorite towns, family stories, food and wine, anything but murders, the ones he investigated or the ones I did. By the time we were walking back to the 4Runner, the soft light of twilight alpenglow was settling in and the moon was already full in the evening sky, washing the streets in purple light almost as bright as day. We took our time. He opened the car door for me. My hand had stopped throbbing, I was pleasantly full, and the wine and painkillers had left me in a mellow mood.

We turned onto Aspen Street. I saw a few hikers heading up towards Coronet Falls, clearly outlined against the road. I watched the hikers, who had stopped to look at something near my driveway, turn and start up the trail again, walking briskly, heads nodding in conversation. Connor swung the 4Runner into the gravel drive with practiced ease, then slammed on the brakes, just short of a crumpled figure, left arm outstretched, at the edge of the drive.

"Stay here," Connor ordered as he opened the door, but he might as well have saved his breath. I was out of the car in an instant, standing beside him as he felt the neck of the prone figure. I was looking down at a rough brown tunic with a spreading dark stain. The figure was so still, his eyes so wide open and unseeing, that I knew in an instant that Captain Bedsheet was past help.

I have always wondered what I would do if I came upon a fresh murder scene. I've attended too many over the years, but always escorted, always prepared, always firmly in command of my role as advocate and spokesman for the dead. I always wondered what I would do if I happened on one suddenly. Now I knew. As Eoin Connor stood up, I buried my face for the second time that day in his soft, plaid shirt.

****

Sweet Mother of God, her hair smelled good. Fresh, like a meadow after the rain, some sort of flowery scent. And she fit into his arms like a key in a lock. It had been a long time since he held a woman like that. He tightened his embrace and cradled the back of her head in one hand, felt her shudder with the realization of the dead man lying in front them.

And it had been a long time since he'd seen death so fresh and so personal. He'd made his living for thirty years or so writing about death in all its cruelty and vengeance, but always as one removed. It was different when you were there. Pictures and reports and interviews, they were clinical, sterile, something he could manipulate and craft to tell the story inside. This was dimensional, uncontrolled, totally present. It even smelled of death, loosed bowels and sticky blood.

He remembered the last time he'd seen it, in the doorway to a poor council flat in Belfast, when a bullet had come whizzing in to lay waste to Tam Murphy, his cousin's friend. The Peelers had been tipped to raid the flat of Seamus Devlin, one of the local IRA heroes and no relation to Bernadette, though he'd let you think he was. They mistook Connor for Devlin in the dark hall of the council building where Devlin lived. Connor bolted for his freedom, dodging down corridors and down a stairwell toward his cousin's flat. His cousin intercepted him and pushed him into the vacant flat across the hall, retreating behind his own door just as the constables rounded the corner.

Connor heard them pounding on the door of his cousin's flat, yelling for Devlin to come out. Then came the splintering of wood as they kicked it in and spilled into the flat, weapons at the ready. They'd caught sight of Tam, of a size with Connor and with the same dirty blond hair as Devlin, but just a boy, slow of pace and slow of mind, overgrown for his age, not even shaving yet, as he stepped into the living room from the tiny kitchen, a glass of water in his hand. They fired without warning. Connor had just eased open the door to surrender himself to spare his family when the bullet hit. He saw it from across the hall, over the shoulder of the pig who pulled the trigger.

Tam's youthful blue eyes widened with surprise, and the blood flowered on his shirt, and he was gone, and all hell broke loose as the RUC realized they'd shot an innocent boy. He never really knew what happened, why he died. Neither, really, did anyone else, except Connor, who took advantage of the chaos to slip down the back stairs, noticed by a dozen pairs of suspicious eyes as he made his way into the August sunlight.

Devlin had taken a shine to Connor's little sister, Molly, and neither heaven nor earth could dissuade him. Connor had called on Devlin that morning, to try to convince him to leave his sister alone, and found him gone, decamped to the states to raise money for the cause, leaving the flat just in time for the Peelers to mistake first Connor, then Tam for the prey they sought, the man they wanted to kill. Connor had paid for that bullet and that death, first with grief, then with dishonor as rumor began to circulate that it was his rash action that tipped the Peelers, that it was his fault young Tam died. Rumor from the mouth of Seamus Devlin, rumor even his own sister began to believe. Rumor that gave his wife the excuse to bolt. He paid the price for that single shot with his reputation, his peace, his marriage, even his chance at any other.

And so had Tam's parents paid the cost, over and over, every day for the rest of their lives. Tam's blood had stained the worn rug they could never afford to replace and never would. That stain, the one his mother cleaned and brushed in hopes of ridding herself of her pain, then left because she wanted the world to remember, would be there until it was hidden by their own coffins, stoking the fire of their anger at the soldiers, the English, God, and all of creation. That bullet killed more than just poor Tam, and it was, in the end, a mistake.

That was the trouble with guns, they made killing so impersonal, so efficient. It was the same with the poor sod on the gravel of the drive. He never knew what hit him. At least with a knife or a club or naked fists there was a chance to see your attacker face to face, to argue, to plead, to fight back, at least to understand. With a bullet, it was so swift and so silent and so complete, there was no time to do all those things that in the last second of life you were supposed to do. *Poor sod*, he thought again, and repeated it. *Poor sod*.

Jane needed to find another line of work, at least until she got over Dead John. She never got to see death in its intended form, slow, contemplative, giving a person time to inventory a life, make amends, savor the last, prepare for the journey. All she saw was the horror and violence that had destroyed her own life over and over again. And she was just as powerless to stop it for others as she had been for herself. If she didn't get past the grief and the hurt and the guilt soon, he feared she'd be lost forever in the dismal mire of brutality and sorrow that was her daily ration at work.

He felt her stiffen, felt the steeling of the resolve in her body as she prepared her mind to deal with it all again, with senseless death and bloodshed. He savored the feel of her against him, knowing it was just a matter of time before she pushed him away again.

CHAPTER SEVENTEEN

JUNE 13, EVENING

It took me a minute or two and several deep breaths to collect myself again and turn away from Connor's arms to the work that now lay before me in my own driveway. My gaze automatically went from the body backwards toward the road where I could see the start of a trail of blood that ended more or less at Bedsheet's sandaled feet. I knelt for a moment. The blood had congealed, and the body offered no resistance when I lifted the hand to get a sense of how warm it was. Not cold, but not 98.6 either. He had been here a little while. There was no crowd and no 911 response. I could only surmise that there hadn't been anyone on the street when he was shot. That didn't explain why those who passed hadn't checked him out, but no one had; I'd seen it with my own eyes. I'll never understand the detachment of some people.

I retrieved my cell, holding it in my bandaged right hand so that I could dial it with my uninjured left. The Center is on speed-dial, and Quick answered on the first ring. From the sound of it, he was downstairs in the office lounge rather than in his quiet apartment on the fourth floor.

"I need you to call the sheriff and send Lucy up to my house. There's been another murder."

Quick's voice was concerned. "Not any of yours?"

I was grateful for that. "No, it's not, Quick. One of the local new age preachers, the fellow that runs around in a tunic and cloak. The one that was in with Houston's lawyer."

"Damn," he said, then, "He was a nice enough guy. Goofy, but nice. Who'd want to do that?"

Not expecting an answer, Quick was just thinking out loud, something those who work in the morgue get used to doing, as there's really no one to hear us and just the sound of a voice, even one's own, is comforting.

"I'm on it," he continued.

I could hear him calling to Lucy Cho as the phone clicked off.

I heard footsteps as yet another group of moonlight hikers headed up Spruce. Five of them, raucous, two of them unsteady on their feet, loud, joking, physical in their camaraderie, with playful shoves and hugs, oblivious of the rest of the world. Sizing them up as trouble, I turned to Connor.

"Help me," I directed and motioned him to follow me without giving him a chance to answer. I confronted the hikers, three women and two men as they reached the corner below my house. "Turn around, go back. The trails are closed. There's been an accident — you can't go up there."

The women stopped chattering, hesitant, stepping back and ready to comply with my order, but I knew that wasn't going to be the end of it. The shorter, scrappier of the two men cocked his head and thrust his chin out, taking a step in my direction so that we were almost toe-to-toe. He'd been drinking. A lot.

"Who says?"

His sour breath washed over me and I winced. He moved even closer, invading my personal space. I hate that. I straightened my spine and squared my shoulders. I reached in my back pocket for the badge that is with me every waking hour of every day, my identity, my life, such as it was. I flipped back the leather cover and pushed it under his nose.

"I do. I'm the medical examiner; this is a crime scene and I am in charge. Now turn around and leave. Immediately."

"No way."

He pushed my hand aside and I dropped the badge. He kicked it like a soccer ball, and it skittered away to land at Connor's feet. I saw him bend over to retrieve it. His expression was cautious, but he was watching both of us intently. He took a protective step closer to me.

I'm pretty good at verbal intimidation and I present an imposing presence, but physical confrontation is neither my style nor my strength. Usually one of my uniformed brethren backs me up when I clear a scene; few people are willing to risk a night in the hoosegow in exchange for crime scene interloper status. Without that support, the drunken little lout wasn't impressed. He pushed past me, which I expected. He was stronger than he looked and more aggressive, which I didn't expect. I lost my footing and sat down hard on the gravel, landing square on my bandaged hand. I yelped in spite of myself.

He laughed at that and turned to signal his friends to follow. When he turned back around, he walked right into Eoin Connor who grabbed his arm. From the look on the man's face, it wasn't a gentle grip. Connor's expression was fierce.

The man tried to pivot and took a wild swing at Connor. I watched as Connor blocked with his right arm, and with remarkable ease, caught the man's hand and twisted him around so that his free arm looped over his head and pivoted him around. Then Connor brought his left arm up sharply against the man's chin, pinning him against his chest. It was as smooth and sophisticated and complicated as a tango move, and it was totally incapacitating. And proof positive that Eoin Connor hadn't always been a man of letters, I thought.

"No, you don't," he said evenly.

The man wriggled and shouted at Connor, who remained placid and completely in control. I was impressed, even as I sat on the gravel rocking in pain and cradling my injured right hand. I hoped I hadn't torn any stitches. The other four stood rooted, eyes wide, jaws gaping. I heard the sound of the sheriff's SUV and saw it spin around the corner, the Center hearse right behind. Jeff Atkins, one of the more seasoned deputies and a regular at Baked for its taco special, propelled himself from the Jeep and helped me to my feet. I was glad for his fondness for Mexican food; it was the reason he'd arrived so quickly. I was dusting my pants off as my pinioned assailant shrieked at Atkins.

"This man's assaulted me! You can see that! Let me loose! Arrest him!"

The wriggling got more frenetic, Connor more placid, like a patient old dog enduring the aggravation of a new puppy, though a look of amusement was creeping onto his face. He shifted his weight just a little, and his prisoner found himself standing on tiptoe.

"Jeff, please arrest this man for trespassing on a crime scene, and while you are at it, throw in assault. He pushed me down and took a swing at Mr. Connor, here, who was kind enough to help me out." I turned to the bystanders, who still hadn't said a word. "Isn't that right?"

I'd probably end up dropping the charges, but not until he'd cooled his heels and sobered up in jail. And not until he signed a release that would prevent his suing Connor — the least I could do for his Good Samaritan act was to keep this aggressive nitwit from trying to bilk him out of his hard-earned money. An occupational hazard, I suspected, of the famous and wealthy. Not that Connor needed my protection. It seemed for the time being, I needed his.

They nodded dumbly, and their faces reflected the hope that they weren't about to join their drunken friend in the sweet embrace of San Miguel County's finest.   Jeff's partner started taking names and statements, and I directed him to my porch, if nothing else to get them out of the way. Lucy had already pulled crime scene tape out of the hearse and strung it across the road, tying it off to a fence on one side and a tree on the other. The hearse and the SUV effectively blocked the cross street, so we had a modicum of control over the site, which was a good thing. The drunk's commotion was beginning to draw a crowd.

Jeff finished cuffing and Mirandizing the man, then shoved him into the back seat of the SUV, then strode to the stretched tape to address the onlookers.

"You all need to leave. Now. Everything's under control and there's no reason for you to be here. Out. Now."

A couple of hangers-on looked as though they were thinking about defying Jeff, then thought the better of it and sidled off. Only Pete Wilson was left.

"Pete, you'd better stay where you are. Dr. Wallace has already brought charges against one person tonight. She won't have to prompt me if you cross that line."

He pointed at the yellow tape. There was no love lost between Pete Wilson and Jeff Atkins.

"Wouldn't think of it, Deputy," he said. "But I'll be here when you're done and I'll have questions."

Jeff bristled, and the verbal peeing match would have gone on had there not been a ruckus from the trailhead farther up the road. A slim teenaged girl in shorts and a cropped, faded sleeveless tee-shirt burst out of the woods, yelling. Jeff and I jogged up to intercept her before she got to the spot where Lucy was stringing the tape across the top of the road. Jeff reached her before I did and put a calming hand on her shaking shoulder. I'd no sooner reached them when two others, also girls, escorting a tiny, white-haired woman, appeared. One of them supported the woman by her elbow, the other carried a rifle gingerly in her left hand, as though she were afraid it would bite her. Jeff and I simultaneously and vigorously instructed the girl to stay put and ran to meet the others.

They were already talking, together, in that peculiar, high-pitched tone that teenaged girls get when excited, the one that penetrates to the very back of an adult's skull. Jeff relieved the one girl of the gun, handling it carefully by the side of the barrel and motioning to Lucy to come and fetch it. A model of efficiency, Lucy already had her gloves on and trotted up to take it. It looked like a .22. There was a neat depression at the base of the stock, so clear and sharp it looked as though it might have once been inlaid. It was a peculiar design, sweeping curves drawn into little points. Into the stock. Flames? Lightning? How odd. It was an older gun, well-used and businesslike; it was not the sort to have some sort of ornament either carved or embedded into it.

When we finally got the girls calmed down, Jeff was able to sort out their story. They had been coming back from Coronet Falls when they found the old woman who was getting herself up from a muddy patch in trees on the edge of the trail just below the trailhead. The rifle was lying on the ground beside her.

"She said she'd been walking along when some man just ran out of the woods, right across the rail. He knocked her down and dropped the gun, then ran off, heading towards Judd Weibe," the taller, heavier of the two girls concluded, naming the long trail that ran for several miles, a popular hiking spot in the summer.

Jeff turned to the woman, inquired if the girl's report was accurate. She nodded, running her hand across her face. Her shirt was torn, and her khaki pants were stained with red soil where she had fallen on her right side. Her hands shook.

"He was not so tall, nice size, like you," she said. I saw Jeff wince. His height was a sore subject to him.

"Hair? Eyes?" Jeff asked.

The woman furrowed her brow. "Brown hair, long, dirty." More reflection, then, "Bah. His eyes, I don't know."

She had an accent, unplaceable. Not German, not French. Eastern European of some kind. I knew her from somewhere but couldn't quite place her.

Jeff paused for a moment, and I knew he was trying to decide how much further to pursue this. The chances of hunting someone down on Judd Weibe were slim at best, and a man of medium height with dirty brown hair was not exactly a rarity in Telluride. The woman began to cry quietly. The girl who had been talking put an arm around her. She invited that sort of familiarity; she looked like everyone's favorite grandmother, tender and vulnerable. Only in possession of a .22 rifle that almost certainly killed Bedsheet and might have killed Cosette Anira and Sig Monson and Jim Webster. One that we could do a ballistics match on. Perhaps my luck was improving. I took a moment to intervene.

"Are you hurt? Did he hurt you?"

The thought of sudden impact on fragile hips worried me, but she looked intact, if a bit disheveled.

She looked up at me, sharp eyes in a lined face tanned by too much sun, and though she had been crying, her eyes were barely moist.

"Thank you. I am fine. I did not fall hard. At my age, you learn how to take care."

The voice caught again, but the eyes were still sharp and focused. I took her hands in mine and dusted them off. The knuckles were arthritic, the palms calloused, but they were strong and intact. No real scrapes, just dust and grime, a bit of adherent gravel. The fall could not have been too hard. The skin on the back of her hands was tissue paper thin, with several resolving bruises, the curse of older women. My mother-in-law called them the devil's pinches, because she could never remember the injuries that produced them, so slight were they.

"Jeff, let me take her and the girls to the house. They can have a cup of tea, sit in there where it's quiet and out of the way. We've got to get to this scene. Besides," I added, "It will keep them out of Wilson's way."

Even without hearing the conversation, he would have a pretty good idea of what was going on just by watching, and I knew his eyes were on us.

Jeff nodded, and I motioned for the girls to come with me. I found Eoin Connor sitting on the porch lower steps, legs extended, reclining, his back resting on the edge of the deck watching intently but without the concern that had earlier marked his face. This was now entertainment for him, and he had a front row seat. I had almost forgotten he was here, but gladly pressed him back into service. He stood up as I approached.

"Will you do me a favor?" I asked. It was mere preliminary; I knew he would, and I didn't wait for an answer. "Take these ladies into the house, let them get cleaned up. Jeff — the deputy — is going to need to talk to them more, but right now, we've got to get this," I waved a hand, the bandaged one, in the general direction of the body, "taken care of."

Connor nodded and took the old woman by her hand.

"There's tea in the canister on the center island. And don't let anyone in, least of all Wilson," I called after him.

He paused as he opened the door, patient and understanding. "And do you take me for a fool, woman?"

Even though he was right, I bridled at his statement and my temper returned.

"That's Dr. Wallace to you. Call Father Matt, too, would you, please? He can help find her husband."

I remembered where I had seen the woman before. I had sat next to this woman and her tall — not nice size — and taciturn husband week after week in the balcony of Saint Pat's, but I didn't know her name or anything about her. Father Matt would, though.

"Happy to, Jane."

Connor's grin broadened, and I refused to rise to his bait a second time in one conversation. We would discuss proper forms of address at some later and more appropriate time.

I was just starting back towards the car and the body, which Jeff and Lucy were photographing, when Isa, Pilar, Lupe and the kids came up the street, in the company of Ben. I hurried to the side of the deputy who was guarding the scene.

"It's all right," I told him. "They live here."

He looked a bit askance at me, but let me usher them past and into the house, with instructions to help make everyone comfortable and to the deputy to let Father Matt through.

"Looks pretty simple," Jeff told me when I returned. "Two shots, mid-back, left side. Lucy didn't see an exit wound. Probably that rifle those girls brought down. Looks like he was in the middle of the road when he was shot, maybe looking over the creek there, who knows? That would put the shooter up in the woods above the road, likely as not."

I knew there was a small clearing there off the trail to the right, surrounded by a thicket, but with a clear view of the road and not far from where the girls said they had found the old woman and the gun. Lucy and I would come back in the morning to check it out, but I was certain that was where our shooter had lurked. Few people bothered to glance up away from the road, and there was enough cover that he could have remained almost hidden until the critical moment. Our shooter was clever and patient.   Here, a clearing, a copse of trees in Ophir, a hill in Town Park, perfectly situated. Same M.O., different locales. Only the site where the killer had hidden when he shot Cosette Anira remained a puzzle. It was somewhere up Spruce Street. A balcony? A roof? I still wasn't sure.

More puzzling was how the shooter picked his victims. Then again, how did the shooter know when and where to find them? I stopped. Was Bedsheet a trusty? I had no idea. If not, it was back to the drawing board. There were still too many questions and too few answers.

I helped Lucy and Jeff get Bedsheet into the body bag, onto the gurney and into the hearse. He was wearing the same tunic and robe. As Lucy zipped the bag, I noticed the big silver pin that held the tunic together. I didn't recall its being there when Bedsheet had been in my office; I wasn't certain, but its presence bothered me. It looked like a variation of the endless knot, but an odd shape, neither round nor oval, all swirls and connections, a surprisingly expensive thing to see on Bedsheet's brown vestment.

By the time Lucy closed the back door on the hearse to go back to the scene and take a second and last set of photos, my hand was throbbing again and my head ached. *Time for another of those blue capsules*, I thought. I left her to finish the processing with Jeff and retreated inside. When I glanced over to the perimeter of the scene as I mounted the porch steps and pushed open the front door, Pete Wilson was still there, leaning up against the tree where the yellow tape was secured. I had to give it to him, the man was patient.

My living room looked like a disaster shelter, and in a way it was, stuffed with people making themselves at home in unfortunate circumstances. Jeff's partner had commandeered my kitchen to take statements and was talking to one of the girls over a cup of coffee. Apparently Lupe had brewed a pot. Pablo was playing on the floor with the cats. Ben was showing pictures from a book — I hoped it wasn't one of my medical ones — to Mariela and Ignacio. Isa and Pilar were refilling cups and passing slices of cake, to which Connor was helping himself from the recesses of my easy chair. Father Matt was leaning over the old woman, deep in conversation. He looked up at me when I came through the door. His glance lacked its usual warmth and he looked uncomfortable. In spite of myself, I wondered whether he had been with Marla Kincaid when he got the call from Eoin.

I was still pondering this when Jeff escorted a tall, white-haired man, with a back as straight as a ramrod, into the room. The man wore creased jeans and a pressed shirt, and took off his straw cowboy hat as soon as he entered the hall. He came straight at Father Matt, bowing just a bit as he thanked us for taking care of his wife. He walked her out of my house, a protective arm around her, and the sight of it pierced my heart.

As the old woman had been the glue that held the crowd together, people drifted away. Isa and Pilar took the children upstairs. Ben collected dishes and disappeared into the kitchen. The two young women finished their statements and left, subdued and shaken, one of them calling a friend — presumably male — to come escort them home. I wondered what the streets of Telluride were like now.

Eoin Connor loitered by the door, silent and observant. I wondered if this was how he collected ideas for his books. If this case turned out to be the one that proved a serial killer at work, he'd have another best-seller without ever leaving town.

"I'll be by tomorrow," Jeff said to me as he raised a hand in acknowledgment. "When do you think you'll do the post?"

"First thing."

I always did my cases as soon as I could, finding no reason to wait, and in spite of my doctor's order, it would be my hand that held the knife. I was always amazed when a high-profile death led some pathologist to say that the results of the autopsy wouldn't be available for weeks. Ridiculous. I'd know everything I needed to know tomorrow by noon, toxicology and ballistics notwithstanding.

"Good enough. See you after lunch, then."

Jeff touched the rim of his hat and was gone, leaving me alone in the hall with Eoin Connor. He made to go himself, and I put out a restraining hand, the bandaged one. "May I offer you a drink? I owe you at least that, you know."

And I wanted to know more about him. He'd been there for me all day, solid and reliable. Taking me to the clinic. Holding me when we found Bedsheet. Subduing that drunken bum. Stepping in to take care of all the stray dogs that had happened on the scene. Without a complaint and without a question. I'd sold him short, I'd snapped at him when he was trying to inject a bit of levity into an impossible situation, and I regretted it. Time to make amends.

"You owe me nothing, Jane Wallace, but I'll have a whiskey, if you are offering."

His voice told me he meant it, that I was not in his debt. I knew better. I suspected he did, too, that he was being kind himself.

"I am."

"Well, then be generous."

He put out his hand to accept the drink, three fingers neat, then sat down in the same place he had on the night we met.

"Sláinte."

"Cheers."

"Quite a good break, finding that rifle."

I had the feeling he was prodding me for information. I remembered the newspaper article and Ben's admission.

"Better than not, that's for sure," I said as non-committally as I could. "I wish I could place that woman."

"Ivanka Kovacs. She and her husband have a big sheep ranch down valley. Near some place called Aldasaro. They run a shop in town. You ought to know her. She goes to church at St. Patrick's. Sits in the balcony, just like you. I've seen her."

I remembered. At one time, there had been competing ranches, but little by little, all the other ranchers had sold out, trading sheep herding for real estate development. The Kovacs' ranch was the last of the holdouts, the smallest of the lot, but still substantial in an area where real estate sold for the same price per square foot as a well-provenanced Old Master. They were still running sheep on the remaining pastures outside of town. They'd managed to keep the ranch a viable concern by becoming a sheep-to-sweater operation, using the wool from their flock to create hand knits that had captured the eyes of the Hollywood glitterati that frequented Telluride. They had a shop at the end of Colorado and another in Ouray and a third on Rodeo Drive that sold incredibly high-end, extremely delicate sweaters, shawls, afghans, hats, and gloves. And he was right. She did sit in the balcony, three seats down from me, with her tall husband.

"One mystery solved at least," I said.

"Are you all right, Jane Wallace? It's been quite a day for you."

I debated for a moment. "All right? No, not really." I paused, wondering just how honest to be and settled for a half portion. "I'm just frustrated that we can't seem to make any headway in these killings." *And frustrated that the men in my life seem to be tied up in this knot, one way or another,* I added silently.

Then we settled back into the living room and talked for nearly an hour over a glass of Jameson's about nothing in particular. I nursed mine as long as I could. After the day's events, I didn't want to be alone, and it felt both strangely familiar and naggingly uncomfortable to be sharing thoughts with a man and a Waterford glass. I suppressed the discomfort and let myself get lost, just for a few minutes, in the sound of Eoin Connor's voice. I didn't think John would mind.

****

As he walked home, Father Matt remembered the first time he met Jane Wallace.

He'd just been assigned to the parish, the first time the diocese had enough money to put a resident priest full time in this little town, home to a few Catholics, many tourists, a growing crop of itinerant Hispanic laborers and their children, and those locals who didn't care much one way or another whether there even was a church in town, let alone a priest.

"The parish is endowed," the bishop told him. Endowing a parish was almost unheard of, but he suspected that in this day and age, secure income couldn't be turned down. "And the donor asked only that we find someone energetic and unconventional to be assigned."

The smile on the bishop's face wasn't entirely comfortable. There was a limit to how unconventional a priest ought to be, and he knew the bishop wasn't sure that the man who stood before him was close enough to the center of the pack to be trusted on his own in a distant parish.

But the bishop had shaken his hand, given him a folder full of background information, and sent him off to spend two weeks with the deacon in residence, who was about to depart for yet another ski town. The priest two towns away would be glad to lose this particular parish from his 300-mile weekend circuit of the faithful scattered about Western Colorado, especially when winter came.

It was on the fourteenth day that she had walked into the church in the late afternoon, dipping her fingers in the font and making the sign of the cross before walking rapidly toward the stairs to the loft. The deacon had called quietly to her and she raised her head, startled.

"Jane, meet Father Matt Gregory. He's the new priest for the parish."

Interesting, he had thought. One usually introduced the parishioner to the priest, not the other way around. It was his first clue that something was different about this woman. She extended a hand, smiled again, but it was a smile without meaning. Not forced, and not insincere, just not complete, lacking something essential.

"Jane Wallace," she said. "Pleased to meet you."

She showed no need to fill the following silence, just let it lay between them. He'd learn later that it was one of her tricks, one of her techniques to keep the rest of the world at bay, and he would learn to cultivate a similar reticence with her. This time, he leapt in to speak.

"Matt Gregory. I hear you are the founder of my position — thank you. I am excited to be here in Telluride. Thank you." He cringed inwardly. Too many thanks. He stopped, blushing in spite of himself and hoping the beard hid it. She didn't respond immediately, but turned her quick eyes to the deacon. He backed up a step as if afraid and held up his hands, palms out.

"Talk to the bishop. He's the one who told him, not me."

He wondered only briefly why the deacon was so deferent until she looked back at him.

It was those eyes, so black he couldn't tell pupil from iris. She barely blinked, and they never wavered. There was a glint of anger in them even though she held her smile and her voice was warm. *He would have to learn to read those eyes if he wanted to survive here,* he thought.

And he had, slowly but surely. She had mastered her voice, her face, her body, all of them subjugated to her lawyer's tricks, but always her eyes gave her away. He'd learned that about a month after he'd officially arrived. She had been there dutifully for Sunday Mass and often during the week, and dropped in at odd hours to sit in the pew she'd been heading for when he first met her. She sat there, silent in her participation, under the watchful eye of St. Anthony, whose statue guarded the choir loft. But she never came forward to receive Communion. It puzzled him, and no one had given him the first clue why, so he had asked when he'd managed to catch her alone late one afternoon, as she was rising to leave the loft. He sprinted up the stairs, two at a time, meeting her at the top landing.

He knew parts of the story, of a husband killed unexpectedly at the hands of someone called a friend, of great grief, of sudden dislocation, of worried and grown children. There were rumors of lawsuits and vast fortunes to which he was willing to give great credence, having seen what she contributed, but no details to help him figure out what was wrong. He played the odds that she was in that state of being angry with God for her loss. He would learn not to do that with her, because she was never with the odds, but it had still been early days then.

"The Church can be a great help to you if you let her." It was a platitude and he knew it, but he could think of nothing else. He was sure as soon as he said it that it was meaningless to her, if not to him. She completed the smile then in sadness and condescension.

"Yes, I imagine she can," she had replied in a voice with no tone at all. "But no, Father, there's nothing you can do."

Silence again, and just when he'd about given up and was going to try to coax the conversation in another direction, she spoke, looking away and into the distance and not at him. It was the only time he'd yet seen her give up the advantage of quiet.

"'Forgive us our sins as we forgive', isn't that what we pray, Father?" Her voice was matter of fact and unconcerned as though she were addressing a lack of postage for a parcel to be mailed, or the dearth of fresh corn for the evening's dinner as she added, "I do not forgive John's killer. I will not. And I will not go to confession for something I am not sorry for."

Her eyes gave her away when she finally turned to look at him. This was no matter of indifference. He looked in those eyes and was surprised to see nothing but hurt so palpable it struck him dumb. Not anger, just hurt and sadness so deep there just wasn't an end to it.

"Will not or cannot?" he found himself asking her. "There's all the difference in the world, Jane. If you cannot, perhaps if…"

She'd stood up then, cutting him off into silence as the rest of the sentence trailed away. She looked down at him, and collected the rest of her features into impassivity. She turned quickly away.

"Thank you for your kindness in asking," she said as she started down the stairs without a look back in his direction, boot-heels clicking on the stairs.

Oddly, she sounded as though she meant it, but it drifted back up the stairs, almost an after-thought. He'd scared her away; amazing!

He managed not to blurt out his incredulous and totally inappropriate questions by imposing his mental, priestly filter. Father Duncan had once told him that was his biggest failing as a priest, not having that necessary brake between thoughts and voice, but one common to the inexperienced, overcome with time and patience. Apparently, he was making progress.

Unwilling, he wanted to ask, or unable, he asked himself again.

There was all the difference in the world. His own heart stirred in memory of his own naked pain of not so many years ago when his twin sister Sarah had died. *All the difference in the world*, he thought, and his own sadness returned, if only for a minute, when he'd walked into that house. He wasn't sure whether it was sadness for himself, or for that poor man who had been shot, or the others milling about, or Jane Wallace, who looked so lost in the middle of it even as she managed outwardly with the practiced ease of an Army drill sergeant with a bunch of fresh recruits. He smiled at the analogy. Jane Wallace was a lot like Sergeant Blair, his own nemesis. Tough as nails outside and complex as a philosopher's dissertation inside.

He opened the door to the rectory, smiling at Isa's admonition that he needed to keep it locked. There wasn't much inside to steal; he lived a frugal life. Mostly books, and the kind he kept no one around here would be much interested in. He'd have to remember to turn off lights as well. The small sitting room was bright. And sitting in the corner was Pete Wilson, thumbing through a copy of the *Summa Theologica*.

"I hope you don't mind that I let myself in. The door was open. I have a few questions to ask you."

Wilson's smile was a lot like Jane's, Father Matt thought, missing something. Only Wilson's smile had no warmth about it.

CHAPTER EIGHTEEN

JUNE 14, MORNING

I hurried down Aspen St. toward Colorado Ave. I was late for my Steaming Bean Breakfast with Father Matt. He'd started asking to meet me for coffee about a week after he'd cornered me in the choir loft and surprised me by probing into my life. I'd been unprepared and off balance, and the meeting had left me in tears.

At first, he asked me either to make amends or find out the answers to the questions I hoped I had deflected, but he pleaded the simple need for society. I found this implausible, then as now. As in every parish on the planet, the women faithful made it their business to see to it that he was well cared for. Fr. Matt made an offhand comment in his homily shortly after arriving that he didn't know how to make pot roast, and within hours, there was a parade of casseroles and at least two cookbooks on their way to the rectory. It had been so obvious that it had garnered public attention and made the front page of one of the papers as a human-interest/welcome-to-town story.

He always arrived at the Bean as they opened the doors, grabbing in order, a triple shot mocha and the green bus bench in the window so that passersby would have a view of him. I smiled to myself as I passed by the window myself and saw him there, cup at his side, head bent looking at the latest edition of the daily, long legs crossed, body studiously arranged in indifferent repose. He would have had a great career as an actor, I thought, had God not gotten hold of him first. Then again, I reflected, maybe he had the best of both.

I ordered my own coffee, plain, old, garden-variety dark roast without frills and without additives. I refused to call it "Americano," the affected café-speak for an old standby. I filled my cup from the pump dispensers on the side, grabbed a pair of muffins, and sat across from Fr. Matt on the other bench, made from an old school bus seat, shoving the green web seatbelt out of the way. I plopped a poppy seed muffin next to Fr. Matt's cup. He looked up with half a smile.

"Thanks," he said as he peeled the paper from the muffin.

He had a ritual for eating muffins — as far as I know, he had a ritual for everything. He was one of the most organized men I had ever met. First peel the paper, then disengage the top. Eat the bottom, save the top for last. I wonder what it said about me that I just did away with the paper and ate whatever part presented itself first. He was distracted this morning and ate his muffin Jane-style. I wondered what was wrong. I glanced down. Instead of his usual black slacks and loafers, jeans and sandals poked out from his cassock.

"You're out of uniform," I said.

He glanced ruefully down. "Laundry didn't come back on time. I ran out of pants. I spilled scotch on my last clean pair last night."

"Out for a drink after the chaos?" I asked.   "Certainly understandable. You should have joined Eoin Connor and me."

I squirmed a bit at the memory. In the clear light of day, all of yesterday made me uncomfortable, especially ending up in Eoin Connor's arms and sharing a whiskey with him in my quiet house.

"No. At home. It was a hard day." His response was short and tense.

Bad sign, I thought, *a priest drinking alone*. And Father Matt's demeanor did little to reassure me. I tried to make light of it for his sake and mine. More for mine.

"You know, it's all right to wear jeans now and again. It's practically a uniform in Telluride," I said, looking down at my own favorite, faded pair. I'd had them for years, and they were just the right shade of pale blue with a hint of white over the knees.

He shook his head, folded the paper, and uncrossed his legs so that the cassock covered more of the pant leg.

"Nope. Just not right." He shook himself as if to dispel his mood and pressed on with the morning pleasantries. "How are you doing this morning?"

I debated giving him a real answer instead of the usual formalities. Over the months, Father Matt had lived up to his title, becoming a real support in my life, though I tried not to acknowledge it myself, let alone let it slip to him. I looked forward to our breakfasts, and to his random visits to the Forensic Center on various pretenses. How odd it felt to have such a relationship with anyone, let alone a man nearly a generation younger than I. Fr. Matt was older than my oldest pair, but almost young enough that he really could have been my son, had I had an out-of-wedlock child at seventeen like my own mother. I thought of how hard she'd struggled all alone to raise me, momentarily sorry that she hadn't lived to enjoy the fruits of my successes.

"Ahem." Father Matt's polite cough brought me around. I was free-associating far too much lately, losing the thread of what was going on around me in random connections of thought.

"Fine." I took the easy way out. "You? What's on the agenda for today?"

"Worried about these murders, like everyone else. Nice that you are the oasis of fine-ness among the rest of us nervous types."

His brow furrowed for only an instant before he displayed a disarming grin. His heart wasn't in it. The good Father was troubled, and not as good an actor as I thought. Still, this was one reason I had to quit wool-gathering. Conversation with Fr. Matt required battle strategies. One minute, superficial pleasantries, random thoughts, one little mistake and bam! There I was, outfoxed and outgunned. At least I had ceased to be irritated either at his directness or at his persistence. I suppose that meant he was making some progress, or I was.

"Nothing seems to come together. Other than the fact that rich kids are being killed, nobody knows much." I felt safe dropping that little bit. It was common knowledge.

"Seems that way." He took another sip from his cup and changed the subject. "I did wonder how things are going with Isa and Pilar."

This time my smile was genuine. Isa and Pilar had proved to be one of the genuine lights in my life since Fr. Matt had foisted them off on me.

"Very well. We're working on getting their status regularized, but that might be difficult. My biggest problem is keeping them from working around the house. The immigration lawyer told me that I can't be seen as giving them employment, not even lodging for work, without risking her status and my hide. I swear, those women—Pilar especially—are not happy unless they are cleaning something."

"I doubt that. They just want to pay their own way. Surely you understand that." His voice was becoming more animated. Clearly, talking about the murders bothered Father Matt.

"Nice," I chided him for chiding me. "Of course, I understand. I also understand that both of them have cleaning jobs that more than validate their worth, thanks to you, and I understand involuntary time in the warm hospitality of the feds and loss of my law license. I am not sure they do. When I got up this morning, Pilar was already doing laundry. It really can't go on. You have to do something about it. I guess I'm all right being your local immigrant shelter for the time being, but really, Father Matt, there have to be some ground rules."

Thinking about it, I realized that I was more worried about taking advantage of their gratitude than I was being hauled off to court.

"I'll talk to them," he said, waving his empty cup at me. "Another?"

I hadn't finished my first and shook my head. As Fr. Matt went to the coffee bar, Eoin Connor walked into the Bean.

"Eoin," Fr. Matt said, a broad smile splitting his face with genuine affection I found surprising and surprisingly, a little annoying. "Join us! What can I get you?"

Connor shook the extended hand and looked over toward the bench where I was seated, glaring.

"No, thanks," he replied, inclining his head in my direction with what I was certain must be a knowing look at Fr. Matt.

"Nonsense. She doesn't bite. Sit down, what do you want?"

"Regular coffee. Strong. Black," Connor replied.

More annoyance. That was my drink he was ordering. He wasn't permitted to like my kind of coffee. Couldn't he drink tea? Though I admitted to myself that tea didn't seem the right drink for someone so obviously and thoroughly masculine in the old, pre-feminist sense of the word. *Rats, wool-gathering again.* I shook my head to clear it, and gestured for Connor to come and sit. At least wandering thoughts were thoughts of something other than this string of murders.

Connor stepped onto the platform in the window. Wisely, he took the seat nearest the window. *Two big men on that bench might be crowded,* I thought, but the climate would be more pleasant for him over there and it served Father Matt right for inviting suddenly unwelcome company.

"I do bite," I said.

I needed to re-establish some boundaries after last evening. Something to counteract the rush of pleasure Connor's presence gave me as he took his seat on the other bench.

"I've no doubt at all about that," Connor replied easily. "The literary muse dictates that I risk it anyway. This saves me having to track you down later today. I need the photographs from the Putnam case. Can you make me some copies?"

I thought for a minute. It was a legitimate request, and the photos were at least theoretically in my custody as medical examiner.

"Weren't they in the file Ben gave you?"

Connor shook his head. "Not a one. I need to see the ones that were entered into evidence and compare them with the rest of the photos I have — I'm wondering what kind of selection went on in choosing them for trial."

I found myself drawn into his question because it seemed so simple.

"They were chosen to make a point for the prosecution," I said. "I can tell you that even without looking at them."

"That I know, too. But there must be something they left out because they didn't need it. I might find some of that useful. Everyone knows the outcome of the trial — there's no Putnam sportswear anymore, no more Putnam jeans because Putnam's lover is marking time on death row."

I looked down at the denim of my pants. I had forgotten they were Putnams, probably collectors' items by now. I tuned back to hear Connor continuing.

"In any case, the real story is outside that. I want to know the why, the how, the good, the bad. Is Putnam the innocent in the tale? I think I know his virtues and his vices, but it's not always as simple as it seems. The pictures sometimes tell a story that the participants forgot."

That was true enough. I had seen the power of crime scene photos many times over the years, starting with my first trial. A woman had been murdered by her boyfriend. We tied him to the murder by matching the imprint of the buckle on his harness boot with a bruise on her side. Just like we would link Pelirojo to Isa by the mark of his ring.

I wasn't, however, sure what Connor meant by the power of the photos to set context. For me, their gift lay in what they proved, not what they suggested. No matter, he was entitled to them.

"I'll ask Ben to take another look. The prosecutor almost certainly still has them. I'll have him call you."

Having put the conversation to rest, I cast about for Father Matt, who was taking far too long.

He was standing by the coffee bar, talking animatedly to a well-dressed woman in pressed white shorts and a tight and low-cut sleeveless blouse, all designed to show off her perfect tan, flawless skin, ample chest and too-yellow curls showing the merest hint of dark roots. She had a multi-carat diamond band on her left hand and an older but equally perfectly tanned and well-preserved man at her side, and she could have been Marla Kincaid's older sister, so much did she resemble her.

Connor had noticed, too.

"Well, now," he said, a smile in his voice. "What's the good Father up to now?"

I felt a flare of irritation. Whatever it was, it was not important.

"He's a priest. He's up to nothing." The woman chose that moment to embrace Father Matt soundly, standing on tiptoes to reach up and bestow a kiss on his bearded cheek, then standing back, looked up at him with a decidedly adoring gaze, his two hands in hers and his mocha growing cold on the counter.

"Aye, now, you're right," Connor said. "Looks like a perfectly ordinary conversation to me."

He looked at me with devilment in his eyes over the rim of his cup.

It was nothing. It had to be nothing. Fr. Matt was a priest, entirely unconnected to those around him in any permanent, human sense. If he could live unconnected, so could I. I had staked my life on that; it was one reason I valued his friendship so much: another solitary soul making his way among the pairs and pairs around him. It had to be possible to live out a life without people to depend on, to live with, to share a house and a bed and a life with. It had to be possible to be solitary and happy. It had to be. If he could do it, so could I, but if he was just as encumbered by the traps of relationship as everyone else, what hope was there for me? My connection was gone, dead, buried.

"But he's a priest," was all I could say.

"He's celibate, not blind, and not made of stone. She's a fine looking woman," he added with an approving glance in Father Matt's direction.

The woman had disengaged herself and was waving as she exited the open door held by the older man. I scowled at Connor, willing him to leave and not to upset my world any further with his observations and innuendoes.

My mind was still spinning when Father Matt stepped across my outstretched legs to squeeze into the seat next to Connor.

"Well done, lad," said the Irishman, clapping Matt's shoulder as he sat. "And just who was that? Are your vows in jeopardy?"

"Not anymore. She was my fiancée when I was a foot soldier for Uncle Sam instead of the Church Militant. Dumped me for the stockbroker she interned with. Two husbands ago. Drove me right into the arms of Holy Mother Church."

He laughed, and I was surprised that it sounded full of good humor; he had clearly shifted mental gears again.

"It took me a while to get over it all, but it turned out for the best."

"Celibacy has its merits," Connor agreed. "There's something to be said for not answering to a woman."

"Indeed." Father Matt looked quizzical for a moment as he took in the seating arrangement, then settled in again. "Answering to the bishop, however, is not much easier. Must be nice for you—no wife, no boss, just you."

For an instant, I could have sworn I saw a cloud pass over Eoin Connor's face, but his reply was light.

"Long loneliness is better than bad company. I get on." He sipped his coffee again, and I regarded him with curiosity. He continued, "Fortunately for me, there's never a famine in crime. And this place is a ripe field indeed. That was some bad business last night."

"It was. We were just talking about it, nothing much to connect the deaths except money." Father Matt looked thoughtful. "Except for that man last night. He didn't look particularly rich to me."

Connor beat me to the punch, laughing and leaning forward to slap Father Matt on the knee, brushing against me in the process. "You've a lot to learn about this place, Father. The richest of these lot still dress like bums. That young fellow, as it turns out, was the grandson of one of the original principals of the Chicago Mercantile Exchange. Paul Kessler. Daddy is a hotshot lawyer and kingmaker in Chicago with aspirations for Washington. Seems he and that climber were boyhood buddies — their fathers worked together."

"That was fast work," I remarked. "At least we know that the pattern holds. Such as it is. Being rich in this town is no particular distinction."

Father Matt frowned. "I expect more from you, Jane," he chided. "Most of the people in this town are making a living just like anyone else."

"Only better."

Having engaged the idea, I wasn't about to let it go. If I couldn't figure out the tangles of these murders, I could, at least, be dogged about the things I did know. And among Telluride residents - not the workers that kept the town going but lived in nearby, and cheaper, places - poverty was at best a relative term. A bit like Marla Kincaid's functional indigency.

Father Matt was forced to concede the point. "Only better. So what's the reason? Why is someone so dead set," he cringed at his inadvertent malapropism "...on killing rich folks?"

"Individually," Connor added. "I suspect that there are those in town that would ditch the rich on political grounds, but only as a class. Do you think that's what's driving this?"

He seemed genuinely interested, as anxious to puzzle out the meaning of these deaths as he was to figure out what the photos of the Putnam murder told him about the victim's life.

"No idea," I admitted. "There has to be something that connects these people, at least in the mind of the murderer."

As if reading my mind, Father Matt said, "I assume the rifle that Ivanka brought down matched the bullet."

"Probably. I hope so."

The ballistics on the Kessler murder weren't back yet. If the bullet matched the one taken from Cosette Anira, Tom Patterson could still peddle his one-shooter theory. If it matched the rifle, then we'd have some chance at running down the owner from a registration. Some. Not much. When I left the Center, Norman, Lucy and Jeff were hot on the trail; there would be an answer by lunchtime. I hoped it would be one I liked.

"It is odd," Connor said. "This feels somewhere between a serial killing and a mass murder. Sort of like a school massacre, only strung out over time. As though anger, not some other compulsion — sex, thrills, money — is the motive. Makes it harder, I would expect."

I reflected on that thought. Connor was right. Some serial killings are linked by some common physical trait: girls with long brown hair, for instance, or some overtly sexual connection, like prostitutes or johns. Those are almost always personal, kinky, and have sexual overtones. These murders felt intensely personal because they were so uncannily linked to wealth, another kind of killer altogether. Despite my words to Father Matt, a series of random assaults in Telluride was at least as likely to involve a working man as a remainder-man. This was more like the enraged office worker who comes back with a shotgun after being fired. Something I didn't yet understand had given rise to truly murderous rage.

"I don't think so," Father Matt said.

I bristled at his tone more than his words, then reminded myself that he was talking to Connor, not me.

"It seems so random. Indifferent. As though the killer doesn't care whom he kills as long as he kills. Like that kid who got his jollies dropping concrete blocks off overpasses onto oncoming cars." He paused. "It's almost worse."

Connor pulled a pipe out of his pocket and began tamping tobacco absently with his thumb. He clamped it between his teeth, and with a dismissive wave, shooed away the anxious barista who hurried toward him.

"Don't worry, lass, I'm not going to light it. I just need it to think."

I was surprised at how articulate the man could be without actually moving his jaw. He continued without missing a beat, echoing the thoughts in my own mind.

"No, lad, those kinds of murders are really local, not very imaginative, and not very daring. Dropping a concrete block from a deserted interstate gives a man time to run off before anyone figures it out. Thrills, to be sure, but the thrill of a coward. Shooting from a car makes for an easy escape."

He leaned forward, elbows on his knees, unlit pipe in his right hand, punctuating his comments like a professor addressing a class.

"Same kind of killing, all of these, shot with a rifle, and a damn fine shot at that. But look at them: Town Park, broad daylight, lots of people around. Same with the one down from the church and the one last night. Gutsy. Only the climber doesn't fit in that regard, almost as if the shooter saw an opportunity he couldn't pass up."

He paused. "Then again, if the one-car accidents and that explosion are connected, it argues that the killer is decompensating. Likely to be more killings, faster, more risky. Bad for the town, but eventually he'll slip up."

He impressed me in spite of myself.

"Not bad for a crass crime writer," I said, then added, "What makes you think the others are murders other than Wilson's wild speculation?"

I hoped he might tip his hand and either confirm my fears that my last-born was the source of the annoying leak to the press, or reassure me otherwise. I should have known better. Connor just sat back, smiled and put his pipe back in his mouth. "Wilson makes sense, but if it's just the shootings in town and in Ophir, the logic still holds. Revenge, not random. Only perhaps the killer is completely in control, in which case it's going to be a long hard spell before he's caught. Which would you prefer?"

He waited, one eyebrow cocked but with the good sense not to smile.

Before I could answer, my cell phone buzzed, and I held up a hand in excuse as I answered. It was Norman with the ballistics report.

"Bad news," he said in his laconic voice. "The bullet from the victim came from the rifle, but the others didn't. Two guns."

It didn't much matter what I preferred. Two guns. Two shooters. Copycat or tag team. Take your pick. Either way, it was going to be, as Connor said, a long, hard spell.

****

They finished roofing the garage just before noon. The day was hot and sticky, and the work was hard. Roofing gave no shelter up in the sun. There were no trees, especially in this end of town, to give even a little bit of shade. Sweat trickled down Raul's back between his shoulder blades and ran stinging into his eyes. His ball cap was drenched, a blurry line of white showing the ebb and flow of perspiration as he worked.

The lady who owned this house drank something dark and sweet and very strong that she had called a sol y sombra. She'd had it in one of those odd glasses with the short stems, with the mouth much smaller than the bowl, and had nursed one drink all afternoon. She'd taken care to offer it to them one Friday at the end of the day. He sipped it and felt it burn all the way down, liquid fire, too much for a tired man. No wonder she had nursed it along all afternoon. He'd preferred a cold beer and told her so. Sol y sombra. Today, all sol, no sombra.

"Diego!" He called to his partner nailing the last of the shingles in place. "Vámanos."

It was a good stopping point, and they had business to conduct for Pelirojo. Diego lifted his head and nodded in acknowledgement, taking his straw hat off and drawing his red kerchief across his forehead. He stood and hopscotched across the roof, climbing down the ladder just after the balding man in the blue tee-shirt who had called his name. They met a third man, Luis, by the burn barrel. He was older and a little taller, barrel-chested, with a drooping dark mustache. He acknowledged them with a squint and a scowl, authority and anger in his bearing. He was Pelirojo's right-hand man, mean, hard and cunning just like Pelirojo, but without the size and the connections to be anything more than Pelirojo's peon. Still, not a man to cross.

Diego listened in silence as the two other men conversed in hushed voices about the woman who was causing Pelirojo all the trouble, and how he had instructed them to take care of her. A chill went down his spine, fear mingled with anger and helplessness. He wanted to stop them but had no way. He made good money as a roofer, but most of it went home to his mother and baby sister, who had no way to survive since Papá had died. He'd gratefully accepted a place to stay at the big house, needing the comfort of familiar sounding voices and the smell of home-cooked food. He had been so lonely and so homesick.

The little one, Isa, had been particularly kind, always setting aside a dish of food for him, so that no matter how late he came in, there was something warm and good to eat. She didn't say much; she was shy, but she would smile at him when she passed him his plate, and his world sang.

He never heard exactly what had happened, but the fire in his belly told him that Pelirojo had finally decided to take her like he took anything else he wanted. Diego had wanted to stand up to him, to beat him for what he did and to make him pay, but the plain fact was that he was afraid. Afraid of being killed, for Pelirojo was twice his size or better and without a conscience. Afraid of being sent back, for everyone knew that if the police ever got their hands on a Mexican, it was into jail and back across the border. He couldn't afford that, so he had spent the days since in miserable, shameful silence. Only the work on the roof, sweating out his disgrace in the hot sun helped, and that not for long.

The two other men finished their negotiations and looked around the work site casually. It was lunch break, and the dozen or so workers on the site had sorted themselves out into various spots of shade, opening lunch boxes and drinking from cold, dripping bottles of water. One of the older men had started up a small grill and was making fajitas his daily habit. The smell of cooking meat and onions drifted across the site and made Diego's mouth water. It went dry again as he heard the voices calling him on, arms beckoning and faces threatening.

"Vámanos. Isa nos espera." *Come on, she is waiting.*

Diego's reluctant steps followed the two as they headed up the street to the big green house that stood near the entrance to the trail that went up the mountain. The men had assumed an air of casual friendship, chatting about nothing, gesturing at each other, just workmen walking among ever-remodeling neighborhoods, invisible because they were so common. Diego lagged behind, desperate to escape and afraid to do so, knowing what was coming and powerless to stop it.

****

The foreman, a slim, aristocratic-looking man, watched the three of them disappear. Raul and Luis were up to no good, that he was certain of. He'd caught a few words of their conversation, despite their whispers. Something about a woman, a payment. With these two, it always was. It made him angry. His family had come here many generations ago, living in New Mexico, then Colorado, ranching, mining, keeping shops. He still had family in Sonora, and he loved both his countries. It made him angry that these two filled up all the dark and fearful fantasies the Anglos had about Mexicans. They brought disgrace to him, to his family, to his profession, to his culture. He was sorry the boss had ever hired them, but he hadn't been able to find a good excuse to fire them yet. They were on time, and they worked hard. He suspected that the big red-headed guy who had brought them to the site until recently made sure of that.

His eyes narrowed as he followed their disappearing figures. They still wore their tool belts, unusual. Most men couldn't shed them fast enough at break. And there was poor Diego, their lap dog. Diego was a nice kid, honest, hardworking, even taking time on Fridays to go up to the little church nearby for Mass at noon. The foreman knew he sent most of his money home; that was why he'd ended up living with those two thieves.

He saw them turn up a distant street. Something was very wrong, and he couldn't put his finger on it. He decided to follow along, distancing himself far enough back that Diego wouldn't see. He flipped open his cell phone to make certain it was working. You never knew around here. He was gratified. What did that silly commercial say? More bars in more places? He had plenty of bars.

****

Pilar was just finishing the dishes. Señora Doctora had a fine kitchen, but Pilar had never seen her use it. Ever since she had arrived more than a week ago, Pilar had taken it as her own domain. It reminded her of the hotel restaurant she had worked in before coming here: big, efficient, the best of appliances and pots and pans. It gave her great joy to make good things come out of it and to care for it. The lady doctor had resisted turning it over to Pilar, but when she finally had, her tired, sad eyes told Pilar she was grateful not to have to worry about cooking. Perhaps the best was being able to go to the market — the big, fancy one in the Village — and get anything she wanted. Anything.

She still couldn't imagine the luxury of making something other than rice and beans for two of the day's three meals. And the lady doctor complimented her and ate it all, though not enough, not nearly enough.

Ignacio, Mariela and Pablo were playing hide-and-seek in the house.

Pablo had begged to stay home today with the two older ones rather than go to the center at the church, and Isa had indulged him, kissing him before heading off into town to clean one of the big houses near the entrance to town. She would be back soon for lunch. Lupe had gone to Montrose to work for the day and would not be back before dark. That left Pilar in charge of the house and the kids. Missing her own grown brood, that suited her just fine. This was a beautiful house. It was a joy to keep it clean. At first, the lady doctor had tried to tell her she couldn't, something about being arrested for letting her work.

Such nonsense. Arrested for cooking and cleaning! It was ridiculous, and she had told her so. They had squared off in the front hall, making polite arguments back and forth until finally, by sheer persistence, Pilar had won. It was the same technique she had used with her stubborn husband, Dios le bendice, and her children, and it still worked. She wiped the last of the counter clean just as the children piled noisily in to sit at the granite center island, clamoring for lunch.

Pablo was the last to wiggle his way into the tall chair. He was so much like her own. She ruffled his hair even as she scolded him for reaching for a cookie from the jar in the middle of the table. He smiled up at her, slipping his hand back from the tempting vessel. Ignacio, seated next to him, turned his attention to the keys that Señora Doctora had left on the table. He was turning them over in his hand, using them as a noisemaker to taunt Mariela when Isa walked in from the front hall. Ignacio stood up in his chair, welcoming Isa with open arms and a broad smile.

Isa hugged him and extracted the keys from his hands.

"You mustn't play with this, Nacio," she said. "It's not a toy." She showed him the electronic fob. "Besides, this is an alarm. To protect the car. If you push it by accident, it makes noise and the police will come. What will you say to them if they come, Nacio?" She was scolding, but her eyes were kind. It was obvious to anyone how much she loved this one, almost as much as her own son. She laid the keys on the counter and kissed the chubby hands. "Go wash, Nacio. Your hands are dirty."

Ignacio started to argue but decided it was futile. He climbed down from the chair and crossed from the kitchen to the small bath off the hallway. Isa was relieved to hear the sound of running water and turned to greet the other children and Pilar, who was taking lunch meat from the big white refrigerator. Isa gave her a quick hug before pulling the bread from the roll-front cabinet on the counter, and pulling a knife from the block to slice the tomatoes that lay on the cutting board.

She had started on the second one when the back door burst open at the hands of two men. Pilar started and dropped a plastic glass decorated with saddles and ropes and cowboy hats onto the floor. It bounced away, making a hollow clatter.

"Dios mío!"

Pilar stepped back as the men strode into the room toward Isa, confident and menacing. The older, bigger one brandished a hammer from his tool belt. Pilar scooped Mariela and Pablo into her protective arms and backed away toward the door. The men ignored her. The smaller man reached Isa first, strutting and speaking in rapid Spanish.

"So what did you think you were doing, trying to get rid of Pelirojo? After all he did for you. Ungrateful witch."

He pushed Isa roughly as the second man approached.

****

Something flared in Isa, and she whirled around to face him squarely. She was not afraid, not anymore, not living here in comfort and security. The knife went from produce to assailant, opening a gash on the man's right arm, just below the dirty shirt sleeve, then another across his face.

He screamed in pain and dropped back, cursing her as the other pushed him aside, swinging the hammer wildly in Isa's direction. She ducked and the hammer came crashing down on the granite counter. She heard it split and heard him curse with the shock of metal on stone. She stabbed the knife blindly and felt it hit. The hammer clattered to the floor as the second man screamed and caught her by one hand, the other clutching the side of his leg where his jeans were rapidly staining. He pulled Isa aside, wide, making an arc to slam her into the broken counter when the kitchen exploded with sound. Loud, violent, wailing sound, an alarm.

It was enough distraction for Isa to pull away, brandishing the knife in front of her, Pilar and the children cowering in the corner behind her. Panic crossed the faces of both men, brutes but cowards. They cursed again, but ran from the kitchen leaving the screen door to clatter behind them.

Isa stood still for a moment, unsure what had happened, fright washing over her at last in a delayed wave, making her knees weak and her hands shake. She placed the knife carefully on the counter and traced the break in the stone as she tried to collect her thoughts and stop her heart from racing. She was finally brought around by Ignacio, one hand pulling persistently on the hem of her shirt, the other holding the forbidden keys.

"Tia Isa, when will the police come? I know what I'll say."

Isa scooped him up in a hug that Ignacio squirmed to end.

CHAPTER NINETEEN

JUNE 14, AFTERNOON

I was deep in thought, pondering a request from a Hollywood producer to assist as medical advisor for a new medical thriller. It was one of the occupational hazards of my position and notoriety, and provided a lucrative source of income for the Center, though working with directors that had little aptitude for taking direction themselves made for a challenge. At least in these days of electronic media, I could consult from the comfort of my very own book-lined office if I wanted, checking in on distant sets by videoconferencing.

It had the added advantage of letting me mute the rantings of various creative types when I told them something they didn't want to hear. This script was unusual, well crafted by someone who actually had some understanding of medicine. I wondered how the director would manage to foul it up, but it intrigued me enough that I was inclined to accept the job.

I had just turned the page to the climactic scene when Tina put a call through. It was Pilar speaking in rapid-fire Spanish. Although my high school fluency had improved greatly since opening up a halfway house for assorted Mexican immigrants, I still relied a lot on gestures and visual cues. Trying to follow Spanish over the phone was still impossible, and Pilar was clearly excited. My "Despacio, por favor!" got lost in a current of words that I couldn't begin to separate. Except for "Isa," "Nacio" and "Pelirojo." And "Policía." I dropped the phone, yelling for Quick, Lucy, Norman, Ben — anyone — to give me a ride back to the house.

Norman came through, tossing me a helmet that I put on as we barreled down the back stairs to the alley where he kept his motorcycle. It's only three blocks up and one over to my house, but it seemed like an eternity before we reached the drive, and Norman broke every speed and traffic law he encountered on the way. Fortunately for us, the marshall and his deputy were already occupied at my big, green

Victorian manse. I tossed back the helmet with thanks and waved Norman off, not even breaking stride as I rushed up the back stairs and into the kitchen.

I have a big kitchen, but it was full to overflowing. Pilar and the three children were off to one side, the children sitting wide-eyed on the side counter, Pilar interrupting their conversations — in excited, high-pitched Spanish rather than their carefully acquired English — with stern and maternal tones. Isa was standing at the counter by the window, which I noticed with passing dismay, was rent by a huge crack through the middle. The marshall was half-seated against one of the barstools at the center island, talking with a tall and courtly Latin man while a shorter man, obviously a working man in stained shirt and dirty jeans, stood by with fearful eyes. I noticed his hands were cuffed behind him, but he stood quietly in the custody of a wiry deputy about his own height and weight, but as Anglo as he was Latin.

There was blood on the counter and on the floor, and I looked around again in panic. None of mine seemed to be injured, and I wondered with now detached concern what the bloodshed had been.

Only one way to find out.

"Grant," I addressed the marshall, whose back had been to me. He turned and stood up, extending a hand.

"Doc. I was going to call you, just hadn't got to it yet. How'd you know what happened?"

"I don't." I inclined my head towards Pilar, who shifted her weight so that I could see the telephone on the counter next to Pablo. "Pilar called me. All I heard was Isa's name and Pelirojo. And 'police.' What happened?"

The sensitivity police would probably have my innards for not asking if everyone was all right, but dammit, I could see that. I wanted answers.

Isa spoke up. "Pelirojo. He sent men to frighten me. To harm me." She paused, glancing at the children to make sure Pilar had them sufficiently occupied, then dropped her voice to a whisper and added, "To kill me."

The bottom dropped out of my stomach, very much the way it had when they'd called me to tell me about John. When once you realize that "kill" and "dead" are not just terms reserved for other people, it has a way of reorienting your life, and not in a pleasant way. I felt my face go white and pulled out one of the chairs to sit before I fell. I had come to Telluride because it was so distant and so safe. I'd read the police blog in the daily paper. No one died here, at least not by another person's hand. This was supposed to be an oasis of civility and safety. Nice theory not borne out by facts, at least not lately.

I looked at Grant. "And....?" I said. "Who are these guys? Are they the ones? And what about the blood?"

My temper suddenly flared, fear replaced by rage.

"No," he indicated the taller, older man, "Gus is the foreman on a job down at the end of town. Diego here works with him, along with two other fellows. Gus saw them leave the site at noon, figured they were up to no good, followed them. He saw them, all three, come up on to your back porch, then a few minutes later, heard an alarm go off, then saw them all run out of the house like bats out of hell. He caught Diego here, but the other two got away. Called 911 on his cell."

He glanced at Diego. He must have seen the anger in my face, because he backed up a step and began to speak rapidly.

"No, Señora, it's not like that. The other two, they were the ones. They made me come along, but I didn't come in, I stayed back. I didn't do it."

His face was pleading. I looked at Isa.

"It's true. He wasn't one of them."

Her face was pitying but not angry. Diego was a coward, perhaps, but at least in Isa's eyes, not a thug.

My gaze went to Gus. I knew it was Grant's job to sort this out, but my pushy nature hadn't been improved by the fact that had these thugs succeeded, I would have been in charge of the death scene. In my own kitchen.

"I saw him go on to the porch. I saw nothing else."

Gus shifted his weight, but met my eyes and kept his confident bearing.

"When the alarm went off, he was the first one to run away. And the easiest to catch." He shrugged. "One of the others limped, the other was holding his arm. This one is unmarked. Perhaps he is telling the truth."

There was that alarm again. Although the house was equipped with an alarm system, I'd never activated it. Not only was Telluride a place I thought safe, I'd never thought that the house contained anything precious enough to protect, least of all me. Looking at Isa, Pilar and the children, and thinking about Ben, I realized with a start that it did house something — in fact, a great deal — that I did not want to lose. I resolved to call the company in the morning. A panic button would be a nice touch.

"Alarm?" Now I was truly confused.

Grant chuckled, pointed over to Ignacio, now thoroughly occupied, as were the others, with a cookie that Pilar had quietly produced from the jar on the counter.

"That little rascal got hold of your car keys and pressed the alarm button. When I showed up, he ran right up to me to tell me I took too long, the bad men got away. Smart kid. Nervy."

I shook my head, not really able to take it all in. "So what about the others?"

"We'll get 'em. I've got two of the deputies off looking for them, and Tom Patterson has his guys on the lookout. Called Montrose, too. Diego here tells me that's where they all live."

Indeed. The gray ranch house on the edge of town. They might run, but sooner or later, one of Telluride's finest, or San Miguel County's best, would bring them to heel. Good.

Grant stood up, motioned to the deputy.

"Let's go, get Diego locked up."

He glanced back at me. "Will you bring these two down to make a statement? Send your crew up to take blood samples? When I catch those guys, I want to be able to tie this up nice and tight, no escape." He rolled the toothpick that was perpetually in his mouth from one side to the other. "I hate men who bully women."

"Sure thing."

My cell phone was already in hand, dialing the office for Norman to come back up, and I watched as Grant Holmes and his deputy escorted Diego out of my kitchen. Gus followed at a respectful distance, pausing in the door and turning back to me.

"I hate them too," he said, then added something in Spanish to Isa and Pilar that I didn't catch. Whatever it was, from the looks on their faces, it was exactly the right thing.

****

Norman showed up with Ben a few minutes later. I was pleased that my last-born was concerned enough to check in on his mom and those he now regarded as his "bonus" family. He greeted the children with hugs and chocolates from his desk-drawer stash, and sandwiches I had asked him to pick up from Baked in Telluride, Telluride's all purpose bakery and sandwich shop that was down the street from the Center. I had finally convinced Pilar that any attempt on her part to finish making lunch might compromise the police's ability to convict the men that had threatened them.

Reluctantly, she abandoned the kitchen to Norman and we all went onto the back porch to eat. We'd fill Ben in later, after the children were fed and tucked in for an afternoon nap. No sense in causing them any more stress by rehashing the day's events in front of them. I'd already called Father Matt to alert him, and had no doubt that he was even now arranging appropriate counseling for Isa, Pilar and the children.

Good thing. I was lousy at that, I had discovered to my own dismay. It was a wonder my own children had recovered so well from their father's death. I'd certainly been no help. Pilar had taken the children upstairs, and Ben had wiped the last of the mayonnaise from the scraggly, pale mustache he was trying to cultivate in an effort to be hip or be more adult —I wasn't sure which — when I got a call from the marshall.

"Got 'em."

No one could accuse Grant Holmes of verbosity.

"Picked 'em up just outside Ridgway, off the side of a side road."

He chuckled.

"Two flat tires. Nails from the construction site. Who says God doesn't have a sense of humor?" A pause, then, "Thought you'd want to know."

"Thanks," I replied. "What about Diego? Isa was pretty insistent after you left that he wasn't involved."

"It wasn't him," she'd said. "He's a good man, a kind man, just a scared one, a weak one. Pelirojo has so much power, Diego is afraid. We all are. But he likes me, he's kind, he wouldn't hurt me."

I could visualize Grant shaking his head as he answered.

"No go. Diego was there. Gus caught him red-handed. I'm inclined to believe Isa, but I've got to let the judge sort it all out. From where I stand, it looks like a three-man conspiracy. The other two say that Diego was part of it from the start, that he was on his way in when the alarm went off and he got scared and ran."

That part fit, at least. The "scared and ran" part.

"When's arraignment?"

"Tomorrow. Don't forget to get those ladies down for a statement."

"Be there within the hour."

I pocketed my phone and looked over at my son, explaining what had happened. He looked at me, perplexed.

"Why don't you just take the video down to the marshall's office?"

"Video?" It was my turn to look perplexed. "What video?"

Ben pointed up to the overhang of the porch. There, in the corner of the eave was a tiny camera, pointed out over the back of the house.

"There are six or seven of them all around the house. They work on motion detectors, see?"

He stood up, moving across the porch, and sure enough, a tiny light came on and the camera swiveled to follow him. *Bless Tommy Berton, he'd really done the system up right.*

"I never activated the alarm system, Ben," I said. "Too bad, it would have been a big help."

Ben rolled his eyes in exasperation, that how-do-you-find-the-door-in-the-morning-without-my-help look that I thought had passed with his entry into college. Apparently not.

"This is part of the system, but it isn't monitored by an alarm company. It feeds into a recorder that probably cycles through its memory every week or so. It's in the back closet in the laundry room; haven't you noticed it?"

"Of course, I noticed it. I just didn't know what it was. Is."

"Oh, Mom."

It was a never-ending source of amazement how much disdain my kids could work into that one syllable when the situation called for it.

"So how do we look at the tape?"

Another eye-roll.

"No tape. This is digital. I'll find a disc and burn a copy for the marshall. You can save it to the hard drive on your own computer, too. Come on, I'll show you."

I followed my son back into the house, to the closet that housed the little black box that linked up to my silent sentries. *Odd, how one criminal's paranoia might send another to jail*, I thought, as Ben slipped a disc into the system and pressed a few buttons. Not two minutes later, we were sitting at my computer, watching a video of my side door. I saw two men mount the steps, motioning to a third, who came slowly, reluctance and fear obvious in his bearing. I saw the two disappear into the house while Diego stayed behind, shifting, agitated, his eyes casting about the porch, but making no move to enter. In fact, I saw him straighten his spine and start for the steps, only to stop, looking around, startled. The alarm must have sounded. But when it did, he was already on his way off the porch, not on his way into the house.

"Nicely done, Ben." I said. "Who knew? This is great."

Ben shrugged his thin shoulders in his nonchalant way.

"I can't believe you didn't know that was there. You see everything."

Not everything, I thought. *Somehow I failed to see how competent you've become, how thoroughly capable.*

"Yeah, well, we all have our off days." I said. "Besides, this is computer stuff, not crime scene stuff."

Ben grinned. "It *was* this time, and you," he emphasized his statement by pointing at me with both hands and finishing dramatically, "missed it. You're losing your touch, old woman."

"And you're going to lose your cushy job and soft life if you keep that up. I'm still your mom." I smiled to telegraph that I was proud of him. "How about taking that down to the marshall's office? I'll be along with Isa and Pilar in a bit."

"Sure thing. Want me to save the file first?"

He was already punching keys in anticipation of my response.

"Please."

If Ben saved it, I knew it would be there. When I did it, I was never quite sure. Computers were my lifeline, but it was definitely a love-hate kind of relationship, and my ability to erase, lose and never really save important files was legendary among my family, friends and associates. So legendary they referred to any sort of IT disaster as the "Wallace Effect."

As he was leaving, a thought crossed my mind.

"Ben, would the surveillance cover the back parking area where Kessler was shot?"

"I think so. It wouldn't make sense to set up the system and not cover the parking areas. I can check."

"Would it still be on the tape?"

"Hard drive."

"Whatever. Would it still be there?"

"Probably. Probably. Maybe. I don't know," he finally admitted, but the significance of the discovery was beginning to dawn on him. We almost ran back to the laundry room to download the rest of the data.

It took a few minutes to pick out the input from that particular camera. The lens covered the porch, but in the distance, I could see the parking lot and a portion of the adjacent road. Ben fast-forwarded through the images until we saw Kessler standing in the gravel of the drive, looking down over the backyard, probably enjoying the view and the sound of the creek. The image was blurrier than the one from the porch; it was in fading light rather than the broad light of day.

"Go backwards," I barked. "Now. I don't want to see the rest."

It had been enough to find Kessler dead; I didn't need to see it. What

I wanted was to find out whether the video feed would give any clues to his killer.

Ben obliged. The images were intermittent because the system only activated when someone wandered into the actual perimeter of the drive. Even so, that meant there was a record of some of the traffic on the day, including images of Eoin bundling me into the 4Runner and taking me to the clinic. I was shocked; did I really look that frumpy? It was clear I needed a good haircut, and fast.

Scolding myself for vanity, I concentrated on the time between my departure and Kessler's appearance. Because of the angle and the off-on recording, some of the images were fragmentary; I saw portions of legs and arms passing out of edge the frame in the distance. I recognized the shorts of one of the girls who had brought Ivanka down from the trail. The best images followed a dog's appearance in my drive: several young men, one of whom hurried up to retrieve the errant canine from my porch. *Amazing what went on in my absence*, I reflected. As he pulled the dog back with him to the road, I caught glimpses of several others heading up the road, including Ivanka herself, her bulky pack on her back, walking with determination.

I sighed. *Nice try*. What did I expect, someone strolling up in view of my camera, rifle in plain view? Besides, there was no assurance the killer had come up by the house, though it certainly seemed likely. I pushed away from my desk as the Kessler images came into view again.

"Copy that off, too, Ben, would you, and take it over to Tom Patterson. It's not much, but he might find something useful."

"Sure thing." He slipped another disc in. I left him to his machinations and went to my study to call Eric Johanssen. He might just like another slam-dunk client to get off the hook, and Diego was a likely candidate.

****

Tom Patterson replayed the file Ben Wallace had brought over for a second, then a third time. He recalled Ben's story of how they had found it. *Damn*, he thought, *that rascal is smart, smarter even than his mother, and that's saying something*. Ben said he'd delivered video to Grant Hudson, too, video that clearly corroborated Diego's story. Push come to shove, Grant would be letting him go, probably in the morning.

The marshall had called Patterson earlier, partly out of courtesy, partly to feed the law enforcement grapevine, and partly because his attempted murder case interfaced with the rape case Patterson was already working.

In the meantime, though, Patterson knew Grant would have a run at trying to get something out of him that might give the court a better handle on the two other hoodlums they had arrested, and maybe that red-haired bastard that had raped that little Mexican girl. Patterson's fist clenched involuntarily as the thought passed through his mind. He spent a lot of time with criminals, most of them petty in this county, thank God, but there was a special place in hell for rapists and child killers. Dale Cutter was a fine lawyer, and she'd use the information to the best advantage tomorrow in court. So, probably, would that mouthpiece Doc Wallace reportedly had hired for the Mexican. Patterson had no doubt that a duplicate file was on its way to Montrose even now. News travels fast in a small town, faster still now that people carried the internet in their pockets.

She was an odd one, Doc Wallace. She came to town all alone and took up residence, knocking about that big old mansion all by herself, working day and night to convince the state to set her up as forensic guru of the Western Slope, which they had done with great joy once they figured out it wouldn't cost them much. He was glad she had — she was first rate — but she'd remained apart from everything and everyone. Except maybe that priest. Word had it that she was the one that paid his salary. And now lately, she seemed to be running an illegal alien boarding house. It was out of character for her, he thought, but an improvement over that fervent isolation she had brought with her over a year ago. He'd never known anyone so distant, not a cop, not a coroner, not even a killer.

Not even a killer, he reflected. *Well, at least we know poor Diego isn't a killer,* he thought with satisfaction. That would cheer up the little Mexican girl that the other one had tried to murder, at Pelirojo's behest, he was certain. Patterson himself would make a visit to Diego later this afternoon. He smiled with satisfaction. This time they might actually close the noose on old Pelirojo. It pleased him to no end to think so.

He watched the video of people coming and going around Jane Wallace's house the afternoon Kessler was killed. He called in the deputy who'd been there to work the crime scene to look at it with him one last time. Two sets of eyes were better than one. Besides, Jeff was known for his attention to detail. If there were something significant there, he would see it for sure. Patterson had learned in his almost too many years of experience to supplement his own shortcomings with the strength of his staff. Not everyone did.

Jeff brought the sheriff a soft drink — cold sugar and caffeine from the machine in the hall. Patterson liked his sodas like he did everything else: real and rich. He never understood the people who drank caffeine-free, diet sodas. What was the point? Chemicals and water. It was like walking though life half-asleep. For better or worse, Tom Patterson had his eyes open and his mind at the ready. He thought it made him a better cop, but he wasn't entirely sure.

"Take notes, Jeff—I want to talk to everyone you can identify that went up that road that day," Patterson said. "If we can pull images off this, let's make the rounds of the hotels and see whether we can identify the ones we don't know, the tourists."

"Needle in a haystack, Tom," Jeff said placidly. "We've already put out the word, and no one has come forward. If we noise it around that Doc Wallace has a video surveillance, someone's likely to come forward, all right, but maybe just to file a nuisance suit, claim she hasn't any right to film them. Personally, I wouldn't think you would want to run the risk of putting a damper on things like this — too valuable."

Patterson sighed. Jeff was probably right. Patterson himself was as respectful of civil liberties as the next guy, but it sometimes got a little crazy here. Doc Wallace would win a suit if anyone brought one; at least he thought she would, but only after a fight. And she was an attractive target with all that money in the bank. Balance was everything. No need to poke that particular sleeping bear.

"Fair enough. Let's just see what we can find. If we identify anyone, you can tell them someone saw them going up the road that day."

White lies in the interests of justice were okay, even to his Baptist deacon daddy. It was only a small omission to leave out that the "someone" was really a tidy little digital camera in the service of a woman who didn't even know she had owned it.

The two of them watched the file in silence, two, three, then four times over, until they had compiled a reasonable list. It was surprising how many people they knew went up that way that particular day. Maybe it meant that Coronet Creek and Judd Weibe were really local favorites like the guidebooks said. Maybe it meant that Patterson's directive to get to know as many of the residents as possible was bearing a little fruit. In any case, they had a list of five or six names.

"None of these look like they'll know much of anything," Jeff remarked. "I already talked to that old lady, Mrs. Kovacs, and the girls she was with."

"Talk to them again. They might have remembered something."

Patterson forwarded the file to the spot that showed Kessler being shot. He was almost out of the frame. The camera caught the bottom half of Kessler's dusty tunic. He had been looking over the creek from the empty parking space that Doc Wallace invariably used. He had walked back to the road, and the video caught the bottom half of his tunic.

He could almost feel the bullets hit. There was a jerk to the rhythm of the flowing tunic, out of sync with the fluid motion of walking and the breath of the breeze against its folds, then Kessler staggered forward. He fell almost immediately, and the camera caught him reaching his hand out, grabbing some of the gravel in the drive in a fruitless effort to regain his feet or make his way to safety.

"At least this time, Doc Wallace will be able to answer the question about time to death," Jeff remarked.

For reasons no cop ever really understood, the state attorney always wanted to know time of death, always asked how much the victim had suffered. It rankled Patterson. Was quick death somehow better? Was it less odious to smother a sleeping baby than to shoot a sentient man? Murder was murder and Tom Patterson had no use for it. The great measure of the pain lay not in the one who died, but in the ones left behind. That, he supposed, Jane Wallace could testify about with great authority.

"Yeah. Suppose so." Patterson flicked off the video. "Not much here, but I'd better call Doc Wallace and thank her for sending it."

Jeff paused at the door. "Did you see the ballistics report? Two guns at least. Do you think this is a copycat?"

Patterson's temper flared. "Damn it, Jeff, I don't know. Two guns. Two shooters? Two with the same agenda? I can't connect the victims; I haven't got a clue as to who did it. I have no idea why. Until I do, we are not releasing any more information to the press, we are not speculating, and we are working our asses off to figure this thing out. The town is getting to be a ghost town. Anyone who can leave has. The ones who are left are jumpy as cats. And we are not, repeat not, buying into Wilson's cockamamie theory that those accidents are part of this whole pattern. Bad enough people are worried about being out on the streets in town. If they think they aren't even safe in their cars, we're really going to have problems."

Jeff held up a hand and shook his head. "I'm not arguing with you, boss. Still, it seems odd, and Doc Wallace has pretty good instincts. I took a look at the stuff Ben put together and I've got to admit—it's worrisome."

Patterson remembered the spreadsheet the red-headed Wallace kid had left with the disc. It troubled him, too, and the pattern fit. Even he wanted desperately for them to be accidents. The cop in him knew there had to be a reason. These killings weren't just random no matter how much he tried to convince himself. Still, with a County Commission to answer to and a Visitors' Bureau that took a dim view of doing anything to upset the tourism apple-cart at the same time they were screaming for him to protect the public, he was loathe to move ahead until he was sure, and not only was he not sure, he didn't have a clue. It nagged at him that being sure might mean that there was another body in Doc Wallace's morgue. Then again, with nothing to go on, how could he do anything but raise blood pressures? If God himself told him to go out and prevent the next murder, he wouldn't know where to start.

"Get the hell out of here and get started on those interviews," he growled, angry at his own impotence.

Jeff cocked an eyebrow and backed out of the door, closing it softly. Tom Patterson reloaded the file for the umpteenth time. Maybe there was something he missed.

****

The deputy on the other side of the door leaned against the wall, with a worried look on his face. Patterson was still looking at the tape for something he missed. Jeff was trying to forget something he had seen and wished he hadn't. On the edge of the screen, among the parade of people going past Jane Wallace's house, there was a familiar cowboy boot, one with an artful metal tip. Tom Patterson's boot. What had he been doing on the road to the trailhead that afternoon?

CHAPTER TWENTY

JUNE 15

"The slugs are all .22s," I told Tom as I pushed the reports across the desk at him. "And both the one from Kessler and the one from the Hummer match the gun Ivanka Kovacs brought down. The others are different. Same caliber, same class, but not the same gun. Two guns. Two shooters. I think we've got a tag team here, Tom. Two killers with the same agenda but two guns."

Tom looked thoughtful, but I knew he wasn't really reading the reports I had given him. He was trying to find a way around the data, something that would spare him standing up in front of a camera and admitting we had not one, but two, certifiable crazies in town, picking off the hapless and, until recently, unarmed residents of Telluride.

He finally grunted in agreement. "All right, you've convinced me." Then, as an afterthought, he added a hearty, "Damn! Though I suppose it's better than having a lunatic and a copycat. At least a tag team ought to have the same motive, similar history. Find one, we'll find the other. Maybe..."

"Look at this." I pointed to the timeline Ben had prepared, the one sitting on top of the spreadsheet that had started this whole thing with his analysis of the demographics of death in Telluride. "First trusty death was the explosion, isolated up on Silver Pick. Nobody around. One on the jeep trail to Bridal Veil Falls a week later. The next two on the road into town, there at that high curve above the river. Then Town Park, the Ophir Wall and Aspen Street. Then my backyard. The killers are getting gutsier. And it seems they have to know their victims for all of them to be so wealthy. So what's the connection?"

Patterson sighed and held up a hand. "Stop, stop!" He tossed the spreadsheet aside in disgust at the situation, not at himself or me, and certainly not at Ben. "Nothing holds these cases together, at least nothing I can see."

"Ben couldn't find anything either, other than the fact that these people were all rich kids who relocated here from somewhere else."

"So has most of Telluride. You can't swing a dead cat in this town without hitting a trust funder."

"Two killings, in cars, on the road into town. I wonder if that means something?"

"Of course, it does. We just don't know what." Tom leaned back in his chair and put his hands behind his head, looking up at the ceiling. "The murders started in the spring. Maybe they're linked to something else that happened in the spring."

"Like what?"

The legs of Patterson's chair sounded sharply against the tile floor of the office as he brought himself upright again.

"If I knew that, I'd have this solved. Why don't you set that boy of yours on that one?"

He sounded irritated, and I responded in kind.

"No need to be pissy, Tom. If it weren't for Ben, neither one of us would have connected the dots on this. Not all of the dots, anyway."

There was a short silence, then Tom spoke again. "I suppose so. Even so, he's probably got the best shot of all of us at figuring out who is responsible. Turn him loose, please."

"I couldn't stop him if I tried, Tom. He's run a bunch of different analyses, but so far nothing other than the trust fund connection. Of course, there's nothing much to cross-analyze either. Ben can't even figure out how the victims were chosen."

"Maybe they're random, then, after all."

I didn't like that idea. It was hard enough to figure out connections when they were predictable at some level. Random murders were much harder.

"I don't think so, Tom. This is a killer with an agenda. There's always a connection. It looks like someone has a real grudge against trust fund babies. The question is why, and how did the killer find out the victims were trust funders, and how did he know where and when to kill them?"

"You got me. Have Ben keep working on it. Maybe if he and Jeff work on it together they'll come up with something."

I knew Jeff was the sheriff's right-hand tech man. He and Ben spent a lot of time over coffee talking about the latest in computer advances. I had listened a couple of times. It made my head spin.

"I will. I don't need to, but I will." I started out of the office, then paused at the door to look back at Patterson. "Where are you on the Houston murder?"

Our celebrity killing had gotten lost amid the rest of the mayhem my office was handling, and I hadn't touched base with Patterson since the day of the arraignment.

Patterson scowled and tossed the morning paper at me. Wilson had been hard at it again.

"Turns out Houston was a trust fund kid, too. His old man is some sort of genius engineer with a boatload of patents. It is the considered opinion of the local press that Houston's murder fits in this series, too, so now all of Mountain Village is in an uproar. Never mind the fact that Houston was shot in the comfort of his own home, at close range and with a different caliber gun."

He pounded the edge of his desk with his fist in frustration. His foam coffee cup teetered from the impact, and he caught it just as it went over, sending a brown spray across the papers on his desk. He swore under his breath as he grabbed from the waste-basket at the side of his desk.

I said nothing as I watched him mop up the spreading coffee. I'm used to dealing with death, even with murder. It's part and parcel of my work. I am not used to hitting a brick wall in putting the pieces of a murder together.

"The heat's got to be on you, Tom. How is it that you've managed to keep any kind of lid on this, especially with Wilson at work?"

"I've called in every chit I've got. The governor's been on the phone to me twice this week already, wanting to set up some sort of task force, to send in the National Guard to protect the town. I managed to talk him out of it, for now at least. That's all we need to really set off a full-scale panic, especially since about half the town thinks the murderer has to be some sort of deranged veteran." He paused. "Veterans, I guess, in light of the ballistics. Whoever it is, is one helluva marksman. I'm not sure I could make those shots myself."

He made one last pass with the napkin and pointed to a report, now half-brown with stain.

I leaned over the desk, looking at Ben's summary of the range data. The longest shot was the one in Ophir, nearly a hundred yards. Town Park was a little less, about eighty yards. There was no guess at the range on the shot that killed Cosette Anira and no idea where the shot had come from. The dense clump of trees that had almost certainly concealed Paul Kessler's killer was only about 50 yards from where the blood spatter indicated he had been hit.

"Good distance, " I agreed. "But how in the world does this guy get around town with a rifle, shoot people in the middle of the day and never get caught?"

Tom Patterson's voice was glum, but his answer was as good as any I had.

"Ghost, maybe?"

****

Pete Wilson sat back in his chair and looked at his computer screen, satisfied. It was a good try and who knows, in this day and age, it might get him some notice. He had no real desire to go back to living in the city; life in this little Colorado town was sweet. The work wasn't hard, the people were pleasant, and he was something of a celebrity in his own right. Still, he had that urge to be noticed and to shake things up by his own might. That was hard in a town full of celebrities. The local newspaperman was just one more transplanted local among others, part of the great unwashed.

This story might change all that. The town was stewing in its own fear, thanks, he liked to think, in part to his reporting of the murders. Hell, a couple of homicides a day wasn't all that unusual in the Chicago beat, but how rapidly murder and chaos had descended into Telluride stunned even him. People were afraid, afraid in a way that the rich and protected rarely are. They paid good money to be kept safe from predators, and here, in the backwash of a box canyon in Colorado, one had them trapped.

Many of them had left already for what they saw as safer places, but many remained in a show of bravado and self-importance. They'd all be in his debt once he helped surface the killer. *God knows,* he thought, *Tom Patterson sure isn't doing enough to figure this out.* Or that M.E. Then he smiled, because he knew that there wasn't any God to know anything at all. If there was an all-knowing being in this tale, it was Wilson himself. And what he didn't know for a fact, he was going to make so, if he could.

He caught a typo in the story he had just finished and corrected it, then gazed out his office window to the street beyond. It was early morning, but he saw the familiar figure of Father Matt, in his running clothes this time, jogging down the street. His pace was steady and his face drenched with sweat. Wilson smiled to himself and re-read the end of the story he had just corrected.

The lawyers would have at this, he figured, though the chances of a priest suing over a newspaper article were pretty slim, and potshots at Patterson were totally protected. He'd come close to the line, but he hadn't crossed it. And besides, he was certain time would prove him right. He attached the story to an email and punched send.

I was consolidating the multiple piles on my desk into the green canvas bin I kept for purposes of episodic neatness when Eoin Connor strode through the door, handed me a Dasani and a grin, then settled himself in my comfortable easy chair. I dropped the last of the papers into the bin with the resolution that tomorrow, finally, I would get to them. I took my time, silently running my one-to-tens in a couple of languages before I trusted myself to respond. "Good morning to you, too. Do you always take such liberties with another person's office?"

I cracked the top of the bottle, which was sweating now and dripping on my hands. I took a sip and excavated a coaster from underneath one of the remaining piles.

"No liberties. Just wondering about your murders. Have you figured out what's pulling them together yet?"

I shook my head. "No idea, really, none. It's driving me crazy."

I gave up on the tidying and took a seat on the couch opposite Connor, trying not to be annoyed that he had already propped his feet up on the coffee table.

Connor tipped his bottle, drained nearly half of it at one gulp.

"Pete Wilson does." He handed me the morning paper. I ran out of languages halfway through the brief story and was running through my considerable store of multilingual cuss words by the time I came to the end:

Witnesses report seeing the priest coming down from the bell tower of St. Patrick's Church in the aftermath of Cosette Anira's murder. The good father, who manages to stick his ecclesial nose into everyone's business, couldn't be bothered to walk down the street to tend to a dying woman. Could it be because the shot came from the direction of the church? Would it be that Fr. Gregory was reluctant to aid the dying because he knows more than he's telling? The bell tower can hide a great deal more than a tall man.

Then there's the fact that Marla Kincaid has been a regular visitor over the past few weeks to the church offices, in off hours. One neighborhood resident confirms that she was there the afternoon that Mitch Houston was shot, and he saw her leave in the company of the priest. He was later seen that same night in Mountain Village, hurrying toward the gondola. Away, as it turns out, from another dying person. The woman who reported the murder remembers seeing him hurrying toward the gondola as she got off. And Marla Kincaid was seen in Father Gregory's embrace in the Steaming Bean yesterday morning.

A priest who fails in his priestly duties isn't news these days. And cowardice in the face of death is nothing compared to the abuse scandals that continue to be uncovered. But isn't murder higher up in the hierarchy of sin than molesting altar boys? It's interesting to know that in his college days, the good Father Matt was a sharpshooter on his ROTC team, presumably before he felt that call to ministry. Was it the thought of all that killing in his future that made him run to the church? Or was it a false conversion, one that never really took? Is he a comforter or a predator?

He's been identified in the vicinity of two of the murders at the proper time. He's kept company with a woman accused of murder.

Means and opportunity. Maybe the sheriff is waiting for an explanation of motive to bring him in for questioning. How about this, the oldest motive in the world? Gregory wouldn't be the first priest to fall for a pretty face. And he wouldn't be the first man to compound one crime with others in an attempt to cover it up. And what better cover up for one murder than a string of murders that diverts attention. A priest of Rome, he'd be well-trained in that.

And no matter who is responsible for the shootings, the sheriff has been so busy with the shootings in town that the Houston murder has been dropped. The longer Patterson delays pursuing the evidence in Houston's death, the more likely it is that the killer will get off scot-free. Patterson's motives themselves are muddied. He was spotted having a late night beer few days ago with a petite blonde who, from the back, looked a lot like Marla Kincaid.

"That one goes straight for the throat, he does," Connor remarked. "One-tenth fact, nine-tenths pure meanness. Do you think there's anything in it?"

"No." My response was reflexive and protective. "Not a chance. Not Father Matt. Not only is he not the killer, he isn't involved with Marla Kincaid." I repressed the image of Father Matt embracing his old girlfriend for the time being, then brightened. "I'll bet Wilson saw Father Matt with his old girlfriend. She looks a lot like Marla. Case of mistaken identity."

Eoin Connor cocked his head.

"You're letting your heart get the better of your head," he said. "It was clear from his reaction—and hers—that the first time they saw each other was in the coffee shop. Houston was killed long before that."

I wrestled with that reality for a moment before answering. "You're right. Still, I don't think Father Matt has it in him to kill anyone, and that's a flimsy motive at best. You yourself said these murders feel like revenge. And anyway, there's not just one…"

I stopped myself, but Connor finished the sentence.

"Not just one shooter. I wondered if you'd come to that conclusion. There are two guns involved, right?"

"How did you know?"

Connor took out his pipe, raising a warning eyebrow at me, and clamped it between his teeth.

"A good woman, you know, would let me light this, rules be damned."

"You may not have noticed, but I am not a good woman. How did you know?" *Please God,* I thought, *do not let Ben be the answer.*

"Nothing particularly difficult about it. No ballistics report came out in the paper. If all the bullets had matched, Patterson would have played that up. He didn't. Ergo, the bullets didn't match. I'm guessing you have two, maybe three, guns involved."

He tamped the tobacco in his pipe absently and lit it in spite of my scowl. "I can understand why you are worried about your shop. Wilson seems to have a lot of information he ought not."

When I said nothing in reply, he went on.

"I've learned a lot about what coroners release and what they don't. Wilson reported the series of deaths before you were ready, am I right?"

I sighed. "You are. And yes, two guns, but not three. That probably means a tag team, two shooters."

"Three. There are three guns. Houston was shot with a nine millimeter. And he's a rich kid, too, or so my sources tell me. Could it be that he's the first? And if that's the case, perhaps Marla and the good Father are your team. "

I shook my head. "Motive? Marla has a motive for killing Houston, but not the others."

"Decoy murders. Besides, young Marla grew up poor indeed, and I gather was not well treated on her way up the Hollywood ladder. She could have a grudge against the rich."

"Nonsense. She wanted to be rich. She is rich. I don't buy it. Besides, how does Father Matt fit in?"

Connor shifted in his seat. "That's a bit of a tangle, I admit. I have a hard time seeing the good Father as a cold-blooded killer, too, but there are those who won't. I think Wilson is tracking the wrong chase. Patterson is a more likely candidate."

Tom Patterson was a good man, one of the best. I didn't agree with him on this investigation, but that was no reason for Connor to set him up as the murderer.

"Go on."

"Jeff, that young deputy, cornered me yesterday. He saw Patterson's boot on the surveillance tape. And Patterson was in Ophir the morning that climber got shot. And he was here awfully fast the day that Bedsheet was murdered."

"Kessler. His name was Paul Kessler."

Having held the man's heart in my hands, I couldn't bring myself to keep calling him Bedsheet.

"Paul Kessler, then. Patterson got to your place fast that evening. Too fast."

"So what? He must have been in town, and if Jeff is right about that boot, he was. He makes a point of patrolling around on foot to be seen. He's the sheriff. He's always somewhere."

"True enough. But look at this."

Connor handed me a stack of various newspaper articles. I flipped through the stack. The usual batch of gossipy drivel I had come to expect in Telluride, with a few lines highlighted. It was dated from May, three years ago.

Patterson almost lost his bid for re-election thanks to the efforts of local Paul Kessler and his coalition, Trusties for Truth. When asked about his next move now that Patterson has secured his office for another four years, Kessler replied, "We'll be watching him. Closely. It's only a matter of time until we find the information we need to remove him from office and put an honest man in."

This was news to me. I scanned the remaining articles quickly. Apparently Kessler had raised a stink about Patterson's campaign funding an inexplicably luxurious home down valley, claiming Patterson was taking payoffs from rich locals to look the other way at various infractions of the law, major and minor. The hostility — or at least journalistic interest in it — had clearly died down before I came to town.

"There was no love lost between Kessler and Patterson."

"Big deal. Patterson is a fair man."

"Maybe not. Care to know the odd bit?"

I took another sip of water and smiled. It was nice to be able to hash this out with Connor, though I didn't like the way his argument was shaping up. Since I'd picked up his latest book — and one of his first — *In Between the Covers*, snagging the copies fresh out of the front window, I'd come to appreciate the quick mind behind that genial exterior even more. It was a sharp book, and he'd connected the dots with startling clarity. And he wrote with the same understated, musical clarity with which he spoke.

"Sure. What's the best part?"

"Patterson started life as an army sharpshooter before coming to town and taking on that shiny badge. And all the victims were healthy contributors to his campaign. All except Webster."

"Connor, that makes no sense! What politician kills off his contributors?"

"One who can't risk their being pressed on the subject of contributions, for fear of being found out. He accepted contributions from wealthy folks who aren't residents. Who have no stake in the election — but who need a friend in the constabulary."

He passed over another stack of papers, leaning back in the chair. I couldn't decide whether his smile was expectant or self-satisfied.

Either way, the material was interesting. It took me several minutes to scan through the articles Connor had assembled. I had to admit, it was an attractive prospect for the Kessler murder. Still, there was Webster to contend with, and I wasn't enthusiastic about the possibility of more than one deranged killer on the loose. On the other hand, if the two shootings weren't related, then maybe I'd have a slow day tomorrow.

"Occam's razor says not. 'Whenever possible, assign only a single cause — not two or three — to things that can have one plausible explanation.'"

"They taught me that one, even in Belfast, thank you," Connor grinned. "Pluralitas non est ponenda sine necessitate. Besides, if I am right, you can relax. With Kessler gone, there should be no reason to go killing anyone else off. All that remains is to prove Patterson is the murderer."

"Touché." I had a sudden frisson of discomfort. "Wait here," I told him.

I strode down the hall and called to Ben, still in the break room.

"Bring me those things we confiscated at the Webster murder site." Something Connor said about Patterson's boot jostled a visual memory in my mind from the day before.

Ben was back almost before I sat down again, the evidence box in hand. I rooted around until I found it: a tiny, triangular piece of intricate metal. The match to the missing one from Tom Patterson's boot. I showed it to Connor.

"We found this at the Ophir Wall. It's from Tom's boot, I'd swear to it," I said, not liking at all the words I was saying. Not only had Tom been in Ophir, I could link him to the Ophir Wall, too.

Connor took the bit of metal from my hand and turned it over thoughtfully.

"So the razor cuts after all. Webster's daddy was well-connected in national politics. I wonder if Patterson has higher ambitions? I wonder if Webster was one of Kessler's political pals? He could do considerable damage to an aspiring politician if he put a flea in his daddy's ear. More than one murder has been done in pursuit of high office."

He passed the metal tip back to me.

I dropped it back in the box as though it would burn my fingers.

"I still don't believe it. There has to be some other answer." Even as I said it, I knew I'd be asking Ben to plot Patterson's movements, if he could, on the fatal days. *Please, God,* I thought, *don't let Connor be right.*

I handed the papers back to Connor, who looked very comfortable in my favorite chair, feet pushing aside the magazines on the coffee table. He'd switched to wearing sandals, and in typical European fashion, had dark socks on with them. I needed to give him a fashion lesson. They looked dreadful.

Wool-gathering again, and far too personal. I flushed.

"Maybe you and Ben can help pinpoint Patterson's movements more closely on the days in question." I paused. "Marla Kincaid's too, and I guess Father Matt's as well. It really cannot be him, Connor. It can't. There has to be some other explanation."

I didn't sound very persuasive, even to myself. I'd been betrayed by one friend in murder. Was this another betrayal?

I was spared further thought when the phone rang. Connor made to leave, and I waved him down. I wanted to take proper leave of this conversation, and really, I didn't want him to go. He settled back in the chair as I trotted to my desk to take the call.

It was my lawyer.

"Jane, glad I was able to get you."

Rick Glass manages my varied business and financial interests well, but his wheezy voice, tending to break at the most inopportune times, would forever keep him from the courtroom. Good thing for me. He'd very nearly made a second fortune out of the one I'd wrested out of Tom Berton and his corrupt corporate cronies. It would be five years tomorrow that this nightmare began with the verdict against Tommy Berton. I had almost forgotten. How odd that such a stroke of accomplishment and good luck could also be my ruination.

"You need something?"

"Just a decision." Rick hesitated. "I got a call from Kiki Berton. She's having a hard time, Jane, she can't make her mortgage payments."

In one of many creative arrangements that had led to the undoing of the practice once it had a significant judgment to pay, Berton had arranged for his own corporation to hold the note on his house, at sweetheart-low rates. I got the note at ten cents on the dollar in settlement, just as I had the house on Aspen. I'd literally taken everything that Tommy Berton had set aside for his old age: his house, his company, his retreat. Fair enough. He'd taken everything from me.

Now that Berton was in jail, I had no doubt that it meant his wife was unable to meet her bills. Kiki was Berton's third — and trophy — wife. She'd worked as the practice receptionist and married up, promptly bearing Tough Tommy two boys and retiring thenceforth and thereafter from the working world. If I remembered, the sons would be in middle school now. I was frankly surprised I hadn't gotten the call before, and I was surprised that the tone of Rick's voice was sympathetic.

"She's asking for you to give her a few months to sell the house. She's got the house on the market, but things are slow, and the bank turned down her application for a second mortgage to liberate enough equity to pay you and to live on until she finishes her degree and gets back on her feet. She's studying to be a paralegal."

Good for her, but it made no difference to me.

"Until she snags another husband to pay her bills, more likely," I said. Though with another fifteen years and two kids on the adorable twenty-five she had been when she married Tommy, it might be a little harder. "Or is she still married to Berton?"

"Still married. Visits him every time she can."

I was unsettled by the admiration in his words. I was unsettled that she appeared to be a faithful wife to that son of a —

"Well, I'm *not*. Still married," I clarified. And never would be, never again. She might have unpaid bills and a financial crisis, but Kiki had something I didn't: a husband. I'd put Tommy out of reach, but he was still hers. Very well, then, I'd take the house he gave her, clearly and finally. "No. Tell Kiki no extension. And as soon as the law allows, I want you to move foreclosure. When will that be?"

I heard the shuffling of papers.

"She's already several months in arrears. I've sent notices. Not long."

I ignored the disappointment, the judgment in the tone.

"Do it. Is that all you needed?"

"That's it." A sigh, a silence, then Rick, all business once again. "I'll have your quarterly statements by the end of the week."

I thanked him. As I turned from the desk to go back to the couch, I noticed Connor regarding me with a troubled look. He didn't wait for me to sit back down on the couch before he spoke.

"You know, Jane, taking that poor woman's house isn't going to put out that fire in your gut. It's not going to bring back your husband. She's not responsible for your pain — there's no need for you to punish her."

His accent made "poor" sound more like "pure."

I was momentarily speechless. He'd only heard half the conversation. Was he clairvoyant? Then I remembered—he'd been researching me for his next book. He already knew all about Kiki and Tommy and John and me. I felt exposed and vulnerable, and suddenly I was mad as hell, at Tommy, an anger that never left, at Kiki, and more importantly, at Connor, sitting there evaluating me in his own comfortable, unchanging world for another of his books just like he'd been evaluating Tom Patterson and Marla Kincaid and Father Matt.

"Maybe not," I said evenly. "But it will spread it around a bit."

We stared at each other like two cats for a minute or so in silence. We might as well have been screaming at each other. Finally, Connor stood up, the table and my anger separating us as clearly as an ocean.

"That's as may be. But you'll find that spreading it around, you'll have just as much as you did before, maybe more."

His voice was even, too, just as controlled as mine, though for the life of me, I had no idea what he had to be angry about, and I didn't care. He tossed the empty bottle in his hand toward the wastebasket by my desk. It arced, hit the edge and rattled in, both bottle and basket echoing emptiness. He dusted his hands in satisfaction—or was it dismissal?

I listened to the clock John had given me for our fifth anniversary. It was the wood anniversary according to the chart, and the antique timepiece was housed in a gorgeous cherry case. Its comfortable ticking had been a mainstay of our marriage, the soft chimes orienting me when I woke in the night with worries, and cuddled closer to my husband at its sound. He'd given it to me, he said, not just because it was wood, but because it would mark all the time we shared, which, after all, he had smiled, was the important thing.

The clock still ticked, but my marriage and John were both gone. The ticking became unbearable and I finally spoke. Even I was surprised at how hard and cold my voice was. It took Connor aback, I could see it in his face.

"How dare you? I know I have to live with it. I live with it every day of my life. I wake up knowing that, and I go to sleep knowing that, and if I want to make a perfectly respectable decision to foreclose the mortgage of the woman whose husband killed mine, I'll do that, and thank you to keep your comments to yourself."

I felt the red creeping up my neck. My kids always had the sense to leave before it reached my jaw. I wondered if Connor would, too. He did, but not without a parting comment.

"You're not living with it, Jane Wallace. You're dying from it, you stupid girl."

****

Father Matt Gregory had just made the last turn before the shelf road going up the side of Little Cone when his cell rang. He was surprised. Reception was spotty out here.

He supposed that the combination of the open, upward curving road and the cloudless blue sky improved things. He fumbled in the pocket of his jeans for the phone, one hand on the wheel, still making steady uphill progress. He hoped it wasn't anything that would call him back to town. He needed the climb to the top of this little dormant volcano to clear his head of the misery that had enveloped his town and his people since the murder of Mitch Houston and the increasing list of others.

The smartphone's screen flipped to "missed-call" just as he extracted it. He recognized the area code and frowned. *This cannot be good*, he thought to himself. He edged past a dusty green jeep that had pulled as far to the side as space permitted to let him pass. The driver, a middle-aged man wearing an Indiana Jones hat and mirrored sunglasses, raised a hand in greeting. Father Matt returned the gesture.

The road widened sufficiently to permit him to pull off about a hundred yards beyond, where a broad curve bounded by piles of rock provided an overlook of the narrow road below to a colony of marmots. He saw one duck into a crevice as he pulled his vintage Land Cruiser to a stop and heard the whistle-dialog as he waited for the cell to reconnect with the previous caller.

"Bishop's office."

Father Matt's anxiety increased. Bishops didn't call parochial vicars for no reason. He forced a smile into his voice.

"This is Father Matt Gregory. I just missed a call from this number."

"Oh. Father Gregory." The administrative assistant, Mildred Haynes, paused for a pregnant moment. "I just left you a voicemail. The bishop wanted to speak to you, but when he couldn't get you, he left early for a meeting. I'm afraid...I'm sorry, he can't...um...perhaps he can call you later this afternoon?"

Her words brought her image instantly to mind: short, pale, mid-forties, tottering about on four-inch heels, with teased, bottle-black hair and tight skirts and weighed down with costume jewelry, she looked like a comedy-skit caricature of the clueless secretary. In fact, she was as canny as a card shark and known throughout the diocese for protecting both the bishop and his turf.

Father Matt forced the smile from his voice to his lips. *How bad can it be if His Excellency couldn't wait even a few minutes on the chance I'd call back?*

"Look," he said. "I'm going to be out-of-pocket for a couple of hours myself. This is the best number to reach me. I'll keep my phone close." *Of course, it will be close to me in a place where the reception map looks like fine Emmenthaler.*

Five minutes more brought him to a cul-de-sac at the end of the last graded road on this part of the mountain. A breeze ruffled the leaves of the aspens, and a few columbine nodded. Father Matt grabbed his beaten-up red backpack from behind the driver's seat. He rummaged around in it until he found his GPS, pulled up the coordinates for the top of the mountain and clipped the gizmo to his belt.

The first time he'd come up this mountain, he'd gotten thoroughly lost. If it hadn't been for the good luck of encountering another hiker, rare on this peak, he might still be wandering around. He'd bought the GPS the very next day, then hired a guide to lead him up again. The price was worth it; the view from the top of the mountain was beautiful, and except for that first day, he'd never encountered another living soul on this trail. It made him wonder whether that hiker had really been a resident of the pricey subdivision that snuggled up to the peak, or his guardian angel.

The trail was poorly marked and wound upwards alternatively through meadows, stands of pine and fields of scree. By the time he reached the ridge line that led through the boulder field to the summit, his shirt was soaked and he was breathing hard, the exertion a welcome relief from the thoughts that had plagued his every waking moment since Marla Kincaid — pretty, persuasive Marla Kincaid — had first walked through his office door.

He stopped to sit on a boulder, eat a handful of trail mix and swig some water, still cool; the ice cubes hadn't quite melted. He closed his eyes and tipped his head back, feeling the sun warm on his face for a moment before he stood, stretched and untied the red bandanna from his belt. He poured some of the water onto it and wiped his face and neck, then tied it loosely inside his collar. Slinging his pack back on, he started out across the field of rocks with careful determination not to think about Telluride or the murders or Marla Kincaid.

It took him almost an hour more to make the summit, but finally he reached the cairn of rocks that hid the pickle jar that held the notepad and pencil, the humble record of successful summiteers. He signed his name and the date, noting with satisfaction that no one had been here since his last climb a month ago. He thought of this particular spot as his own. He placed the jar carefully back in its place of repose. Then he made the sign of the cross, said a prayer, and sat down to eat his long-overdue lunch and think.

Mountains clear the mind, make it easier to sort out difficult problems. *Moses went up on the mountain for answers, and so did Patrick*, he thought. *Maybe I can find a way out of this mess up here.* He shook his head, and a wry smile twisted his lips as he thought, *If not, maybe I can just stay here.*

He had just finished the double-chocolate brownie from Leona's Cafe when his cell phone shrilled again.

He considered ignoring it, but his curiosity and a sudden sense of unease that rose unbidden out of his ruminations compelled him to answer. The worried conscience never rested easy, not even on top of the world.

"Father Gregory."

The bishop's raspy voice sounded distant and matter-of-fact. Father Matt noticed the lack of obsequies and answered in kind.

"Bishop. I'm sorry I missed your call."

"Yes. Well…"

A pause. Father Matt's eyes narrowed and his heart started to race. The bishop was a loquacious man, if a clever and sometimes manipulative one. Silence was not his style. Father Matt heard him clear his throat and resume.

"Father, some disturbing news has come to my attention. I'm afraid it involves you."

"Disturbing in what way?"

Father Matt needed to pace, but the rocks wouldn't permit it. Instead he rocked back and forth, rooted to the spot, fearing what might come next. He had done his best, that he knew, but the boulder forming in his gut told him it wasn't going to be good enough.

Another discreet cough.

"Father, have you seen today's paper? Your paper, the local one…the…"

Father Matt could hear papers shuffling in the background. The mess on the bishop's desk was legendary.

"No, I haven't."

His voice was calm, but his words were sharp. Not good. He heard the shuffling stop.

"Perhaps you should. There's a story in it about you, and it makes some serious allegations. Allegations I cannot ignore." The bishop coughed, then resumed. "I assumed you would have seen it." A pause. "I really did. Otherwise I would have come in person." Another pause, then, more to himself than to the priest on the other end of the line, Father Matt heard him say, "I really should have come."

Father Matt ran a hand through his hair. The act expended just enough energy that he was able to answer calmly, with no note of the anxiety he felt betrayed in his voice.

"I'm sorry, Excellency. I haven't had time to read it today. There's been a lot going on. I spent the morning on parish business, said Mass, and then decided to take a hike. What is the article about?"

He steeled his nerves for the answer, his mind racing to figure just how much trouble he was in, how badly his well-intentioned actions had been misplayed in the press. He was framing his defense, mentally taking stock of just how close he had to come to the line of truth when the bishop answered. Time, he needed time, to sort this out. It could all still be made right. He knew it could.

"It accuses you of murder, Father Matt. Rather credibly. It seems you were seen coming down from the belfry of the church the day one of those poor unfortunates was killed, and it seems the shots came from there. There's also a suggestion that you have been...seen with...the girlfriend of one of the people who has been murdered."

Still another pause, and when he resumed, his voice was gentle.

"I want you to know I am certain this is a complete misunderstanding, but it seems you are in the middle of a murder investigation. Mildred has been fielding calls all day long." The bishop sighed. "I have no choice but to suspend you until this is sorted out. I'll be sending the vicar general tomorrow. He needs to meet with you, needs to ask you some questions. You probably need to get a lawyer. I'll..."

But the bishop was talking to himself, the smartphone sailing in a clean arc across the bright blue sky to bounce and shatter on the rocks below the summit. Matt Gregory plucked the glass jar from its hiding place and sent it cascading after, shards of glass spreading like bright drops of water in the afternoon sun, then stumbled to the edge of the mountain, dropped to his knees, put his head in his hands and wept.

CHAPTER TWENTY-TWO

JUNE 17, EVENING

It was just after five when I finished the last of the reports on my desk. I was tucking the last of them back into its dark green folder when my eye caught sight of the coffee stain on the wall next to my door. I'd hurled my favorite coffee cup at the wall after Connor left. I decided that I'd had most of the day to cool off, and called Tom Patterson to find out about the case against Father Matt. I caught him just as he was leaving.

"What the hell is all this about, Tom?"

"What's what about?"

I heard him bark orders to someone in the background and waited for him to return his attention to the call.

"You know damn good and well what. Father Matt. The article in the paper this morning."

He answered with a long sigh. "Doc, you know how reporters are."

"I know how reporters are and I know how cops are. What the hell is going on?"

"Wilson came by a few days ago, claiming he had some information on the case. We had to follow up on it. No choice."

My temper rose and I counted to ten. "Tom, I'm going to ask you one more time. This is part of a murder investigation. I run the forensic lab for the state in this area. Why is it that I am just now finding out about this from the..." I counted again. Swearing was coming far too easily to my lips these days. "...local newspaper." I emphasized the words.

"Doc, we just investigated yesterday..."

"Without any of my techs there, apparently."

"We found a .22 round, unspent, on the floor of the belfry. It's bagged and ready."

I closed my eyes in exasperation.

"I repeat — without benefit of my team there. No prints. No trace. No photos."

"Photos." He interjected. "Carter took them. There was really nothing to see — the floor had been rained on day before yesterday, pretty hard, and it was pretty clean except for a few leaves and that bullet."

"Fingerprints?"

"Come on, Doc. The priest's fingerprints are all over that bell tower. Why waste your time?"

I counted again. I get so very tired of excuses for not doing what needs to be done. I expect it in some quarters, but I thought I'd cured Tom Patterson of it.

"Tom," I finally said evenly. "When this office investigates a case, we do it thoroughly, and we do it the same way every time. EVERY time. And, unless I misread the authorizing legislation that established the Center, we get to call the crime scene shots. Not you."

There was a long silence. Patterson and I had collided over this before when I had first arrived in town and he had failed to call me to a DUI scene. Net result, the inebriated driver walked because there was no one there to draw a blood alcohol, and by the time one was drawn in the ER, there was sufficient wiggle room for his expensive lawyer to argue his way out of a conviction. The Center was something new and different in law enforcement, in some ways neither fish nor fowl. The powers that be had made it very clear that having a central, well-trained forensic laboratory was a priority, and the Western Slope Forensic Center was the prototype. Calling it into being had stepped on plenty of law-enforcement toes, some of those toes in well-appointed, silver tipped boots that used to have the free run of crime scenes before I arrived.

When he finally replied, his tone was stiff and formal. "I understand, Doctor Wallace." Emphasis on the doctor. "I'll see that the evidence gets over to you right away. It won't happen again."

The line clicked dead before I had a chance to say, "Thanks, and see that it doesn't."

I clicked on Outlook and dashed off an email to Lucy and Norman, telling them to get themselves over to the church and process the bell tower at the first opportunity, then thought the better of it and deleted it. There was still plenty of light. I grabbed the forensic kit and headed out the door to process the scene myself.

Then I stopped. I was already ass over teakettle in conflicts in this case, and the scene was already compromised. That I know Father Matt is no secret to anyone, and there was no need for my hard-headedness to make things worse than Patterson's had. I stepped back to my desk and dialed Lucy's extension. She picked up on the first ring and agreed to accompany me to the church to do the grunt work. I went along to work off the nervous energy that shattering my coffee cup had failed to dissipate.

As usual, I found the door to St. Patrick's open. Lucy and I walked into the silent, dark interior, afternoon sun streaming in through the windows and dappling the floor.

Lucy looked around slowly, taking it all in, her eyes wide. They lingered on the massive font in the middle of the floor, then on the crucifix.

"First time in a Catholic church?" I asked.

She nodded. "My family is Buddhist." Meaning, I supposed, that she was not, like so many of her twenty-something peers, having abandoned the faith of her parents for nothing much. She cocked her head, then added, "I saw pictures in art history, of course, and in museums. I didn't think they actually had stuff like this in real churches. Real American churches," she amended.

I chuckled, the sound reverberating in the stillness.

"Well, they do. And most of the time we aren't in the business of processing them in a murder case. Let's get busy." I started up the balcony stairs. "If there's an interior access to the belfry, it will be here."

My first glance at the ceiling identified it, a pull-down stairwell in the middle of the ceiling. I pulled it down over the middle row of seats, and a few sticks and leaves fell out onto the worn plush upholstery. I let go of the pull-rope and knelt down in the aisle, taking note of the detritus on the floor. Clearly the maid gave short shrift to the balcony, all to the good in this case.

"Process everything from this seat over three more, Lucy. You never know what might have fallen out when the good sheriff and his men went a-hunting up there."

Lucy nodded, then helped me pull the stairwell into place between the rows of seats. We snapped on our gloves and our chic, blue booties. I peered up into the recesses of the bell tower.

"Let me go first," Lucy said.

Before I could respond, she had clambered up the narrow stairs and was standing above me.

"Not much room, but enough. Come on up," she said.

I smiled to myself, glad that my forensic techs felt enough confidence to order the boss around when necessary.

By the time I poked my head into the belfry, Lucy was already looking carefully at the perimeter of the wooden square that housed the great iron bell that called the faithful to Sunday Mass and irritated the neighboring heathens who were sleeping off Saturday night's excesses. I stepped carefully around the opening and looked out over her to the expanse of street below. This would indeed have been the perfect place to shoot at passersby. And it wouldn't take a sharpshooter to hit the mark.

It took us about forty-five minutes to inspect, sweep, process and bag all the potential evidence — contaminated though it was — from the ten-by-ten square. At length, Lucy stood up, pinched the last bag closed and stretched her back.

"Prints?"

"You bet. At least dust the rails and the uprights. That's the most likely place for the shooter to have put his hands."

She nodded and started to work. Ten minutes later, my compulsive nature was rewarded with a palm print on both rails.

"Nice," Lucy remarked as she lifted them with an artisan's appreciation for a work of great beauty.

I looked at the spot, imagining how the hand must have been laid on the green enamel of the wood, still shiny and new from recent renovation. I leaned out over the edge and indicated the outside of the rail.

"Betcha there's a couple of fingerprints out here," I said.

"Betcha you're right."

Lucy leaned out over the edge, worked her forensic magic, and soon enough produced two full prints on the far side of one rail and one on another. I watched with satisfaction. At least there was something, and Tom Patterson was wrong. There weren't prints everywhere. Just on those two rails. Now all that remained was to figure out whose they were.

I helped Lucy pack up the rest of the forensic kit and followed her down the rickety stairs. The fading afternoon sun had left the balcony in shadows, and there was still the little matter of the seats to process.

"I'll get the lights," I told her as I headed downstairs. "Do you need help with this?" I called back.

I knew the answer before her. "No, thanks" reached my ears as I searched the wall by the front doors for the proper switch. It took a few moments to find the right one out of the six.

"That's it, thanks," floated down from the balcony as the door to the church swung open and Father Matt walked in. He was dressed in khaki pants and a sweat-stained tee-shirt. His face was weary and his shoulders stooped. I hadn't seen him since our breakfast in the Bean. It pained me to see him so haggard.

"Jane. It's you. Why are you here?" He ran his hand through his hair and attempted a smile. The attempt failed.

I pointed upward. "The belfry. We had to process the scene. For what it's worth." I stopped, unsure what else to say. Part of me knew beyond a shadow of a doubt that this man could not have shot anyone. Another part of me remembered the betrayal of a man I thought close enough to be my brother. The two parts of my mind did battle, and the result was a standoff. I sighed, hating the uncertainty and for the moment, hating my job. "Father, I'm going to need your fingerprints."

Father Matt closed his eyes for a long moment, and when he opened them again, I thought I saw them well with tears. He shrugged.

"Let's go then," he said, as he held the church door open for me, and I walked out into the gathering evening.

****

One advantage to black clothes, thought Father Matt, *is that fingerprint ink won't stain them.* He'd wiped his hand absentmindedly on his khakis when Lucy Cho had finished printing his right hand, leaving a smear just above his knee. He wondered, as he walked back to the rectory, whether he'd ever wear his cassock again.

The door was unlocked as it always was. He glanced around the untidy room without turning on the light. His eyes came to rest on the chair Pete Wilson had been sitting in just a few nights before. Maybe if he had kept his door locked, Wilson would never have cornered him, never have written that article. Perhaps Isa was right. He needed to be more wary.

Too late. He knew the drill. Even the slightest whiff of suspicion, and a priest was yanked from his parish, guilty until proven innocent. He'd stopped at the gas station outside of town and called back to the bishop's office on his way back from his hike. The vicar general was coming tomorrow and, until further notice, Father Matt was relieved of his faculties. He was forbidden to celebrate the Mass, hear confessions, present himself as a priest in any way at all. He flopped in the chair, resting his elbows on the arms of the chair and tilted his head back to look at the ceiling, at nothing in particular.

He sat there, thinking and praying, until it was fully dark, the only light spilling in from the street lamp outside the window. Then he stood up, looked at the crucifix bathed in shadows on the wall and flipped on the light. He needed to pack. The bishop made it clear he couldn't stay in the rectory. It wouldn't take long. He wouldn't need any of his black clothes.

CHAPTER TWENTY-THREE

JUNE 19, MORNING

It was a miserable morning. Even if I hadn't looked at the calendar to know it was the anniversary of John's death, the ache in my very soul would have told me. I'd woken up just before dawn, tossing and fretting, unable to get back to sleep, much to the dismay of my two cats. My thrashing about eventually drove them, complaining, from my bed to find more hospitable digs, presumably with Ben or Pablo or Isa. After an hour or so of restlessness, spent uneasily in the twilight between sleep and full consciousness, I gave up, showered, pulled on jeans, a frayed white shirt and hiking boots, and headed into town.

There was nothing to draw me to the office, so I headed up the trail to Bear Creek Falls, hoping to exorcise the restlessness with a good long walk. I stopped to look back over town as the trail rose, quiet and deserted, above Town Park. Telluride wakes up late on its best day, and no one was about, not even the construction workers, mostly Mexicans, who were building several new, expensive and expansive homes at the edge of town. One lonely dog, a golden retriever, trotted across the street, the only sign of life.

Ordinarily such a peaceful scene would have given me some rest. Today it only irritated me. I headed up the trail, pacing out the distance with military rhythm and purpose, pushing through the winded fatigue that set in almost as soon as the trail took an upward pitch. I had lived in Telluride long enough to be acclimated to the elevation, but still found the first mile of any walk to be pure torture, all burning lungs and unwilling muscles. I had learned from experience not to give into it, to keep on by force of will. Eventually, my breathing would even out, my legs would warm up and my strides would become regular and easy, allowing me to put energy into thinking rather than moving. It was all a matter of will, of getting past the resistance that my body has to changing gears, to accepting challenges.

I had not quite accomplished the break-in mile when I heard a noise behind me, a regular stride, approaching quickly, but a softer sound than that of hiking boots. I turned to see an early morning jogger effortlessly making his way up the trail, clad in green shorts, white singlet and garish orange running shoes. He lifted a hand in greeting without ever breaking stride, and I watched his form disappear around a bend in the trail, envious of such physical prowess. Awash in self-pity, I wondered why even the simple act of taking a walk to a pleasant spot in the woods was such a trial for me these days.

John and I had loved to walk in the woods, even on the steamiest days in Florida. We'd wake early, before the sun was up in the middle of summer, and stroll through the hammock park that bordered our home, listening to the coo of doves and the drone of cicadas. Sometimes we'd take one of the children, and John would point out things along the way with his artist's eye, things I saw but missed, being caught up in the patterns instead of seeing the pictures. But most of the time we'd walked alone, in our private start of the day, just as the quiet evening time drinking Jameson's ended it, the children safe in the care of one or another relative that had showed up miraculously in need of assistance just when we needed a mother's helper.

The children, my kids, were all that I had left to link me to John. "How will we manage?" I had sputtered. Medical school and residency and law school loomed ahead, and I wasn't at all certain how children would fit in those plans.

"You'll see," was all that he would say. "It will work out. Trust me. Trust God."

And it had worked out. Children hadn't come until I was past the brutal part of my law and medical classes and had already embarked on the relatively gentle schedule of a pathologist. We found a rambling old Victorian near the hospital with more than enough room for a large family when we finished training and started to make our way in the world, so that I could work from an office in the garage and still cover duties in the hospital. A wide assortment of relatives, friends of relatives, and relatives of friends turned up on our doorstep to stay with us and lend a hand.

Looking back, I knew that it had often been chaos, with all the usual childhood illnesses and problems, with intermittent crises in both of our practices, with lousy partners and incompetent hospital administrators, and the deaths of parents, and a miscarriage, too much debt and too little income — but it had all worked out and I had loved it. I had loved John, and not a single moment of it seemed a trial to me. It had all been joy because of John, my other half, the true mate of my soul, who had led me, uncertainly and sometimes unwillingly, from fear into generosity, from hiding into life.

Such trust. In me. In God. In the Church. In everything and everyone. It had been his undoing, and mine. He never saw Tommy Berton coming for him in the parking lot that day, never had a chance to duck between cars because it never entered his mind that the car bearing down on him was actually meant to kill him. I'd learned to trust and to live with John, but Tommy Berton shattered it, and I would never get it back. *Damn him.*

By the time I reached the falls, the jogger had passed me coming back. The sun was full up, I was sweating, and I was hungry. I splashed cold water on my face, and turned around, half jogging myself, almost enjoying the jarring twinge that my heavy-soled boots sent through my shins with each step.

****

I was in no mood to cook breakfast for myself. I headed for Leona's, a small bakery and cafe that had opened only a few months before. I usually avoided it because it served a side portion of politics along with the food, and I was generally averse to, and irritated by, propaganda about global warming, the evils of Republicans and the virtues of sexual liberation, and so tended to vote with my pocketbook and eat at establishments that realized on what side their economic bread was buttered. This morning the smell of frying bacon overcame me and I ducked inside.

And ran right into Father Matt, already seated at a table, cup of coffee in hand. He motioned me to the table and pulled out a chair.

"Join me."

He looked as glum as I was, and he was dressed in jeans.

I sat down gratefully, and he motioned for the waitress to bring a cup of coffee. She acknowledged his wave, but languished near the pass through, and waited until the cook put up a plate before she poured the coffee. She brought it with the plate, putting a plate of scrambled eggs and sausage, garnished with a slice of ripe tomato on a bed of lettuce, in front of Father Matt.

Breakfast has never been my favorite meal, and eggs are far from my favorite food. I've learned to eat them, at least, but to say that I am particular in their preparation is to understate the case. The eggs that Father Matt was about to tuck into looked rubbery and overdone. I decided to opt for my fall-back breakfast instead.

"I'll have a BLT, please," I said as I took a sip of coffee from the mug. It was lukewarm. Great.

The waitperson — a prominent sign on the restaurant wall declared that the servers were to be addressed in politically correct terms — looked up from her pad.

"Sorry. That's lunch. We're only serving breakfast."

She adjusted the ring in her nose, raising unpleasant hygienic possibilities in my mind.

"Excuse me?" I asked, incredulous.

"We don't serve lunch until 11:30. This is breakfast. Do you want a menu?"

I looked at the toast that Father Matt was using to wipe a bit of egg from the plate and the garnish that lay untouched on the side. I tried again.

"Don't you serve bacon for breakfast?" I asked reasonably.

"Sure."

"And toast? Wheat toast?"

"Uh-huh."

I pointed to Father Matt's plate. "And what's that?"

"Tomato. Lettuce. We use it to garnish the plates."

We were making progress. "So can you explain to me why you can't make a BLT for me?"

"We don't get the mayonnaise out until lunch."

God help me, the woman was serious. I sighed. It wasn't worth it.

"You going to eat that?" I asked, pointing to the side of his plate.

"All yours," he answered around a bite of sausage and toast.

"Okay, then bring me an order of wheat toast and a side of bacon." I extended the cup to her, "and some hot coffee." I'd give up the mayo in penance for the suffering souls in purgatory. I forced a smile. "Please."

"Sure."

Another adjustment to the ring and she was gone, snapping her gum as she left.

"Gotta love it," Father Matt said as he followed her retreating form. "What brings you here so early?"

I toyed with a flip answer, but decided against it. John's presence was too close. If I held Father Matt at bay, I was afraid I would push John away too. I answered honestly. "Couldn't sleep. It's the anniversary of John's death. You?"

"I couldn't sleep either. The bed at the Victorian is a bit short for me."

It took me a minute to realize why he wasn't in his usual cassock and why he was staying at the Victorian.

"Surely the bishop doesn't believe..."

"It doesn't matter what he believes. He has no choice. Bad enough to be accused of... impropriety. He can't leave an accused murderer in charge of a parish, not even one this small."

"Give it time. It will all sort out. I promise."

It sounded hollow, even to me. How could I promise anything when I knew nothing? His sad expression told me he knew better. Over the time I've known Father Matt, we've developed the habit of quiet with each other, feeling no pressing need to talk when words are not the issue. I waited for him to find the words he was looking for.

"You know, Jane, it took me a long time to quit running and enter the seminary. But since then, there's nothing I wanted to be except a priest. It's who I am. Only now, it looks like it's not what I am going to be, ever again, and I don't know what to do about it." He took a deep, ragged breath, somewhere between sigh and sob.

"You know that's not true, Father." I was surprised at my conviction and my candor. The walk must have jarred something loose in my soul. I reached my hand across the table and covered his. It was warm and soft, the hand of one unaccustomed to physical labor. The hand I expected from a priest. I realized with a start that, though I had shaken that hand many times, I'd not really felt it ever before.

"And I know how you feel. Believe me, I do. My life changed in an instant, too, and I know what it's like. Only for you, it will get better, because we'll find out who's shooting people, and it isn't you and you aren't...you aren't..."

I found myself unable to go on. My heart ached with a pain so physical it nearly doubled me over, but I was determined not to succumb to tears, not again and not here.

Father Matt slipped his hand out from under mine to rest it on top of mine, heavy and protective.

"No, Jane, I'm not. And you and Tom will figure it out. I just have to be patient. Sorry to burden you with my worries when you have so many of your own. Are you all right?"

I sighed. "I'm not. I'm a mess. I can't sleep. I can't get on with life. My kids are worried about me. I'm miserable, and I'm making everyone around me miserable. I can't even do my job right anymore." I paused again to collect my thoughts, and drew in a sharp breath. "I just miss him," I concluded in a small voice.

Father Matt didn't answer. He just left his hand on mine until the waitress returned with the bacon and toast. Then he slid it off and assembled my sandwich, cutting it on the diagonal and shoving the plate across to me.

"Eat," he commanded. "And listen. Not a word, Jane. Just listen to me. John died. It was a tragedy, a terrible waste of a life. But it's over, and it was his life, not yours. Like it or not, you're still here, and you still have a life to live. You still have gifts, and you have people who love you, and who want to love you and you have things to do. You cannot let this eat away at you anymore. Time is running out, Jane."

Oddly, no tears threatened; I just felt hollow and alone. I swallowed a bite of sandwich and took a sip of the fresh cup of coffee, as lukewarm as the first. It was fitting. It was how I'd spent the last three years, lukewarm. Never hot, never cold, just lonely and tepid.

"I can't," I repeated for the hundredth time. "All I can think of is Tommy Berton and how he destroyed my life. It fills every minute I'm not actively thinking about something else. Believe me, I wish it didn't."

"Jane, look at me," Father Matt said. His face was serious, his voice gentle. "It doesn't have to. Tommy Berton killed your husband. You're destroying your own life."

I put down the sandwich and wiped toast crumbs from my mouth with my napkin, the pain in my heart searing now and almost beyond endurance. I opened my mouth to reply, to tell him that I was doing no such thing, but the pain was too much.

He continued. "I don't think I have ever known a more strong-willed person than you, Jane, especially when it comes to people around you. You had the will to stop a handful of corporations from bilking people out of millions of dollars. You had the will to bring your husband's killer to justice when the police said it couldn't be done. You had the will to start a new life and a new career in a town where you knew no one, and that suits you about as well as a bicycle suits a fish. It's time you used that will to start healing yourself. Forgive yourself, because you didn't cause John's death. Forgive Tommy, because you must. Forgive John for leaving you alone. Make the act of will, Jane, and the healing will follow. Will yourself past it. You're running out of time."

I couldn't respond to him, and he felt no need to say more. We just sat, drinking that awful coffee, he sharing my anguish and I taking small comfort in his concern even as I doubted his solution. At length, I drained my cup, left a twenty-dollar bill on the table for our meals, and walked with Father Matt into the bright light of a summer day.

Our company and our silence lasted until we reached the intersection of Spruce Street, where he turned to go up the hill to the church to meet the vicar general as I continued on, as alone again, in fact as I was, in spirit.

****

The walk up the hillside from the Telluride trail was longer than it looked but worth it. The rifle broke down to fit in the simple, black backpack, indistinguishable from the ones that all of the tourists who hiked up and down the mountain carried. Reassembling the gun was easy in the cool shade of the trees, out of sight of everyone. When it was over, a few moments to break it down, put it away, then it would be a quick walk down the gentle trail back into Telluride, unremarked. In time to hear the dreadful news that there was another shooting. What a tragedy.

The little glen had a perfect vantage, in the woods, away from the line of sight of the gondola — though if you looked hard it was visible. That was how the shooter had found it, riding up to Mountain Village with some tourists. Hidden behind some rocks but with a perfect clear view of that roof garden, close enough to town as the crow flew and with a serendipitous outcropping to steady the barrel. Not that it was needed. Eyes and hands might get older but the will, the precision never left. It was the will that counted in the end. Many people had the physical skill to be a good shot, but not the will. The will is what made the difference: the will to wait, the will to be steady, the will to take another creature's life. It would be a long shot but an easy one; all that was needed was to wait.

This was the last one. It was time to put the anger away, the spleen vented, the pain at bay for a bit. Time to resume life again, life such as life was. Life that stretched ahead, gray and lifeless, empty of meaning since she was killed. Life was a shadow, a shell, no joy, no pleasure, nothing.

It had built up month after month following her death until it had spilled out in murderous rage on the anniversary of her death, and it had surfaced again year after year since. In a way, it was the only time that life stirred inside, when one of those clean shots found its mark and someone else had to share the pain and not know why. It was all that made life worth living, worth getting up, putting on the coffee, working, even drawing the next breath. Only death made Bella seem alive again, or at least not so terribly and finally and stupidly gone. Only the faint sense of satisfaction that came from extracting payment for a life too soon gone made anything else bearable.

This shot had to be right, because that woman doctor was determined to ferret out the reason for the deaths. She'd discovered the pattern, so carefully concealed — or was it the incursion of sloppiness that made it discoverable? No matter, get rid of the woman and the problem would be solved. Things would go quiet again; soon, they all would have forgotten.

The woman doctor had even been smart enough to figure out the ones that were so carefully arranged to look like accidents. She had to be stopped, because if not, she'd never let go, so great was the drive within her. She'd said something about a dead husband — that had to be the source of her stubbornness — and the shooter knew from experience that such personal pain created a persistence that would never, never end.

It was a beautiful day, the air crisp and clean from the rain the day before, and the surrounding meadow smelled sweet with crushed grass and wildflowers. Like childhood summers so long ago, so far from this quiet canyon in Western Colorado. A brown rabbit ran across the path, zigzagging from tuft to rock, finally disappearing into a hollow at the base of an aspen tree. The sky was the same as it had been then, blue and clear, dotted with clouds, but everything else was different, from the town, full of rich, lazy and spoiled children with no sense of place and no sense of responsibility, to the forest that surrounded it.

Both were impermanent, the town made all of wood, not proper stone and brick, and these pale, fragile aspens that came down in the least wind, or in no wind at all, more like weeds than trees, not thick, strong oaks that stood for generations. No real businesses there, no honest work, only frivolous shops and restaurants serving people with nothing more to do than waste their time and their money in idleness and self-indulgence. The devil's very workshop. What sort of place made its name and its living on skiing and biking and jeep tours and hang gliding and building enormous, expensive homes for rich people with no children to fill up the many bedrooms? A hundred years from now, and this place would be the same ghost town it was after the silver ran out and before the ski lifts and chamber of commerce. Nothing to show except excess, the kind of excess that killed souls. The kind that killed Bella.

Down the mountain, in the valley, the door to the roof garden opened, and a tall figure crossed under the arbor to sit in the sun at the corner nearest the mountain, just as she did every sunny day at lunch. She was unaware of the rifle that swung up to come to rest on a ledge of rock, held by determined hands and pointed at her. Good. The shooter's right hand stretched in anticipation, bringing the index finger slowly and purposefully toward the trigger.

CHAPTER TWENTY-FOUR

JUNE 19, LATE MORNING

The morning dragged. I heard from all of the children, anxious for my state of mind, each probing gently. Adam, Zoe, and Luke called. Ben dropped by the office, anxious at having arisen to find me gone so early. Beth sent flowers, too much like me to risk talking. Seth sent a long email from Rome, including a Mass intention for his dad. Instead of making me feel better, their concern weighed even heavier on my heart. They deserved a mother who wasn't a burden on their spirits, but hadn't been dealt one. I worked through a stack of correspondence and long-neglected cases.

On top was a handwritten letter postmarked in town. The script was textbook-perfect cursive, the mark of someone my age or better. Kids today all printed, the legacy of easy access to word processors. I slit it open, and a scented piece of stationery fell out. I scanned it quickly, astonishment and irritation growing. It was a letter from Marla Kincaid's father.

Thank you for taking care of my daughter, it read. *She's doing okay now, and I'm staying here until she can come home with me. No matter what, it was good of you to get her to the hospital. We are hoping the baby will be okay.*

The letter trailed off as though the writer had run out of words, and it was signed with an abrupt *Spencer Kincaid.* I tossed it aside, having no desire to be reminded of yet another murderer angling to go free. After that were a dozen or so letters from lawyers soliciting assistance with various kinds of lawsuits, and a huge stack of reports from the various assistant medical examiners who took care of routine cases in the distant reaches of the Western slope. I had convinced the powers-that-be to construct a network of local pathologists who could be expected to handle uncomplicated cases, natural deaths, obvious accidents, while calling me in on more complicated matters.

We'd spent nearly six months giving them a crash course in forensic pathology, but it was paying off. As pathology revenues fell, most of them were glad of a little extra income, and knowing that there was expert help a few hours away, most of them were paying more attention to the matters of life and death in their communities. Already one of them had discovered the smothering of an elderly man that would have been unremarked and unnoticed in years past, and the greedy nephew who killed him was marking time awaiting trial.

Still, it meant that I had to review all the death reports from several counties, and I was a week behind. It took most of the morning to go through them, and I was glad of a break and a cup of coffee, hot this time. I poured it from the pot in the break room. I sat down at the table, where a newspaper lay open and folded on the table. I glanced at the date. A week ago. Surely my staff kept up better with the local news than that.

The paper was opened to the letters page, where the ongoing controversy about the prairie dogs that had taken over the valley floor after the town had condemned and taken it over and removed the ecologically damaging valley cows raged on. About half of the town wanted to protect the rodents, who had turned the once luxuriant meadow into something resembling a minefield with their network of burrows. Others, objecting in equal parts to the unsightly mess the colony had made of the landscape and to the inconvenience their burrows meant for anyone or anything trying to negotiate the terrain, wanted to flood them out. I smiled at the predictable, unintended consequences that the reflexive ecologic preoccupation of the local citizenry inevitably produced.

I flipped through the rest of the paper, enjoying a decent cup of hot coffee for a change as I caught up on local goings-on. There was a write-up on the coming art show at the New Sheridan, with a couple of photographs of some of the submissions. There was an update on proposed changes to the historical and architectural review standards. There was a screed from a local progressive politician, the only kind in Telluride, condemning the "corporate disease monopoly" and calling for mandatory, universal, socialized health care. There was a piece on the activities of the local kids enrolled in the town's summer enrichment programs, including photos of them picking wildflowers — permitted only because they were instructed to pluck as many ox-eye daisies as possible given that the state had classified them as noxious weeds. Leave it to Telluride to take the joy out of a harmless childhood activity and turn it into just another opportunity for indoctrination.

Father Matt was right. This town just didn't suit me. I sighed and turned the page. Paul Kessler, dressed in his tunic, his cloak secured with a large silver pin, stared back at me from the page. I skimmed through it. It was one of those local-color profiles, a pleasant little homage, done in question and answer format.

Q. What brought you to Telluride?

A. The energy here is just so amazing. It's even better than Sedona, I think, because we're closer to the heavens, higher up. The mountains focus it, and the valley channels it. It's an amazing place to live.

Q. How long have you been here?

A. Five years. I came here from Chicago when I finished college. My old man wanted me to go to law school and join the family firm, but my grandfather left me enough money to live on, so I came out here to find my spiritual source. Big cities kill the soul...

Most of the rest of it was an exposition of Paul Kessler's hodgepodge philosophy, but my heart skipped a beat at the last line. Kessler was explaining the connection of his religious philosophy to the lunar cycle, and how he liked to plug into the great energy of the moon.

...The best time is when there's a full moon. I always go up Coronet Creek to the falls at night when there is a full moon. The moonlight off the water is spectacular, and it's the best place to meditate. I reconnect. I get to be part of the great Universal. It sets me right.

There it was, in black and white. All of Telluride knew that Kessler would be going up Coronet Creek last Thursday night. And all of Telluride knew he was a trusty. I picked up the phone in the lounge to dial the downstairs office where Ben worked. I was surprised when Lucy picked up instead.

"Ben's on the roof," she told me. "He works up there every day it's nice."

Would I never get used to the eccentric work habits of this new generation? Visiting the garden had become a routine for him, a place of quiet beauty and refuge. Besides, my last-born had always chosen eccentric places to work, as often as not, sprawled on a floor or literally up a tree instead of sitting quietly at a desk. I liked the garden, too, as a respite from my office. I particularly welcomed it today, welcomed the chance to sort out my thoughts and emotions amid the flowers.

The sun was bright, and the day was warm. I stood for a moment in the shade of the trellis, allowing my eyes to adjust to the sunlight and watching a hummingbird dance among the fuchsias. The flowers were at their peak, pots of marigolds and lilies of the valley, hearts-ease and Dutchman's breeches, bachelor's buttons and columbines, old-fashioned flowers that my mother had loved and that provided a riot of color against the dun-colored brick of the building. A pot of ivy spilled out of the top of a small fountain by my favorite chair, the water cool and inviting.

One of the staff, all of whom who live in the apartments in the Center and use the rooftop in the evenings, had left a red plastic cup, and it rolled around the base of the fountain in the gentle breeze. I stooped to pick it up with a little irritation at the carelessness of the miscreant who left it and called to Ben. As I expected, he was draped crosswise over a lounge chair, computer in his lap, reflective sunglasses and a visor providing the requisite shade for him to see what he was doing. I called to him.

"Ben!" He looked up, startled, and rearranged himself into a more conventional pose as I walked over. "Do me a favor and get copies of all the editions for the month of June for both of the papers in town. I might just have figured out how Kessler's killer — and James Webster's, and maybe the others — identified his victims. I might have found the link in the chain I needed to convince Patterson that I was right."

His reply had the familiar distracted quality that meant he was hot on the trail of some computer issue and was only half-listening to what I had said. The fact that he was still peering at the screen confirmed it.

"Sure thing, Mom. I'll get right on it."

In a motherly routine born of long experience, I asked him, "Get right on what?"

There was a pause. He'd surfaced and realized he had no idea what I had told him.

"Uh..." he faltered.

"The local papers. All of them, every day, from both newspapers, for the whole month of June. Come to think of it, for the last week of May, too."

"Okay. Sure. Do you need hard copies?"

Now it was my turn. "Huh?"

"The papers are both online. Do you need the hard copies, or can I find what you need on the internet?"

"Doesn't matter, I guess. Take a look at all our recent trusty deaths, and see whether the victims were written up in the paper in the week or so preceding their deaths."

I paused. He was still absorbed in the computer. I cleared my throat and he looked up again, smiling, quick to answer this time.

"Sure thing, Mom. I'll get right on it."

"Thanks, babe," I said, then added, "I love you."

As I leaned over to kiss his cheek, I was overcome with a sense of foreboding so palpable it made me shiver. I straightened and cast a look around the roof, then beyond the building to the mountainside and its lacing of trails.

The defining trait of a pathologist is to know when something is out of place. It's how we can find the ten cells in a thousand that are cancer, it's how we put the puzzles of life and death together. Something gnawed at me. Something was wrong, out of place, not right. A brief flash of brightness caught the corner of my eye as Ben stood to hug me. Instead of dissipating the dread, it intensified it. Ben paused in response to my tension.

I saw the flash again, and it triggered something inside me. I squinted into the distance and saw a hiker; the flash was a reflection from his mirrored glasses. I relaxed a bit, having resolved that bit of inconsistency. The day was quiet in the noonday heat, the streets still emptier than usual. I took a deep breath and looked at my son and smiled.

A moment later, in the distant, quiet center of my mind, where most of my thinking goes on without my knowing it, I froze with fear, the dread having returned with a focus. Ben, my Ben, my own last-born, was a trusty, too. Not a remainderman, but a trust fund baby. All my brood were, funds established in the aftermath of their father's murder. Suddenly, I wanted him inside, safe, and secure.

"Ben, I really need that information PDQ. Go on inside — I'll get your computer for you. Now, Ben, please."

I needed time to think, to decide whether I was being overprotective or just plain crazy. I struggled to keep the tears out of my voice. First John. Then Adam's near crash. Now this. I felt myself unraveling.

Ben looked at me quizzically, but he was used to my outrageous motherly demands, and he must have seen something in my face that softened him and made him hug me again. He brushed my cheek with a kiss.

"Love you too, Mom. See you downstairs — how about I make dinner tonight for you, special, just you and me?"

He glanced at me one last time with that indulgent look John had dubbed "humor the crazy lady" and then went inside. I watched the steel door close behind him with a sense of relief that he was gone, but a residue of unease remained.

I paced back and forth a bit, trying to think but my mind continued to be restless. Thoughts of John kept interrupting my attempts to reason out the string of murders that plagued me and thwarted my attempts to rest easy about my son. The thoughts were so real and persistent it was almost as if he were with me. The thought of John only raised my anxiety instead of calming it. I kept shoving him out of the way, that act of will Father Matt talked about, but he kept coming back, insisting. I wondered if I finally had lost my senses. As I leaned over to pick up Ben's laptop, I heard John's voice.

"Jane. Leave. Now. Go back inside."

I heard his voice as clearly as I ever had. I looked around. There was no one there, least of all John. I stopped in my tracks. Another flash caught the corner of my eye, from another direction, brief and evanescent as lightning.

"Now, Jane! Now! Go!"

There was no mistaking the urgency, even if it couldn't be John.

A chill went up my spine, and the garden wasn't a place of repose any longer. Now it menaced me, taunting me with memories of my dead husband and fears for my son so vivid I couldn't bear it. I turned abruptly, away from the wall that overlooked the Telluride Trail.

They say you never hear the shot that hits you. I can vouch for that. I heard no sound, but felt a sudden pain in my right breast, hot, incapacitating. My hand went to the spot and came away sticky, and I couldn't breathe. I fell on my knees, doubled over, trying to catch my breath in the shelter of the wall, making mental inventory of what might have been hit, given the entrance wound. If I was lucky, nothing too vital.

I stayed there in the shade of the wall as precious minutes ticked by, too afraid and in too much pain to move. I'd examined countless gunshot wounds, but never considered how they felt, except in response to questions on the witness stand. Next time I'd give a better answer. Yes, it hurt. Yes, the victim was in pain. As a matter of fact, it hurt like hell, like nothing I had ever experienced before.

I finally struggled to my feet, splinting my side with my right arm to ease the pain. I still couldn't breathe well, and blood was now starting to drip from my side — never a good sign. I paused at the trellis before wrestling the door to the stairwell open, hoping there wouldn't be another shot, all too aware that I was an easy target. It was a shock to realize someone wanted me dead. *Why? What had I done?* I wanted to confront my assailant, drag the answers out of him, a response I found oddly comforting. *If I could be angry, I couldn't be dying, right?*

I lurched forward through the door to the safety of the building's interior, leaning against the wall to make sure of my balance before going any farther. A gunshot wound was bad enough. A broken neck from a fall would be much, much worse. I tried to smile at the irony of my forensic examination of my own plight, but it hurt too much. I paused again, hoping to gather some strength, but I couldn't. The pain kept coming in great waves, and my breathing was increasingly shallow. I was shaking.

I started down the steps, cursing myself for once again leaving my cell phone on my desk. The pain increased with every step, and I could feel the blood dripping onto the steps as I stumbled down them. *Just my luck*, I thought. Only Ben knew where I was, and no one would find me. I'd collapse and bleed to death in this damn stairwell, and no one would ever find me.

As I came to the first landing, another wave of pain, worse than any of the others, brought me to my knees. I sank onto the cool tile, grateful for its reassuring feel on my face, something other than the pain in my chest. My breaths were shallower now, not enough to sustain movement, even down stairs. It would be so easy just to lie here, just give it up, let it go. The voice again.

"Get up, Jane. Only five more steps." John's gentle encouragement. *"Come on, Mrs. Doe."* His pet name for me. We were the Does. John and Jane.

I pulled myself up by the rail. One step, two, three. I collapsed again on the fourth step, gasping in air as hard as I could but getting no relief. The door to the third floor tantalized me, so close, so unreachable in front of me. I closed my eyes, gathering my strength and my will to reach it. I pulled myself up again, not quite to standing, doubled over but mobile again. Fifth step. Landing. My hand was on the lever of the door, and I pushed with all the strength I had left.

A buzzing rose in my ears, my head started to swim, and darkness started to close off my vision like an encroaching tunnel. Where was the light? Wasn't there supposed to be light? Where was John? Wasn't he supposed to meet me?

"Oh, dear God," I whispered, as the last of the light slipped away and I fell into darkness, "I am so sorry."

****

Connor couldn't believe that he was driving like a bat out of hell along the highway to Montrose, couldn't believe that he cared so much, that she was — as far as he knew — hovering between life and death and there was nothing he could do about it. Damn the road, damn the cell-holes that kept him out of touch, though he doubted he'd be able to get any information, anyway. He'd given her son his number as he climbed aboard the life-flight, his eyes red, his hands shaking. Damn the man who'd shot her.

It would be almost an hour before he knew anything. Sixty interminable minutes. He gunned his car past a camper-truck, chugging along the Divide, oblivious to the notion that there might be something coming the other way. Damn them, too, they'd just have to get out of the way.

She'd managed to get down the stairwell to the third floor and had collapsed through the door, a motionless heap, her blood staining the floor outside the lounge. That Navajo tech had roused the troops and called everyone he could think of, thanks be to God, and he'd been among them. He'd arrived just as the paramedics were pumping her full of fluids and calling for the helicopter. She was pale and silent, eyes closed, a purpling bruise on her temple, her right breast obscured by an enormous wad of bandages, what he could see of her shirt stiff with the blood she'd spilled onto the floor.

He'd touched her hand, warm and limp, before they pushed him away to load her onto the gurney. Her son was sobbing like a child, and he'd put a strong arm around him. "It'll be fine, Ben, she'll be fine." Ben hadn't been able to say a word, had just gone with the paramedics, still weeping. The priest had arrived in time with another cleric in tow, and that one anointed her before the helicopter lifted off, and the two of them had stood there, silent, praying, watching it disappear down the valley.

And now here he was, racing to see what happened. As if getting there a minute earlier would make any difference at all. She was in God's hands, God's and the Blessed Mother's, and the doctors'. It reminded him of too many such trips in Belfast and Derry. Most of those had turned out badly, and how often he'd stoked the anger that came out of the following grief before he realized how futile it was. He'd done exactly what she had been doing, and he'd chastised her the last time they spoke, and they'd parted badly. And now he might never get the chance to apologize.

Why did it matter so much? She wouldn't give him the time of day, so tied up she was in that dead husband of hers. She was cross and businesslike and temperamental and enchanting and brilliant and altogether lovely, with those black eyes and curly hair she'd never bothered to darken once it started to gray. There was a spark of life in her that was compelling, that demanded response, even now, in the midst of her despair. It was something that Dead John must have known and loved, something he could still see himself as hard as she tried to hide it. Something her own anguish hadn't yet extinguished.

He sighed. Even if she did give him the time of day, not much good it would do him, him having no standing to court her even if she were inclined. Not since Fiona had abandoned him and then lied about it for spite, and not since Holy Mother Church ruled that the marriage was valid, nonetheless. It had never really bothered him, not until now. Now, for some reason, it mattered. No, not for some reason. It mattered because *she* mattered. Perhaps he would ask the Tribunal again, if she recovered. Perhaps Fiona would be honest this time.

He wanted her to live, wanted her to bridge that awful distance she had set up between her and the rest of the world before it made her hard and set and bitter and used up in sorrow. He wanted her to get past all that anger, all that sadness, and he wanted to be the one to help. He wanted that life to be there, revealed, visible, warming, engaging. He wanted...

He realized that what he wanted didn't matter as much as what really was and what was going to be. It was the same lesson he'd learned that August morning in Ulster so many years ago. *Let it go*, he told himself, and began the prayers his mother had taught him as a boy. It wasn't the same as praying at his bedside, with his mother's hand on his back, but it would have to do. *Hail Mary...*

He made the turn onto Highway 550, pushing the accelerator another fraction and throwing in an intercession for open roads and no police.

CHAPTER TWENTY-FIVE

JUNE 21

I couldn't decide which hurt worse: my head, my throat or my side. I finally settled on my side. A dull, persistent ache that was like the drone on a set of pipes, always there, constant, never changing, over which the pain in my throat when I swallowed, and in my head when I even thought of opening my eyes provided a varying, if unpleasant, melody line. I was pretty sure that meant I was still alive, though my mind was foggy enough I wasn't entirely certain. I strained to think, which pained me in yet another way, sorting out what happened. I remembered the roof garden, hurrying Ben away, that peculiar flash and then being shot, that was it. I remembered the stairs and passing out. I even had a vague and impossible memory of John's voice, and that was the last full fabric of recollection I had.

But there were bits and snatches after that. I remembered hearing voices, feeling hands — strong ones — maneuvering me even though I saw nothing and said nothing, and could not even respond with a purposeful movement. I remembered the sweet smell of something unexpected and the touch of a soft hand on my face, my hands. My hands. I strained to remember: was there a rougher touch as well, gentle, but not so soft? I gave up trying to sort it out, but the impression of it remained.

I remembered coming around in a bright, cold recovery room, a familiar spot. Surgery. There must have been surgery. I remember trying to sit up, a firm hand on my shoulder, pain everywhere, and then the closing in of darkness again, this time with a dizziness of mind that somehow reassured me this was just sleep. Much needed sleep.

And now this. The pain in my head subsided, secondary now to my raw throat. Did I dare open my eyes? I lifted one lid cautiously, forcing the other one shut in anticipation of the pain of light.

There was no pain, and the light was soft. I opened both eyes, and shifted my head, looking around, orienting myself to the surroundings. I was in a hospital bed, in a private room, rails up, pillows under my head, uniform, thin cotton blankets tucked military style around me. I must have been sedated. My bedclothes never looked this good after a night's sleep; they are all tussled and knotted from my fretting through the night. An IV in my left hand, something bulky on my right side — a chest tube? Ugly blue print hospital gown that — by the feel of it — was open along my back. Great.

I ventured to lift my head a bit more and saw a figure in a chair next to the bed. I wrinkled my brow in confusion. It wasn't John; John had a beard, and anyway, John was dead, I knew that, but who was this man, slumped in the chair, head on his chest, snoring gently? Silver hair, cheeks stubbled, cotton shirt. A cold pipe on his lap, cold, but a pipe, nonetheless. I wondered once again how he smuggled it in, and moreover, why? Connor? *What was Eoin Connor doing at my bedside?*

I croaked out his name. My scratchy throat and the ache in my side made it not much more than a whisper, but he heard it and was up in an instant. His pipe clattered to the floor as he stood, but he retrieved it in a single smooth movement and was standing over me, smiling, laying a gentle hand on mine, the one with the IV in the back of it. It was the rough hand I remembered through the fog. What had Eoin Connor been doing at the Center when I was shot?

"What are you doing here?" I finally managed. It was an effort to speak; my mouth was dry and nothing seemed to work quite right.

"Waiting for you."

It was a simple answer, but still foggy, I struggled to process its meaning. I must have looked perplexed, because he continued.

"Ben's off at the airport getting Adam — isn't he the daredevil in Alaska? Turns out there's quite an alliance of flying priests and parishioners — he's coming in on someone-or-other's Lear jet. Literally hitchhiked his way across country in the air."

Connor's head shook in admiration, and he smiled to himself.

"Ben didn't get through to Beth until he already knew you were out of danger, so he told her to stay home and finish her classes. Zoe's sick in bed with morning sickness so bad she can't get more than a few feet from the bathroom, but Ben keeps her and Seth — that's the one in Rome, right? — updated by texting."

He was reading from the screen of his phone, unable, I supposed, to keep up. Not surprising, given my far-flung family. But something he said jarred me into complete wakefulness, my heart racing, unaccustomed pleasure rising.

"Morning sickness? Zoe's pregnant?"

A grandchild. My Zoe. My only married child, Zoe, wife of Zach, who worked in advertising in Manhattan. Zoe, who wanted to start a shop in Brooklyn, where they lived, one that would be a haven for mothers and their children, with books and toys and storytellers and a soda fountain. Zoe, the first girl to steal John's heart clean away when she put her tiny hand around his fingers that first day in the hospital. Zoe was pregnant?

Connor's face flushed, aware that he'd made a misstep. He stammered out a reply. "I'm sorry, I thought you knew, Ben didn't tell me..."

His voice petered out, then resumed again as he valiantly changed the subject, jerking his head in the direction of another, more distant chair.

"And that one, that one drove straight through from Oregon when he heard, came in last night after midnight, exhausted but wouldn't hear of leaving."

I lifted up a little higher and saw Luke's form draped over another chair, wedged into the corner of the room. He was wearing the paint-spattered tee-shirt and jeans that were his trademark; he hadn't taken time to change but had come right from whatever construction job needed his artisan's skill. He covered the seat and the arms of the chair like an overgrown cat. Tears again, but this time grateful ones. Connor pulled a tissue from the box on the bedside table and dried my eyes.

"You've quite a brood," he said as he pressed more tissues into my hand for future use. "And he sleeps like a stone, that one. I've never seen anything like it."

I laughed, but only briefly, because it hurt.

"That he does. When he was a teenager, a tornado took out a tree right outside his bedroom. The whole house shook, and Luke slept right though it."

I paused, not quite knowing what to say, nor how to say it, overwhelmed at how my children had dropped everything in their own lives to surround me, but overwhelmed too that this stranger — and one I'd been more than churlish to — had done the same.

"Eoin." I finally said, using his Christian name with him for the first time. "Thank you for being here."

His hand closed over mine, and he looked as though he was going to speak, but Luke stirred in his chair. Realizing that I was awake, he bounded over to the bedside, elbowing Connor out of the way in his enthusiasm. He grabbed my hand in his and leaned over to give me a kiss. He smelled like work, salty and with the faint aroma of paint, sweat and dirt, my workingman son. An unruly brown curl fell over his face, and his cheeks, like Connor's, were stubbled from lack of shaving.

"Mom! Are you all right? You scared us to death."

"I'm fine. Or I will be. Or at least, I think I will be," I amended as I realized I really had no idea about my medical state. Connor would know. I lifted my head to peer around Luke, who still held my hands firmly, and called out his name.

But he'd slipped out, leaving me alone with Luke. I was surprised at the empty twinge it added to the symphony of my bodily aches and pains as I settled back on the bed to listen to my carpenter son's welcome voice.

****

Luke was still there, and Ben had returned with Adam when the doctor came in to check on my progress, breaking up a slightly tearful and very noisy reunion as all three of my sons tried to edge each other out in telling me news and asking me questions, just as they had when they were children. This time, I noticed that Ben more than held his own, a certain confidence in jockeying with Adam and Luke that he had not displayed before. And it was Ben who sat protectively — if illicitly — on the foot of my bed, imposing himself as protector and guardian. How life changes.

The doctor was a tall, balding man whose age, about my own, I found reassuring. He shooed my protesting sons out the door, closed it, and returned to my side. In the best bedside manner, he held my wrist in his fingers as he read from the chart and introduced himself as Dr. Butcher. *Bad name for a surgeon,* I thought.

His routine reminded me of those first classes in medical school, introducing us to patient care. An aging professor, notable for having been the man to administer the first dose of penicillin in the U.S., instructed us to take the patient's hand whenever we came into a room. You can learn so much, he had told us. If it's warm, fever; cold and clammy, shock. Feel the pulse, look at the nail beds. Is there cyanosis? Clubbing? Pitting? It's all a clue to what is happening inside.

I doubted my hand revealed much other than I was alive, had good vital signs, no interest in manicures, and had recently crushed a wine glass, but Dr. Butcher's touch was comforting if for no other reason than that I could feel it. Most of the hands I touched in the course of my professional life, after all, were past feeling. They were cold and stiff, and almost anything I wanted to learn I had to wrest from them by force and intrusion. The enormity of my experience was beginning to settle in. My hand was warm, and it connected me at that moment to the man who had saved my life.

He dropped my hand with a smile. "Good to see you back with us."

Yes, indeed, it was. Very nice. I nodded in agreement. "What happened?"

"You know you were shot, yes?"

"Yes." I paused. "What did it hit?" I could ask with some confidence, given the fact that I was alive to talk about it. In my world, that alone meant I was pretty well off. As, in fact, I was.

"Odd trajectory," he said, lapsing into medical-ese, undoubtedly having been filled in by someone — my guess was Ben — about who I am. "Downward path. Small caliber, not sure what, .22 maybe. Not my area of expertise, I left that to your staff. They haven't gotten back to me."

He motioned me to lean forward, listening for my breath sounds with a stethoscope he had recently retrieved from a freezer.

It certainly was, I thought. Even as I emerged from the cloud of the last few days, I knew my shooting was related to the rest. Though given that the gun that killed Kessler was locked up in the San Miguel County Sheriff's evidence locker, I knew it couldn't be the same one. I wondered who shot it. Come to think of it, if Connor was right, how did I know that gun was even locked up? I wondered how many medical examiners investigated their own shootings. As many as survived them, I guessed, then wondered what sort of exclusive club that might be. I had every intention of starting that investigation. Just not today.

The surgeon moved the flat, round head of the scope around my back, obliged me to cough and breathe deeply, then, satisfied, snapped the earpieces out, draped it around his neck and continued, arms folded across his chest.

"Entry at the upper, outer quadrant of your right breast—just. It nicked your right lung, carved a pretty good furrow, actually, that dropped your right lung right away and took us a while to fix. But we got to try out our VATS on a gunshot wound; you were our inaugural patient. And all things considered, there was remarkably little damage. Your lung came right up, not much drainage. You're a remarkable patient."

I remembered reading that the hospital had recently acquired video-assisted technology for surgery. Who knew I'd get to try it out? I wiggled my shoulders and chest a bit. It was uncomfortable, but nothing like the old intercostal incision would have been. *Hooray for robots.*

Dr. Butcher smiled broadly, the smile of a surgeon satisfied with a good case and a new toy, an expression I had seen on John's face many times.

"That — and the fact that you took a pretty good knock on your head when you fell through the door — probably explains why you were unconscious so soon. They put a tube in you before transporting, you had a chest full of blood, and they tell me you left a good bit on the floor where they found you. It took a couple of units to get you back where you belonged."

He paused, pointing to his own right side as he continued, "The bullet tracked along the back of your chest right along a rib. It didn't hit anything major, liver, big vessels, none of that. Just sort of ran out of speed because of the rib it connected with and finally ended up just under the skin of your back, waiting for us to come and get it. We did. It looked in pretty good shape, by the way."

He made a few notes on the chart, then resumed his narrative.

"I had to put you in ICU for a day, because you kept trying to pull out your tube and IV. We just shut you down for your own good. I moved you to the floor just this morning, you're doing so well." He paused. "You were lucky. Most of the time a .22 wreaks utter havoc. Remarkable."

How well I knew, and knew why. I sent up a prayer of thanks to my guardian angel and to John.

"When can I go home?"

"I want to pull your chest tube, and we'll see. Maybe tomorrow."

Suddenly, I wanted desperately to be away from the hospital, surrounded by my children and my dogs and cats. In familiar surroundings. In my own bed. In the chaos of my own life. My life. The one I was lucky to have, even without John by my side. Just as suddenly, I never wanted to see the house again and wanted my children anywhere but Telluride. "How about you pull the tube and if I'm okay in a few hours, you send me home with a 24/7 nurse and my vigilant family."

I'd figure out somewhere other than home to go, but Dr. Butcher didn't need to know that. He furrowed his forehead and shook his head. "I don't know..." he began. "You're looking pretty good, but I'd rather...."

I didn't let him finish. "What do you expect to happen to me tomorrow?" I pushed, trying to back him into a corner.

"Nothing much. I just want to watch you."

"Nothing much can happen at home as well as here. Isn't your fancy new VATS supposed to get me home sooner?"

"Not that soon. What if you collapse a lung again? Too risky."

"I could always sign out against advice."

Dr. Butcher smiled, showing the gold edge of a bridge on the left side of his mouth.

"Mr. Connor told me to watch out for you. 'Stubborn as a setter,' he said. I'd have said mule, but I got his meaning. Let me check your wound, and we'll see."

He pulled back the covers and lifted my gown to look at the bandage. Then he called for the nurse, and between them, with scrubbed and gloved hands, they changed my bandage and eased the tube out of my right chest.

Remind me to testify that that isn't a walk in the park, either. I gasped as it finally snaked out, then took a tentative deep breath. Everything moved as it should. There was enough discomfort to offer up, but not much more, and my headache was receding. I was elated and laid back on the bed, smoothing the dreadful gown and the rumpled sheets. I smiled as sweetly as I could, and was surprised at how weak the smile was and how grateful.

"Can you find Mr. Connor for me?"

****

Connor arrived a few minutes later without my boys in tow.

"The lads went for a bite of lunch," he explained. "They won't be long."

I struggled to sit upright for a moment before Connor stepped to the bedside and adjusted the head of the bed, smiling.

"Not much of a patient, I see," he said.

Embarrassed at such a silly lapse on my part, I cast him a sharp look.

"Doctors usually aren't," was all I said. My side hurt where the tube had been pulled, and I found I was hungry myself. I took a breath, winced at the pain again, and continued. "I need a favor, Eoin. A big one." I consciously used his first name; it was less forced than I expected.

One wiry brow lifted in surprise, but he said nothing. Instead, he turned aside just long enough to pull up a chair and settle himself with an expectant look on his face, still silent. Damn the man, he was going to make me work for it. I decided on the direct approach.

"It wasn't me the shooter was aiming for."

The words lay between us for a long moment before Connor's expression changed from expectation to puzzlement.

"You were the only one there. You're trying to solve the murders. Seems reasonable you'd be a target."

"I was a substitute. It's Ben he was after. I know it."

Connor leaned forward, hands folded, elbows on the side of the bed. He stroked his upper lip with his thumbs, then rested his chin on them before he spoke.

"Ben's a trusty. He's one of the marked." Tears welled up. It was so much worse to hear someone else say it than to hear it in the recesses of my own mind. I nodded, cleared my throat and continued.

"Ben takes his lunch on the roof nearly every day. The shooter would have no idea that I'd be there. He wanted Ben. He wanted my boy."

I paused, my constricting throat making it impossible to continue. I would not cry. I would not.

Connor shifted a bit but remained quiet, giving me time. I felt the time tick by inside me until the tightness receded, and I dared my voice again.

"The boys can't go back to town. They can't be there, not even for a minute. I can't lose Ben, any of my boys. I..." my voice trailed off, tears threatening again.

This time Connor stood and looked down at me for a moment, expressionless except for the furrowing of his brow. Then he covered my hand in his, the rough touch I remembered from the fog.

"I'll have them come with me," he said. "I've plenty of room." Then his placid features split in a wicked grin. "Of course, you'll be coming, too. You know they won't abandon you."

He paused a moment, clearly relishing the prospect and giving it time to sink into my own horrified mind.

I flushed as I realized he was right, which produced a laugh, then a pat on my hand, more kindly than I expected. When he spoke, he trotted out his brogue for effect, underlining that I had been outmaneuvered. "You poor wee thing," was all he said, but I saw his smile and heard him chuckle as he went out the door in search of my boys.

****

It took most of the day to make the arrangements, but Ben finally lined up a private duty nurse with the help of a buddy from the Medical

Center. Dr. Butcher insisted on ambulance transport, just in case, and wouldn't let me move until the nurse called from the house to let him know that she had arrived with the necessary back-up IV bags and tubing, with the doctors and paramedics at the Medical Center on alert to put in a chest tube if my lung collapsed again, just in case. I rode in the back of the ambulance, annoyed and restless that I couldn't see the passing scenery. I made the fresh-faced EMT provide me running commentary as we passed along the valley to Ridgeway, across the Dallas Divide, and wound up the twisting valley toward Eoin Connor's place in Mountain Village.

The ambulance made its slow and deliberate way to a back drive, near a service door. It appeared I would be brought in like yesterday's laundry. I was gratified that the drive was underground and surrounded by high, stone walls. I never wanted to be out in the open again, even here, where no murders — except for Houston's — had occurred. I considered that ill-fitting fact again for several minutes in spite of myself as they bundled me out the back — out of commission but not off-duty. It spared me worrying about more present concerns, like the safety of my sons.

Ben walked by my side and held my hand as the attendants bumped me up a few steps and rattled me into a service elevator, where they punched the buttons for the top floor. *Fine digs,* I thought to myself. Writing must pay pretty well.

We made our way through a laundry area smelling of bleach and pine, around several corners and down a back hall, the unseen vitals of the luxury building. Eventually, we emerged into a posh hall, all log and leather. I passed under an elk-antler chandelier and counted the lights for amusement. Fifteen, before I was turned down another hall and lost sight of it.

Connor opened the door before we even arrived. The gurney rolled into a spacious room with a cathedral ceiling, all logs and antlers, like the hall. Logs, antlers, and my brood. My whole household.

I was immediately surrounded by a noisy, relentless, loving crowd. Straps finally loosened, I sat up and swung my legs around, pausing to let myself equilibrate before trying to stand, overwhelmed at the sight. The room was crowded with people. Three of my four strong boys, Ben at the fore, offering me his arm with the advice to "Take it easy, Mom.

We've got you set up in the study."

Adam and Luke, now freshly showered in chinos and a blue polo, stepped respectfully back to let him take his rightful place. I noticed as I passed that Adam's close-cropped hair had a few threads of silver in it. He'd gotten at least a few of my genes, it appeared.

Behind the boys was Isa, with Pablo in hand, Mariela and Ignacio standing shyly beside Lupe. If my nose was any judge, Pilar was at work in the kitchen. Father Matt, looking on, quiet and thoughtful, still wearing those unfamiliar jeans. A competent-looking middle-aged nurse in blue scrubs and white clogs stood by. I looked around as Ben's strong arm guided me to an easy chair across from a bank of windows that looked out over the mountains now awash in alpenglow. A cherry desk with a computer and towering stacks of paper was in the corner next to a matching filing cabinet with one drawer partially open and a file protruding from it at an angle. Photographs were strewn in a semi-circle to the right of a comfortable-looking Scandinavian desk chair upholstered in trade-blanket wool.

Apparently I was invading Connor's writer's sanctum, and he felt no compulsion to tidy it up. That small fact somehow made me feel better, safer, more ordinary. I looked around to thank him, but he had disappeared.

Ben settled me in a chair and propped my feet up on the ottoman. Caroline, the nurse, shooed everyone out, then checked me over, pronounced me well, and dashed my hopes of a good dinner by reminding me that I was still on clear liquids for another day. It was pure anguish to eat green Jell-O and tepid chicken bouillon while the rest of them crowded into the study, plates on their laps, enjoying tamales and chiles rellenos, talking over each other in English and Spanish, to ask me questions or to catch me up on what had been happening. Pure, unadulterated, wonderful, healing anguish.

It was two hours later when the last of the dishes had been cleared, Father Matt had made his excuses, the women had disappeared with children in tow, and Ben, Adam, Luke and I were left alone in the study as the shadows outside deepened. We made small talk, carefully avoiding both the subject of their father's death and my own close call. Ben caught the boys up on the trustafarian murders, unaware, I hoped, that my close call was really his.

The hoopla that had accompanied the swift departure from this mortal coil of Mitch Houston elicited great interest from Adam, who then regaled us with stories of Alaska. Luke, ever the quiet one, mostly listened, interjecting his approval now and again, or asking the odd detail about one of his brothers' elaborate yarns. I sat aside, there but so very separate, watching with great satisfaction as his brothers teased out of him where he was working (a new condo complex in Newport) and what he was doing (learning to play the banjo, dating a nice girl named Ella who worked in a dairy making artisan goat cheeses).

I shifted in my seat, still a little uncomfortable on my right side, but contented in a way that I hadn't experienced for a long time, the tiniest warmth beginning in the very center of my being. I was happy just to be the observer in this family tableau. An observer, but an engaged one, a living one.

There was a lull in the conversation as Caroline came in to check me out again. She had just pocketed her stethoscope when I heard footsteps behind me. I tried to crane my neck to see who was approaching, but my side still hurt too much.

"You have company, Mom."

Ben motioned to his brothers, nodding his head in the direction of the front hall, and they got up to leave, each giving me half a hug and a kiss on the cheek as they left. Ben was the last, his kiss on the top of my disheveled hair, the same kind of goodnight kiss I used to give him as a boy. Caroline pocketed the thermometer and stood up as Eoin Connor materialized in the corners of my vision.

I gave a quick prayer of thanks for whoever invented the digital thermometer. With any luck, Caroline would take the hint and be out of my hair in a minute. She was, with a reminder to Connor that I needed rest and to call her when I was ready to make my way to the bedroom. I might need rest, I thought, but just now, the last thing in the world I wanted to do was get to sleep. I tried to rise, but Connor put a restraining hand on my shoulder.

"Are you daft? You wouldn't stand for me when you were well. What makes you think you need to now that you're only half a furlong from death's door itself?"

His teasing words were a welcome sign of normalcy. He winked and went immediately to the sideboard where a bottle of scotch — no decanter for him — beckoned, pouring two fingers neat before turning back around to me.

"I've time for a wee dram," he said as he settled onto the couch opposite me, smiling broadly now, and motioning to the glass of half flat ginger ale at my elbow. "I see you're well-supplied yourself."

I made a face. "What I wouldn't give for a drop of that," I said, then sighed. Deep breaths still hurt.

"True enough. Nothing like a bit of holy water to mend one's innards. Sláinte."

He sipped, looked at the glass, put it down, and turned his attention to me.

Fully, completely, utterly to me. The room was suddenly very close and far too warm, and I had to suppress the urge to run — not that I had the ability. Time ticked by in silence as we exchanged glances, my face flushing deeper by the minute as I considered his kind eyes and patient look. I lost the battle.

"You never did tell me how you managed to convince the nurses to let you into my room," I said, breaking my gaze and feeling my face flush even more deeply as I reached for the ginger ale, hoping to maintain a bit of dignity.

I felt like a schoolgirl sitting across from the new boy in class, hoping he'd not find me completely hideous. I felt just as I had that first day in medical school when I went into my anatomy lab and met the handsome, interesting intern who'd been assigned to help us learn the mysteries of the human body. The handsome intern who'd laughed when I couldn't make that first cut into the skin of my cadaver, who had taken my hand in his and demonstrated the force it took to get through the skin.

"Like this," he had said. "Press down, let your finger guide the rest of your hand as you make the cut. It takes more than you think to get past someone's skin."

The intern who'd stolen my heart and fathered my children.

"Oh, that."

Connor's words interrupted my thoughts, brought me back into time.

"You'd be surprised what a small lie — abetted by your son — will do. As far as Dr. Butcher knows, I'm your cousin, just here from the Auld Sod itself."

There was that Irish manipulation again, broad accent showing forth as he recounted his tale to me, no doubt in the very words and accent he'd used to charm Dr. Butcher, "...at my wit's end because my dearest cousin who lived next door and the only one that's left besides meself — has just been gunned down in cold blood in this wicked excuse for a country." He smiled again and lifted his glass.

My eyebrows raised. "I gather that nobody reads much in that hospital, least of all Dr. Butcher."

Connor was so famous, I couldn't imagine him pulling off such a ruse. His was a striking face, a memorable figure. He was a celebrity, after all. I couldn't imagine anyone not recognizing him, conveniently forgetting that a scant month ago, I hadn't known him from Adam. The original one.

"You must know how to play the game, dear Jane. Of course, he knew it was a lie. The point is, it was a lie he could use as a plausible excuse to give me what I wanted. Actually, what Ben wanted. He was crazy with worry but couldn't spend every moment with you. He needed help. I was happy to oblige."

Another sip of whiskey.

"Well, I'm glad you did." I paused, gathered some courage, and continued. "I've behaved very badly to you. I'm sorry. I can't imagine that you'd—that you'd be willing...that you'd..."

I stumbled over my thoughts. What I wanted to say was that I'd been a perfect ass, and in the same circumstance it would never have occurred to me to sit up at the sickbed of someone who had been so...well, mean. I tried again.

"I behaved badly," I repeated. "I am so sorry. Please forgive me. Perhaps I can start again?" I looked up, straight into those arresting green eyes again, and they were both serious and smiling.

"You've a bit of the harridan in you, there's no denying it," he said.

"But then, there's not a dish worth having without its measure of salt."

He paused just a breath more than a moment, making me anxious for what would come next. I wasn't sure what it would be, and worse yet, I wasn't sure what I wanted it to be. I was relieved to hear his voice take up the conversation again and pleased by what he said, inexplicably pleased.

"That's enough of that—not another word. We'll just get on again, shall we?"

He raised his glass and drained it in one draught, put it down carefully and regarded me seriously, no smile lingering in his eyes. The pleasure I had felt began to wither. Silence grew again until finally he broke it.

"I'm not above a white lie, Jane Wallace, when it suits me, and isn't dangerous. But here's the truth. You worry me. You've been to the brink and back, twice over now, and I can't bear the thought of your going back again. Your husband is dead, God be good to him, but you're not and I'm glad."

His candor made me uncomfortable, and I looked away, unwilling to meet his gaze any longer and afraid of what he might see in my own eyes. Connor rose and stepped to the side of my chair. Leaning down, he took my chin in his hand, and turned my reluctant face towards his again.

"I don't know you at all, Woman, and I'm going to."

I cast my eyes down, unwilling to look at him. This felt somehow intimate and reassuring, and it disoriented me.

"Don't shut me out. Don't shut them out. It's a hard life sometimes, that I know. But don't shut us out."

His thumb ran across my cheek, and he kissed the top of my head, just as Ben had done.

"I've taken a room in town for the time being. I'll call tomorrow," he said and was gone.

I sat looking out the window into the darkness for a long time, thinking before I called Caroline to help me to bed. It did not escape my notice that Connor had given me over his own room, and the bed I was going to was his. I wondered how I would sleep.

****

Eoin Connor strolled up Pacific, slow and thoughtful. He stopped in the light of a street lamp in front of the tee-shirt store and pulled out his pipe and tobacco. He stuffed the bowl automatically, by habit and not by intent, tamping the tobacco with his thumb and lighting it with a match struck on the side of the lamppost. He ignored the frowning glances of those who passed, cursing mildly when the first match wasn't enough, and lit another. So absorbed was he in the process that he failed to see Father Matt, engaged in similar activity, leaning against the building on the downhill side.

"Another sinner, I see."

Father Matt's voice almost startled him except for the fact that he'd trained that response out of himself years ago. Eoin took a couple of satisfactory puffs, then cradled the pipe in his hand. He tried, usually unsuccessfully, not to reply through clenched teeth, even to another smoker. It smacked of rudeness, and Father Matt had become a friend.

"Hopeless, I'm afraid," he admitted. "I didn't know you indulged. Not so common these days."

Father Matt finally succeeded in lighting his own pipe and stepped up into the light to shake hands.

"I'm not sure when I got the habit. My uncle has a pipe and I admired him. It seemed natural. Nasty habit that it is, it's a certain comfort. No one's perfect."

"True enough." Eoin took a puff from his own pipe. "You're out of uniform."

Father Matt tamped the pipe and puffed again.

"Haven't you heard? I've been relieved of my faculties. The bishop thinks it's poor form to have a murder suspect in charge of a parish."

"You're in good company, lad. Patrick had the same thing happen to him. He was cleared. You will be, too."

"Any progress on the murders?"

"No, not really. Tom Patterson is holding this close to his chest, and try as she might, Jane hasn't figured it out. She's like a terrier, that one. Every time she thinks about it, she grabs hold of the case and gnaws on it, but nothing yet. And before you ask, no, I've no ideas either. Remember, all I do is tie up the strings other people tease out into a pretty bow at the end. I'm no good at working these things out myself."

"Is that so?" Father Matt was applying yet another match to the bowl of his pipe, and had no compunctions about talking around the stem. "I've read your books. You're good enough."

CHAPTER TWENTY-SIX

JUNE 22, MORNING

I woke early, as soon as the first bit of light began to come through the window and my pain medicine wore off. I sat up gingerly, sore and weak, but otherwise not much worse for the wear. Connor's bedroom was decorated in an odd mixture of styles, unsuited to his very masculine presence. The king-sized bed had an ornate, old-fashioned iron frame with well-worn glass doorknobs as finials on the tall, pink posts. The side tables were overdone French provincial and the armoire a beautiful art deco piece with elegant, feminine curves setting off the design inherent in the birds-eye maple. A deep green flokati rug covered the hardwood floor. The green was picked up in the geometric design of the drapes, which were otherwise a riot of colors and a mess of ruffles. It was strikingly ugly. I gave thanks that Kiki Berton was a better designer than this. This, I would have been compelled to redo. I'm indifferent to my surroundings, not numb.

I swung my legs over the side of the bed and allowed my swimming head to clear before I tried standing up. I was still tethered to an IV pole, and it rattled as I stood up and grabbed it, suddenly intent on reaching the turquoise and gold bathroom. I might as well have pressed a buzzer. Caroline materialized in the doorway with a chastising look on her face.

"Let me help you."

I wondered how she got there so fast; was she sleeping in the hall?

She must have seen my confusion because she added, "I was on my way to check on you. Time for your medicine, if you want it. Sit down for a minute, and let me get you some water, then I'll help you to the loo."

She was sharp and businesslike and was back with a gold-rimmed glass decorated with gilt grapevines before I had a chance to protest. I took my pill dutifully; the truth was that my side ached fiercely. Then she guided me to the toilet with a gentle hand under my elbow. I was grateful she gave me the dignity of taking care of myself after that, closing the door with an admonition to wait for her, and she would help me back to bed.

When she did return, it was with a thermometer, a stethoscope and a glass of cold milk. Once she confirmed that I wasn't febrile and that my lungs and guts sounded as they should, she handed me the glass.

"Ben told me you like to start your day with a glass of milk. He made sure we had some for you; I gather Mr. Connor isn't much of a milk drinker."

She paused long enough to count the beats of my heart, her fingers firm on my wrist. Funny, taking a pulse is such a simple and routine thing, but it utterly defines how dependent a patient is. Just as it had in the hospital, the feel of fingers on my wrist brought me an unfamiliar sense of calm and protection. I hadn't realized until I woke up in the hospital and Dr. Butcher took my hand how little I touched living people these days, how much my grief had isolated me physically. I hadn't realized how much the laying on of hands can heal. What we touch touches us in the deepest ways, and I hadn't been touching live people much lately.

Caroline dropped my wrist. "You're doing well, but I expected that. Dr. B is first rate. Would you like to come out into the living room? I think you can see the sunrise from there, and it doesn't look like you're in any mood to go back to bed."

She helped me on with a robe, no small feat when there's an IV line involved, and we rattled our way to the living room. I settled on the burgundy leather couch, propped my feet on the log coffee table, and watched the sun turn the sky purple and pink and gold in turns. There were dark clouds already; it would rain by the end of the day. Good. The sound of rain and the dreariness of a gray sky has always refreshed me. I can handle storms; it's relentless sunshine that depresses me.

Caroline provided me a cup of coffee, made a few notes in my chart and disappeared.

"Holler if you need something."

I would have welcomed the company, but I suppose the habits of the hospital die hard: don't spend more time with any one patient than you need to, because there's always someone else with a demand on your time. And don't get attached. John always managed that last one well. His attachments were at home. Compassionate surgeon that he was, his patients were just that. The fact that I'd never managed to keep the two roles straight was only one of the reasons that I worked in the morgue and he had worked inside people's heads.

The clouds scurried across the sky, and the gold faded to gray as the morning darkened again with the approaching weather. The first fork of lightning brightened the horizon as I heard the door open behind me. I craned my neck, but it didn't take much of a detective to know who it was.

"Ah, the patient is up and taking nourishment."

I smiled, genuinely happy to see him. "Up, but no nourishment yet. Unless you count coffee and milk. Caroline is my nurse, not my cook, and the boys aren't up yet. I was just enjoying the rain, but I suppose I should get something to eat."

I realized that I was hungry. Really hungry, my long-forgotten appetite returned with a vengeance. I started to stand, but Eoin's hand on my shoulder restrained me.

"It's my kitchen. I'll thank you to stay out of it. I think I have the makings of an Ulster fry."

"It seems I'm superfluous," I replied as he poured himself coffee and refreshed mine, finishing the pot that had been on the stove.

"Let people take care of you for a while," he said. "You're worth it."

He started to busy himself in the kitchen, but I called him back.

"Take either my coffee or the pole. Let me sit at the counter while you work. The rain can wait."

Eoin took the coffee cup from my hand, and I dragged the pole behind me with my good hand. It followed like a sorrowful puppy. I noticed the bag was about empty; I hoped Caroline would not feel compelled to hang another. I sat on one of the upholstered bar stools that stood at attention along the granite bar and watched as Eoin Connor made breakfast.

I was surprised at the quality of the pans he pulled from the cabinets and the ease with which he handled them. I was utterly astonished by the contents of the refrigerator. It was full, and the contents had the look of being the result of everyday life, not just provisions laid in for my arrival.

"What's an Ulster fry?" I asked.

He answered without even a glance in my direction, intent on cutting rounds from two tubes, one light, one dark. There were eggs in a bowl, and strips of meat that looked like Canadian bacon were already on the stove next to links of sausage. The aroma was almost unbearable.

"The world's best breakfast. Designed to keep an Ulster farmer working in the fields all day long. Eggs, sausage, bacon, white and black puddings, toast, marmalade."

"Pudding? I'm generally game for unconventional breakfasts, but pudding?"

Eoin waved his knife at the rounds on the cutting board, far more than were needed for the two of us.

"Not like dessert. A sort of porridge loaf. One made with blood, the other with pork, if you're well-heeled enough to have it. When I was a cub, we just made it with oatmeal and spices."

"I'll pass on the blood one, thanks."

"Nonsense. It's good, and in your current state it's good for you. Source of iron, don't you know."

He dropped the rounds into a second pan and finally looked over at me, flourishing the knife for emphasis and smiling.

My eyes welled with tears. It was just the same kind of gesture John would have made. He was the weekend breakfast cook. Always making something special for the children and me: French toast, beignets, even an elegant dish called eggs champagne, reserved for adult birthdays and childhood milestones. I was wiping my eyes when the sound of my boys yanked me from my nostalgia into the present. Leave it to the smell of food to rouse them.

They each hugged me in turn, calling out greetings to Eoin and pitching in. Ben rooted around in the refrigerator and came up with fruit. Luke started another pot of coffee. Adam got out plates, fussy things with a stylized castle in the center, surrounded by vines and curlicues. They matched the garish cup I was drinking from.

"Looks like that bag is about done," Caroline said behind me. "How about I take out that IV? You're doing fine."

No more lines, no more pole, one more step towards normalcy, whatever that was.

"You bet." I extended my hand eagerly and only winced a little when she slid the thin tubing out of the back of my hand. I don't know why, but that particular discomfort has always been out of proportion for me, hurting much more than it was intended to, more than the injury deserves. More pain than necessary for such a simple procedure. I flexed my hand with satisfaction after Caroline was done, regarding the folded square of gauze she had taped over the site with great pleasure.

Caroline continued. "I talked to Dr. Butcher. He says if everything continues to check out for the rest of the day, there's no need for me to stay. Just to make sure you're back for a follow-up visit in his office next Monday. And be sure to take it a little easy. And call if there are any problems. *Any* problems."

It seemed to be the day for repetition. Did everyone think me incapable of understanding on the first pass? She packed up the remains of my IV to discard in the red biohazard container that had accompanied me from the hospital.

"So you're released from bondage."

Even with all the chaos and his back to me, Eoin Connor didn't miss a detail, a writer's habit I supposed, as much as a medical examiner's. John had been alert to anything that related to neurosurgery or to his loved ones, but was blissfully oblivious to the rest of the world. He never understood my inability to shut out information, good or bad, never quite knew why everything I encountered affected me. It had been a rough place in our otherwise placid marriage, my moods and worries, something he never really grasped.

I realized with a start that I'd had a negative thought about my husband. An honest one, but a negative one. *Was that another change?* I wondered. John was stepping back down into reality from the pedestal I had put him on, by my leave or without it, and I found the thought comfortable. I had loved all of him, even the things that drove me slightly batty. Better to keep hold of them all.

For the second time that day, I felt a storm of emotion. Indignation and annoyance, followed in close succession by a blush of shame, the warmth of gratitude and something very like affection. This time, I wasn't quick enough to sort them out. Eoin turned to look at me, fork in hand, and found what must have been an expression of mixed bewilderment and apprehension. His brows furrowed as I struggled to find the right thing to say to make light of the moment.

Nothing sufficiently brilliant surfaced, so I just nodded, and took a sip of coffee, now stone cold, for cover.

"I've never known a bachelor with such a well-stocked kitchen," I finally said.

It was unsatisfactory. I wanted to pour out my heart to him, if only because he was near my age, and he'd been through enough of life to understand, had probed and explored enough murders, analyzed enough victims, laid bare the lives of enough survivors to understand what was happening to me. I wanted him to listen and to explain, but there was no asking, not here and not now.

His brows relaxed. He smiled and handed the fork to Ben with instructions to finish up breakfast.

"That's because you knew bachelors that wanted wives. If I hadn't learned to cook, I would have starved long ago." Then he added, "Just like you to bite the hand that's trying to feed you. I'd hate to think that you had some sea-change just because of a missed appointment with a cold morgue slab. The world needs its share of cynics."

The smile broadened, and I knew he understood; he was just teasing. Not wanting to press any further, he changed the subject as he watched Ben fiddle with the sausages.

"I think we can grant that you are right about Father Matt. He was with the vicar general the day you were shot; he's definitely in the clear, not that that will hold any weight with Pete Wilson. Or the bishop. There's still the little matter of Marla Kincaid and Mitch Houston. Father Matt isn't off the hook for that one yet."

He sat down on the stool next to me, cradling his coffee in his big hands.

I shrugged. "I know. One murder at a time, please, and Houston's,

God forgive me, isn't the most important one. His really was a one-time event, crime of someone's passion."

Connor shrugged and leaned forward to rest his forearms on the counter, hunching, then stretching his back. "It would surely help to know what the connection is." He wiped a hand across his face and glanced at me. "We already know they were all wealthy outsiders. It turns out they all were written up in the paper shortly before they were shot, for one reason or another.

Paul Kessler was the subject of one of those profile pieces. Sig Monson did one of those cutesy little sidebar quotes, and it made it very clear he was very rich. Cosette Anira was always in the paper because of her business. Both papers reported on James Webster's newest climbing opportunity. The fellow whose cabin blew up — I'm still not sure that one belongs, but the timing is right — he was mentioned in an article about the visual arts commission. It wasn't exactly a secret that they were all rich and prominent in one way or another. But no other connection I can find beyond that, and the fact that they supported Tom. As far as I know they didn't even know each other."

Eoin Connor might be less suspicious of the sheriff, but I wasn't sure. I kept thinking how easy it would be to get that gun out of the evidence locker. More than that, I wondered why Patterson hadn't stopped by to pay me a call. The fact that my normally sociable colleague had not been by to visit me nagged at me.

"But you weren't written up, were you?"

I shook my head. "I haven't been in the paper for months. Even the report of Webster's death didn't mention me. If the murderer is picking his victims from the paper, I don't fit. And neither does Ben," I added in a low voice.

I still hadn't shared my suspicions with my sons.

"Which means you're overlooking something else. You were picked because you've done something to make the murderer uneasy. Uneasy enough to want to shoot you." Connor's face was serious.

"That's the school solution," I said, "but for the life of me, I have no idea what that could be. I am completely in the dark on this one." I paused. It almost had been for the life of me. Or the life of Ben. I pushed the thought away and said, "I was too close just because I was doing my job." Patterson loomed as a suspect again, but I deliberately shook off the thought of him as suspect. "Maybe you should take a look at the files and see if I am missing something. About all I can say for sure is that my shooting makes it clear that these deaths really are related."

"I'll see what I can do," Connor said, posing like a leading man waiting for his fawning fans and making me giggle in spite of myself. "Famous writer that I am."

He rose and took his cup and mine to the sink, returning with a cloth to wipe up the damp ring his cup had made on the stone counter. We chatted amiably about his book, and his habit of rising to write at three or four in the morning when insomnia overtook him. About the boys when they were younger, stories of Adam raising a great roar of laughter as they always did. About the latest in Telluride gossip. We were so lost in conversation that Luke had to touch my shoulder to tell me breakfast was on the table.

After breakfast, Connor and I sat on the balcony. The storm had cleared, so he wiped the chairs dry and left the boys to cleaning the kitchen. Caroline was gone for the time being, Dr. Butcher having been pleased with my progress.

"I find it odd and more than slightly chilling to be considering a potential assailant every time I think about moving out of the house," I said as we took seats in the dappled shadows, looking out over the wild green of the rising mountain. The sight was familiar and comforting, and it fit Connor's presence with me. He was becoming a rather pleasant habit. "I've got to get Ben to a safe place. I told Luke and Adam it's best for them to go on back this afternoon, so they'll be safe, but Ben is still a target. And if you're right, he's still in danger."

"It won't last. We'll find the bastard who shot you."

His expression darkened, and I was impressed that this was now a personal quest, not one he was going to be content to leave solely in the hands of Tom Patterson. I wondered if he still harbored a bit of suspicion, despite his strong words earlier. It worried me that I was relying on a man I didn't quite trust to solve the crimes and to see that I was safe in the bargain. I shuddered a bit at the thought of Tom Patterson's being in charge of the investigation. Eoin caught my shiver and patted my hand. I turned mine to take hold of his and held it tight for a moment. He picked up the conversational ball in a teasing tone, but sober as a judge underneath.

"So there was a sea-change, after all. Not content to be alone anymore? Not going to shove the rest of us into a closet?"

He was as direct as Father Matt and John and my oldest son. Was there something about me that invited such presumption on the part of men?

"I am not. Gone all soft and emotional, that's me."

There was an ungentlemanly snort of laughter from the other chair.

"Dear Dr. Jane Wallace, pathologist extraordinaire, you've always been soft and emotional, that's your problem. You just need to find a way to manage it without the illusion of a cast-iron fence around your heart."

My usual smart reply flitted across my brain; good that it seemed to be working properly. But this man deserved better than that, and so did my beloved John. I was silent for a long time, turning what he said over in my mind. When I finally spoke, it was with a clarity of understanding I hadn't enjoyed for some time.

"It was the only way I had of coping when John died. It's not the only way I have now."

"I've seen it before. I've seen it save people and I've seen it destroy them. You came very close to destruction, Jane Wallace."

"I know."

"See that you remember. Something tells me you're a bit hard-headed, that it might take a more than a few times to teach you a lesson. You've still a heart full of proper grieving to do, the real kind. It's not going to be easy."

Damn the man. My eyes welled with tears, and I had thought myself finally past them. He sighed heavily, but with a smile on his face, and passed me his handkerchief. It still smelled of peppermint.

****

Lucy Cho clicked on the icon that would set the computer matching prints and turned her attention to the bullet that had come out of Dr.

Wallace's back. It felt strange to be working on the bullet that had almost killed her boss, but that, she figured, was all part of the job. Though she had to admit, for all the hype of Hollywood and real-crime TV shows, being a medical examiner was just about the safest job in the world, if you discounted the risk of hepatitis C and HIV. The old guys in the field, and they were all guys, the ones who wrote the books and gave the lectures, were odd by anyone's standards.

Forensic work was a nice gig: job security, because there were always going to be creeps in the world, and because few people wanted to hang out with dead people and crime scene junkies for a long time. Lucy had not been in the business long, just short of ten years, but she had seen people come and go, burned out by the repetitive nature of the work and the brutality of the circumstances. Lucy liked the predictability, and the cases didn't bother her. Except this one. She would have hated to lose her boss, if for no other reason than she didn't want to lose her job here.

She had just seated the bullets in the comparison scope when the computer beeped, signaling that the fingerprint matching software had finished doing its job. She hesitated a moment, then walked back to the computer and looked at the screen. No match. Good. Dr. Wallace would be glad to know the priest's fingerprints weren't in the belfry, but it left the question of whose were. She would run the prints against some databases later; for now the fact that these weren't a match with the exemplars was all she needed to know.

There were no surprises on the bullets, either. The scratches matched the ones on the bullets from the Town Park killing, but not the ones from that crazy hippie that Dr. Wallace found in her driveway. The unspent round the sheriff found in the belfry could have matched either, from the looks of it, but Lucy knew looks would not be enough. She finished her examination of the bullets, made the appropriate documenting photographs, and printed out the fingerprint data. Then she searched through her files until she found the photos she had taken the day Dr. Wallace was shot, the photos of the rims of the bullets from the belfry and those from the rifle the sheriff had brought by for comparison. She smiled at the images. They were crisp and detailed, and Dr. Wallace was going to find them very, very interesting.

CHAPTER TWENTY-SEVEN

JUNE 22, MIDMORNING

I shooed the men off as soon as the kitchen was cleaned up. I read for a bit and tried watching some television, but daytime TV is even more inane than I remembered. Uncharacteristically, I wanted company. I was toying with the idea of trying to scare up Father Matt when I heard a knock on the door.

"Coming," I announced.

I stood too quickly and had to grab the arm of the chair to keep from swooning. I might be good to go from Dr. Butcher's perspective, but I was still about a quart and a half low.

"Coming," I called again, adding, "just not very fast," under my breath as I went.

Lucy strolled in when I opened the door. It was around lunchtime, and Lucy was not one to miss a meal. She dropped a folder on the kitchen counter with one hand, licking pale green frosting off the fingers of the other. I have no idea how she keeps that size-2 figure given the amount of pastry she consumes. To her credit, it's the good stuff, mostly from the artisan patisserie in Mountain Village, nothing junky; but she has to consume at least a thousand calories a day in cake alone.

"Interesting stuff there," she said as she examined her fingers for any remaining bits of sugar. "For starters, the prints don't belong to the priest."

"Father Gregory. He has a name."

Lucy sent me a sidelong glance, cocked an eyebrow, and wiped her left hand for good measure against her jeans.

"Father Gregory. Not his."

"Well, that's something." I tried not to let the relief show in my voice. In the standoff in my mind over whether Father Matt was guilty, one of the desperadoes blinked.

"And I've been thinking. There was a lot of rain a few nights ago, just like this morning. Lots of it. It's not unusual to get prints off wood these days, but usually it's inside. Outside the elements tend to degrade the prints over time and a good, hard rainstorm really wreaks havoc. I was a little surprised to find prints, to tell you the truth, especially ones that were this good."

"Go on." I could practically see the wheels turning.

"I'm thinking these are pretty fresh prints. Like, maybe made after the rainstorm. Not before."

"Well, now, that raises all sorts of interesting possibilities."

Lucy grinned. She is something of a shark when it comes to evidence. She loves putting the pieces together. "Yeah, well, there's more. I got a little, tiny partial on the casing of the bullet. There's not really enough to stand up in court, but I'm pretty sure it matches one of the prints from the railing."

My turn to cock an eyebrow. "How sure, Lucy? We don't play in hunches here. Peoples' lives depend on it."

Lucy pouted. "Not a hundred percent, that's for sure. But not a hunch, either. Maybe seventy-five percent sure? Anyway, either way, it doesn't belong to the priest."

"Father Gregory."

"Yeah. Whatever. Anyway, the reports are there. I did a full spreadsheet comparison on all the samples we have. Houston's is an outlier because it's too heavy. Nine millimeter is my guess. It's an outlier. So is the one that's from the bell tower, but it's a different kind of outlier. The rim markings on it are different from the ones on the casings on the bullets that were left in the rifle that was used to shoot Bedsheet."

"Paul Kessler."

Lucy ignored me.

"So, best I can tell, there are two different sources for the .22 bullets. The rim markings on the one from the rifle are odd. I can't match them to anything. Maybe they are recycled, I don't know, but it doesn't look like it. They are definitely not from the same batch as the one from the belfry. And I just got the printout of ammo sales you asked for, that's in there too."

"Thanks, Lucy. Good job. Buy yourself a napoleon on me."

Lucy paused at the door to look back over her shoulder and grin. "No good source around here. I'll have to settle for a profiterole."

I glanced over Lucy's reports, not expecting to find anything different, and I did not. Relieved as I was that this seemed to clear Father Matt, it still didn't explain the .22 round in the belfry. I pulled out the ammunition sales list.

One of the great things about the computer age is that it's incredibly easy to track purchases of just about everything. All it took was a few well-placed phone calls and a little unaccustomed sweet talking on Ben's part to get the local purveyors of ammunition to give us a record of who had bought .22 rounds for the last two months, right up until the day I was shot, if the printout dates were to be believed. I started going down the list, increasingly annoyed that none of the viable suspects appeared, but relieved that that included Father Matt. I noted that a sizeable delivery of ammunition had gone to the local very high-end shooting club, Fauxhall. I was surprised that they bought their wares locally.

I was ready to give up the search as futile by the time I came to the last page, the most recent dates, all of them after the shootings began. Fortunately for me, my compulsive nature wouldn't permit me, because in the third line from the bottom, I found an interesting entry, an unexpected but not unfamiliar name. I checked the date against the calendar, the date of the shooting of Cosette Anira and the timeline in the newspaper article. Then I sat back and smiled. One of the desperadoes in my mind holstered his gun and slinked off.

Some of the pieces were falling into place, but only around the edges. I looked at the reports again, underlined one of the entries, and sent Lucy off to the hardware sporting goods store in Norwood to get hard copies of the receipts from the purchase. Then I called Jeff Atkins. I was hoping he'd remember the name of the boy in charge of the gun locker at Fauxhall, where the rich and the famous and the nervous went to learn how to shoot. It was time I had a chat with him about his clientele.

****

Jane would have his head if she knew that he had taken the boys to town, but they wanted to shop for something for their mother. Grown men, all of them, and they hadn't got past the little boy stage of wanting to bring a fist full of daisies to their mom to show her they loved her. Typical of boys. Hard to say the words, but everything they did gave voice to the fact that they adored their mother and worried about her. As soon as the gondola let them off, they were off in a pack, arguing good-naturedly among themselves about what to get. The last he heard, it was flowers.

He debated what to do with his time. Jane needed some time alone, and he was in no mood to work on his book, anyway. It was too soon after breakfast for him to be hungry and too early in the day for a drink. He walked up to Pacific in the general direction the boys had gone and decided to window shop.

There were people on the streets, but not nearly as many as there should be for a fine summer afternoon, and people hurried from place to place rather than linger on the street to talk or to enjoy the sunshine that had followed the storm. Even the reporters from the national media were keeping a low profile. Not one of them qualified as a remainderman, but not one of them really believed that was the basis for the killings either. There was something about people being picked off in broad daylight that made them nervous.

The print media were happy to feed off Pete Wilson's filings, as far as he could tell. He didn't watch television so he wasn't sure how this was playing outside Telluride, but the lack of news trucks meant it wasn't of particular note. As he passed the glass doors of the Forensic Center, he saw Pete Wilson at the reception desk, no doubt trying to figure out where Jane was. He took some satisfaction in having spirited her away from the spotlight. His condo was a bit secluded, and the two burly guards he hired — one for each end of the hall — assured him that there would be no unwelcome intruders. Jane needed a bit of peace.

Peace, and a new wardrobe. Eoin Connor wasn't overly concerned about female fashions, but even Irish farm wives dressed better than Jane Wallace. Ben had brought up some things for her: shapeless, faded jeans, white shirts, and a nightgown that would have looked out of place even in a 1950's sitcom. *A pity, she is a fine looking woman,* he thought. He paused in front of the White Deer. The window was full of sweaters — out of place in the summer heat — but beautiful. They reminded him of home and he decided to go in.

The store was beautiful. A Victorian settee and side chair were settled around a tall, stained glass floor lamp. There was a calligraphied sign: the tired husband chair. Several hutches and chests of drawers were scattered about, and sweaters draped invitingly out of them. Shelves held scarves and hats, and the knitwear was supplemented by a variety of purses, a baker's rack of lanolin-based toiletries, and local artwork on the walls.

He wandered the store, not quite taken with anything until he came to the back, where a stack of shawls lay highlighted in the light of a crystal chandelier on an oak table. The one on top was a confection of winter colors: mauve, turquoise, dull gold, and sage green. Connor picked it up and drew it out to its full expanse. The pattern was lightly woven, making the piece look like a spider's web reflecting the changing lights of an evening sky. He nodded approvingly.

A salesgirl materialized out of nowhere.

"Very beautiful," she said. "For your wife?"

Eoin smiled. "I'm not married."

"Your girlfriend, then. Very beautiful. She will thank you very much if you buy her this."

The salesgirl was a well-endowed brunette with an Eastern European accent. She took the shawl from his hands and draped it across her shoulders, then around her neck, then over her head, then around her hips in a well-practiced display of options for the vacillating customer.

"Just a friend. I'll take it."

He followed the salesgirl to the register. On the way, she stopped at a display of brooches and picked one off the stand. It was a round silver Celtic knot. Symbol of the continuity of life, every ending a beginning. She held it against the shawl.

"It is beautiful too. Beautiful against the wool." She started to demonstrate again, but Eoin put up a warning hand.

"That's fine. Wrap it up. I'll take them both."

He had just finished paying when Ben walked up. He folded his arms across his chest and looked Eoin Connor right in the eyes. Connor was impressed. The boy had spunk. He was still rangy, not filled out yet, a scrawny shadow of the man that was going to be, but he had nerve, and here he was, challenging him man to man and in public.

Connor smiled slightly. It wouldn't come to blows, of course, that wasn't the point. But Ben might need to learn that however young and fit he was, it wouldn't do to lock horns with someone like himself. *I might be older than you, you wee...* he caught himself before the usual expletive; he'd have to make more of an effort to subdue his working class language if he were to have any chance with Jane. *But I could still take you in a fair fight... and I don't fight fair.*

He waited to hear what was on Ben's mind. It wasn't long in coming.

"Do you love my mom?" Ben asked.

Connor was taken aback. It was just like Ben, still not much more than a teenager, brash and impatient, thinking that everything happened in a rush. He hadn't had the time to learn that some things develop ever so slowly and are the better for it. He was still at the stage of tossing his heart in first and letting his head follow sometime after. Still, he deserved an honest answer.

"Not yet," Connor answered, "and not like you mean. I don't know who she is, she doesn't really know, herself, so no, Ben, I don't."

Blue eyes regarded him warily. "Don't you hurt her."

Ben squared his shoulders unconsciously, setting himself up as white knight and protector.

Connor laughed at that. "I can tell you this much, Ben. That I'll not do. I'll not hurt her, I promise. She's had enough of that for a while." He stopped.

There wasn't really any way to explain how complicated it all was. There was no way to tell Ben that he longed to get to know Jane and to love her with great abandon, but wasn't sure she'd have him in her life in any form. *Not that this upstart needed to know that in the first place,* he reflected. And how to explain that the absent Fiona threw a spanner in the works, even if Jane *would* have him? For now, he was content to ignore the problems.

"The only end I have in mind, Ben, is to enjoy her company, for whatever it is, for however long she'll have me. I've no designs, good or bad."

He glanced up to see the other two standing at a distance in the store, heads together, watching. He could see the curious looks on their faces. *Another rite of passage for young Ben*, he thought. They sent him over to talk. He tilted his head toward them in acknowledgement, and Adam waved a cautious hand in his direction.

"Before Dad died, long before really, since he didn't — well, let's face it — Dad didn't know he was going to die — he took all us boys out to lunch one day." He smiled in spite of himself at that and continued. "We went out to this really great restaurant on the ocean and had crab and shrimp and oysters, just us. When we were done, he got really serious and told us that one of these days, there'd come a time when Mom needed us to take care of her, and he wanted to make sure that we understood it was our job if he wasn't there. That he expected all of us to be the men of the family, and that he trusted us and never to forget it."

Connor was torn between admiration and annoyance for Dead John. Admiration because he was an old-fashioned husband who clearly took his obligation to his family and his wife seriously. Admiration, because he'd handed her specifically to his sons. Annoyance because this one had been too young to understand, and the weight of it showed clearly in his face even this many years later.

"My dad did the same thing. Big responsibility. I was glad I had older brothers; it made it easier."

The boy's face relaxed in the comfort of shared experience.

"It sure does. When Dad died, Adam and Seth were right there with her. When they had to go back to seminary, Luke took construction jobs around town for about a year. She came out here alone — and I was elected to come out. We're all worried about her. She's not getting better. She's not, and there's nothing I can do. I've let Dad down."

He stopped abruptly.

Connor recognized the turmoil in the voice, the unwillingness to trust speech for fear that it would let loose unmanly emotion.

"I understand," he said, and he did. Not from the perspective of losing a wife, for that he'd not done; she'd lost him. But he remembered the awful, isolating grief that had enveloped his mother after his own father's death, and the terrible sense of impotence they all had in dealing with it. But his mother had followed her husband to the grave in only a few short months. Jane had half a lifetime left. "You didn't let your dad down, you did just what he asked. This isn't something you can fix."

"She used to be really fun. Not like Dad, she always worked harder and longer and she was always more serious. But she could be fun." He paused. "She never even smiles anymore."

Connor paused to consider his words carefully. No room for missteps here. Ben was too shaken by his mother's near death to realize that she'd already turned a corner. Ben would have to realize that himself, in his own good time.

"It's like a part of herself died, Ben. It's not like it is for you. You loved your dad, and you miss him, but you're a separate person from him. She's not, not anymore, probably not since long before your dad died. That's what people mean when they talk about two becoming one. She has to get on by herself and it's hard for her."

"Will she ever get better?" The troubled eyes were earnest, the face glum.

Connor returned his direct gaze. "I'd like to think so. I care about her, too."

"I know. I'm sorry. I didn't mean you didn't. I just needed to be sure, you know?" Then, abruptly, he changed the subject. "She won't even go to communion. She never missed communion. What's wrong? She won't talk about it." It was like Connor had opened a dam. "Will she ever get better?"

The question was more earnest than before, the eyes more troubled.

"I hope so." *Dear God,* Connor thought, *I hope so.*

Ben looked at him, his jaw working but no words coming, clearly uneasy with what he wanted to say and afraid to say it.

"Spit it out, lad. What's on your mind?" Eoin Connor wasn't prepared for the response.

"Is it true, what they say in church? That she can always come back? That it isn't ever too late? It's important. Adam says yes, but he's supposed to. Is what he told me true?"

Connor was taken aback by the concern of one just out of the nest wrestling with what he'd been taught and what he now thought, or what he thought he thought. And here his poor mother had pulled the very rug out from underneath him just when he needed it most, and they were both adrift.

This question, however, Connor could answer with confidence.

"Every last syllable, lad. Every last syllable."

Satisfied, Ben held out his hand and Connor took it. It was a strong grip, the grip of a man and not a boy.

"Okay, then. Just remember, don't you hurt my mother."

I was writing a note to leave on the counter thanking Connor for his hospitality when he came in. The carryout bags in his hands explained why he straggled in rather than on the heels of my boys.

"And what do you think you're doing? Where are the boys?"

I bristled at his tone, not able to tell whether he was angry or worried. Either way, it was none of his concern.

"The boys are gone. I sent them off. Luke is taking Adam to Portland. I booked him a flight from there to Juneau, but they had to leave this afternoon to be able to make it to Alaska, and Ben's along for the ride. I wanted them safe."

Connor closed the door behind him and put two bags on the counter, one brown paper smelling of food and the other a red and white one with grosgrain ribbon handles.

"Well done, Jane. I suppose that means you're leaving, too."

"No need for me to stay now."

"Unless the killer really is after you."

"I'll be fine in the house. I don't feel much like getting out, anyway, and Isa and Pilar will take good care of me. I don't want to impose any more than I have."

Connor pursed his lips and gave a brief nod. "Fair enough. Have a bite with me before you go? I've brought Chinese. More than we need, I expect. I bought enough for those ruffians of yours. You'll be doing me a kindness. Otherwise I'll be eating this for weeks."

"I doubt my appetite will make much difference, but yes, I'll stay."

We sat down on the couch where we had watched the storm earlier. Connor laid out a veritable Chinese buffet, supplemented it with a beer for himself and fizzy water for me. We ate right from the containers. I was surprised at his skill with chopsticks.

"Did the boys figure out why you were in such a hurry to get rid of them?" he asked, gesturing in my direction with a container of mu-shu pork.

"Who knows? Probably. I think they were just glad to have some time together. I suspect they'll spend it plotting how to take care of me. It's interesting, isn't it, when the children start to worry about the parents?"

"Worry they do. Ben especially." Eoin looked as though he wanted to say something else but changed his mind. Instead, he got up and retrieved the fancy bag from the kitchen counter. "I brought you something from town."

I expected more explanation, but none came. I set the container I was eating from aside and took it, wiping a bit of sauce from my mouth with a paper napkin.

The bag was tied together with more ribbon, and the contents were shrouded in layers of tissue. I pulled out a delicate knitted shawl in a riot of winter colors. It was beautiful.

"It reminded me of Ireland," he said simply. "I thought you might like it."

I put the soft wool to my face. "Oh, I do. Much more than that awful tee shirt you bought me."

"So I hope," Eoin laughed. "There's more."

I dug around in the paper until I found something heavy. It was a silver brooch, made on intertwining lines, strangely familiar. I held it in the palm of my hand and looked at it, trying to remember where I had seen it before. In frustration, I looked heavenward, and my eyes landed on the antler chandelier. Suddenly, pieces began to fall together in my mind. I looked at the logo on the bag again: a white deer.

"I have to go to the office. Right now. Things are starting to make sense. Can you take me? Please? And I need Father Matt, too. This involves him."

I stuffed the shawl and the brooch in the bag and headed for the door without waiting for an answer.

Fifteen minutes later, both Eoin and Father Matt stood behind me, watching me shuffle the pictures from the crime scene on the glass blotter of my desk: Paul Kessler lying on my drive. The entrance wound in his back in all its clinical detail, spreading stain on rough tunic. Finally I found what I was looking for: A shot taken of the rifle that Ivanka Kovacs had said the assailant dropped as he shoved her out of the way. And a distance shot of the death scene, taken in the light of the flood-lamps the sheriff had brought up, that showed Ivanka Kovacs and her husband leaving my house. Ivanka was shouldering her backpack, and she was turned, so that the profile of the oversized pack stood out clearly, soft and nearly flat against her back.

I stabbed my finger at the picture. "See that?" I asked.

Father Matt and Eoin shrugged.

"Sure. Ivanka Kovacs. She was there, I helped take care of her. The killer pushed her down. The backpack broke her fall. What about it?" Father Matt said.

"Okay, now I need you to look at something else." I fished my keyboard out of the middle drawer of my desk and I pulled up my documents screen. I paused for a moment, perplexed. Where had Ben saved that video? I tried a couple of prompts, with no success. "Damn," I said under my breath. "Where is it?"

"What are you looking for?" Eoin asked.

"A video. Ben saved a video from my security camera from the day Kessler was killed. I sent it down to Tom, but as far as I know he doesn't think much of it. He doesn't know what to look for."

I kept punching keys in increasing desperation. Where was Ben when I needed him? Why was it so hard to find things on this beastly computer?

Eoin pushed me gently aside. "Let me." He punched a few buttons, emitted a couple of reflective noises, punched again, and the video magically appeared on my screen. Once again, I was watching the intermittent parade of people who passed within camera range of my house that Thursday afternoon.

It took longer than I thought for Ivanka Kovacs to come into view, but there she was, backpack on and in profile as she turned to look down the street.

"Pause it," I commanded Eoin, and he did, an amused look on his face. I pointed to the screen. "Look at that backpack. Now look at the crime scene picture. Notice anything?"

It only took a second for Eoin Connor to see it. "Her pack. It's bulky on the way up, flat when she's leaving your house."

"Exactly." I said, relieved that he'd seen the same thing.

My relief evaporated when Father Matt followed up with, "So what?"

I indicated the other photo, the rifle with the inlaid stock. "See that? It's not an ordinary gun. It comes apart for carrying. See?" I indicated the joint. It breaks down into relatively small sections. Small enough to fit in a backpack." I waited for the penny to drop.

Father Matt looked at me, confused and concerned. "Jane, are you trying to tell us that Ivanka Kovacs had that rifle in her pack? That she's the killer?"

I could tell the idea seemed preposterous to him. It had to me, too. Serial killers are dysfunctional loners, not sweet little old ladies running knitting shops in tourist towns. Still, it all fit. It had to be right.

"I think so," I responded slowly, suddenly unsure of my self. "Look, see how big the pack was going up, sort of irregular, and how flat later on? Something was missing — why not this? "

"Jane, it could have been anything. Lunch. A bag of birdseed. A jacket. Anything. You can't tell what's in there from the shape of the pack. Besides, Ivanka Kovacs must be nearing eighty. She couldn't possibly shoot that well anymore, even if she once did. Whoever shot you was a sharpshooter."

I bristled. "She's sharp as a tack, she works on that ranch, she doesn't even wear glasses — have you ever seen her with glasses? What makes you think she couldn't pull off a shot like that? Especially with a scope — the rifle has a pretty impressive scope on it."

I could see Father Matt wrestling with the possibility that one of his flock was a black, black sheep indeed. Anxious to press my advantage, I remembered the image of the deer. "And wait a minute…take a look at this." I typed Ivanka Kovacs into the computer search engine and scanned the results. The article I was looking for, one I had read shortly after coming to town, was the third one down. "That's the connection. Ivanka was a biathlete in Hungary. She knows how to shoot. And the funny design on the stock, it's not flames or lightning. It's antlers, just like the ones on the White Deer logo."

Father Matt looked at the bag and slid the photo of the rifle from underneath the others, looking back and forth from one to the other.

"There's a resemblance," he admitted, "but it also looks a lot like the Hartford logo and a zillion other images of a buck. I'm not so sure."

I looked to Connor for support. He was considering the photos, moving them back and forth as he thought, chin in hand, glancing from time to time at the computer screen. Impatient, I scanned the other hits from the search engine. One of them was from the White Deer online catalog, the usual corporate back-story.

"Look here," I showed them the photo of the young Kovacs couple. "See? They were crack shots. Look at the guns in the background. They're a matched set. That would explain why two guns." I shuddered, remembering the analysis Lucy had come in special to run the Saturday after I was shot.

Conner looked at the picture intently. "I don't know, Jane," he finally said. "It could be. The stocks are turned away. There's something on them, you can just see it, but there's no way to prove that it's the same." He put down the magnifying glass he'd taken from the rubble on my desk and used to examine the photos more closely. "Still…"

I could tell his writer's mind was turning over the possibilities. He waved me out of my chair and took a seat in my desk chair. He flipped through the pages of the files, Father Matt reading over his shoulder. I watched them confer over this bit of information and that, wanting to step in, to plead and convince them, but knowing that they were my jury now. I'd made my argument. Time to see if it held up. *Please, God, it would.*

Eventually, Father Matt straightened up. His face was dark, concerned, but I couldn't tell why. It wasn't until Eoin swung around in the chair, his eyes meeting mine, that I knew they saw it, too. It took us the rest of the night to figure out how to prove it.

****

Connor pushed open the door of Jane Wallace's office, put a paisley wrapped box on her desk, and made himself comfortable in her chair. He wanted the desk between him and the door. He figured it was only a matter of time before the sheriff came by, and he didn't want to miss the fireworks, even if Jane was gone, but there was no sense risking physical violence. He had probably already risked jail, given that Jane was under a gag order in the matter of these murders. Strictly speaking, it didn't apply to him, and that's what he would argue, but he'd probably have to do it from behind bars.

He propped his feet up on the old wood desk, careful to avoid the package, at ease doing so because he'd caught her with her own boots amid the files more than once.

It was refreshing to know a woman who slumped in chairs, scattered books in piles on the floor and propped her feet up on whatever was handy.

He glanced around the office as though seeing it for the first time, taking it in now that he knew more about the woman who inhabited it. Nice, too, to know a woman who decorated in something other than lace and chintz. Her office was paneled in wood, with two walls of bookshelves on which the books were neatly arranged, unlike the ones he'd seen at her house. Perhaps she had more respect for her working tomes. He admired the leather Chesterfield sofa and the antique prints on the walls. It was a room he would be comfortable in. Idly, he hoped he'd have the chance.

She had courage, he'd give her that. She was right about the murders, of course, but proving it was something else. They had talked long into the night, her lawyer's mind turning the evidence over and over, casting it this way and that, finally deciding to her disappointment that it wasn't substantial enough to get a warrant for a search.

"No search, no evidence, and no arrest."

He couldn't tell whether she was disappointed or afraid. She had reason for both. Disappointment because he knew her well enough to know that she was one of those women who was a fixer. It was the core of her motherhood, and he suspected of her life with Dead John. It was her job in life to make things better for the people she loved, and that drive had transferred to her job now that the kids were grown and her husband gone.

The fear was worse. The fear that the killer would try again, to kill her, to kill others. The fear she would never clear Father Matt's name. The disappointment might motivate her, but the fear drove her. A month ago it wouldn't have. A month ago she wouldn't have cared.

It was that drive that led her to propose the interview. He'd met with the reporter, Pete Wilson, in the Sheridan Bar. It was pleasant duty, another comfortable room. It was posher than the pubs back home, with the oversized TV screens and the heavy metal music blaring from the speakers. In Ireland, TV screens were smaller and the music more congenial.

No matter. He made his way past the bar to the little alcove between the main saloon and the pool room in the back and settled onto one of the faded, green, velvet settees. Between the music and the crack of pool balls in the billiard parlor, no one would overhear. It was a perfect spot for what he had to do.

He was ready for his second drink when Wilson walked in. The reporter had asked what he was drinking.

"Scotch on the rocks."

Wilson returned with two glasses, one scotch on the rocks and one draft beer.

"I thought you'd be drinking Jameson's or some other Irish stuff," he said as he put the glass down in front of Connor.

"You know the difference between Scotch whisky and Irish whiskey?" Connor asked.

Wilson shook his head. "Nope."

"The letter 'e'," Connor said. "Sláinte."

He drained half the glass. Setting this interview up had seemed like a good idea when he and Jane had talked, but now he was not so sure. If it didn't work, if it didn't flush out the killer, he would have signed her death warrant. It had better work. It had to work. He drained the glass.

The reporter looked at him curiously. "You're thirsty this evening."

Connor was in no mood for dissembling.

"Let's get on with this, shall we? I've a scoop for you. There is a serial killer at large in Telluride, and he's bound to kill again tomorrow."

Wilson tried to look nonchalant, but his jaw actually dropped. He recovered his expression and spoke cautiously. "I'm all ears." And he was. The reporter was leaning forward, tape recorder at the ready, oblivious to everyone else in the bar. "Go on."

Connor spun the tale of the murders with little embellishment. The facts were clear enough. He watched Wilson's face go from mild skepticism to interest to outright horror as he listened. *Thanks, Da*, he thought. *I learned how to hold an audience from the best.* By the time he'd gotten to the details of the second murder, more or less, Pete Wilson was savoring the prospect of an above-the-fold story that would reverberate around the world once he wrote it.

As he drew the conversation out, his writer's mind crafted the recitation and pushed the reporter toward the story he and Jane had pulled together. The story that, if Father Matt was right, would bring the murderer to justice.

"But there's more, there's more." Connor shoved his glass across the table towards Wilson. "Fill me up again, and I'll tell you what it is."

Wilson practically sprinted to the bar and returned with amber liquid covering the ice.

"Why haven't we heard about this before?" he asked.

"The sheriff is holding it close to his chest. So's that female coroner you have here. Sharp as tacks, and she's got it figured out, just a few loose ends to tie up. The sheriff is afraid she'll steal his thunder, won't let her talk to you lads from the paper."

"So why are you telling me all this? You've no skin in this game. Unless you're planning on writing a book."

"No book. I've got no great love for the law. I've been on the rough side of the constabulary's hands one too many times." Connor winced inwardly. There would be hell to pay when Patterson read this if Wilson was any kind of reporter at all. He'd dropped enough choice quotes. "But she—that coroner woman," Patterson wouldn't be the only angry one, he reflected. He hoped Jane would understand the hyperbole. "She's got it figured out, tapped on to the evidence that will put the killer away."

"I'm all ears." Again. He had been ever since Connor opened his mouth. Ears and hands with pencil scribbling frantically.

"Remember the gun from that Kessler killing? It's one of a matched set. Special kind, too. Breaks down for travel. The kind those crazy alpine athletes that ski and shoot use. Not too many around here. Only a matter of time. As soon as the ballistics reports are done, there will be a search warrant, end of story."

They'd talked a few more minutes — small chat, nothing more. Pete Wilson was studiously calm, but Connor knew the signs of a writer with a story that needed writing. He knew the reporter was twitching to get back and put his report to bed. Wilson finished his beer, paid the tab, and walked out. Connor had waited until he was sure Wilson was gone, picked up Wilson's empty glass with his handkerchief, and paid the barmaid a handsome tip to let him keep it.

He brought his mind back to the present, and he sat waiting for the explosion that was sure to come. If he remembered correctly, it was the sheriff's custom to have coffee and a muffin at the bakery; he'd probably see the newspaper there. He had to give Pete Wilson credit. As newspaper stories went, it was good. Tight, all the information there, and he didn't bury the lead. And it was no more fictional than his usual stories. But the lead wasn't the important part. That was the little tickle about the gun, and God bless him, he had worked that in, almost word for word, in the last paragraph.

Downstairs, a door slammed, and he heard a roaring voice. A minute or so later, there was the sound of a man stomping down the hall. The office door flew open, and Tom Patterson, red-faced and indignant, filled the doorway.

"Connor," the sheriff roared when he recognized Connor at the desk. "Where the hell is she? Where is Dr. Wallace?"

Connor was calmly filling his pipe with tobacco. *The last one I'll have until I make bail*, he thought. *Better make it count.*

"Gone, Patterson. She's gone."

CHAPTER TWENTY-NINE

JUNE 24

I looked out over the wing of the hired jet. Dawn was beginning to peek over the horizon, pink and gold and cloudless, like summer mornings in Florida generally were. Things in the tropics always started out well, full of promise. It was only later that clouds arose and storms battered, I reflected. Meteorology, a metaphor for life. I smiled. I was nervous about this trip but looking forward to being back where all this had begun. My former life, the one that had been so brutally interrupted, and the one I needed to come to grips with.

After Connor and Father Matt and I had hatched our plan, I went home and slept the sleep of the innocent. I spent the next day rattling around the house, getting under Pilar's feet and waiting for Connor's call, the one that told me he had managed to plant our story with Pete Wilson. In the meantime, I chartered a plane; I still had unfinished business back home.

The charter plane had left at 2:30 in the morning in order to get me to the airport in my old hometown in Florida by breakfast. Good thing. I had a lot to do, and I wanted to be home by nightfall. I hadn't asked Dr. Butcher about flying, and I knew that there was some risk, but I was willing to take the gamble. I needed to get back home to tie up loose ends. I could finally see the path out of my misery ahead of me, and ironically, it led right back to where the misery had all started.

Connor called around midnight. My Hispanic bonus families were in bed and asleep. It had not been worth my going to bed, and sleep would not come anyway, but because of my own ghosts, no one else's. I sat with a family album on my lap and a glass of Jameson's in my hand, thumbing through the pages, smiling at the memories of my perfect life, my children, my beloved John. I was careful not to let my tears mar the photographs.

Connor was right. I still had grieving to do, and it was not easy. It was not easy to look back at those happier times, birthdays, school plays, Sunday afternoons in the pool, at posed photos of John and me at one of those boring, pretentious fundraisers our town was famous for.

My heart ached for those days. But it was an ache, that's all. An ache I could live with, not a crippling pain I was going to die from. I wasn't sure, but it might even be an ache I could get better from, one of these days. But first I had to put my ghosts to rest.

It was nearly one when I freshened up with a sink bath—no showers yet — and changed. I had taken time that afternoon to have my hair cut, and it hung curly and silver just below my chin. I'd even braved the ministrations of the stylist to tame my brows, though I had balked at her suggestion of a new makeup wardrobe. I put on a silk shirt and pleated slacks, also new, and tied a silk scarf around my neck.

My eyes fell on my jewelry box. I had brought it with me but hadn't opened it since I moved into the house. I lifted the lid. Inside were my treasures from John. I put on the pearl earrings he had bought me for our wedding. They lay next to a rosary I had finished making for John the night before he was killed. It was made of rough cut green stones. Zoe had found an ad for cheap, uncut emerald necklaces, and the stones had attracted me: rough, rich, textured with depths of pattern and light that reminded me of John who still delighted me with undiscovered charms after so many years of marriage. I'd ordered two, torn them apart, and assembled a rosary from the pieces. I had forgotten it even existed. I had never gotten the chance to give it to him.

I passed the stones though my fingers, feeling them run heavy across my hand. I turned over the cross. I'd engraved it to him in the manner of lovers, using our nicknames. He would have cherished it. I sat down in the rocker by the bed, in the quiet, and prayed the prayers, the first time since I had been shot. The creak of the rocker accented my words. The feel of the stones was soothing. It was a beautiful rosary. It deserved to be prayed.

I held the heavy crucifix in my hands and remembered how hard it had been for me to embrace this devotion when I had married John. His father, Hugh, had given me away on my wedding day, my own father having abandoned my mother when he found out she was pregnant with me. Just before we were to walk down the aisle, he had pressed a cobalt glass rosary into my shaking hands, had taken me aside to the Mary chapel, and knelt and prayed with me. He told me he'd done the same with his two daughters when they married.

"Janie," he'd said. "Jesus gave us His mother as our own. I want you to have her as a wedding gift."

Hugh made a point of praying the rosary with me whenever John and I came to visit. Most of the time, it would be at the kitchen table, John, his father and I, late at night, after we had driven across the state after work on a Friday, John's mother bustling around us to make us a late dinner. Hellos, hugs, the rosary, dinner, and then swapping tales of patients and surgeries and autopsies until the small hours, my patient mother-in-law having retired as soon as she laid the food before us.

I had prayed that cobalt rosary by Hugh's bedside when he was ill and through tears with John at his casket when he died. As I now moved my fingers from bead to bead on the rosary I had made for John, I felt them close to me: John, Hugh, and Mary nudging me closer to healing and home. The rosary had been my anchor in the days after John's death, a prayer I could make when my heart was too raw and my mind too numb to pray. It remained my lifeline in the many months after, a connection to the husband who was no longer at my side. Mary understood senseless death and betrayal, and she was still faithful. Why was it so hard for me? Perhaps because Mary met her grief with faith and obedience. I still kept trying to wrestle mine to the ground by will and intellect.

I lost track of the prayers, repeating them decade after decade until I heard the hall clock chime two.

I dropped the beads into my pocket, collected my purse and phone—I had not been without it since the day I was shot — set the alarm for the house and headed for the 4Runner. The automatic floodlights came on as I walked across the porch. I had a spasm of fear as I saw a tall figure leaning up against the driver's door, until I recognized the glow from a pipe. Connor. He straightened up as I approached. I hoped he could tell I was smiling.

"How did you know I was leaving?"

"Have you never heard of the second sight? We Irish are famous for it. Clairvoyance runs in our blood."

"I'm not so sure about second sight, unless it goes by the name of Pilar or Isa." I rested a hand on his forearm. "Thanks for being here."

"The least I can do. That way I can be assured of your jailhouse visit when Tom Patterson has my hide for your little scheme."

"Count on it."

We fell quiet, and the silence grew between us. We were so still that the motion-activated flood went dark. Eoin Connor's form loomed in the shadows, oddly reassuring and disconcerting at the same time. I was becoming accustomed to the smell of his pipe.

The floodlights flashed back on as Connor took his pipe in hand and placed it carefully on the roof of the 4Runner. He took my hands in his own rough ones, raised them slowly toward him. He regarded them for a long minute, and then bent his head to kiss them gently. I heard the sharp intake of my own breath.

"Take care, Jane Wallace, and come back whole." He let go of my hands as gently as he had taken them, retrieved his pipe, and walked down the street. He was whistling softly.

I remembered the sound with pleasure as the wing of the plane dipped, reflecting bright sunlight onto my face, and the plane began its descent.

****

The Berton place was one of those monstrosities that had sprung up all over town, covering every inch of waterfront — ocean, intra-coastal or river or man-made pond — with faux-Mediterranean palaces. They were all at least three stories, because codes prevented living space on the flood plain in any new construction, and they all crowded the lot lines. John and I had made great fun of these temples of narcissism.

They were massive: cathedral ceilings, oversized rooms, entire walls made of glass, two full baths for each master suite, and walk-in closets the size of our first apartment, each new builder trying to outdo the last in grandeur. But they were all alike. Same ochre barrel tile roof. Same linen with dark accents exterior. Same curving entryway and porte-cochere. In trying to be so very current and so very individual, their owners, like teenagers trying to be cool, had succeeded only in raising the bar of conformity. I had much preferred our quirky Victorian then, and I found as I stood in front of the carved door to Kiki's house, that I still did.

I raised my hand to press the bell, but hesitated. This was going to be much harder than going to the prison would have been. There I could be, if not superior, at least justified. I had a legitimate, if misguided, reason for revenge on Tommy Berton. I had no such excuse for his wife. I stood a long time amid the hibiscus, ixora and peace lilies in the well-manicured dooryard, before I worked up courage enough to ring.

Kiki answered the door, clad in shorts and a tee shirt, blond hair disheveled, tanned feet bare. Her blue eyes widened with surprise, then hardened. I hurried to speak before she slammed the door in my face.

"Kiki, I'm sorry." *Best to get right to the point.*

She looked at me with suspicion. I could see packing boxes in the expansive living room behind her.

"What do you want? We'll be out of the house by Monday. Until then, it's still mine." She brushed a lock of hair from her face as a bead of perspiration trickled down her neck.

I took a deep breath, which still hurt. A good reminder. "I'm sorry," I repeated, and started to explain but Kiki interrupted me.

"Sorry? Sorry." She repeated the word in a mocking tone. "You're sorry. Well, good for you. You're sorry, and I'm out of a home. You're sorry, and I'm packing when I should be studying for finals. You're sorry, and my boys can't stop crying because they have to leave the only place they've ever lived, the only friends they ever had. You're sorry. Well good for you, Jane. Be sorry. You ought to be. You've ruined my life. What's left of it."

She started to turn away, and I spoke rapidly, knowing it was now or never.

"I know." She jerked around, looking at me again, brows furrowed.

"What did you say?"

At least I had her attention. She leaned on the door, no longer threatening to close it, but made no offer to ask me in. I felt my own sweat trickle between my shoulder blades.

"I said I'm sorry. I know I ruined your life. I meant to. It was wrong. I want to make it right."

There. I'd said it. *Not as hard as I had thought.*

"Go on."

She was interested, but still cautious, head cocked, eyes narrowed.

And still not inviting me in. Fair enough.

"I want to buy your house. For your asking price. My lawyer's working on it."

Relief flooded her face, but she caught herself, evening out her features before she spoke again. "What's in it for you?"

I shrugged. "A house, I guess. And I'll need someone to take care of it for me, so I thought you might want the job. I can't just leave it empty, and I'm not coming back here." I realized as I said it that it was true. This place was no longer my home, and it was no longer my prison, either. I was free to go, and go I would. "Look, I can't really make up for all I put you through these past months. It's just that..." I started to explain, then stopped when I realized it wasn't important. Kiki wouldn't understand, and wouldn't care, and I didn't need to be making excuses. An apology with excuses wasn't much of an apology.

Kiki was still struggling mentally to catch up with me. I guess it isn't every day that your worst enemy rides in on a white horse to save the day.

"You're buying my house? And you want me to be the caretaker?"

I sighed. "I do. I'll buy your house at your asking price. Your first one." I knew she'd had to cut the price several times; the market was slow. "That will give you all the equity you have in it and profit besides. I'll hire you as caretaker for ten years. You live here as part of the deal. That will give you time to raise the boys right here; in ten years they'll be in college. If something happens that makes you want to leave before then, you can, but you don't have to. If things change and you want to buy the house back, I'll sell it back for what I paid for it, and I'll carry the note if you need me to. You don't have to move. Stop packing."

"Is this a joke?"

I didn't blame her. In her shoes, I wouldn't believe me, either. As a matter of fact, in my own shoes, I wasn't entirely sure I believed me. But I was serious, and I told her so, handing her Rick Glass's card.

"Give my lawyer a call. He's working on the papers. He's expecting to hear from you."

Kiki looked as though she couldn't decide whether to laugh or cry. Crying won out. It usually does. I stood there in the heat, uncomfortable as much from the tears that rolled down her cheeks as from the damp silk shirt that clung to my back. I began to realize how helpless men feel at a woman's tears. I made a mental note to apologize to Connor for the times I'd cried on his shoulder.

Southern breeding will prevail, though, and Kiki composed herself enough to thank me through sniffles. She wiped her face with the hem of her shirt, cleared her throat, and invited me in.

"The place is a mess, but I can get you a cold drink. A beer. Wine. Something." She opened the door wider, and stood back.

I'd been brave enough for one day, I decided. I shook my head.

"I don't think so, Kiki. Not today. I'd best not, but thanks. I've still got another errand to run, and I'm flying home tonight."

Home. It came out naturally. Home. I'd never thought of Telluride as home.

She nodded, in understanding as much as in gratitude. I doubt she had any more desire to spend time with me than I did with her.

****

My own home was only about a mile from Kiki's waterfront mansion. I pulled into the drive, unprepared for the emotions that gripped me. Unprepared because I had spent so much time pushing memories away. Now I stood in the driveway looking up at the very embodiment of them. My tears trickled down, and I made no effort to wipe them away. Better to get them out, once and for all.

I looked around the yard. Monroe had always kept it up well, and his attention hadn't slipped even without John's watchful eye to keep him in line. The bougainvillea arbor over the brick entryway was clipped and flourishing. I smiled, remembering that it was that arbor that finally convinced John that his weekend gardening skills were not enough for this lush and formal yard. He'd done battle with the overgrown vine, cutting overgrown shoots and wrestling invading Virginia creeper in an effort to make it presentable for the housewarming party we had planned just after we moved in. As he cut one branch, a second snapped back, catching him in the face, narrowly missing his precious, beautiful surgeon's eyes.

I'd tidied the cut and confiscated the trimmers, and Monroe had come into our lives the very next week. He tended the yard with the love of a father for his children, and it flourished. And even though John wasn't the one personally responsible, he prided himself in the perfect lawn, the neat hedges, the arbor, the rose garden, the gardenias under our bedroom window, the pond lilies in the water garden out back.

I touched a fuchsia blossom as I put the key into the door and opened it. The entryway smelled of oil soap, the carved mahogany hall tree that had been a birthday gift from John empty of hats and coats and just-collected mail. A clue that no one lived here. My house had never been this neat. It had been strewn with the detritus of life: cat hairs and dog bones, schoolbooks and toys, stacks of books and magazines. The never-ending series of maids and houseguests for hire had not been able to keep up with it.

Afternoon sun filtered through the living room drapes, mottling the oriental rug: a wedding gift from one of John's aunts who was breaking up housekeeping and wanted to keep it in the family, and the mate to the one in my office in Telluride. The bookshelves that surrounded the fireplace were empty, and I could see the odd board that marked a repair John and Luke had made one summer afternoon, when my habit of stacking books two and three deep caused one of the shelves to collapse.

I moved through the arched doorway into the dining room. I ran my hand over the table, remembering all the family dinners here. John and I had insisted that everyone be home for dinner, and we all sat around the big table together. John's neurosurgical practice often kept him away, but I'd keep him a plate, and we'd sit together in the candlelight as he ate, exchanging stories of our days.

"I miss you." I said softly.

And so it went. I walked through every room in the house, recalling the joys and sorrows of living there, the friends and the family who had shared our home and our lives together. The house was unbearably empty, sterile, holding only furniture in showcase perfect order with none of the little things that made it a home. No misplaced shoes. No childish drawings. No thrift-store treasures borne home by my children for birthdays or anniversaries or "just because I love you, Mommy and Daddy." I used to get angry with John because he hoarded everything, adding to the inevitable clutter that comes from six kids, two parents, and assorted others sharing the same living space. Now I missed it all.

"John, you've got to set a better example," I'd chide him, especially when trying to make order out of the room Adam and Seth shared. It was a close call among the three of them who was the messiest.

"Mom, I can find things if they're on the floor. The only time I lose them is when you clean up," Adam in particular would say.

"It's mostly Adam's junk," Seth would counter.

And John would make it all worse with his own rationalization. "Tactile memory, Jane," he'd say. "I can't remember anything on my own. But if I have something to hold in my hand, it all comes back. This isn't junk, it's my peripheral brain." And then he'd kiss me.

I'd never understood until now. This house, the furniture in it, the very walls reminded me of John, and I could feel his presence almost as close as it had been when he was alive and we shared this place together. I felt his arms around me, his breath on my neck, his hand in mine. Tactile memory. Not my peripheral brain. My peripheral heart.

****

He looked at the clipping for the thousandth time, folded it carefully and put it, creased and smudged, back into the breast pocket of his starched, white shirt. He noticed that young men today did not wear such stiff shirts, but it was his habit from long ago, when starching a shirt kept it cleaner, more presentable, longer. Laundry was hard in those days, and he'd wanted to spare his new wife the trouble of so much washing, so much ironing. She had worked as hard as he did, and for so little. These days it was easy. She sent his shirts to the laundry in town, and they came back, stiff as a board. When he picked them up, the girl behind the counter invariably remarked.

"Isn't that uncomfortable?" she'd ask. "There is so much starch. It's almost like wood."

No, not uncomfortable. Familiar. Reassuring. A nice thing in one's old age, like a warm blanket on a cold night. And this was a nice place to live, not like Hungary had been in his youth under the Communists. He had learned quickly to lie, to hide, to submit his actions to the authorities. Guile and deceit and selfishness were a way of life, but he'd managed to keep his heart true. True to his country, his faith, his wife. Not easy when everything around him was trying to rip it away. Not easy when it took almost total devotion to selfish needs just to get by, day by day. It took a strong man to survive.

Or woman. His wife was as strong as they came, deceptive because she was so small. So delicate when he'd married her, not any bigger than a minute, frail as a breath, and beautiful as the dawn. A cloud of blond hair, huge brown eyes. The hair was gone white now, thin and flat, but the eyes were the same and every time he looked into them, he saw his loving, young bride, on the clear summer day in Szombathely, in front of the Franciscan church. How had she changed so much? How had he not noticed? Had she changed, or had she just grown more like herself in spite of his love for her? Harder and more determined.

She had always been better than he was at playing the Communist game, at getting what she wanted from those who ruled their lives with their power and position. She was good at using her charm and her wits to feed and house them when he had not been able to work himself. She had moved them as far up in a closed society as she could until she could move them no farther. It was she who had planned the escape, figured the route, marked the time, arranged the distraction that kept the border guards away long enough for them to ski into Austria and freedom in the middle of a blizzard. She had been the one to find her uncle, Lazlo, in far away America, had bullied him into sponsoring them to come to the country where their only child, their son, was born. Free. American.

They had made a good life here in this place. Not like home at the foot of the mountains and the beginning of the plains, this was more rugged, more isolated. The ranch had been hard work, re-learning ancestral ways, wresting a living out of the high meadows and the stupid, stupid sheep. But they had done it. Raised their son, the only one, to her great dismay, for she had wanted a legion of children.

They had endured and prospered. They had sent the son to college, to marry, to return with a wife who loved him enough to come live in this solitary place, make a living and have a child of their own. A granddaughter who would eventually take over the ranch. The granddaughter who nearly broke their hearts with her wild ways, with no thought of home or family. A granddaughter who left the mountains for the city, never wrote, never called, never responded, never cared.

Until her own parents died one winter when their car skidded off the road and into the icy river. Then she'd sobered up, come home with some gray in her hair and some pain in her heart. She was the one who'd figured out the only way to save the ranch was to expand it; it was she who'd cajoled her grieving grandmother into selling her knitting, had found an entire squadron of talented artisans to copy her designs and make beautiful things from the wool and the mohair and the cashmere; who'd connected with all those rich and famous people she'd met in the wild days, had made a name for the ranch and the store, and brought life back to the dying land and to her loving grandmother. She had even met a man and was pregnant with an unexpected baby when she had died.

It had been her death that pushed his wife over, back into the self he thought she had left behind in Hungary. She had seen too much death. Friends who opposed the invaders and were shot to death in the streets. Friends who disappeared in the night, never to return. Aging parents who died for lack of food and care. Her son and his wife, whom God flicked from the side of the road for no reason one harsh winter night.

And then her granddaughter, her brilliant, beautiful hard-working granddaughter, dead because some spoiled and drunk young man crossed the center line and sent Bella into eternity while the drunk walked away unscathed. It was too much. Unable for so many years to push back, she had finally taken out a lifetime of frustration, anger, disappointment and hurt in a few well-placed bullets. It pained him that she turned her anger outward and never once came to him.

But then, she wouldn't. It wasn't in her. There were simply things that she never spoke about, subjects that she never raised, even to him. He wondered whether it was because she wanted to protect him or because talking would cause her too much pain. He didn't know. He just knew it was part of her character to know things, but not to know them, never to acknowledge them, never to let them out into the light of day. Never to share them, always to be solitary and a little broken. Perhaps it was the result of being the Hungarian daughter of a Bulgarian father, even her name a little different, not quite right. But he had loved her then and he loved her now.

He would have loved her through it, held her, coaxed her through it if he'd only known. If he'd only recognized. He hadn't, and now it was too late for her and for him. Such a waste. It was what he hated most about the Communists and the Nazis before them, those predators of their precious Hungary. They wasted human life, and they had poisoned her, and now she did the same.

He'd known she had never really ceased mourning Bella, but he hadn't known how deep her mourning was. Not until he read the article in the paper about the lady doctor who was investigating the deaths. It spelled out a story in such detail that he could not ignore it, especially when he read about the rifle. The one with the inlaid deer. The white stag.

He had always been proud of her prowess with the rifle — she was better than he was — and they both had competed for their country in biathlon in hopes of winning a few more favors, a bit better treatment from the overlords. Never did he dream that she would turn her skill, undimmed even after all these years, to such terrible use. His face flushed with shame at the thought at the same time that his heart ached for the woman he had lost to such darkness.

He took the long, polished, oak case from the closet and opened it. A single rifle lay in there cradled by the velvet lining, an empty space where the mate had been for so many years. He closed it and took it outside, putting it in the bed of the red pickup, wedging it against the toolbox that spanned from side to side, so that it wouldn't rattle, and he covered it with one of the rough blankets in the bed so she wouldn't see. A tuft of airy, white wool spotted the dark surface, and he pulled it off absently, then called to his wife.

"Ivanka! Hurry! I am ready."

It was time to go into town.

CHAPTER THIRTY

JUNE 25

I slept late the next morning, exhausted in mind and body from my trip back East, though the private jet made it easier. I blushed at the expense, but the fact of the matter was, I could afford it, and it meant I was able to do what I had resolved to do before I lost my nerve. Now it was done, the pages turned, and when I woke, my mood was lighter than it had been for many months. And my two cats were sitting on my chest, purring and licking my face, something they had never done before. Perhaps they sensed the change.

I bathed and dressed quickly, still annoyed that I was forbidden showers until the stitches came out, probably tomorrow. Caroline had not accompanied me to Florida but had waited anxiously at home for my return. I had sent her away last night, arguing reasonably that if the plane ride hadn't done me any harm, I was well enough to manage on my own. And I was. Still tired, still a little sore, but up and taking nourishment. All good.

The thought of nourishment reminded me that I was hungry. I'd had one of the elegant little sandwich and cheese plates that the plane stocked, but that was a long time ago, and it was all I had eaten yesterday. I wandered into the kitchen to find Pilar at the stove, the children in a noisy assembly about the table, chattering in a mixture of Spanish and English.

"Buenos dias, Señora Doctora." No matter how hard I tried, the women insisted on using my honorific. Both of them. I tried again.

"Jane, por favor, Pilar. Que es para desayunar?"

She was removing a cast-iron skillet from the stove, turning the burner off as she shifted the massive pan with ease to a cold burner. It smelled of onions. Wonderful. My stomach growled.

"Tortilla de papas," she replied as she bent to remove something from the oven. "Ignacio! Sientate!"

Her special potato omelet. I took my place at the table, patting the chair beside me for Ignacio to join me. He had a way of testing Pilar's limits that reminded me of Adam. I smiled conspiratorially at him.

"Be good, and you'll get a bigger piece," I whispered.

"No fair!" shrieked Mariela. "I'm bigger."

"I'm hungrier," Pablo weighed in.

"I'm the mom," I countered. "I win."

I tickled Mariela and she giggled. Pablo crowded in for his share of attention, clambering onto my lap and putting his arms around my neck.

"Not the mom," Ignacio said in a solemn, authoritative voice. "Tia Abuelita."

Auntie Grandma. It fit. Pilar placed a plate in front of me, then the children, then herself: fragrant eggs and warm flour tortillas. We held hands and Pilar graced the food. Life was good. Very, very good.

****

I took my time walking to the office. The morning was cool, and rain clouds were gathering over the peaks, a welcome difference from the hot, muggy South. I dropped into Baked to pick up some muffins for the staff and ran into Tom Patterson filling his oversized coffee mug.

"I was just on my way to see you," he said.

"Hang on, and I'll walk with you."

I paid the young woman behind the counter and took my bag. Thanks to Pilar, I wasn't tempted to sample the contents. I'd be lucky to be hungry again by dinnertime. That woman really knew how to cook.

Tom held the door for me as we left. The tables on the porch were filled with people. Most of them were reading the paper, talking excitedly about some news or other. I caught a few words from a burly man in a shirt sporting the logo of a local construction company.

"They got him. Her. The killer."

I turned to Tom. "You made an arrest?"

His face was stern. "I'm asking the questions here. Just where the hell have you been?"

"Not that it's any of your business, Sheriff, but I went to Florida. I wasn't aware that I was grounded."

Patterson sighed. "Not grounded. But gagged. Apparently it should have been bound and gagged, you and that Irishman both. Just what did you think you were doing, giving that interview to the paper? Setting it up. Wilson said it was your idea, not his."

We'd reached the door of the center, and he pushed the expanse of glass again, permitting me to enter first. Tom Patterson might be chewing me out, but he was still a gentleman.

I dropped the muffins with Tina, forgetting too late that I'd bought her favorite lemon poppy seed, which would thwart my plans for random drug testing for a while. Come to think of it, maybe that's why she liked them so much. On the other hand, she was pleasant most of the time and competent enough. Maybe it was time I learned that I don't have a dog in every fight.

"I'm taking the stairs," I said, ducking Patterson's question. "Let's finish this in the office."

Tom dogged my footsteps up the three flights to my office, opening that door for me, too. He stood belligerently in front of my desk, demanding an answer with his mere presence. He was too mad to ask again.

I picked up a stack of messages, stacked in neat order next to an enormous package. Who'd left me a gift? Medical Examiners weren't usually the recipients of largesse, unless it was booby-trapped. Patterson grunted, unwilling to be put off anymore, and I abandoned my train of thought.

"You weren't listening to me. You also weren't getting anywhere. I figured the only way you were going to get anything at all was if someone delivered it to you on a silver platter. Like me. So I decided to rattle the cage. I gather something showed up?"

"You could say that. Janos Kovacs showed up in my office yesterday morning with the mate to that rifle, saying he read the story in the paper. He had some cock-and-bull story that that little wife of his has been killing people. Problem is, turns out he was right. Ballistics matched the rifle to the slug they pulled out of you. We arrested her as soon as we got the results. The only prints on it are hers. Open and shut."

"All of them? Even the fire up on Silver Pick? Was that hers, too?" I didn't much care, but I knew Ben would pester me until he found out.

"That one, too."

"How? Ben was sure you couldn't set off a tank that way."

"You can't. She shot through the window of the cabin at Cooper, hit his kerosene lamp. That started a fire pretty quick. I guess it caught the curtains. Anyway, Cooper ran out the front porch towards the woods, and she plugged him there. She said she was almost back to the main road when she heard the explosion."

"Ben was right then. It exploded from the fire."

"Lucky for her. Damn near hid the murder," Patterson continued. "Anyway, it was her."

Ivanka. I'd been right. I knew who, I knew when, I knew how, I just didn't know why.

"What made her do it?"

"Damnedest thing. She had a granddaughter, apple of her eye. She was set to take over the family business when she was killed. Run off the road by a drunk three years ago, June 30."

I felt a chill run up my spine. June 30th. Around the time John had died. She had been working out her own grief at the same time I had. In the same terrible way. She'd just been a little more obvious about it.

"Ivanka never got over it," Patterson continued, "and when the anniversary rolled around again, she snapped. Decided to take out her revenge on anyone with any money she could find. Clever, too. You were right. She was responsible for that string of accidents on the highway into town. She'd lie in wait on the rise there, wait for an expensive local car to come by and shoot at it. Sometimes she'd get the tire, sometimes the windshield; she probably even hit the driver once or twice. Anyway it was enough to send them over. She's a helluva shot." He pondered a moment, then added, "Of course, it was a little easier because the cars were coming straight at her because of the road. All she had to do was keep steady and she was bound to hit something."

Oh yeah? I thought. Ivanka was a marksman, a good one. The cars might have been easy, but tagging Webster and me had not been.

Kessler, closer, was an easier shot. Still, I doubted Tom Patterson would do as well.

"What did she have against me?"

"She knew you were investigating the deaths. Wilson let that slip in the article on Kessler."

Fair enough. But how had she known to lie in wait for me to come out onto the roof garden of the center?

As if reading my mind, Patterson continued. "She overheard you talking to that priest of yours the night of the killing. You mentioned that you take your lunch on the roof on sunny days. All she had to do was wait. She had all the time in the world."

Patterson took a swig of coffee. "I'll give her this, that Kovacs woman is cunning. Crazy as a road lizard, but cunning. When we came to get her, she went off like a bottle rocket. It's a good thing you were gone. She'd spent the whole day before up on Telluride Trail, waiting for you to show again."

"Then why are you giving me a ration of grief for leaving town? Sounds to me like I saved your sorry bacon. And kept myself out of the hospital, too."

Patterson allowed himself a brief smile.

"Maybe so. Don't let it go to your head. And next time I tell you to do something and you don't, I'll skin you alive."

"I'll report you to PETA," I retorted.

It was over. I realized it was finished. No more murders. I went white and weak at the knees, and sat down suddenly and hard in my chair.

"You okay?" Patterson's voice was concerned. When he saw I was not swooning, just seated, he hurried on. "Listen, you did a great job, really. We can't afford to lose you. Just please leave the police work to me. I'm not as incompetent as you think."

So that was it. Wounded pride, not hidden guilt, and then that fueled by my spectacular indifference to the people around me on full display.

"Never said you were, Tom." At least, not out loud and never again. "Don't think you are. And if dabbling in police work nets me a trip to the hospital, I am more than happy to leave it to you."

"Fair enough." He acknowledged my words with the hat he had so carefully removed when we entered the building. His momma had really raised him right. "Take care of yourself."

I closed my eyes for a long moment. "I intend to." Another moment to gather my thoughts and I spoke again. "She didn't kill Houston, though." I pushed a file across the desk at him. He looked at the papers in it and whistled long and low, then smiled. He saluted me with his hat, a smile on his face, the first real one I had seen in weeks.

I started to rise, but he motioned me down. "I know the way out, and it looks like I have business to attend to. Nice job, Lady Doc."

"Lady Doc?"

"That's what they're calling you in the paper. I like it, mostly because I know it's going to drive you crazy. Wilson's getting a bit of payback because you kept him out of the Kessler scene."

He waved again as he closed my office door.

Lady Doc, huh? Not such a bad name. And if towns were like families, a nickname meant I'd been accepted. In spite of myself, I was part of this eccentric little community. And I would make sure that the lady part fit. I had some fences to mend in town.

After Tom left, I turned my attention to the box that occupied most of my desk top. It was one of those stage-style boxes, wrapped in paisley and bound with pink grosgrain ribbon, top and bottom separate so that I could open it without tearing it apart. It was beautiful if a bit jarring in my wood and leather office. Zoe would love it, would find a place to use it for special letters, clippings from papers, pressed flowers, and all the other sorts of tactile memories she so carefully hoarded, just like her father. So much John's daughter.

Of course, Zoe wouldn't be crashing into it as soon as she found it like I was. She had this habit of setting her packages aside, savoring them, drawing out the enjoyment for as long as she could. I was just as much a scientist with my presents as I was with my autopsies. For me, it was important to know, completely and as soon as possible.

The contents were obscured by several layers of pink tissue paper covered with tiny silver stars. On them lay a square, cream-colored card, which I opened. *Meet me at the Peaks for lunch, Woman. I'll be there at one, and we have work to do on my next book. E.*

I smiled in spite of myself and started pulling back the layers of pink. There, in the box was a beaten up pair of men's figure skates, the laces knotted together and laid carefully on top. The black leather was scuffed and wrinkled, but the blades were bright and sharp. I took them out of the box and turned them over in my hands. *What in the world was Eoin Connor doing, giving me a set of ice skates — men's no less — in the middle of summer?* It made no sense.

Until something on the side of the blades caught my eye, something engraved in florid, curling script. *Lucifer.* Satan's first name. Or one of them. Hell had frozen over, and I had the Adversary's own ice skates.

I laughed out loud, so loud that Lucy, on her way to get coffee from the break room, stuck her head in. Clearly, my laughter was an unfamiliar sound. Seeing that I was fine, she smiled, gave me a little wave, and went on her way. I started to put the skates back, then thought the better of it. There was an empty nail on the wall by the door, and I hung them there. I liked how out of place they looked.

I glanced at my watch. Just over an hour until I was to meet Eoin at the Peaks for lunch. I called out to Tina as she passed my office. She stuck her head in the door, wiping poppy seed crumbs from the corner of her mouth.

"You need me?"

"No, just wanted to let you know I'm leaving for the day. I have a couple of errands, then I'm meeting..." I fumbled, not sure what to call Eoin, and settled on weasel words. "...a friend for lunch. I won't be back in. I'll see you tomorrow."

Tina looked puzzled for a moment, then smiled.

"Okay, works for me," and she was gone.

My eyes lingered on the doorway for a long moment, then caught sight of the skates hanging on the wall. I shook my head, smiling, as I dialed Father Matt.

He answered on the first ring, bellowing in the phone so loudly I had to hold the receiver away from my ear.

"Turn the volume down, Father! You're going to make me deaf!"

The faint "sorry" from the earpiece told me it was safe to try again. I cradled the receiver against my shoulder as I picked up the green folder from my desk. "Are you free? I have some interesting news for you." I flipped through the five or six pages in the folder.

"News?"

"About the murders. Something that might be very, very interesting to a former prime suspect."

I didn't tell him I had another item on the agenda. I figured I'd deal with that when I saw him face to face. He deserved at least that.

"Sure, I guess. Can you give me about twenty minutes? I'm just leaving down valley."

"Meet me at the church, Father. Thanks."

I cleared the line and dialed the number on the first page of the file. Pete Wilson wasn't as prompt as Father Matt had been. He answered on the fifth ring with a brusque, "Yeah?"

"Hello to you, too. I need to come by and talk with you. Matter of some importance, a big, big story. Do you have a minute?"

I put the file down and held the receiver in my hand. I was surprised at how tightly I gripped it. I had rehearsed this moment in my mind all morning. I was surprised that the repetition had not drained any of the power out of the moment.

I could almost hear Pete Wilson sit up straighter.

"I'm just about to head out to Norwood..." the newshound's desire for a scoop was almost audible; he said the words without conviction.

"Believe me when I tell you whatever it is can wait. I'll be there in five."

I didn't give him time to protest and cradled the receiver. Then I took a deep breath, ran my hand over the face of the file one more time, picked it up and left the office.

Tyler Lee, the editor, was leaning against Wilson's desk engaged in earnest conversation when I arrived. Other than those two, the office was empty. Early lunch for the Fourth Estate.

Tyler extended a thin, manicured hand. "Good to see you, Dr. Wallace."

I'd only met the man once, when I first came to town but he impressed me as kind, competent, and overloaded, given that he had to share his time between Montrose and Telluride running two very different local papers.

"You too, Tyler."

I glanced down at Pete Wilson, who didn't bother to conceal his curiosity. My message had to be delivered in private; Tyler had to go. I turned back to him and smiled my best Southern Belle smile.

"Tyler, I hope you don't mind. I have something I need to discuss with Pete and it's of a personal and...delicate nature. I would prefer it if we could speak privately."

As soon as I said it, I knew I had overplayed my hand. Tyler Lee is a Virginian. I missed the proper tone by a Richmond mile. Out of practice.

Still, he's a Virginian and a gentleman who would never, ever contradict even a counterfeit lady. I wondered how he managed a newspaper with such sensibilities.

"Why don't you two use my office? I'm going out to lunch."

He smiled at me, but the look in his eyes told me he'd want answers later, if not from me, from Pete Wilson. Good. Maybe I hadn't overplayed it after all.

Pete Wilson pushed his chair back.

"I'm off to Norwood to cover the rodeo. I probably won't be back until this evening."

"Check in when you have a break," the editor said. "You've got my cell."

He nodded his head vaguely in my direction and was off. I was right. His editorial nose smelled news. The local M.E. never, ever comes calling on the press.

Lee's office was tidy and spare. His diplomas were hung neatly on one wall, and there was a shelf with a scattering of awards on it. His taste in art ran to modern, abstract and colorful. The reds in the canvas behind the desk — I recognized it as a Fonteyn — matched the red leather of the chair Pete Wilson sat in as if he owned it. He waved a hand at the barrel chair opposite him across the desk, also red.

"So, what's this about?" He reclined slightly in the chair as though he were contemplating putting his feet up.

I hesitated for a moment. There is a fine line between reproof and revenge. I'd spent enough time on the far side of that line lately. I didn't want to cross it again. Still, I felt my pulse starting to race and the familiar knot in my stomach I used to get in front of a jury. I stood there, silent for a long enough time that Wilson began to get fidgety. He sat up in the chair again, leaned on the desk, and motioned to the chair once more.

"Sit down. Please. What is it that you wanted to tell me that was so all-fired important?"

One deep breath, drawn in slowly so as not to make a sound. I steeled the muscles of my abdomen. Showtime.

"You smarmy son of a bitch. Next time you decide to frame a man, you had damn well better make sure he's guilty."

Pete Wilson blanched, then recovered. But he pushed the chair back from the desk, trying to gain distance. I still had not sat down.

"I don't know what you're talking about."

"The hell you don't."

I threw the folder on the desk, then felt in the pocket of my jeans. I pulled out one of the .22 rifle slugs I had bought at the hardware store in Norwood. "Catch." I tossed it to Wilson. He bobbled it and had to retrieve it from his lap.

"What's this?"

"A bullet from the same lot as the box you bought to frame Father Matt."

"I don't know what you're talking about." This time he didn't blanch, but he tossed the bullet onto the desk as though it were red hot. "I helped you break this case. I was wrong about Father Matt, but you have to admit the evidence was impressive."

"There was no evidence."

"Someone saw Father Matt coming down out of the bell tower on the day Cosette was shot."

"Who?"

I'll give Wilson credit. He didn't even squirm. "A source who wants to remain protected. I don't have to reveal him. Her. Them." His struggle to reconcile political and grammatical correctness amused me and annoyed him. "Not even to you."

I counted to ten in Irish. Connor taught me while I was recovering at his place.

"No, you don't. But I can tell you. There isn't one, at least not a direct one. Father Matt was in the belfry all right, but it was the day after the murder, not the day of. My guess — and it's an informed one — is that you overheard him telling Ben when they had lunch together at Baked. Your favorite lunch spot, I believe."

"So *you* say." Emphasis on the "you."

Wilson's eyes were beginning to shine. It seemed he liked a verbal donnybrook as much as any lawyer.

"So I say. I also say that the bullet the police found there was planted. By you."

Wilson chuckled and leaned back in his chair again, hands behind his head. "Prove it."

I leaned forward to tap the folder and remained there for a long moment, invading his personal space.

"It's all there. The receipt from the hardware store in Norwood where you bought the ammunition for starters. Really, Wilson, you shouldn't pay for things like that with a credit card. Were you thinking of expensing it to the paper?"

"They sell a lot of ammunition in Norwood."

"So they do. This lot happens to match the bullet from the bell tower. Same rim markings."

"Lots of that ammunition floating around."

"Not much of it bought the day before your article came out. It's not hunting season. No reason to buy bullets this time of year."

"So I bought some bullets. Big deal. Circumstantial. What else you got?" Wilson's tone was still cocky, but he'd dropped his arms and was pushing against the desk. The knuckles of his hand were white.

"You know, that nice enamel on the trim takes prints really well. We got two sets, palms and fingers, from the rails in the corner. Are you scared of heights, or did you just want to take a minute to gloat?"

"Not my prints."

"Wanna bet?" I flipped the folder open to Lucy's report. "Read it and weep."

Wilson looked at me hard, then slowly leaned forward to look. The muscles in his neck tightened, and he remained silent.

"You ever watch what a bartender does when he's bored?" I asked. No answer, not even a look. "He polishes glasses. Nothing better than a nice bar glass to take a set of prints from. Usually get part of the palm too. Remember that night you had a drink with Eoin Connor? The night he planted the story with you? Lovely prints from that. Matched right up."

"I never gave permission."

"Stuff it." My tone announced I was done playing games.

Wilson stood up, his hands wide apart on the desk. He leaned pugnaciously forward until his chin nearly touched mine, like something out of a bad movie. I steeled myself not to move.

"Circumstantial. You can't prove anything."

He glared at me, and I held his eyes without blinking for a long moment before I laughed.

"You're right," I said as I backed off, sliding the folder out from under Wilson's right hand. "All circumstantial. Not much proof at all. But I know you did it."

I sat down finally in the barrel chair, trying to suppress the smile that threatened to play around my lips. Wilson relaxed a bit and crossed his arms across his chest in a look of triumph.

"You can't prove anything. Circumstantial," he repeated.

The smile broke through. I fluttered the folder. "You really ought to know better, Pete," I said. "I suggest you ask Tommy Berton just what I can do with circumstantial evidence. While you're at it, you might discuss with him what happens when you lose a civil suit after a slam dunk conviction for a crime."

Wilson blanched again. I was well aware my reputation preceded me. For once it was nice to play it to positive effect.

"What are you going to do?" he finally asked. His voice was firm but his words lacked bravado.

I smiled. "Not sure yet. I haven't given this to Tom Patterson. When I do, he'll have no choice but to file charges for obstruction of justice. Time in the big house for that, you know. Then there's the possibility of a lawsuit on behalf of the good Father and the diocese for defamation."

"A priest would never sue."

"He would if he had a good lawyer advising him and it was a big-ticket, slam dunk case. And he does, and it is. I wonder whether Father Matt has any experience in running a newspaper?" I smiled a predatory, lawyerly smile at Pete Wilson, who, to his credit, had not yet sunk into the chair again. Nor had he turned his eyes away. I thought I detected a sheen of sweat on his brow. He was tough. Almost as tough as Tommy Berton. But not quite. And I was tougher now than I had been then.

I stood up and looked him in the eyes one last time, and in his eyes I saw fear. Not regret, just fear.

"There is no statute of limitation when obstruction is related to a murder charge." A slight shading of the truth in this particular case. "Ten years if it's not. I have lots of time to make up my mind. And if I were you, I'd try real hard not to piss me off."

I turned abruptly and walked away before I crossed that line. Tough enough and whole enough to stop short of mayhem, at least for today. But I toed right up to it when I turned back at the door and looked at Wilson one last time.

"Have a nice day, Pete. Tell Tyler thanks for the use of his office."

I walked out into the sunlight and turned in the direction of Spruce Street.

My heart began to pound as I approached the church, a familiar feeling on the way to confession, and confession was what I was after.

Enough to keep me out of the Church, if that were all I knew. But I knew that the feeling I would have after was more than worth the anxiety beforehand. Time to clean up and get on with life.

I put my hand out for the knob, but the door pulled open before my hand reached it. I found myself standing face to face with Janos Kovacs in the small vestibule. Desperate to get out of his way, I moved to one side, and he moved in the same direction. We did the avoidance dance for a moment, then stopped, regarding each other warily. His face was tired and lined, his expression full of pain that I recognized. Pain that I had in some measure caused and that wouldn't end for a very long time. Maybe never.

What do I say? I asked myself. *What do I say to the man whose wife is sitting in jail now, likely never to get out?* That I know the prison he finds himself in all too well? That I cannot imagine being the one to bring in the evidence that would convict the other half of my life and tear her away from me? I didn't know what to think. Would he blame me, or did he shoulder this terrible burden all by himself? I waited, half-afraid, unable to make any gesture.

Then he did the most extraordinary thing. He extended a hand to me. I took it tentatively, not knowing what to expect.

"Peace be with you," he said simply and quietly. I noticed he dropped the "h."

With reflexes born in years of attending Mass, I replied, "And with your spirit." His other hand closed over mine and squeezed, holding it tight and warm for an instant too long, then letting it go. His tanned face creased in a shadow of a sad smile. He stepped out of the vestibule and was gone. I heard his footsteps on the stairs and listened until they were lost in the distance.

Father Matt was waiting in a pew, sunlight from the windows burnishing his brown curls. They were unruly at best, and lately they had gotten impossibly long. If he didn't have a haircut soon, he'd have dreadlocks. *Probably better to fit into town,* I thought. He saw me and stood up, a questioning look on his face.

"I got here as soon as I could. Should we go to your office? I'm not supposed to use the facilities here."

I looked around. The church was empty except for us, silent as only a church can be, the warm mid-day light coming in through the windows dappling the aisle with patterns and colors. I shook my head.

"No. I think I'd rather just talk here. It's private enough."

I took a seat on the pew next to where Father Matt had been sitting and patted the wooden bench. He sat back down, hands resting lightly on his knees, and didn't say a word. I held the folder I had just threatened Pete Wilson with in my two hands, looking at it and gathering my thoughts. It was hard to know where to begin. I finally decided that cutting to the chase had a certain appeal.

"Pete Wilson is the one who framed you. I can prove it."

For an instant Father Matt stiffened, then relaxed. His hands lifted from his knees briefly, fisted, then straightened again, slowly. His mouth twitched, but he still said nothing, just looked at me with those big, brown eyes. I reached across and placed my hand on top of his, and repeated myself.

"I can prove it, Father. Beyond a doubt."

Father Matt stood abruptly and paced about the floor, from the front to the pew and back, three times, then four, his hands now clasped behind his back, the fingers of the free hand working powerfully. Finally, he stopped in front of me and simply asked, "Why?" I noticed the corners of his eyes were damp.

I shrugged. "Didn't say. Who knows? Does it matter?"

"Yes, it matters!" he thundered. "Of course, it matters!"

I recoiled a bit, and he stopped, closed his eyes. I was familiar with that particular ploy. Sometimes it helps to shut out the world when you want to collect yourself after someone has scattered you to pieces. I spent a lot of the first year after John's death with my eyes closed.

At length, he sighed and opened his eyes again.

"It matters to me," he corrected himself. "I don't suppose it matters other than that."

Good man. He'd toed up to the line, too, but hadn't crossed it. He was better at this than I was, but I was learning. I patted the bench again.

"I just came from his office. He knows that I know. I haven't told Tom Patterson yet. I thought I'd talk to you before I do that. What Wilson did was obstruction of justice, pure and simple. And defamation of the worst kind."

"I suppose he can go to prison for it?"

"If I tell Patterson, yes."

"If you tell. Don't you have an obligation to tell him?"

"Probably. If it ever came out that I hadn't, I'd probably lose my law license. Might starve to death for lack of a proper job."

I hoped a bit of levity might help. It didn't. Father Matt was on his feet again, pacing more furiously this time, muttering to himself, and pressing his fist into the palm of his hand. He stopped again, this time in the middle of the church.

"For the first time, Jane, I think I understand," he said. "You...he...I...." his words trailed off in confusion as he punched his palm with such force, I was afraid he'd hurt himself. He sighed again.

I sat back on the bench and stretched out my legs. Father Matt sat heavily down beside me. "You're asking me whether you should tell Patterson, aren't you?"

"Up to you," I said. "But no need to decide this instant. I just wanted you to know that it's over. No suspicion. And my guess is that the paper's going to carry a retraction, if for no other reason than to cover its own corporate self. Do you want the details?" I held up the folder. "This is a copy for you. I have the originals in my office."

Father Matt took the folder and held it gingerly, at a distance, then set it aside. "I think I'll wait. I'm too angry just now."

I took a breath. This was going to be the hard part. "There's more."

"More?"

I shifted so that I could look him eye to eye. "About Marla. I know. I had to tell Patterson. He's on his way to take her back into custody, right now, I expect."

This time the look was relief, but his words were the same as Pete Wilson's had been. "I don't know what you're talking about."

"Never play poker, Father. You haven't the face for it. I know you know, and I know you can't say anything. I figured it out while I was looking into that hatchet job Wilson did on you."

"Go on." He sounded cautious.

I smiled. "It's the done thing these days for the glitterati to go over to Fauxhall and learn to shoot," I said. "They order a lot of ammunition, and I went over there to check it out, trying to run down someone — anyone — who had purchased ammunition about the time you were framed. Turns out Houston kept a target rifle over there. A .22 and a sidearm, a nine millimeter Beretta. His name caught my eye, and I did a little digging. Marla Kincaid showed up the afternoon Houston was killed and checked the Beretta out. It was the only one out of all of the murders that was an outlier, and it was complicated only because we picked up on the wrong gun. She killed him, revenge I expect, because he infected her and the baby with HIV."

He leaned forward, put his head in his hands and was still. I placed my hand on his shoulder. He shook his head, and his voice was muffled when he finally spoke.

"I am not cut out for this. The bishop was right."

I laughed and clapped him on the back. "You're not getting off that easy. Sorry, Father, you're in this for the long haul. Welcome to my world. It's not so bad once you get used to it."

Father Matt turned his head to the side and looked askance at me, then smiled. "You are something else, Jane Wallace. Thanks. Thanks."

"Just doing my job," I said. "Now how about you doing yours?"

Father Matt sat up slowly. "No mind games, Jane. I'm too tired. What are you talking about?"

"I'm tired too, Father." I looked past him to the altar and the crucifix. Funny how I'd managed all this time to stay within the four walls of this little church, in spite of my best efforts to the contrary. Something, someone — John? — had kept me here when I had no reason to stay and every reason to go. "I'm tired of fighting Tommy Berton. I'm tired of cleaning up the fruit of revenge — mine, Ivanka's, Marla's, who knows, maybe yours. Go get your purple stole. It's time to scrape the barnacles off this hull. The bishop has reinstated your faculties. I want you to hear my confession." I handed him the fax I had received after my early morning call; it helps to be on the big donor list when you want to have a conversation with the head man.

He looked at me for a moment as though without understanding, then a half-smile crossed his face. He stood up, and I watched him as he opened the back door and listened to the sounds of his steps in the hall that led to his office. When he returned, he had the stole in his hands, kissed it and put it around his neck.

I watched him contort himself to fit in the old confessional, the one the previous priest had used as a storage closet. The processional bells on the outside wall jangled slightly, and I heard a muffled invective, no doubt from some appendage knocking against the confines of a space made for much smaller men. As cramped as it was, I knew he preferred it to the bright, new reconciliation room.

So did I. It's always easier to talk to a screen than it is face to face. I'd been brave enough, long enough. I welcomed the chance to be momentarily anonymous. I glanced up at the loft, thinking of all the times I had sat there under St. Anthony's watchful eyes. "Looks like you found something else — a lot — that was missing," I whispered as I opened the door and knelt on the velvet cushion. Then I closed the door, made the sign of the cross and began. "Bless me, Father, for I have sinned..."

****

When we were done, we walked together out of the church, back into the sunlight. Father Matt's phone rang just as he let the door close behind him.

"It's the bishop," he said. His face hardened for a moment. He pocketed his phone with an air of indifference, and we listened to three more tones before it went silent again. Father Matt looked for a long moment at the blue folder I had given him before he pulled his phone out again, this time with purpose on his face. He pushed redial, and as he listened for life on the other end of the line, he looked at me. I noticed his eyes were almost the same color as Janos Kovacs'. And not nearly as kind. Father Matt was in the same boat as Janos, but with two tormentors, not one.

He held both of them in his hands just now: one in a folder, one in a phone. I wondered how he would respond.

"He didn't just attack me, Jane. He attacked the Church. It's one thing to come after me. But I can't let him come after the Church I love. Go ahead. Tell Tom," was all he said to me before turning his attention to the phone again.

I left before the bishop answered. That promised to be an interesting conversation. I was sorry to miss it, but it was almost one and I had another man to meet.

****

The lobby of the Peaks was washed in sunlight and one of the bellmen greeted me as I walked through the massive, glass door. A guest padded through the lobby wrapped in a white terry robe, coming or going, I thought, from the spa. I frowned in spite of myself, regretting the pervasive informality that made nightclothes as acceptable in the lobby of a fine hotel as an evening dress would have been. Then I remembered that I was headed to meet Connor for lunch in that same fine hotel in boots and jeans and would be accepted for the same reason: my money's green, and the hotel wanted as much of it as could be pried out of visiting wallets. Some things are not worth making waves over.

Indeed, I thought to myself. Some things are not. I wasn't sure that Pete Wilson fell into that category yet, but probably. Besides, I might get more mileage out of the knowledge held close to my chest than I would satisfaction at his downfall. Fr. Matt said to tell Tom. He didn't say when. My smile broadened. I might have gotten past the greater part of my stubborn need for control and revenge, but there was still enough left that I was my own irascible self.

The Great Room was emptying of the early diners, waitstaff clearing tables here and there in anticipation of a second wave of custom. I caught sight of Conner, settled in a chair at a table for four that was tucked into a corner, far enough from the expanse of windows that none of the tables near it was occupied. He stood as I approached, then held the chair for me as I took my seat. A charming custom of chivalry John taught our sons, and one I had sorely missed since he died.

An open bottle of red wine was on the table and Eoin's glass was half full. He topped his own off and filled mine, in that order, then replaced the bottle in its terra cotta holder. I listened to the silence grow, unsure of what to say and unwilling to break it. He looked at me with a glance that told me he was both amused and perfectly capable of waiting me out. He took up his glass, raised and tipped it in my direction, still silent. I followed suit.

"Sláinte, is it?" I was surprised at the tentative sound in my voice.

"Indeed. Sláinte! I see you got my gift."

I felt myself flush. "It's hanging on my wall. Do you remember everything that's said to you?"

"Writer's curse." He took another sip from his glass, and his face lost its humor. "I heard about the arrest. Well done, Jane Wallace. You were right."

"That's my job, being right." My flip answer sounded hollow. I hastened to amend it. "It is my job. It used to be enough to be right. Not so much anymore. What an awful business." I took another sip of wine. "I ran into Janos at St. Pat's. Considering the circumstances, he was very kind to me." *More than I deserved,* I thought.

Connor regarded me with a curious look, head cocked to the side and eyes narrowed. Then he sat himself up straighter, tilted his head back and smiled that broad, infectious smile of his. "Can't wait to hear it. It will make a fitting ending to my new book."

"About the murders? It's too soon, isn't it? Not even gone to trial. Surely you have to wait. I thought you asked me here to try to convince me to..." My voice trailed off when I realized how self-centered I was about to sound, how presumptuous.

"Oh, indeed, Jane Wallace, I did, I did indeed. Tis your story I'm going to tell next, and a great work of literature it will be, too."

I smiled in spite of myself as I heard his accent broaden, a sure sign of impending manipulation. For once I didn't mind. I had a lot to sort out, about John and me, about death and life.

"Well, talking it out with you is probably as good as seeing a shrink," I said. "And a lot cheaper."

I was rewarded for my candor with a laugh, so genuine and deep that I saw diners turn to look for its source. I looked down, uneasy at being the center of attention. Eoin Connor just took another sip of wine.

"So it is, Woman, so it is."

He reached across the table to pat my hand and retrieved a tape recorder from the chair to one side of us. He clicked it on and placed it in the empty place where my plate would go, if the waiter ever came. I suspected Eoin had instructed him to keep his distance at least for a while.

His voice was serious and kind and almost devoid of accent as he spoke.

"Now then, Jane Wallace. Tell me about this John of yours."

And so I did.

Acknowledgements

This book would never have happened without the faith and assistance of so many people. So my thanks…

To Doreen Thistle, my friend and agent, for asking me to write the first chapter after seeing my *Second Home Telluride* columns and for coaching me through the creative process. You saw in me something I never saw in myself.

To the Corvisiero Literary Agency for taking me on and leading me through the labyrinthine world of publishing.

To Danelle McCafferty who saw the first and very rough draft of Jane's story. Your good advice led me to see clearly what kind of book I wanted to write.

To Deacon Dennis Dorner, who helped me have the courage to go ahead and rewrite it that way and trust the results to Doreen (and God).

To my Irish priests, Msgr. Leo P. Herbert, Fr. Liam Coyne and one who wishes to remain nameless, for helping me bring Eoin to life, especially to the nameless one for Eoin's sometimes colorful language.

To Deacon Matthew Gregory, for permitting me to pirate his name for Father Matt.

To my son Nathan for proofing the climbing aspects of the book and to Bruce Laird for taking custody of the law enforcement references. Any mistakes are mine alone. They gave me great advice.

To my daughter, Lorna, for cheering me on when things got bleak. Only another writer knows what giving birth to a book is like.

To Bertin Glennon for his insight and direction as Jane's journey (and my own) evolved over the course of the book.

To Full Quiver Publishing for the chance to see Jane come to life in print.

To all those who read early drafts and offered suggestions. Your good humor and insights kept me going, especially my Telluride friends.

Jane finally learned what I have long known—that little box canyon is a special place.

And most of all, to Steve, who believed in me and endured late nights and a distracted and sometimes nutty wife as I worked on this book nights and weekends for such a long time. You have always believed in me. You still are not Dead John.

Dr. Barbara Golder
Lookout Mountain
January 2016

About the Author

Dr. Barbara Golder is a late literary bloomer. Although she's always loved books (and rivals Jane in the 3-deep-on-the-shelf sweepstakes), her paying career gravitated to medicine and law. She has served as a hospital pathologist, forensic pathologist, and laboratory director. Her work in forensic pathology prompted her to get a law degree, which she put to good use as a malpractice attorney and in a boutique practice of medical law, which allowed her to be a stay-at-home mom when her children were young. She has also tried her hand at medical politics, serving as an officer in her state medical association, lobbying at a state and national level on medical issues, writing and lecturing for hire, including a memorable gig teaching nutritionists about the joys of chocolate for eight straight hours, teaching middle and high school science, and, most recently, working for a large disability insurance company from which she is now retired.

Her writing career began when she authored a handbook of forensic medicine for the local medical examiner office in 1984. Over the years she wrote extensively on law and medicine and lectured on medicolegal topics. On a lark, she entered a contest sponsored by the Telluride Times Journal and ended up with a regular humor column that memorialized the vagaries of second-home living on the Western Slope.

She currently lives on Lookout Mountain, Tennessee with two dogs, two cats and her husband of 41 years.

Full Quiver Publishing
PO Box 244
Pakenham, ON K0A2X0
www.fullquiverpublishing.com
Bookstores: For bulk orders, please contact us at: fullquiverpublishing@gmail.com

To contact the author: ladydocmurders@gmail.com

Author website:
http://ladydocmurders.weebly.com/

Made in the USA
Lexington, KY
09 August 2019